SPECTACULAR

PRAISE FOR

BLOOMSBURY'S LATE ROSE

"Pearson imagines the life of the early 20th-century English poet Charlotte Mew in this novel. Charlotte and her sister Anne have always been close. After their two siblings, Henry and Freda, were institutionalized for mental instability in 1894, the sisters swore to each other that they would never get married or have children, in order to avoid passing on what they saw as a family curse. Now, in 1909, the nearly 40-year-old women are still single, living with their ailing mother, her maid, and other tenants in a modest house in [the] Bloomsbury area of London. Charlotte ... begins to express her rich interiority in her poetry.... She's finally building the life that she always wanted as an independent, artistic woman — but things become complicated when she falls in love with a woman herself. Pearson writes in an elegant prose that summons the era of the novel in precise detail.... In its pacing and style, the novel earnestly evokes the works of Edith Wharton and other writers from the period without ever stumbling into parody or awkward pastiche. **In Mew's story, Pearson not only uncovers central questions of first-wave feminism, but also finds an opportunity to resurrect an intriguing and worthwhile real-life poet for posterity. A rich, enjoyable historical novel with compelling themes.**"
— *Kirkus Reviews*

"This beautiful story transported me to a different era. Charlotte Mew is a haunting heroine: brave, talented and tormented. I loved her, and **I loved this novel.**"
— Susan Breen, author of *Maggie Dove's Detective Agency* (Penguin Random House, 2016)

"Waiting politely in the shadow of history, poet Charlotte Mew finally steps into the light to take her place amongst the Bloomsbury writing elite thanks to this **elegant, painstakingly researched and beautifully written** novel by Pen Pearson. This is a truly vivid and wonderfully insightful reimagining of Mew's professional and personal triumphs and tragedies. Written with such skill that I found myself walking the Edwardian London streets alongside Mew, this novel does what great historical fiction should: it brilliantly illuminates the past."

— Tracey Iceton, author of *Herself Alone in Orange Rain* (Cinnamon Press, 2017)

BLOOMSBURY'S LATE ROSE

A Novel

Pen Pearson

ISBN 978-1-7329139-4-3

Front cover illustration by Kelly Airo

Book design by Scribe Freelance

Chickadee Prince Logo by Garrett Gilchrist

Visit us at www.ChickadeePrince. com

First Printing

PEN PEARSON

Bloomsbury's Late Rose

A Novel

Pen Pearson lives in Aberdeen, South Dakota, where she teaches at Northern State University. Her writing has appeared in various journals and anthologies, including *New Writing* and *The Working Poet*. She has published two books of poems, *Trespass to Chattel* (2009) and *Poetry as Liturgy* (2010). *Bloomsbury's Late Rose* is her first novel.

BLOOMSBURY'S LATE ROSE

A Novel

Chickadee Prince Books
New York

*To my late father, George, my mother, Ruth,
and my siblings, Jim, Pam, and John*

PROLOGUE (1894)

The late August sun peered through the bedroom curtains as it set in Bloomsbury.

"Ma says it's from Father's side of the family," Anne said.

"And Father says it's from Ma's," Charlotte replied.

The sisters, both in their early twenties, sat on Charlotte's mattress. Anne picked at the tufted fringe of the chenille counterpane. Charlotte twisted the gold ring on her middle finger.

"It doesn't matter whose side is to blame, does it?" Anne asked.

"Not for us," Charlotte admitted. She studied her younger sister's hands as they fiddled with the fringe. "Are you worried that we might join Henry and Freda in the hospital?" Charlotte asked.

"Not as much as I worry about our future as wives and mothers," Anne said, "if everything the newspapers say about insanity being inherited is true."

Charlotte hesitated, then said, "You must see that we can never marry."

Anne's fingers quit worrying the fringe. "Because marriage would result in children," Anne said. It was a statement, not a question. She looked at Charlotte.

"Children who might inherit the family curse," Charlotte said, meeting Anne's eyes.

"Isn't curse too strong a word?" Anne asked.

Charlotte remembered their brother and sister as one and then the other was taken from the Mew family's home. She said, "Henry's and Freda's fate can't be viewed as a blessing."

"We could make a pact," Anne said, returning Charlotte's gaze, "a pact to never marry. Then we wouldn't have to worry about children, and whether they're cursed or blessed."

Charlotte nodded. "It's the only sensible thing to do."

"We'll have our art," Anne said. "You, your writing, and I, my painting."

"And we'll have each other," Charlotte said.

"That's what's most important," Anne agreed.

THE QUIET HOUSE (1909)

CHAPTER 1

Charlotte carried her umbrella. She stood on Gower Street, in Bloomsbury, waiting for an omnibus with her sister Anne.

"It mustn't rain," Anne said, "not on Henry's birthday."

"It might not," Charlotte conceded, but she was doubtful.

The horn-handled umbrella was more than half Charlotte's height. If asked about its company, she would say it was better than most, with her sister's company an exception. Anne, three years younger, stood a head taller. She carried a mixed bouquet of bright flowers in one hand and a carpetbag in the other. Both sisters wore woolen stockings under their long skirts, and topcoats over their shirtwaists and suits. A cameo brooch adorned Anne's high collar; a blue tie, Charlotte's. Their galoshes Anne carried in the carpetbag.

Charlotte and Anne's family resemblance began and ended with their fair complexions and fat earlobes. Charlotte had the petite figure and heart-shaped face of a fox, which framed large, deep-set eyes as alert as a startled hare's. Anne was softly rounded and as self-possessed as a roosting hen. Anne often complained that her ears stuck out like a Welsh corgi's. "But your eyes are the loveliest shade of violet," Charlotte, whose eyes were only gray, argued. Anne's eyes were indeed stunning, and every other feature except her comparative height was more feminine than any of Charlotte's features. But it was Charlotte, just short of five feet and with the hoarse voice of an unseasoned cello, whom people remembered, whether or not they could recall her name.

It was the end of March. Of course, it might rain, but it was more likely to mist or drizzle. The afternoon sky looked as if London's best linens had been washed in the Thames with King Edward's blackest stockings and hung from the bulwarks to dry. On the pavements, horse-drawn and motorized omnibuses jockeyed for right of way. The horse-powered buses, ubiquitous a few years before, were scarcer in number and, Charlotte thought, old-fashioned, much like herself.

Omnibus passengers were part of the street scene, particularly those who climbed the winding stair at the rear of the omnibus and took seats on the upper deck, as Charlotte and Anne did. The steep faces of Gower Street, monolithic institutions of stone and iron railings, hugged the pavements. The omnibus pulled into the fray of traffic, and the sisters were threaded through a narrow chasm past the British Museum on Great Russell Street and the heart of central London to the city's southern rim and their ultimate destination.

On an omnibus or in the underground, Charlotte felt almost thankful that her youthful prayer for fame had been denied, so that she could study people from behind a mask of anonymity. Today, a woman sitting catty-corner from Charlotte knitted what looked like the lid of a soup tureen but must have been a baby's bonnet. Three children jumped or climbed onto her lap, sometimes two at once, as the woman held the needles at arms' length. A thick wedding band squeezed her ring finger, while its fingertip ably tensioned the blue yarn feeding the needles from a misshapen bag at her side. With her right thumb, Charlotte twisted the gold band on her middle finger in sympathy, the same finger that wore a thimble when she embroidered years ago, the same thumb long familiar with Middle C on the Mews' piano.

Next to her, Anne sketched the bouquet of flowers with a charcoal pencil and sketchpad, her attention absorbed by the imitation of life. Occasionally she would look up, but only long enough to guess their progress.

The omnibus, emptied of all but three passengers, stopped on Linden Grove Road in Southwark, four miles south of central London, opposite two pairs of colossal pillars and a wrought-iron gate that opened onto a road stretching to the horizon. That hour the gate stood unlocked, its arms swung open in welcome. After helping each other step into galoshes, Charlotte and Anne walked through the gate purposefully, sure of their way despite a creeping fog, down what might have been a country lane if Nunhead wasn't the second largest cemetery of London.

The cemetery's vastness, expansive as heaven itself, was counterbalanced by overgrown flora. Towering trees and squat shrubs grew as thick as a fairytale forest. Large monuments to the great dead, themselves forgotten, stood censured by the erasures of time and neglect. Headstones listed to one side or pitched forward, while vines crept over untended graves. The fog crowded among the trees and lay over the gravel lanes and footpaths. Without knowing where one was going, it was impossible not to get lost.

Ahead on the lane, a figure raced toward them through the fog. Charlotte might have mistaken it for the shadow of a scudding cloud if there had been a sun. Anne turned to Charlotte. "Do you see what I see?"

Charlotte stopped. "That depends on what you see."

Anne stood beside her. "I see a child running toward us."

A boy, about six years old and dressed in a sailor suit, stopped short before them. "Eddie's gone missing," he panted. Not looking where his hand pointed, the boy waved at a bramble patch whose branches held the promise of summer blackberries.

"And who might Eddie be?" Charlotte asked politely.

Without comment, the boy raced back up the lane while yelling, "Eddie," his figure and voice merging with the fog. A string, for a kite or a pull car, hung unoccupied from the boy's hand and reached just to his bare feet.

"Stranger things," Charlotte said, and the sisters walked on.

Henry lay in the Victorian section of the cemetery among autumn's rusted bracken. Like the graves to either side, his headstone's gray existence was relieved only by lichen and an inscription. The fog blurred the stone's edge, so the marker appeared to hover just above the ground. The inscription's square letters, which said that Henry Mew was born in 1865 and died in 1901, were as black as the hard-won tarnish of a silver teapot.

The sisters stood on either side of their brother's grave without speaking.

Breaking the silence, Charlotte said, "Something's different from last year."

"Last year, the day was sunny, the bracken was green, and there was enough wind to fly a kite," Anne said.

"I meant aside from spring's late arrival." Charlotte looked down at the grave and recalled the pinecones that the sisters cleared from the grave each year. She walked around the foot of the grave to the plot's perimeter, where she peered through a hedge at a large, ugly stump. "The giant evergreen's vanished," she called over her shoulder. "The one we called 'Bertie' because of its resemblance to King Edward."

Anne knelt beside the grave on an old counterpane, taken from the carpetbag, and tended the grave. Charlotte joined her sister, standing over the grave after propping her umbrella against its headstone. She traced Henry's name with her ring finger and thought of the pact she and Anne had made, fifteen years earlier, never to marry. The sisters' annual visits to their brother's grave reminded Charlotte of the necessity of their pact, yet the sisters never spoke of it, not on this day or any other day of the year. It was as if by keeping the pact, they needn't mention it.

Anne talked as she methodically cleared the leaves and twigs of last year's storms. "If Aunt Fanny were here, she would say the fog is the fairies' way of making mischief for silly townsfolk who choose to waste an afternoon visiting graves."

Charlotte knelt on the counterpane beside Anne and took a white carnation from the bouquet. "Especially as the graves' occupants are frolicking in the woods with the fairies, making dandelion wine for the fairy king's inauguration, of which our dearly departed is a special guest." She held the carnation to her nose and breathed its clean scent.

"What still puzzles me," said Anne, rearranging the bouquet before placing it on the heart of the grave, "is that Aunt Fanny believed every word while insisting it was only make-believe." Charlotte laid the white carnation at the base of the headstone. "She knew reality and truth aren't synonymous. And she never grew up into a foolish human being."

Anne sat back on her heels. "Neither did Henry."

"But unlike Aunt Fanny," Charlotte said, "Henry never had the chance." She put her hand on the headstone to raise herself up, when a crimson mark, just to the right of the stone, arrested her vision. She crawled toward it, then peered around the stone's corner. "Anne, you won't believe this." Behind Henry's headstone lay a scarlet rose as fresh as if a wild rose bush bloomed nearby. The patch of red Charlotte had spotted was a stray petal. Anne joined Charlotte but remained standing.

Charlotte looked up at Anne, whose mouth formed an O. "Fairies?" Charlotte asked.

"Why it must be for another grave, mustn't it?" Anne replied.

The sisters searched for another grave directly behind Henry's. There was a grave to the right, and two graves to the left, but none that accounted for a single rose placed just so behind Henry's gravestone.

Charlotte stood and brushed off her hands. "Another mystery for the ages."

Suddenly, Anne's face shone. "What if Henry has an admirer. Even a sweetheart. A girlfriend who still pines for him?"

"It's possible," Charlotte said without conviction.

Anne's face fell. "The fairies are a more likely explanation," she admitted. "But the rose is certainly pretty."

The sisters again stood in silence.

Anne patted the headstone. "Happy birthday, Henry." She turned and took up the counterpane and folded it before tucking it away in the carpetbag.

Charlotte placed her hand on the cold stone, damp with fog, and shut her eyes. When she opened them, she hesitated a moment, then quickly stooped to retrieve the crimson petal, waxen as the inside fold of a dog's ear, and put it in her skirt pocket.

The sisters heard Eddie before seeing him. Snuffling among fallen branches on the trail of a squirrel, the Irish setter broke through the tall grass along the lane and bounded toward them, his tongue lolling from a side of his mouth. Mud encrusted the feathers of fur hanging from his underside and tail, a collar encircled his neck, and a leash trailed between his feathered legs. Cockleburs polka-dotted his once-sleek coat. He wagged his body and shook his head at the sisters, a grin creasing his face.

Charlotte turned to Anne. "Eddie, I presume?" The setter barked and jumped in the air, happy to find himself among friends.

Before they could search for him, the boy came padding down the lane, the limp string still dangling from his hand. With his other hand, he grabbed Eddie's collar. The setter sat next to the boy and looked up at him.

Eddie's face said he was glad their game of tag was ended and the boy had won at last.

"You found him," the boy said accusingly.

"Truth be told," Charlotte said, "he found us."

The boy turned to leave.

"Wait," Charlotte said, "Where is your mother?"

"Home," he replied.

"Where is home?" Anne asked.

The boy pointed to the horizon.

"Are you alone?" Charlotte asked.

The boy shook his head. "Father's there." The boy pointed again, this time over his shoulder.

Anne looked to Charlotte.

Charlotte asked, "Could we meet him?"

The boy shrugged indifferently.

Eddie led the way, the boy holding the leash as the setter pulled him along, the sisters in tow.

Either the man was unusually short or the grave he dug was deep. They saw the top of his head and then dirt shower from the hole. He whistled a familiar tune. The boy stood over the hole and dangled his string into it. Curse words replaced the whistling. A shovel flew out, handle first.

"You better not been runnin' over the graves," the man said, abruptly hoisting himself from the hole to seat himself on its rim. He pulled a green apple from a rucksack and offered it to the boy.

The boy shook his head and motioned toward Charlotte and Anne, who stood eight feet from the grave. The man looked up at them without comment, as if gentlewomen watching him luncheon was all in a day's work. Despite the inclement day, the man's shirtsleeves were rolled up over his elbows. He bit into the apple and wiped his mouth on a sleeve. Like the setter's and the boy's, his hair was red beneath his cap.

Charlotte broke the silence. "We apologize for interrupting your work. But we wanted to be certain the boy wasn't alone."

The sisters and the man looked in concert at the boy. The boy wrestled a branch from Eddie's mouth with one hand while holding his string in the other.

"Have you been botherin' the ladies, lad?"

Before the boy could answer, Charlotte interjected. "Oh no, he's been a gentleman. We just ..."

"Wanted to be sure he was no orphan," the man finished. He threw the half-eaten apple into the grave, stood up and brushed off his trousers. He turned to Charlotte.

"The missus and I tried tradin' him and his sisters to gypsies, but all they'd give us for the lot of 'em was a horseshoe to hang over our threshold, as though to say without children we'd have all the luck in the world." The man winked at the sisters.

Afraid for half a moment the man had been in earnest, Charlotte breathed out.

The man bent to gather his things, but stopped, a pickaxe in his hand, and studied them. "What brings you to these parts, and on a bloomin' day like this?" he asked, turning his head in the fog. "Come from London to visit country relatives?"

"Yes," Charlotte said, "in a manner of speaking."

"Our brother is buried here," Anne explained.

The man nodded. "The boy's mother tells him if he goes off with his father to work, he mustn't walk on top the property of other folks. That doin' so might wake what lies there. It's not houses that are haunted, she believes, but people. And the surest way to becomin' haunted yourself is by walkin' on a body's grave."

Charlotte looked to Anne, whose eyes conveyed Charlotte's own dismay. It had occurred to Anne just as it had Charlotte that the man had mistaken the sisters for ghosts.

"Our aunt always said any sprites one meets in cemeteries are bound to be fairies, not ghosts," Anne spoke quickly to reassure the man they were among the living, "and that all fairies are well meaning, even those who are mischievous."

"Gypsies, ghosts, fairies. And the only name I'm called is gravedigger because I work 'ere." The man swung his pickaxe around his head before putting it in his toolkit with the shovel and a spade. "If I dug holes in a churchyard, they'd call me sexton and ask me to ring the bell on Sundays." The man hoisted his toolkit and rucksack onto his back and tipped his cap to the sisters in farewell.

"Eddie," the man called. The boy came running, the string still clasped in his hand, but the Irish setter was nowhere to be seen. The boy and the man turned to leave.

"Just a moment," Charlotte said, her hand instinctively grasping Anne's arm for support. The man and the boy turned. "We thought Eddie was your setter."

The man looked down at the boy and shook his head at him, clearly exasperated. The man nodded toward his son and said, "He's Eddie." The boy pulled an innocent face. The man whistled sharply, and the setter came bounding through a hedge, pleased whatever its lot.

"So who's this," Anne asked of the setter, unsure of the punchline.

" 'enry," the boy shouted. The setter barked and rolled onto his back. Eddie put his hands over his mouth and giggled, the string at his lips the last word. As if the boy's conspirator, Charlotte tossed her head and laughed out loud. Then Eddie, with the gravedigger and with Henry, disappeared a second time into the fog.

Before the sisters arrived home, the heavens would open and the rains pour down. For now, each lost in her own thoughts, they made their way up the lane to catch the omnibus back to Bloomsbury in time for tea.

Finally, Anne mused aloud, "What do you think Eddie had on the end of his string?"

"I think," Charlotte said wistfully, remembering Henry as a child and the evergreen that had overlooked his grave, "it was nothing less than the whole world."

CHAPTER 2

An oversized wooden door shut heavily behind Charlotte and Anne, enclosing them in a cool, dark vestibule, where the strains of a pipe organ filtered to them from the nave. Each year, in the same week that they visited Henry's grave, the sisters attended Sunday services at Anne's church, St. Mary's, located a block south of Gordon Street.

Reverend Cecil stood before the nave's entrance. He held his hands together in front of his vestments and greeted them with a ceremonial air. "Ah, if it isn't the sisters Mew," he said, taking Anne's outstretched hand in his while looking down at Charlotte.

"We could hardly be anyone else," Charlotte replied, then bit her lip.

"Quite true," he said. "It's good to see you, Charlotte, after so long. You mustn't let my senseless comments keep you from God's house." He turned to a family of four, dismissing the sisters.

Charlotte and Anne made their way up the center aisle to a pew on the left, halfway between the entrance and the lectern. Charlotte took her seat while Anne pulled down the kneeler and knelt, bowing her head and resting her folded hands on the pew in front of her.

Charlotte's eyes settled on the imposing stained-glass image of Christ beyond the altar. Three sheep lay at his sandaled feet, his right hand leant on a staff, and his left hand was raised, its palm toward Charlotte. On the altar, a gold crucifix stood, and to either side of the altar, urns overflowed with red and white carnations.

A woman in black edged herself laboriously into the pew in front of the sisters before sitting down with a harrumph, interposing herself between Charlotte and the crucifix. The woman took *The Book of Common Prayer* from the pew and a handkerchief from her sleeve, which she used to dust the worn red volume, as if dispelling germs callously left by less conscientious parishioners.

Eyebrows raised, Charlotte looked to Anne, who mouthed, "Mrs. Mendelssohn." Charlotte nodded, the organ's notes rose dramatically, and the mace bearer proceeded up the aisle, followed by Reverend Cecil. Behind them, a tall, thin man peered above and beyond the procession, as if wanting to head it rather than take up its rear. He darted into the pew catty-corner to Mrs. Mendelssohn's, his hat in his large, rectangular hands. Charlotte recognized him as Mr. Wheeler, whom Anne had aptly nicknamed the White Rabbit.

During the sermon, Mr. Wheeler sat as upright as a schoolboy and nodded at key points in the sermon, while at the same time Mrs. Mendelssohn shook her head. Mrs. Mendelssohn wore a black shawl whose horseshoe lace hung over the back of her pew, and each time Mrs. Mendelssohn shook her head, the black lace shimmied.

Charlotte looked at Anne to see if she noticed, but Anne was glancing timidly over her shoulder. Charlotte turned and saw a man's eager face staring in the sisters' direction. She looked back at Anne, who had turned her head and now listened attentively to the sermon.

Anne served on the altar guild with Mr. Wheeler and Mrs. Mendelssohn, and she frequently described their squabbles over Sunday tea. But Charlotte couldn't recall Anne ever mentioning a dark-complexioned man with soulful eyes. Confused, Charlotte tried to focus on Reverend Cecil's words.

"In this Lenten season, on the eve of Christ's crucifixion — his suffering on the cross until death — we mustn't lose sight of the work yet to be completed here on earth in God's name.

"Christ's sacrifice of his life for our sins does not free us, as indulgent Christians willfully believe, to live our lives as we did before Christ redeemed us. To commit the same sin a hundredth time, while expecting Christ's blood to hide you from God's sight, is folly. God knows who you are, and He sees your sin."

The red and white carnations held Charlotte's gaze.

"Unwilling to leave her life of sin behind, Lot's wife disobeyed God and looked back. Offered a new life, a life free from the corrosive forces of carnality, she turned away from God's vision of the future toward her old life in Sodom.

"Sinner, I say to you, though redeemed by Christ's crucifixion, you must leave your old life of sin behind. You must not look back. You must look forward to the work left to do in God's name."

Each urn appeared to hold one huge red or white carnation without discernible rosettes. The brilliant red carnation struck Charlotte like a knife's blow.

"Christ's passion was for mankind. Will you repay his suffering by turning away from his Father's will for your life? Think of the consequences if Christ had turned away as you have.

"Never forget. Everything is God's. Everything."

Mrs. Mendelssohn shook her head, the black lace shimmied, and Charlotte's gaze was broken.

Reverend Cecil prepared to give the benediction, but when he raised his right hand, opened his mouth, and took a breath — all in slow motion — a sharp cry and then a loud kafuffle came from the rear of the church. When she turned, Charlotte saw a man's prostrate figure in the center aisle. It was the man with black hair and penetrating eyes whom Anne had glanced at during the sermon. Half the congregants looked on confused while the other half rushed to action, crowding around the man. Anne clutched Charlotte's arm as they stood together in their pew.

"Stand back. Give him room to breathe," Mrs. Mendelssohn demanded, taking the situation in hand. She had trained as a nurse in her twenties, Anne once told Charlotte, with the hope of doing missionary work in the Congo. The crowd thinned. Charlotte could see Mrs. Mendelssohn loosen the man's tie and collar, then take his pulse. Reverend Cecil stood over her and the man as though he were the Angel of Death. Meanwhile, Mr. Wheeler officiously shooed milling congregants to the front of the nave. When Anne hesitated, Charlotte led her forward, and the sisters joined the procession, the crucifix drawing Christ's sheep nearer, before the flock suddenly veered right into the narthex.

Mr. Wheeler silenced the murmurs of the newly gathered congregants and asked that they bow their heads in prayer. "Dear Lord," he began, "one of St. Mary's parishioners, your devoted servant Mr. Antony, has been struck down. We ask that you raise him up and make him well again. In your name, Amen." Mr. Wheeler lifted his head and touched an oversized handkerchief to his lips, and the murmurs recommenced.

Anne wore a veil of despair. But it was anger that spoke when Anne, avoiding Charlotte's eyes, declared, "It doesn't matter that he's an Italian immigrant and a butcher. Mr. Antony is worth twice as much as any man here. Why isn't it one of them who was taken ill?" Anne looked around accusingly, then hid her face in her hands and wept.

"There, there," Charlotte said and pulled Anne to her side. "Everything will be all right, I promise." Charlotte looked from the sisters' solitary union to the islands of families around them. She saw each man as a substitute for Mr. Antony, whose name Anne had never spoken to Charlotte before today.

Mrs. Mendelssohn entered the narthex. Instead of addressing the expectant congregants with news of Mr. Antony's health, as Charlotte anticipated, she sat down two tables away from the sisters' table. Mr. Wheeler went to Mrs. Mendelssohn's side and stood listening to her, looking from table to table, nodding his head as she spoke. Surely, they know how he is, Charlotte thought. We're all waiting. Just tell us.

Anne hiccoughed but no longer wept. Mr. Wheeler left Mrs. Mendelssohn and joined several men circulating among the tables. A distinguished man in a gray suit stopped at the sisters' table, a pad of paper and fountain pen in his hand. He nodded at Charlotte and glanced at Anne, who hiccoughed.

"Please sign here," he said, holding out the pen and paper. A note, Charlotte wondered, of condolences for Mr. Antony's family?

"What's this for?" Anne asked, suddenly composed, looking up at the man and then across at Charlotte's bewildered expression.

"The council meeting, of course," he said.

Anne shook her head, confused.

The man persisted. "We're taking an official count. We need enough parishioners to make a quorum." He moved the pen and paper toward Anne.

Anne hiccoughed. "I'm sorry. We're not staying for the meeting."

The man looked at Charlotte as if she were to blame for everything. Mr. Antony. The failed quorum. The late spring. "Please yourselves," he said and abruptly turned away.

Anne rose, followed by Charlotte, and they headed toward the nearest exit. Mrs. Mendelssohn, like a farsighted battleship at full speed, steamed toward the sisters in pursuit. Charlotte stood her ground to confront her. "What about Mr. Antony?" Charlotte demanded when Mrs. Mendelssohn reached them.

"Yes, Mr. Antony," Anne echoed.

Though Charlotte's height, Mrs. Mendelssohn managed to look down at the sisters through the lower half of her spectacles. "The man who was taken ill?" she asked.

"He collapsed," Anne insisted.

"That's what we're all waiting for, isn't it," Charlotte asked, "to learn how he is?"

Mrs. Mendelssohn's demeanor stiffened. Her chin fell to her chest, and she looked at Anne over her spectacles. "If you please," she said slowly, "we're here to safeguard our parish against the diocese's threats to disband us."

Anne hiccoughed at Mrs. Mendelssohn, then turned to Charlotte and nodded. "I remember now. It's just that with Mr. Antony having been taken ill, I thought ..."

Charlotte put her hand on Anne's arm and addressed Mrs. Mendelssohn. "If you please," she said, looking over Mrs. Mendelssohn's spectacles into her black eyes, "Mr. Antony, tell us how he is."

Mrs. Mendelssohn frowned. "Mr. Antony," she said to Charlotte, "is perfectly fine. He'll be back at his butcher shop in no time." She paused meaningfully. "Thanks to me." She looked at Anne. "Let's hope we can say the same for our parish in a year's time." She turned to leave, but paused. "No thanks to you," she added, then left the sisters standing alone.

CHAPTER 3

The sisters took the short way home, walking along the west side of Gordon Square toward Gordon Street. Charlotte waited for Anne to speak of Mr. Antony, but instead Anne took up a comfortable refrain as though nothing unusual had happened.

"I'll take the butterflies and the flowers," Anne said, "and you can have the birds and the trees."

"An agreeable arrangement, I think," Charlotte said, "although the birds and the trees might not agree."

"Wek's a bird. Will you take him with the rest?" Anne asked.

"Wek is a category unto himself, as everyone he's met knows."

"And the sky?" Anne asked, "Who will have the sky?"

"The sky," Charlotte said, "we must share, whatever the weather."

In the entry, the sisters took off hats and coats, and Charlotte stamped her feet to let Jane know below stairs that they were home.

Jane had the best training for domestic service — a tutelage from Nurse Goodman who, having brought up the Mew Children, lived long enough to move the family from the Doughty Street house to Gordon Street and train her successor, Jane, before dying in harness as she had hoped for. Thus, Jane didn't need to attend the Domestic Economy School either to learn "housewifery, cookery, and laundry" or to comprehend the irony that the school operated short hours Sunday through Friday, and on Saturdays and holidays, was closed — a fate wholly opposite of the girls it trained, when half a day a week was all the leisure each girl was afforded once she found a position.

But the perks of domestic service allowed girls such as Jane to live-in. While doing so meant longer hours and little autonomy, it also meant, in Jane's instance as the maid-of-all-work, the queendom of below stairs, the basement level of the Gordon Street house, where she cooked, laundered clothes and linens, slept, and spent what free time she had reading comic strips in the pantry.

In the front room of the ground floor, Mrs. Mew lay propped on her invalid's sofa, as the sisters expected, but her arm covered her eyes as if she were sleeping. Wek, Mrs. Mew's African gray parrot, eyed the sisters from his cage beside the sofa. Charlotte nodded to Anne, who drew the curtain over the bay window, where the white sun of early spring crept in like a late guest.

"Who's that?" Wek asked, and Mrs. Mew started. "What time is it," she demanded, looking around.

"We didn't mean to wake you," Anne said.

"I wasn't sleeping, child. I was resting my eyes." Mrs. Mew looked down at the Sunday newspaper folded haphazardly beside her.

Jane entered with the tea tray. "We're out of Earl Gray, so I laid on breakfast tea," she said.

"I'll pick up more tomorrow," Charlotte said.

Mrs. Mew sniffed. "You said that Friday."

"I could nip out if you like, Mrs. Mew. Haggerty's is closed on Sundays, but Barney's is open. It'll take just a quarter hour," Jane offered, setting the tray on the tea table.

"You might have thought of that before you began, my dear. Complete tasks in their proper order. That is what Mrs. Kendall told her maid. I pass on the knowledge to you with the hope that our household might run as smoothly as my mother's."

"Yes, Mrs. Mew," Jane said. "If you please, ma'am, I'll return to the scullery. I still have the coal shuttles to scrub." She curtsied before dismissing herself.

Ignoring Jane's comment, Mrs. Mew searched in her cushion for the red pencil she used for her crossword.

Charlotte thought, as she had a hundred times, that Jane was a godsend.

The sisters took their seats, and Anne served tea to Mrs. Mew, then Charlotte, and last herself. Mrs. Mew sat up on her sofa but kept the afghan in steady tow over her legs. She took her tea in an oversized teacup, twice as big and in a different pattern than the regular cups of the tea service, but treasured by Mrs. Mew because the unique cup had belonged to a favorite aunt.

"How is Reverend Cecil," she asked, intoning her preference for gossip over news.

"He asked after you and said he will send a lay pastor this week to administer communion," Anne said.

"And not come himself," Mrs. Mew said.

"He means well," Anne said.

"Meaning well and doing good are two very different things," Mrs. Mew said. "He wouldn't miss the Last Supper, excusing himself later by saying he meant to come, I assure you." Mrs. Mew looked at Charlotte. "You're unusually quiet."

"Only tired," Charlotte explained.

"Anne, you're quiet as well," said Mrs. Mew, looking at one sister and then the other over her teacup, hungry for conversation, not biscuits.

In the entry, the grandfather clock struck 11. Wek bobbed in rhythm with each chime and fanned his wings.

Sitting up suddenly, Mrs. Mew said, "Church dismisses at 10. Where have you girls been?"

Wek squawked, "Where've you been? Wek is so very handsome. Isn't Wek handsome?"

Charlotte looked at Anne, who studied the teacup in her lap. Neither sister answered.

"That's enough, Wek," Mrs. Mew said. But she had lost the conversation's thread. "I hope you girls haven't forgotten," she said.

The sisters sipped their tea knowingly.

"I would see to it myself," Mrs. Mew continued, "as with Henry, but in my condition" (Charlotte and Anne knew all about Mrs. Mew's condition) "I fear the journey would prove far too precarious."

The conversation was as well-rehearsed as the grandfather clock's chime. It began each March, after the sisters visited Nunhead Cemetery, and continued until they returned from the Isle of Wight in September.

"We understand, Ma," Anne soothed her, "and we haven't forgot. It's marked on the calendar, in September, the same as every year."

"And you'll tell me everything," Mrs. Mew demanded. "You'll keep nothing to yourselves."

"Of course, Ma. We always tell you everything," Charlotte lied.

"Our dear girl, Freda, must know I'm lost without her," said Mrs. Mew.

"Of course, Ma," Anne said. "You can depend on us."

CHAPTER 4

Charlotte wasn't sure whether she had slept or dozed. When she woke, the patch of sky in its window frame was the shade of spent coal. She lay in bed under the counterpane sewn and embroidered by Charlotte in her twenties, so long ago she might have only imagined it.

In November, she would be forty years old. Charlotte's thoughts ranged over the last twenty years. Her run as a fiction writer and essayist with the aim, early on, of fame, and later, and far more urgently, of money. That utter foolishness in Paris, not so long ago, her dumb heart quickened, then duly chastened. It seemed now as if she were waiting, but for what?

She swung her legs over the side of the bed. Sitting on the hard mattress — penance, she thought, for the easy sleep unappreciated in youth — she retrieved her pocket watch from the nightstand. 5:30. She had slept, but she felt more restless than rested.

Her room, her very own room in the Gordon Street house, was spartan. There was a dresser of drawers, a wardrobe, a vanity that doubled as a writing desk, and two steamer trunks, both appointed with leather straps and buckles for the rough waters of a sea voyage, but neither of which contained anything of value.

The wardrobe was a child's, fine for Charlotte since she was child-sized herself — from her diminutive stature to her size 4 boots, which she had worn for ten years and whose heels she had replaced three times. There was little money to spare for new clothes, and any money spent on clothes was spent on Anne, for whom fashion mattered. Gone were the full skirts and crinolines, fitted bodice, and stiff, upright collar of the Victorian era. Today, the fashionable Edwardian woman wore the less confining shirtwaist and a more fitted, ankle-length skirt, which was slightly less cumbersome than its predecessor.

Charlotte shed her nightgown and dressed in a shirtwaist and skirt (one of three she owned, each in an identical twill fabric of brown, blue, and black, and expertly altered by Anne to resemble the current fashion). Later she would dress her hair in a chignon, how she had worn it for years, despite the changing styles. First, however, she would smoke a cigarette, a less-than-genteel habit for women, but a freedom, Charlotte swore, more important than the vote. Luckily, neither Ma's hearing nor sense of smell was acute, or Charlotte would have to escape to the attic rooms or forego the cigarette until her walk through the Gordon Square garden later that day.

She sat at her desk, positioned by the window overlooking Gordon Street and the Gordon Square garden, catty-corner from the Mews' home.

From a desk drawer, she took out a red leather pouch of tobacco and a packet of cigarette papers. She rolled a cigarette, licking its thin edge, and then lighted it with a match scratched on the sole of her shoe. She inhaled, feeling guilty, because she knew she must quit (Nurse Goodman's voice in her ear), but in her guilt, she also felt at home. She exhaled and watched the plume of shame rise toward the ceiling. In her left hand, she fingered her long braid, just beginning to reveal strands of silver.

When she was a child, Uncle Richard would sneak up behind her and pull her braid. When she turned, he would say, "That's what the boys'll do. Wait and see, Lotti. Boys like petite girls best." Then Uncle would tweak her nose and wink, as if theirs was a secret like no one else's.

A knock came at the door, startling Charlotte.

"Miss Lotti?"

Charlotte rose. "Just a moment, Jane." She stubbed out her cigarette and smoothed her hair and skirt.

"Yes, Jane?" Charlotte said after opening the door.

Jane was dressed haphazardly in her maid's uniform, over which she wore a shawl that Charlotte had never seen, and whose corners she clutched in her right hand.

"Mr. Boynton, it seems," Jane grimaced and frowned.

"Yes, Mr. Boynton?" Charlotte said encouragingly.

"It seems Mr. Boynton has ..." Jane put her left hand to her mouth.

"Perhaps you should come in," Charlotte said and moved aside so Jane might enter.

"I couldn't," Jane said, removing her hand from her mouth.

It was one thing, Charlotte surmised, for Jane to strip the bedsheets on laundry day or lug the carpet down the backstairs with Charlotte's help to air it in the back garden. It was another thing to enter the room for polite conversation.

"It's just that," Jane whispered, leaning toward Charlotte as if to share a secret, "Mr. Boynton has lost *his teeth*." She stood back and clapped her hand back over her mouth.

Charlotte imagined Mr. Boynton, missing his two front teeth, looking under his pillow for something left in their place by the tooth fairy.

Charlotte looked past Jane into the hall.

Jane, exasperated, said, "And so *his tuba*."

"Yes?" Charlotte dared to ask.

Jane, impatient, burst out. "He can't play his tuba without his teeth." She fingered the corners of her shawl in pantomime, as if the shawl were Mr. Boynton's tuba.

Charlotte understood. It was no less than a crisis of monumental proportions, at least to Jane. "Are we to help him find them?" Charlotte asked.

Relieved, Jane nodded and dropped her hands.

Charlotte said, "I'll be with you shortly."

Mr. Boynton sublet the third floor of the Mews' house, one large room to the front of the house, overlooking Gordon Street, and three rooms to the back. It was understood when Mr. Boynton took the rooms that Mrs. Mew shouldn't meet him on the front stairs.

Now Charlotte climbed the backstairs and joined Jane on the third-floor landing. Jane stood with a feather duster in one hand and a dry mop in the other, as if they were swords drawn for battle.

"What on earth?" asked Charlotte, nodding toward Jane's implements.

"It's just that," but before Jane could explain, Mr. Boynton announced himself by slamming the door of a room just off the landing. He hurried toward them.

"I'm sorry I'm disturbed," he said, putting his hand to the center part of his well-oiled hair. "I mean, I'm sorry I've disturbed you," he corrected himself.

"You needn't apologize, Mr. Boynton," Charlotte said as reassuringly as she could. "Only tell us how we are to help."

Mr. Boynton looked at Charlotte just as Jane had. "Find my teeth!" he shouted, evidently confounded by Charlotte's obtuseness. Jane's expression begged Charlotte not to ask Mr. Boynton to describe his teeth to them.

"Of course," Charlotte answered calmly.

Charlotte was hesitant to compromise Mr. Boynton's privacy. Then again, she told herself, she was searching for the man's teeth at his request.

The three back rooms revealed nothing, or rather, produced no teeth.

In the front room, the early morning sun seeped through the story-length windows. Entering behind Mr. Boynton and Jane, Charlotte started. She saw Mr. Boynton's parlor table, a pair of armchairs, and a tuba on its stand. Then she saw her father's drafting table, facing the yawning windows as it had for more than ten years, and alongside it, facing the doorway where Charlotte stood, Henry's table, a study in miniature of their father's. Of course, it was only the play of morning light, but there Henry sat on his swivel chair, a pencil behind his left ear, another pencil in his hand. He winked at her, twirled the pencil between his fingers, and hunkered down to work.

Mr. Boynton's teeth were nowhere to be found, for she and Jane (with Mr. Boynton at Charlotte's side, pointing under the cushions of the settee and shaking his head each time Charlotte came up empty-handed) overturned and self-consciously plumped every throw pillow in the front room. They searched in the joins of the chairs, on the mantle, and beneath and within the coal shuttle. The teeth, and their whereabouts, remained a mystery.

Defeated, Mr. Boynton sunk into the chair next to his beloved tuba, and, mimicking his hand's placement on his head an hour before, rested his hand on the tuba's horn and sighed.

Jane promised Mr. Boynton she would look again later, once Mrs. Mew was installed on her sofa and the dusting completed. Inconsolable, Mr. Boynton looked to the carpet for answers, then at the mouthpiece upturned in the palm of his hand. Charlotte was hovering in the doorway in sympathy with Mr. Boynton, far away and utterly lost, when beside the tuba she saw the smiling keys of the Mew family's piano and heard its Middle C echo down the years. Without Charlotte, the voice of Middle C intimated, it was as mute as Mr. Boynton's tuba without Mr. Boynton's teeth.

CHAPTER 5

Charlotte helped Ma down the stairs each morning: Ma's right hand on the banister, her left arm supported by Charlotte. "Don't forget Wek," Mrs. Mew said. Jane couldn't forget Wek, and she did not forget Mrs. Mew's walking cane, but hooked it through the bars of Wek's cage and carried them together behind Charlotte and Mrs. Mew. (Ma wore her cane like Charlotte wore her umbrella, mother and daughter willing to accept sunshine but more optimistic about continuing showers.)

During that morning's processional, Charlotte thought of young Queen Victoria's walk down the royal staircase, always accompanied, lest she fall. Born in 1836, Ma was one year old when Victoria, at nineteen, assumed the throne. Imagine all the changes Ma witnessed through the long years of Queen Victoria's reign. Imagine the happiness of Victoria's marriage to Albert, a happiness, unfortunately, Anna Maria Kendall had not shared with Fred Mew.

"Don't fuss. You mustn't fuss. You always fuss so," Ma scolded as Charlotte tucked her in an afghan. Before Mr. Boynton's tuba and the street traffic, the motorcars and omnibuses overtaking London's streets as if their perpetual right of way, 9 Gordon Street had been a quiet house. Charlotte listened again for Middle C, but heard only the faint strains of Jane singing below stairs. Ensconced in view of the portrait of herself as a young woman of nineteen, Mrs. Mew was contented working a crossword and muttering to herself, a freshly pressed and scented hankie in one hand, a red pencil in the other. Anna Maria Kendall, as Mrs. Mew was called when she was nineteen, wore the Gordon Street house outside-in. Sitting on her sofa in the front room, she was ever conscious of their address in Bloomsbury, so the address might as well hang on the lintel as on the doorpost.

Fred Mew, despite his many faults (chronicled arduously by Ma through the years), had at least got them up from Doughty Street to the more fashionable Gordon Street in 1890, when Charlotte was just twenty-one, and the Victorian world was dissolving, as if Queen Victoria's Golden Jubilee, three years earlier, was the welcoming of a more liberal era and not the solidifying of a conservative past. Still, like the Doughty Street house, which sat just off Mecklenburgh Square and thus feet short of a truly good address, the Gordon Street house, though a grander house on a wider street, was likewise one house short of Gordon Square.

After helping Ma down the stairs with Charlotte, Jane promised to let Charlotte know should she lay her hands on Mr. Boynton's teeth. They giggled conspiratorially at Jane's expression. "Lay her hands on," as if Mr.

Boynton's teeth might be rectified by Jane's healing touch. Following her usual breakfast of soft-boiled eggs and toast with marmalade, Charlotte returned to her room to spend the morning "scribbling," what she called her writing ever since she had failed to write anything worth publishing. Fifteen years earlier, Charlotte had a brush with fame when a short story of hers was published in *The Yellow Book*. Since then, she had published a number of essays in mostly dull women's magazines, earning some pin money, but fame had eluded her.

Charlotte addressed a letter to the trustees of Nunhead Cemetery. She must know the fate of "Bertie," the evergreen tree felled sometime this past year. She gave its approximate distance and direction from Henry's grave and the height of the tree as she remembered it. The description was clinical and inadequate. As she struggled to find the right words, Charlotte imagined Mr. Boynton's sitting room above her own room and saw, just as she had that morning, Henry's drafting table alongside Fred Mew's, the faint sun lighting the table's roughhewn surface.

Charlotte fingered the grain of her desk, imagining it was Henry's table and her hand was his hand. She heard, as she listened, Uncle Richard ask his nephew, did he want to be a builder, like his father? She looked up from her desk into the past and saw Henry, ten years old, shake his head, slowly moving his chin from shoulder to shoulder.

Uncle Richard said, "He knows what he's not going to be." Uncle laughed and looked around at the rest of the family. Encouraged, Uncle went on. "Does Henry want to be an innkeeper or a brewer?" Henry shrugged his shoulders. "How about a farmer like your favorite Uncle? C'mon, Henry. Don't you want to slop pigs?" Henry shook his head. Aunt Fanny smoothed Henry's cowlick. "So, what'll it be," she asked. "Will you be my special beau?"

Henry looked up at Aunt Fanny, wonder and desire shining in his eyes. "I want to be the man in the public gardens. The one with a big rucksack on his back. And I want a pole that paper sticks to like magic." Henry, his most secret desire wrested from him, dropped his head in shame at the exposure. "Your son wants to be a trash picker, Fred," Uncle Richard said, shaking his head. Their father only laughed, whereas Ma harrumphed and stuck her nose in the air at the indignity of it all.

No one asked Charlotte, Anne, or Freda what they wanted to be when they grew up. They would be ladies first, Ma told them, then wives and mothers.

Charlotte signed off her letter to the trustees and prepared an envelope. She doubted whether the cemetery kept records of the fate of a single tree, given the massive forest of Nunhead. But she wouldn't know unless she wrote. She raised her head, envelope in mid-air, and listened. *She wouldn't know unless she wrote.* There it was again, the melodic and insistent voice of Middle C, bobbing on the distant waves of time.

She laid down the envelope, picked up her fountain pen, and, on a fresh sheet of paper, wrote "Requiescat." She closed her eyes and imagined Henry's ideal resting place as he might have drawn it. First, in descriptive phrases, she sketched images of Nunhead and the countryside of the Isle of Wight. The birds and the trees, the road and the sky, and a soft bed of daffodils. Then she listened to the sounds and to the beats of the words and phrases, searching for poetic form. But instead of lines of charcoal measured with a ruler, she measured her lines in verse.

> *What threat of old imaginings,*
> *Half-haunted joy, enchanted pain,*
> *Or dread of unfamiliar things*
> *Should ever trouble you again?*
>
> *Yet you would wake and want, you said*
> *The little whirr of wings, the clear*
> *Gay notes, the wind, the golden bed*
> *Of the daffodil: and they are here!*
>
> *Beyond the line of naked trees*
> *At the road's end, your stretch of blue —*
> *Strange if you should remember these*
> *As we, ah! God! Remember you!*

It was incomplete. Words dropped from the ceiling or snatched from the sky. But they were the first words she had written in years in what she recognized as her own voice — strained and hoarse, perhaps, but also insistent, even melodic at turns. She sat back in her chair, unsure of how much time had passed with the flow of words. By the patch of sky through the window, she thought it must be noon.

It was because Charlotte loved the sky that she and not Anne made the front room of the first floor her bedroom, what was once the family's drawing room. Its three large windows faced east and each morning welcomed the sun. Because Anne worked in the afternoon and into the evening, she insisted that a back room facing west (and with only two much smaller windows) suited her. Moreover, she argued, any time she liked she might go to the small plot of land at the foot of their backstairs (euphemistically termed "the back garden") to paint "en plein air." Thus, Charlotte had taken the front room for herself.

Now she crept down the hall to Anne's room. Anne, a night owl, slept in, whereas Charlotte, a "morning" dove, as Anne affectionately called her, woke at the first notes of birdsong.

She tapped on the door.

"Come in," Anne said, sounding bright and fully awake. Charlotte entered a room half the size of her own. Anne, still in her nightgown, was sitting up in bed, sketching.

Without looking up, Anne said, "I dreamt last night of the Isle of Wight and of Uncle's and Aunt's farmhouse. But instead of small hillocks behind the house, there were mountains, their peaks in the clouds, and as the clouds moved to the east, the mountains moved to the west. Isn't that the oddest dream?"

Charlotte, having taken a seat on the edge of Anne's bed, looked at the sketch when Anne turned it toward her. In the background were charcoal clouds and rust-colored evergreens. In the middle ground stood the farmhouse, a two-story clapboard ... without the red shutters or the blue door Charlotte remembered so well.

Anne interpreted her sketch. "It's Uncle's and Aunt's house, and yet it's another house ... where another family lives when Uncle and Aunt aren't there ... but when they are there, the landscape changes, as in a diorama."

Anne handed Charlotte a brilliant blue pencil. "Shade in the door, so then we can say that we both built it." Charlotte laughed and took the pencil. First, she wrote *door*, scribbling lightly where she saw the door. Then she drew a rectangle around *door* and shaded within it until the letters disappeared.

Charlotte turned the sketchbook toward Anne, who studied the door. "In the dream, there wasn't a doorknob. I looked and looked because the mountains were moving, and I wanted Aunt to see, and you, and Henry. But you were all inside the house. For some reason, though, Freda wasn't anywhere." Charlotte took the sketchbook, picked up a gold pencil, and asked, "May I?" Anne nodded, so Charlotte drew and colored in a doorknob. On top of the blue, the gold was muddy, as if burnished. "There," Charlotte said and handed the sketchbook to her sister. Anne smiled. Charlotte had placed the doorknob in the sky, near the peak of the most distant mountain, as though it were a doorway to the heavens.

Anne turned the book's page to begin a fresh sketch, and Charlotte looked around the disheveled room. Canvases were stacked on top of one another in precarious towers. Paint boxes and rags lost themselves on a table among jars of brushes. Another table, with a canvas propped up by encyclopedias, served as an easel. The smell of turpentine hung in the air, along with the conversation the sisters might have about Mr. Antony. Charlotte wouldn't intrude on Anne's privacy, but she would listen willingly if Anne chose to share her thoughts.

"I wonder if it's healthy for you to sleep here," Charlotte said.

Anne laid down her sketchbook and looked at Charlotte. "You mustn't fuss over me. I am blessed with more, after all, than artists who reuse canvases they might like to keep."

"But wouldn't you like your own studio?" Charlotte asked, forever the elder sister responsible for the younger.

"If we could afford it or if I could sell my paintings for a profit to pay the lease ..." Anne's expression softened. Charlotte wanted to ask Anne what she imagined her studio would look like, but thought it might be cruel. Instead, she said, "I'm going to wrestle with the household accounts for the next couple of hours."

That was Anne's cue. "And I'm going to read the paper to Ma." Anne's soft expression vanished. "I only hope she won't ask me to solve the crosswords that stumped her this morning. Yesterday, she got stuck on "9 Down," and you were at the market and Jane was no help."

Charlotte stood up. "What was the clue?"

"Acute shame or embarrassment."

Charlotte paused, her hand on the doorknob. "How many letters?"

"Seven," said Anne expectantly, "and the first letter was C."

Charlotte opened the door, and then said, "*Chagrin*, I should think." But before leaving, she turned to Anne. "I nearly forgot. Mr. Boynton has lost his teeth. If you find them, whatever you do, don't tell Ma."

CHAPTER 6

In the morning room, at the back of the house on the ground floor, Charlotte sat at what she jokingly called her seat of authority, a wheeled chair with a wooden seat made only slightly less uncomfortable by a thin cushion and a thick catalog of building designs on which she placed her feet. For her legs "mustn't dangle," as Nurse Goodman said.

To be contrary, Charlotte had retorted, "Monkeys' legs dangle, and they're not scolded."

"Monkeys," Nurse Goodman said, "haven't the good fortune of a nanny to keep them from being caught out."

To be caught out, Charlotte knew, was to give oneself away without hope of recovery. For Nurse Goodman and Mrs. Mew as Kendalls (Nurse Goodman, though a servant, was by circumstance a Kendall) appearances were irrefutable markers of not only social class but also moral decency.

Charlotte's reign as Gordon Street's exchequer was more difficult as each year passed. An annuity of 300 pounds must cover the household expenses, which, unlike the annuity, increased each year. There was the lease on the house, the rates and taxes, and the cost of coal, gas, and lamp oil. There were soap and brushes for cleaning, and small change to replace worn linens and bathing towels. There was bread and meat, potatoes and greens, butter and flour. And, of course, they must have tea, and Charlotte her tobacco, papers, and matches. (Smoking was an expensive as well as a nasty habit, and she must quit.) A pittance was set aside for toiletries and various household sundries. Charlotte insisted on a clothing allowance for Anne. Then there were Ma's doctor bills and Jane's wages. (No middle-class household was respectable without at least one maid-of-all-work.) Charlotte and Anne made do with homemade ointments and poultices, distillations and infusions, outlined in *Culpeper's Herbal Remedies* for the common cold, sore throat, fever, and "female troubles." Most frustrating for Charlotte were the endless outlays for repairs to the kitchen range and the boiler, both which conspired to undo number 9.

The tenants, Mrs. Caroline McHardy, a widow, in the second-floor rooms, and Mr. Boynton in the third, were necessities. (Charlotte counted the Mews' lucky stars that the terms of the Gordon Street lease allowed them to sublet.) The tenants had access to the kitchen as well as the privy, using these rooms when at all possible during hours "the lady of the house" would be asleep in her room or at rest in the parlor. If they needed the front room or the dining room to entertain, they must discuss it at least a week in advance with Charlotte (who would discourage them). Most important, except in dire emergencies, they must use the backstairs. Jane provided a weekly dusting and bedding change, but tenants were responsible for their own laundry, cooking, and dishwashing. (Certain cookware and serving dishes in the kitchen were reserved for tenants' use and kept separate from the Mews' crockery by Jane.) Last, because Jane hadn't refused, and it seemed important to make a concession, Jane served the tenants afternoon tea in their rooms.

Mrs. Mew knew of the tenants, of course, but they were never mentioned, not by Charlotte, Anne, Jane, nor Ma herself. The arrangement left two floors strictly to the three women — the first floor, where each of them had a bedroom, and the ground floor, which housed a parlor (kept pristine for the most important occasions), the front room (where Anna Maria spent her days on the invalid's sofa), the dining room, and, finally, the morning room, above the scullery and adjacent to the backstairs. There, besides settling the household's accounts once a week, Charlotte planned the week's menus (with Jane's assistance and final approval) and kept a housekeeping schedule, which she and Jane had followed since Fred Mew's death over a decade ago.

Today, as she reconciled the household accounts in the morning room's gathering western light, Charlotte saw she had less sway than an exchequer. She hadn't the power to raise money except by subletting rooms. She had only the power to decide which bills to pay down and which to put off. Worst of all, Charlotte desperately wanted Anne to have a studio. A windfall not long ago prompted Charlotte to write the holders of the Gordon Street lease for permission to build a studio in the back garden. But the trustees refused, and the windfall was eaten up by overlooked necessities. One mustn't grudge the score, mused Charlotte, signing a check for the rent. But she promised herself that the next windfall would go toward a studio for Anne, no matter what the cost.

Afternoon tea was served promptly at four, except when it wasn't. Today, because of Mr. Boynton's teeth, Jane was behind in everything. When she entered the front room with the tea service, her face was flushed, and tendrils of damp hair escaped from her cap at the temples.

"Sorry, Ma'am," she said to Mrs. Mew, "but ..."

"No excuses are required," Anna Maria interrupted, "because they remedy nothing. But you may pour out my tea if doing so will relieve your guilt."

Except for the sugar she ladled in, Ma took her tea black. Charlotte and Anne preferred theirs with milk, which they poured into their cups. Jane hurriedly poured out tea in Mrs. Mew's favorite teacup, and Charlotte winked at Jane when Ma laced the tea with two heaping teaspoons of sugar, "plus one," she said, "to grow on."

After Jane excused herself, Ma asked, "What's got into her? I've never seen anyone less focused on the task at hand." When Charlotte and Anne glanced at one another, Ma said knowingly, "Oh, female troubles. Kendall women always have struggled with the curse." To Ma, Jane was a Kendall by association, just as Nurse Goodman had been.

Satisfied, Ma sipped her tea. "Your lay minister was here late this morning," she said idly to Anne. "You must have heard the bell. Jane saw him in, and he administered communion. His name escapes me. Mr. Cunningham, I think. But I must say, though forgettable himself, the parish news he shared was memorable indeed."

Charlotte set her teacup in its saucer and held her breath.

"He told me how fearful the entire congregation is that the diocese will close the parish due to dwindling membership and funds."

Charlotte breathed out and glanced at Anne, who looked equally relieved.

"I don't think the situation is as dire as Mr. Cunningham suggests," Anne said. "Reverend Cecil met with the altar guild in January to assure us that the huffing and puffing of the diocese and the gossip among the congregants were just so much wasted breath and energy."

"Mr. Cunningham also told me about the man who collapsed during Sunday's service. Now what was *his* name?" Ma tapped her chin with a forefinger, pretending to be deep in thought.

Charlotte looked at Anne from the corner of her eye. She appeared to be studying the weave of her skirt. Charlotte braced herself.

"Ah, yes. I remember now." Ma narrowed her eyes over her teacup. "It's strange neither of you girls should mention Mr. Antony's collapse. I imagine Reverend Cecil will think twice the next time he delivers the benediction." Ma turned her gaze on Anne. "And I imagine that you must have been more alarmed than anyone if everything Mr. Cunningham said is true." Ma sat back with the smug expression of a cat whose mouth reveals the tail of a mouse. Charlotte looked at her sister, who was red as Ma's crossword pencil, and felt the embarrassment and panic she witnessed in Anne's face as if it were her own.

Charlotte said, "I think ..."

Ma sat up abruptly, as if propelled by Charlotte's words, spilling her afghan onto the floor. She looked down at the dregs in her teacup, then quickly set the cup before them on the table. She looked accusingly at Charlotte, then at Anne. "What is this," she demanded. Charlotte froze, and she could feel Anne, seated next to her, go cold as well.

"Anne, take my cup, and tell me what you see."

Anne hesitated before leaning forward. She gingerly picked up Ma's favorite teacup.

"What's there? What do you see? Tell me this instant."

Anne tilted the cup and glanced in, but remained silent.

"I'm not asking you to read my fortune. Just tell me what you see."

Charlotte knew as well as Ma what Anne saw. She knew, too, with the evidence before them, that Ma would accept nothing less than the cold truth. Anne looked to Charlotte and Charlotte nodded.

"Ma," Anne said, "I'm afraid it's Mr. Boynton's teeth."

Once Jane had cleared away the tea service, Charlotte escaped below stairs to the kitchen. Mr. Boynton's teeth were in Charlotte's skirt pocket, tucked in her handkerchief.

"The last place I thought to look was in your mother's teacup," Jane explained to Charlotte, shaking her head in disbelief.

"I'll wash," Charlotte said, "you dry, and then we'll return Mr. Boynton's teeth to him."

Jane picked up a cloth. "I bet Mrs. Mew was furious."

"Only aghast," said Charlotte. She rolled up her sleeves and ran water into a basin from the tap. She washed Ma's teacup first.

"I'm so very sorry, Miss."

"Jane," said Charlotte gently, turning toward her, "Mr. Boynton's teeth in Ma's teacup was not your fault." Charlotte handed Jane the offending cup, or rather, the cup that had held the teeth Ma found so offensive.

Jane took the cup and thoughtfully dried it. "I'll never look at this cup the same way. How do you suppose ..."

"It was hardly mischievous fairies," Charlotte said. "Mr. Boynton must have meant to place the teeth in his own cup and got Ma's cup by mistake."

"What did Mrs. Mew say?"

"That she never wants to see the teacup again."

"Should we give it to Mr. Boynton for his teeth?"

Charlotte wiped her hands on a dry cloth and took the teacup from Jane. "And risk Ma finding his teeth in her cup a second time?"

"You're not going to ..."

The cup fell from Charlotte's hands onto the stone floor and shattered. She fetched the broom and dustpan from the pantry.

When Charlotte had deposited the shards in the dustbin, Jane said, "I never did like that teacup."

They looked at each other. Jane began to giggle and covered her mouth with her hand. Charlotte caught Jane's giggles as if the hiccoughs, and they giggled until Charlotte's cheeks ached and Jane doubled over. For the moment, they forgot Mr. Boynton.

But Charlotte, try as she might, couldn't forget Mr. Antony. And what had Mr. Cunningham said to Ma about Mr. Antony and Anne?

CHAPTER 7

Spring had arrived late in London, but the pale green luminescence of June's early days assured Londoners of summer's punctuality.

The Gordon Square garden's wrought-iron fence, marking the garden's boundaries, joined its four gates, which stood open from morning until night. Anne identified bluebells, cow parsley, and violets among the beds lining the inside perimeter of the fence, along with shrubs and undergrowth left untended so that the garden's fauna might nest. Besides the ever-present blackbirds and pigeons, numerous wrens, robins, blue tits, and magpies made irregular appearances, as if spirits materialized from an invisible clime.

In late spring and summer, bleeding hearts and bridal wreath poked through the railings, so that passersby might sample the garden's offerings without entering its gates. Today, however, Charlotte was not among them. Though she passed the bridal wreath scenting the sidewalk with its white clusters of tiny flowers, she turned into the north entrance and strolled along the dirt paths before taking her favorite seat on the east side of the garden.

From the west entrance, a central path forked into two smaller paths, and Charlotte liked to think that on any day she might take one path and the next day another, and thereby try on every experience the great world held out for her. Over one of these forked paths, a tree pitched sideways. Charlotte held as much sympathy with this tree as she did with the towering plane trees standing sentinel around the garden's perimeters. The dignified presence of the plane trees — abiding, stalwart, and silent — must be similar to God's, Charlotte thought, if God, indeed, existed.

One day, when the Mews had only just moved to number 9, Henry and Charlotte, strolling in the garden at dusk, swore they saw a fox or its red shadow hurry into the undergrowth. Before it disappeared, the fox had looked at them, over its shoulder, as if bidding them to follow.

"A gray squirrel, I'll believe, even a brown rat, but never a fox, not in this neighborhood," Nurse Goodman said.

Father laughed, then he said that Bloomsbury had gone to the dogs, just like the snobs who once considered Bloomsbury a fashionable neighborhood had predicted.

"Just don't tell Ma," Charlotte said. "Everyone knows what a good address means to her."

"Because she's a Kendall," Father snorted. "Well, let the Kendalls go to the dogs."

Charlotte saw Nurse Goodman bite her lip, for she, even more than Mrs. Mew's children, was loyal to Mrs. Mew. Not only did the Mews' house on Gordon Street fall just short of Gordon Square, its garden was public, unlike the garden of Mecklenburgh Square, which was reserved for residents' use. Henry, Charlotte, Anne, and later, Freda, might stand outside the garden's railings trying to glimpse through the shrubbery the goings-on inside. Of course, it was worse for them than Ma because they imagined it was a garden for all children to play in, not one for only those children who lived on the square.

Mrs. Mew could never see it from the children's point of view, insisting the great wrong had been done to her alone. Fred Mew took her from her parents' home on fashionable Brunswick Square and put her on "Dowdy Street," as she mispronounced it, not four streets from where she once lived in style and comfort, and worlds away in respectability. (When Fred Mew proposed, she was twenty-eight, an old maid. What was she to do?)

Today, as Charlotte sat reveling in her senses' apprehension of the garden, an old man shuffled toward her bench and took a seat at the other end. He stared at the numerous pigeons and lone magpie feeding on the lawn.

The man said, "Funny how there's just the one white spot on its wing in a sea of black." He nodded toward the conspicuous magpie. Charlotte glanced around to see if the man was speaking to someone else.

"'Course it'd be even funnier were it on the one wing but not the other," he continued, still not looking Charlotte's way.

Charlotte studied the magpie's hijinks. "It's difficult to tell," she said, "as we usually see only one side."

The man grunted. "Right, you are. I hadn't thought of that myself." He looked at the book in her lap. "Emily Brontë. You know her, do you?"

"You've never read the Brontë sisters?" Charlotte asked.

"Can't say as I remember hearing of them, but I never thought much of letters and books, not even newspapers, for that matter." He nodded toward the daily paper at his side. "Stories are all the same at my age. Doesn't matter who tells them."

"Are you from London?" Charlotte asked, knowing he wasn't.

"No, no," the man said, as if the idea were absurd. "Yorkshire," he pointed to the sky. "Been here too long though to care much where I roost."

Charlotte wondered if he referred to London or to life.

"What do you think of your new king," he asked, as if Yorkshire and old age were countries unto themselves. Charlotte smiled to herself. Ma, too, thought of King Edward as new, although he had sat on the throne nearly a decade.

"He'll have to do," Charlotte said.

"Just that," the man agreed. "I've not much time for the royals now. Time was when I couldn't pass Buckingham without doffing my cap to old Vic — I mean, of course, our queen."

"Of course," Charlotte said.

The two fell silent, as though king and queen themselves, and practiced in holding down two ends of the universe without consultation.

Charlotte thought of the old man and of Emily Brontë, both from Yorkshire and yet worlds apart. Charlotte knew what it was like to be tired of life and irritated by the human race. She also knew what it was like to be set aloft by a buoyant, yet turbulent heart, the winds of romance tearing at the sails of her soul. And she knew what it was like to be frustrated one moment and transported the next, as if a child unable to sleep the night before Christmas because it stood just outside the gates of an enchanted realm.

The man stood suddenly, startling Charlotte from her thoughts, but before shuffling away as he had come, he doffed an imaginary cap to Charlotte. She nodded, the man turned, and Charlotte thought, whether or not she accomplished anything else that afternoon, the day had been well-spent.

She picked up the newspaper, lost still in the haze of her reverie. The flapping of pigeon wings above Charlotte's head announced the bird's droppings on the newspaper's front page, as well as on the shoulder and the lapel of her best wool suit. "Pooh," Charlotte said, irritated. The magpie, still policing the garden's lawn, bobbed its head as if having got the pigeon's joke. Deciding she'd been singled out in a game of tag, Charlotte laughed with the magpie and the pigeons, delighted they counted her among themselves.

When she arrived at number 9, Anne, her violet eyes shining, greeted her in the entry. In one hand, she held a piece of letterhead and an opened envelope. Anne took no notice of her sister's disheveled appearance, embracing Charlotte with her free hand and shouting in her ear words Charlotte couldn't make out but instantly knew the meaning of.

"Which painting?" Charlotte asked.

Anne gushed on and on about her painting of wild flowers, newly chosen by the Royal Academy for its autumn show, and how it was unworthy. Just the same, it was her favorite, and she'd accept nothing less for it.

Charlotte couldn't have been happier if her poem "Requiescat," drafted the day Mr. Boynton misplaced his teeth and posted a month ago to *The Nation*, had been chosen for publication.

Suddenly, Anne exclaimed, "I nearly forgot, there are three posts for you." Charlotte put them in a pocket of her suit without looking at them, recalling what happened when she stopped just long enough to glance at the newspaper.

"Why look at you!" Anne exclaimed.

"Yes, I'm afraid a pigeon got the better of me."

Anne laughed, until Charlotte added, "You, too, I'm afraid."

Anne looked puzzled.

Charlotte explained, "Remember embracing me before I'd even got through the door?"

Anne walked to the entry's mirror. Charlotte joined her, and they peered at themselves standing side by side. Like Charlotte's, Anne's face, hair, and collar showed the distinct trace of a pigeon's leavings.

"The Italians say a pigeon's leavings are a good omen," Anne said.

Charlotte wondered if Anne had learned the expression from Mr. Antony. She said, "When in Rome, perhaps."

Anne laughed, then Charlotte laughed, and their self-portrait reflected their mirth.

Ma called from her sofa. "What are you girls laughing about? You sound like a couple of old hens."

"Nothing, Ma," Anne shouted. But they had the giggles, and they chortled still louder, at which Ma said, "You girls and your hysterics."

That afternoon following tea, Charlotte sponged her suit, using the laundry soap Nurse Goodman swore by, then hung it on a shoulder in her wardrobe. Only a week later, when she needed to run errands, did she think to wear the suit (and carry her horn-handled umbrella, of course, in case it rained).

She discovered the posts while in queue at the butcher's shop, where there was a special on calf's liver. Jane, knowing it was Mrs. Mew's favorite, asked Charlotte to step out to buy a pound, as she was using the afternoon to scrub the pantry shelves and mop the pantry and kitchen floors. Though Charlotte did most of the shopping, Jane, because she knew more about various cuts and quality of meat, usually went to the butcher's. Charlotte thought of suggesting that Anne go, but bit her tongue, afraid what gossip Ma might make of it.

So it was Charlotte, not Jane nor Anne, whom Mr. Antony addressed, wearing his butcher's apron and welcoming smile.

"Ah, Miss Mew, the elder, yes?"

"Quite so," Charlotte replied. "A pound of calf's liver, please," she added.

"Of course," he said, then weighed and wrapped the liver in butcher's block. He placed it in a brown sack, which he exchanged for the shillings Charlotte offered. Before she could turn away, he asked, "Everybody's well in your house?"

"Everybody's well. Thank you," Charlotte said and nodded.

Mr. Antony nodded back as if he expected their conversation to continue, but the man directly behind Charlotte demanded, "Your best chicken fryer, please," so Charlotte smiled and turned from Mr. Antony's imploring eyes.

Outside the shop, she placed the sack and the umbrella under her arm, then took the letters from her suit pocket. The first was an advertisement for "The latest in carpet sweepers — sure to be your last!" (This was addressed to her, Charlotte presumed, because all the bills came in her name.) The second was from Dunham & Sons Law Firm, and the third, *The Nation*. She deposited the advertisement in the dustbin on the pavement before opening the other two envelopes, each in turn, while Londoners wove around her.

Like the advertisement, the law firm's letter was addressed to Charlotte, but it concerned both herself and Anne. Their Aunt Mary Kendall, who had died less than a year before, left Charlotte and Anne two investment properties in Brighton, the letter said. The sisters were to receive a modest annuity of twenty pounds each, of which the first payment would be made within a fortnight. If these arrangements sufficed, the sisters should sign the enclosed document and return it at their earliest convenience, et cetera.

Before Charlotte read the document in its entirety, she knew how the money must be spent, regardless of how loudly Anne protested. To convince Anne, Charlotte would need the help of their old school chums from Gower Street, and, as importantly, a good measure of loving deceit. *The Nation*'s acceptance of her poem "Requiescat," Charlotte thought as she read the editor's note with pleasure, would serve as the ace up her sleeve, and she smiled to herself as London, content with the promise of its future, hummed around her.

CHAPTER 8

That afternoon during dinner, Charlotte dangled the bait.

"Anne," Charlotte said over warmed pot roast from the evening before, "There's a letter in the front entry. It was addressed to me, but it concerns you as well. Could you look at it before Friday? Our signatures are required. I can take care of mine when I settle our accounts for the week."

Anne's knife hovered over the heel of bread on her plate.

"I received the letter the day you got your news from the Academy, but until today I forgot it in my suit pocket."

Visibly excited, Anne changed the subject. "Ma, why aren't you eating. Don't you care for the roast?"

"This meat is too tough for anyone with common sense," Ma complained.

Willing to share his two pence, Wek said, "Too bad."

Jane arrived from below stairs with a fresh pot of tea. Having set the pot on the table, she fussed with the tureens on the sideboard. "Can I help anyone to more greens or roast beef?" she asked.

Ma harrumphed in displeasure.

Before thinking better of it, Charlotte reassured Ma. "There's calf's liver for supper. I bought it fresh today."

Jane added, "I'm preparing it exactly how you like it, Mrs. Mew, with crisp bacon, caramelized onions, and sherry."

Ma harrumphed again, this time in satisfaction, but Anne blushed when Charlotte met her gaze.

"So sad," Wek said, clamoring back and forth on his perch while bobbing his head up and down.

To help execute her plan, Charlotte invited the sisters' closest friends to tea on a Saturday afternoon in June. The iced teacakes and ladyfingers were expensive; however, the extravagance was necessary in light of the occasion's importance. Charlotte feared that unless the day was seamlessly orchestrated to appear commonplace, Anne would balk at the idea of her own studio, and having backed away, might never consider the matter again. But Anne must have her very own space to work among other artists to reassure her that her art mattered. Without it, Charlotte feared, Anne might take to her own invalid's sofa, as Ma had, and much worse, never realize her talent.

Five of Charlotte and Anne's closet friends were chums from Gower Street School, where they'd been taught by Lucy Harrison, the headmistress, that if they had a clear sense of direction, a song in their heart, and a book of poems in their pocket, they'd never be lost or alone. There were the three Chick sisters: Elsie, Harriet, and Margaret, as well as Edith Oliver and Maggie Browne. Elsie and Harriet had both married, but Margaret was single, as were Edith and Maggie. Though Elsie's and Harriet's immediate loyalties lay with their husbands, Charlotte could count on Margaret, along with Edith and Maggie, to attend the tea.

Like the Gower Street girls, Elsie and Evelyn Millard were close friends of both Charlotte and Anne. When they were young women, Anne met Elsie at the Royal Female School of Art, where Elsie discovered her love of landscapes and Anne of still lifes. As talented as her sister, Evelyn worked as a stage actress. Though Elsie married an Irishman and had two young sons underfoot, she was the least matronly of the women gathered, seeming to grow younger, Charlotte thought, as her children grew up.

Elsie and Evelyn were to be Charlotte's primary allies, helping to work the conversation around to the idea of women in the arts owning their talents. When the time was right, Elsie would hold out the apple to Anne. But for things to go as planned, everyone must be privy to Charlotte's machinations. Thus, Elsie and Evelyn, Edith and Margaret, and even Maggie had been informed of the plan. Dear heart, Maggie. Dear, certainly, but also slow-witted. She must be included, however, because she was one of their oldest friends and because her plodding nature made her stalwart. Simply, Anne trusted Maggie's frank manner and guilelessness.

Charlotte, Anne, and their five friends gathered in the parlor and made small talk while Jane served tea. Ma was moping in her bedroom because she hadn't been included. Occasionally, she rapped her walking cane on the hardwood floor above, and Jane, also privy to Charlotte's plan, ran up the stairs to placate her.

"These iced cakes are absolutely scrumptious," Margaret declared. "Wherever did you find them? My bakery only makes crumb cakes and charges an arm and a leg."

Edith said, "And to think of those poor women arrested, starving themselves, unwilling to eat even a heel of bread, all in the name of suffrage."

In recent months the suffragettes, determined to win the vote for women, had taken drastic measures, and newspaper headlines were rife with their activities. Many of the women had been arrested and force-fed while imprisoned.

"I wouldn't think of going without a meal, even to make a point," Evelyn said. "Acting demands enough discipline and self-sacrifice without starving."

"I might *think* about it," Elsie said, "but knowing my children depend on me to feed them would stop me. The boys are always hungry.

They remind me of the koi in Kew Gardens, circling the pond's surface to gobble bread crumbs dropped by visitors."

"It's the force-feeding that chills me to the bone," Evelyn said. "It's barbaric."

"Our pastor says Christ would instruct the suffragettes to put down their placards and eat," Edith said. "But he's a man, after all."

"Your pastor or Christ," Charlotte asked, trying, without success, to introduce levity into the discussion.

"But we all see the necessity of the vote for women," exclaimed Anne.

"Equality, yes," said Margaret. "But why the vote necessarily?"

"Because the vote is the first step toward equal rights," said Anne.

Charlotte, who had never heard Anne side with the suffragettes, was surprised by Anne's outspokenness.

"I disagree. The first hurdle is society's presumption that marriage and childbearing are cornerstones of a woman's identity," said Margaret. "Look at my two sisters. They're married with children. Therefore, society tells them their lives are complete. Because I'm single, our parents live on tenterhooks, anticipating the day I will join my sisters in their holy state, while fearing I'll end up an old maid like my great aunt."

"I'm afraid our mother thinks the same way as your parents," Charlotte said honestly. "But she's given up hope at this point, I imagine." Charlotte looked at Anne, who avoided Charlotte's gaze.

"But what woman doesn't want to marry and have children," Elsie asked. "That's every woman's greatest joy. I love painting, but I would give up my landscapes in a moment for my sons."

"The point is that you shouldn't have to give up either your sons or your landscapes. You must see that when it's necessary for a woman to marry and have children to qualify as a real woman, that it's an obligation before it's a joy," argued Margaret.

Charlotte thought about her own deep desire to have children, a desire she had possessed ever since she was a little girl. Before Henry and Freda were institutionalized, Charlotte had wanted children even more than she wanted fame.

Evelyn asked, "And what about the woman who wants a career, not in addition to her roles as housewife and mother, but as an independent woman of the world?"

Elsie said, "You, for instance, Evelyn. You've succeeded as a professional woman in a man's world."

"But actresses must earn the respect freely given to actors," said Evelyn. "Worse, as soon as we marry, which we're expected, finally, to do, it's taken for granted that we'll quit what we see as our life's work, as if acting were an idle occupation we busy ourselves with while waiting on our natural calling of wife and mother. Actors, on the other hand, can marry, produce ten children, and work in the theatre, and no one questions their right to do all three."

"But political freedom must come first," Anne said. "Once women have an equal voice in the political sphere, they'll find their voices in the home."

Maggie, who had been silent while finishing her plate of iced cakes, said, "I can't see things ending well when a woman would rather have the vote than eat these delicious cakes."

Everyone laughed, and the earnestness of their conversation, for the moment, was abandoned for talk of the latest fashions. However, for fear that seeds of their small talk land on fallow soil, the women again picked up the previous conversation's thread.

"There are opportunities for professional women if one just looks," Margaret said. "Think of Miss Harrison. She had a distinguished career as a schoolteacher and headmistress before moving to Cupples Field for an idyllic retirement."

"With Amy Greener," Edith said.

Maggie tittered, then covered her mouth.

"It's what our American cousins call a Boston marriage, surely," Edith said to Evelyn and Elsie, who hadn't attended Gower Street School with the other five women and didn't know of Miss Harrison or Miss Greener, a fellow teacher at the school.

"Miss Harrison, though no longer our headmistress, deserves our respect," Charlotte said self-consciously. She admired and envied the courage it took for Miss Harrison to live as a lesbian, but she was afraid to let Anne and their friends know how deeply her sympathies with Miss Harrison lay.

"Who are we to say how she truly lived?" asked Evelyn, "regardless of whether or not any of us knew her."

"Or to judge her regardless of how she lived?" added Elsie.

"She was wonderful, wasn't she?" Maggie said dreamily.

Edith, Margaret, Charlotte, and Anne fell into silent agreement.

"Remember the time she caught Charlotte drawing hearts on her folder when she was teaching us long division. I've never seen a face so red," Margaret said.

"You speak of her as if she's deceased. She's still living at Cupples Field, with Miss Greener," Edith said.

"Perhaps Miss Harrison and Miss Greener have the right idea. A life without men," Margaret said.

"But without children as well," Elsie said.

"They had so many children together as teachers," Margaret said.

"But they weren't their own children. It's not the same, surely," Edith said.

Charlotte looked furtively at Evelyn.

"We were speaking of opportunities for professional women," Evelyn said, "when we were sidetracked by nostalgia."

Charlotte and Evelyn looked at Elsie.

"Hogarth Studios houses nearly as many female artists as men, and with its latest vacancy at such a reasonable price, pocket money, really, it's likely to be snatched up," Elsie said casually.

Charlotte watched Anne but couldn't see an appreciable shift in her expression.

Evelyn chimed in. "Painters like Elsie and Anne have to make the most of opportunities for space with their myriad supplies and need for optimal light. We theatre folks only need our grease paint and a captive audience."

"Writers are just as fortunate," Charlotte said. "Time is more important than space. With ink and paper, I might work anywhere."

"Yes, look at the Brontë sisters. They wrote at the family's kitchen table," Margaret said.

"But Bramwell, their brother, was sent to art school where he had a studio, yet he ended his life as a dissolute," Anne politely argued.

"There's no guarantee in any pursuit. But one must have the opportunity to realize her talent, and an artist needs a studio to do so," Elsie said.

Maggie looked up from her second plate of cakes, now reduced to crumbs. "But you don't have a studio, Elsie. And I've been to your house. There isn't room to paint with the boys' things everywhere." Maggie looked around at the women and, meeting Charlotte's gaze, blushed.

Elsie caught Maggie's dropped ball. "I live in the country, and as a landscape painter, the countryside is my studio."

"And I paint flowers," said Anne simply. "I can paint a vase on the nightstand in my bedroom just as easily as in a studio."

The tea had been a disaster. As the women left, filing out one behind the other, each gave a conspiratorial glance at Charlotte in sympathy. Elsie, the last to leave, held Charlotte's hand in farewell and squeezed it. "Be in touch," she said.

Clearing the tea service before reinstating Ma on her sofa, Anne turned to Charlotte. "You weren't able to perform your pantomime of King Edward. We all forgot. I'm so sorry." It was just like Anne to think not of herself but of her sister, mother, or a friend.

Charlotte, with Maggie's second plate of crumbs in her hand, said, "It's just as well. I fear all our talk of women's suffrage would have made poor company for his majesty."

CHAPTER 9

But Anne did lease the vacant studio at Hogarth. She went there on her own — not telling Elsie and not telling Charlotte — for fear that, she confided in Charlotte later, the space had been rented, or it was too expensive after all, or she didn't feel it suited her. Charlotte suspected Anne hadn't wanted to raise Charlotte's hopes by showing an interest, only to dash those hopes.

So a fortnight after the gathering, Charlotte and Anne, accompanied by Elsie and Evelyn, turned the key on Anne's very own space.

Hogarth Studios was in Marylebone, just west of Bloomsbury and north of Soho, and within easy walking distance of Gordon Street. The pink and cream stucco building stood on the corner of Tottenham and Charlotte Streets and rose three stories, including the ground floor, plus the attic rooms. Anne's studio was on the first floor and its tall windows faced southwest, perfect for her habit of painting in the afternoon. Before venturing inside, the four women stood on the corner, and as Anne pointed out the windows of the studio, the women looked up reverently.

Charlotte expected Hogarth to be as noisy as a boy's dormitory, but as soon as the four women entered the ground floor, she was struck by a hushed stillness. As if they were entering the reading room of the British Museum, the four began whispering, and then because that seemed silly, giggling, until Anne, frowning and putting her finger to her lips, shamed them into silence. They were halfway up the first flight of stairs, Elsie and Anne leading the way, when a cacophony broke out on the flight above them, and first one young man and then another, each dressed in painting bibs, rushed by them down the stairs, taking two at a time, and shouting as they went.

On the first-floor landing, the women looked at each other in bewilderment. "That must be the welcoming committee," Charlotte said, and the women burst out laughing. Finally, holding her sides, Elsie said, "I thought one of them was on fire and the other was trying to put him out." Eleanor added, "So much for our respectful silence."

They followed Anne to her door, which she unlocked with trembling hands. Before opening it, she turned to them. "It's not much. I mean, it's rather small as studios go." She ushered them in and followed behind. The mid-afternoon sun washed the studio in an orange glow.

Elsie went straight to the four windows, and looking out, proclaimed, "Not even Turner could fault the view."

"But it's just a street corner," said Eleanor, joining Elsie.

"Exactly," replied Elsie, "and what does a landscape painter know about street lamps, pavements, dustbins, and pedestrian traffic?"

They all laughed.

Charlotte looked at the canvas frames stacked against a wall. Anne, following her gaze, said, "It's a bit messy, of course, since the last tenant left some of his supplies." Charlotte could sense Anne wringing her hands, waiting on their approval. She turned to Anne. "It suits you perfectly."

Anne smiled and began to point out her studio's features. "This is where I'll set my easel," she said, standing in front of the center window. She took three small steps forward. "Here's where I'll place my tables for models — one large table and a smaller one. "And over here," Anne said, walking to the wall opposite the canvases, "You can see I already have my own tea kettle and gas ring. And right here, she pointed to her feet, I'll place another small table and chairs, so that I can invite guests for tea."

"It's all wonderful, Anne," Evelyn said.

"Smashing," Elsie added, rushing at Anne to peck her on the cheek.

Charlotte tossed her head. "Our dear Anne's no dilettante. She's exhibiting at the Academy, and she has her very own studio, with a view."

"That," Elsie said, "deserves a toast," and from her carpetbag she pulled a bottle of champagne and four nested teacups, like rabbits from an oversized hat.

"My first tea party!" Anne exclaimed.

And Anne's studio was christened.

Anne stayed on "to tidy up things," she said, but Charlotte imagined she would stroll around the studio the rest of the afternoon in a joyous haze. After Charlotte parted from Elsie and Eleanor on the corner where the women had stood together only an hour before, she walked to the Gordon Square garden, her own home away from home.

In the garden, from her favorite seat, Charlotte could just make out through the summer leaves Christ the King Chapel to her near left. To her far left stood her favorite purple beech tree.

To her right, students from London University strolled toward her as if the footpaths were country lanes, some stopping to bask under the sun on the lawn, their chatter rising above their heads as wordless notes hung on the summer breeze. Charlotte, alone on her bench, was deliciously pleased. What began as a hen party had ended as a *fait accompli*. Anne, so long without her own studio, had one at last.

Three days following the women's tea, Anne, her hands shaking, had approached Charlotte in the morning room, where she sat balancing the household accounts. Charlotte, immediately sensing the reason for Anne's appearance, but afraid to hope, asked Anne if she had spoken with Elsie in the last few days.

Everything poured from Anne, her excitement mounting, how she had seen the studio by herself and then with Elsie, that it was "a real artist's studio," unlike anything she'd ever dreamed of, but then she stopped short; like Charlotte, not daring to hope.

"Of course, we can afford it, my dear Anne. That's what I've been trying to tell you," Charlotte reassured her.

Anne grew solemn. "But what about you, Charlotte. Your writing. Wouldn't you like your own place somewhere far from number 9?" Anne looked around the morning room. It was where Charlotte most felt her burdens as the eldest daughter.

Charlotte, still seated, took her sister's hands and looked up into Anne's violet eyes. "I've the drawing room, remember, at your insistence. And," Charlotte rolled her chair back from the desk and took her trump card from the center drawer, "I've had a poem accepted by *The Nation*, which tells me that my vanity and steamer trunks have served me well."

Now, seated on her garden bench, Charlotte thought with satisfaction, that was that. She closed her eyes and turned her face toward the perfectly blue sky and accepted the sun's warmth as her due.

When she opened her eyes, Charlotte saw a couple walking toward her, talking animatedly to each other. The man wore a white linen suit and straw hat. The woman wore a dress the same blue as the day's sky. Her face was brown and her hair black. Charlotte, stunned, held her breath. The woman so closely resembled Freda that she could be her twin. When the couple passed, Charlotte saw that the woman's dress was tied in back at the waist. The bow hung down lopsidedly, its tails uneven in length, as if the woman had dressed hurriedly that morning.

Between the tails of the bow, a red blotch, the size of Charlotte's hand, bobbed as the woman walked. A child might believe the woman had been blackberrying and sat on her hands without thinking. As the couple continued walking along the path, the woman's hips swaying back and forth, the crimson stain held Charlotte's gaze. The woman strolled past the purple beech and through the south gate, then disappeared.

Charlotte returned to number 9 in a trance. Inside the door, the chill of the house embraced her. She put her umbrella in the entry stand and hung her felt hat and gray suit jacket on hooks above the umbrella. She stood there, her hands above her head on the shoulders of her suit, unwilling to move. Before she turned around, she knew what she would see. She listened for the sounds of the house to steady herself. Wek chattered to himself in the front room, and Jane sang below stairs. In the entry, where Charlotte stood dazed, the grandfather clock solemnly struck 3.

Charlotte turned and walked to the entry's mirror. Next to it, marked in charcoal pencil, were the heights of the Mew children in 1890, when they first moved to Gordon Street. Henry, aged twenty-five, Anne, eighteen,

Charlotte, twenty-one, and Freda, eleven. Charlotte looked into the mirror. She was thirty-nine. Her hair was beginning to gray, yet her face held none of her mother's lines.

Charlotte blinked. Beside her, reflected in the mirror, stood Freda. Her hair and eyes were so brown they appeared black, and next to Charlotte's porcelain skin, Freda's complexion was a golden olive. Only eleven years old, Freda was nearly as tall as Charlotte. She peeked over her big sister's shoulder (as she had loved to do in fun) and smiled at Charlotte with her beautiful face.

Charlotte blinked again, and her little sister vanished.

CHAPTER 10

The Isle of Wight lies five miles off the southern coast of England. Londoners traveling to Newport, the largest village and heart of the Isle, take the Mid-Sussex train to Southampton, an eighty-mile journey. From Southampton, a boat ferries passengers across the Solent Strait. The strait separates the mainland from "England in miniature," an affectionate term for the Isle much repeated by "overners," those mainlanders who have made the island home.

Once across the strait, the ferry passes between the seaside villages of Cowes and East Cowes into the Medina estuary, lined with quays and boats at anchor, and chugs slowly south to Newport, where Fred Mew's family once owned the Bugle Inn and Mew's Brewery. From Newport, the village of Newfairlee is a short ride by cart, dray or trap, and it was here, at their great uncle's and aunt's farm, where Henry, Charlotte, Anne, and Freda spent their summers as children. Like Newfairlee, the village of Carisbrooke is a short ride from Newport, and it was Carisbrooke, not Newfairlee or Newport, that was Charlotte and Anne's destination this late September day.

On the train to Southampton, the sisters shared a compartment with a family of four. The younger boy, pointing to his father's newspaper, squirmed in his mother's lap. The older boy sat between his parents and looked up at his mother's pensive face as if to read her thoughts. Anne sat forward and stared abstractedly beyond the window at the countryside of the shires, with its hedgerows and fields yellowing in the waning light of autumn. Charlotte sat backward. First London's boroughs and then trees dotting the countryside receded from view, so that Charlotte felt as if she were traveling into the past. Yet all the while signs of the burgeoning future loudly asserted themselves. *The Times'* headline warned that the build-up of arms across Europe signaled war, the women's dresses were cut more closely than was last year's fashion, and the new poles of telephone wires appeared comical against the aged groves of trees.

Charlotte knew the Isle was as doomed to progress as the mainland. The Isle's major industries were once boatbuilding, sailcloth-making, and farming, but in recent years, each was surpassed by tourism. Sea villas sprouted like clover on sixty miles of coastline, and the temperate climate drew islanders and mainlanders alike to walk the coastline's footpaths while admiring the chalk cliffs. There were pleasure piers as well, with vendors of food and games to amuse all ages. But for Charlotte the Isle would always be the quays along the estuary and at Newport, the sailing lore begotten from a world of boats coming and going, and the farm at Newfairlee, with its corn and alfalfa fields, sheep and dairy cows, and haymaking in late September, when Uncle would go to the Saturday Market and hire workers to scythe the hay and then gather it on ricks once it had dried in the early autumn sun.

It was then that Henry, Charlotte, Anne, and Freda left the farm to return to Doughty Street, its furniture hung with Holland cloth in a conspiracy of silence with the grandfather clock in the entry, with no one there in summer to wind it except Fred Mew. Their father often worked from home year-round, but especially in the summer, when the house, free of children's playthings and tantrums, meant his drafting office was as still and as silent as though time had indeed stopped. Their mother, on the other hand, stayed with her sister and her own mother near Brighton, where the Kendalls owned a villa worlds away from London and the Isle.

Once the sisters reached Southampton and boarded the ferry, Charlotte's pulse quickened. The ancient cry of seagulls and the smell of salt on the stiff breeze revived the child of yesteryear who loved the tragedy of mankind failing to tame the tempestuous sea. It wasn't until she stood on its deck and felt the sea cradle and rock the ferry that she could leave London behind. Anne, a landlubber, left Charlotte to make her way to the boat's hull. There she could talk with other women from behind their handkerchiefs, held to their nose and mouth, in part to temper the smell of fish, in part to disguise what seafarers called "going green."

That morning, Charlotte sprinkled her pressed handkerchief with rosewater, Nurse Goodman's routine preparation for ladies traveling, whether over London's pavements or across Hampstead's heath. "You must never forget," Charlotte heard Nurse Goodman caution in her ear even after all these years, "You are Kendalls, like your mother and your grandmother, and thus you are ladies." What she meant, the sisters understood, was that on the Isle, among the Mews' relatives and especially when crossing cow pastures on their way to St. Paul's on Sundays, they were to remember their dresses, which were so clean they might be worn inside out, and the Shining City of Jerusalem, hanging over the Doughty Street mantle alongside the portrait of their mother, Anna Maria, at nineteen.

Charlotte stood at the boat's railing, sea spray unpressing her wool suit, listening to the gulls above the chugging of the ferry, and believed if it weren't for the anonymous life of London's pavements, she might stow away on a ship bound for the high seas. For more than a moment, she guiltily savored the thought of Ma, prone on her invalid's sofa, hearing from Reverend Cecil the news of Charlotte's capture by pirates. (Where Anne had got to, or Jane, Charlotte didn't question in her reverie, nor why Reverend Cecil should be the bearer of her scandalous demise, except that he should enjoy it so.) Ma might enjoy it, too, because she could conclude once again that Fred Mew's children hadn't been spared his negative influence, the least he might do as their father.

"'Don't forget Freda,' Ma says, as if we could." Charlotte started. Anne stood at her elbow, her vision parallel with Charlotte's.

"Or would ever want to, no matter what," Charlotte added, and looked at her sister's hand as it gripped the railing. The ferry, having crossed the Solent Strait, edged into the mouth of the estuary and between Cowes and East Cowes.

"We must make believe we're genies," Anne said, her handkerchief tucked into the sleeve of her shirtwaist. "And return to the bowl of the lamp," Charlotte rejoined. The ferry moved slowly past the quays to either side, boats at anchor and men on shore loading and unloading their hulls with *whoops* and *whoas*.

"What if the genie refused to return?" Anne stated rather than asked. Though it was her turn to speak, Charlotte remained silent. "He could never again grant wishes to whoever rubbed the lamp and released him," Anne continued.

The sisters retold the bedtime story each visit to the island as if Newport, where the estuary began and the River Medina ended, flowing north and emptying into the sea caught between the inlet, were the land of sleep and dreams as much as the center of the Isle of Wight. The telling and retelling of the story began long ago when Henry asked their father to show them the Isle of Wight on a map. Henry was ten, Charlotte, only six, and Anne, three.

Fred Mew looked among his papers in the drafting office. Unable to find one, he sketched a map showing England and the continent, and just off the south shore of England, the tiny island where at sixteen he left his own father to join his brothers in London's building trades. His sons must better themselves, his father told him, not step into harness at the Bugle Inn at Newport, waiting on Londoners vacationing on the Isle, never to vacation elsewhere themselves.

When Henry saw the map, he pointed to the island and said it was shaped just like Aladdin's lamp, and that when he grew up, he would fly there in an aeroplane. Fred winked at Henry and tussled his hair, and from then on, the children spoke of genies and aeroplanes synonymously, sure one was as likely as the other.

Reading her thoughts, Anne said, "Henry might've flown to the Isle after all." Charlotte, gazing into the churning water as the ferry came along a quay at Newport, replied, "If only the lot of the Mews in London had turned out lucky."

The ride from Newport to Carisbrooke by horse-drawn cab was the quickest leg of the journey. To the driver, Charlotte knew, they were "grockles," the islanders' name for tourists, but because of the long summers spent on the Isle in childhood or because, as Mews, the rolling countryside and sea breezes were in their blood, they thought of themselves as "caulkheads," those born and bred on the Isle.

On the farm at Newfairlee, having eaten their breakfast, the children would ask to see that day on the kitchen calendar. On each day a tiny chart told where the tide would be at every hour. "But why isn't it the same every day," Henry asked.

"And how did they know when they made the calendar," Charlotte demanded, certain magic was involved.

"Ask Uncle when he's done slopping pigs," Aunt said.

The cab rocked and slowed as they began their ascent to Carisbrooke. "Anne," Charlotte said, "Do you remember the tidal calendar hanging above the matchbox at the farm?"

Anne looked at Charlotte, who sat next to her. "Should I?"

As the hill on which Carisbrooke stood grew steeper and they inched ahead, Charlotte's back was pressed against the cab's seat. "Henry and I thought it was magic," she said.

"I remember thinking it strange that the sea should draw itself up around the island only to pull away," Anne said. "But it always left gifts, Aunt said, as flotsam and jetsam." Not to mention, Charlotte thought, the occasional drowned sailor washed ashore, or the moon's dropped child, forsaken and left to wander the shoreline alone.

Charlotte bounced forward in her seat as the cab crested the hill and began winding down and through the outskirts of town. Anne steadied herself by resting one hand on the roof of the cab and the other on Charlotte's. Charlotte took her sister's hand in silence and held her breath.

Through the cab window's shifting viewfinder, Charlotte saw Carisbrooke castle, a looming edifice dating to the Middle Ages and impossible to imagine having never existed. Each time she saw its forbidding stone walls, Charlotte believed she was entering a world haunted by long shadows of the distant past. Standing its ground, a stone's throw from the castle, the priory, though medieval as well, struck Charlotte (its tower bobbing into view) as living — and at peace — while the castle was long dead, yet restless in its grave.

Charlotte felt Anne's gaze and turned to exchange a knowing glance. The cab continued past the baker's and fishmonger's, the horse's shoes clattering on Carisbrooke's cobblestone pavements. The September air, sharp and sifted with the acrid decay of leaves, greeted the sisters as they stepped down from the cab with the help of the driver, his grunts ushering them to their ultimate destination.

CHAPTER 11

Outside the dull red brick walls of Whitecroft Hospital, where Freda lived, there was little to suggest the building was anything more than an oversized schoolhouse. The grounds, though hedged with bridal wreath, boasted no trees or flowerbeds.

Inside the tall entrance door, the atmosphere was that of an infirmary. Walls were painted a pale green, and tile floors and slick furnishings smelled of disinfectant. Anne led the way to the reception desk, daisies clutched in her hands and held at her waist. Dressed in nurses' uniforms, the women, their hair hidden in caps, appeared interchangeable and thus impersonal. But the nurse who greeted them almost smiled when she asked, "The sisters Mew to see Miss Freda Mew?" Anne nodded while Charlotte stood waiting just behind her. "The attendant is expecting you," the nurse said. "I'll ask Nurse Ryan to escort you."

The wing for incurables, built once the patients who would never leave these walls outnumbered those who might, lay behind the original structure, and so it was down a long corridor that Anne, then Charlotte, followed Nurse Ryan in silence, Charlotte focusing on the chain of keys banging against Nurse Ryan's leg rather than gaping at the tiny windows of patients' rooms.

The room in which Freda stayed (Charlotte couldn't think of it as Freda's room) was three flights up a narrow stair. Charlotte and Anne queued outside the room as Nurse Ryan waved at the attendant through the small, reinforced window. The attendant, an unsmiling woman in her early thirties or forties (Charlotte couldn't be sure, but thought the latter while suspecting the former), swept from the room into the hallway, her finger to her lips.

Charlotte couldn't imagine that being an attendant was a rewarding occupation, yet this woman was only the second attendant from whom Charlotte received reports on Freda's condition, via the head matron, since Fred Mew died more than ten years ago. Now she advised the sisters, as she did each year, that only one of them should see Freda at a time, and that as Freda's attendant, she must stay in the room. This was standard protocol, to which both Anne and Charlotte consented, because this woman knew Freda better than did either Anne or Charlotte.

But she couldn't know her, Charlotte thought now, as she had each visit in recent years. Not Freda herself, the Freda that Anne and Charlotte knew and loved as their little sister, taken from them just as she turned thirteen, nearly fifteen years ago. Charlotte imagined that attending Freda's funeral would be worse than seeing who she had become, but only on a day, she admitted to herself, when she and Anne weren't visiting Freda here at Whitecroft.

Anne followed the attendant, leaving Charlotte in the hall to sit on a wooden chair, left over, perhaps, from a retired schoolhouse, as it was uncomfortable enough to keep the least attentive student awake. All the doors in this wing were closed, lending an atmosphere of stillness, if not calm, to the long hall, empty except for the occasional attendant entering or exiting a room, quietly closing the door behind her, and the odd wooden chair like the one Charlotte sat on.

She tried not to think of Jane at number 9 contending with Ma and Wek, just as she tried not to imagine Anne watching the woman who occupied Freda's room, hoping for a glimmer of the seemingly irrepressible fire that animated and defined Freda's dark features as a child. Worse, Charlotte knew, was the hope of recognition by Freda of Charlotte and Anne as beloved sisters who would give their own lives to return Freda to herself.

When Charlotte took her turn sitting with Freda, she understood Anne's defeated expression on leaving the room, the daisies still in her hand, gifts either withheld or rejected. Charlotte sat in a corner chair while Freda absorbed herself as though a cat with a moth. The moth, visible only to Freda, flirted with the air in the middle distance of Freda's vision. Freda, seated on a narrow bed and dressed in a worn red sweater buttoned over her nightgown and black stockings pulled up to her knees, sat straight as a toy soldier on a shelf. Her arms were folded across her waist, and as she gazed at the moth, she rocked herself forward and backward.

Charlotte perched on her seat, watching this stranger who she once knew as her sister. She longed to talk to Freda, or at least return Freda's shoe to her. The attendant sat in the chair nearest the head of the bed and knitted what appeared to be a man's muffler, glancing up now and again, not at Freda, but at Charlotte.

Charlotte said hesitantly, "May I talk to her?" (Each year the question grew more urgent.) "Of course," the attendant said in the voice of a lion tamer who tells the curious boy there wouldn't be any harm in sticking his head into the lion's mouth.

Charlotte stood and walked to where the moth fluttered. She looked at the woman whose dark hair and dark eyes were those of her little sister, as was the olive skin. But the thick chapped lips and the heavy eyebrows knitted together were not, nor was the fine dark hair on the sides of her face, running from her temples to just below her ears. She watched Freda's eyes for a hint of recognition and was rewarded when Freda turned her head just far enough to cast Charlotte from her line of vision.

"Freda," Charlotte said. "It's Charlotte." Freda rocked back and forth a bit faster and shook her head from side to side, like a child refusing its porridge. Charlotte edged back toward her chair in the corner, and Freda ceased shaking her head.

"Does she hear me?" Charlotte asked.

The attendant continued knitting but looked at Charlotte. "She listens. She always listens, I know." The attendant looked at Freda, who was fixated on a button of her sweater. "But it's never clear what she hears or doesn't hear."

"Her other shoe, where is it?" Charlotte asked. "I'd like Freda to have her other shoe."

The nurse stopped knitting and looked at Charlotte. "She's happier this way."

"I don't understand," Charlotte said.

"What seems unbalanced to you and me," the attendant said, looking at Freda, "is balanced for her. Some days she dresses herself in one stocking and one shoe. Other days, as you see her, with both stockings and one shoe. But she never wears two stockings and two shoes."

"What about when she walks outside with the others," Charlotte asked.

The attendant hesitated. "When she knows it's time for exercise, she wears both shoes, but no stockings."

Charlotte sat back in her chair, unsure whether the nurse was telling the truth. Was Freda allowed to walk outside without shoes? Worse, was she no longer taken outside? The reports she received about Freda's care assured the Mews that Freda's life was as normal as if she lived at home. She had three meals a day, took walks with other patients on the hospital's lawns (under strict supervision, of course), and was kept busy with activities such as games and crafts when staffing and the patient's status allowed. Most important, Freda was responsible for her own hygiene, such as washing her face and teeth and brushing her hair.

But how could she and Anne know that Freda's care was what was best for her? And if Freda became agitated or violent, did the attendant call for someone to restrain her, with bindings or a chemist's prescription?

As if hearing Charlotte's questions, Freda rose from her bed and began walking back and forth the length of the room, while muttering and pulling her hair. Charlotte watched in alarm as Freda stopped, bit her own lip, and cried out while pointing at the middle distance between where she stood and Charlotte sat.

Instinctively, Charlotte leapt to embrace her baby sister and calm her. Freda turned from Charlotte, shrieking, then struck out at her, knocking Charlotte to the floor. When Charlotte looked up, the attendant had restrained Freda by clasping Freda's arms behind her back and holding them until Freda stood limply in the attendant's embrace. Charlotte found her feet and stood.

As she watched, the attendant led Freda to a child's table in the far corner and sat her down in a child's chair. From the chest of drawers, she took several loose sheets of paper covered with black marks and a beige eraser and placed them on the table in front of Freda. Freda picked up the eraser and began rubbing it over the paper, instantly absorbed by her task. The nurse walked to where Charlotte still stood.

"It doesn't happen often," she said, "but when it does, the eraser and charcoal drawings almost always soothe her. She'll be all right now." The attendant escorted Charlotte to the door, and Charlotte understood she could do nothing for Freda but take the attendant at her word.

Charlotte and Anne stood side by side at the boat's railing. The quay faded as the ferry pulled away and twilight fell on the Isle. Aunt Fanny called this space between day and night "the gloaming" and said it was a fairyland neither here nor over there. Charlotte wondered if Aunt was pulling their legs or issuing an edict because she spoke solemnly but had a twinkle in her eye. "Be careful," Aunt said, "you don't give yourself away." That meant, Charlotte learned from Henry, one mustn't ask to see a fairy to believe in one. Doubt begets doubt, whereas faith makes something that's true, real.

"Ever since we were little, leaving the Isle makes me think of Lot's wife," Anne volunteered. In the gathering gloom and chill of the autumn evening, her voice was reverent. Charlotte remained silent to encourage Anne, who always seemed to wait for Charlotte to direct their conversation. The ferry gathered speed as the estuary widened, and a woman collected her child and hustled him below deck. Charlotte and Anne remained aboveboard as Whitecroft and Freda receded into the distance.

"How could God condemn her?" Anne burst out. "What woman wouldn't look back when she was leaving everything she loved behind? I would have. I would have looked back. I would have!" Anne pounded the railing with the palms of her hands, flinging the bouquet of daisies into the ferry's wake. Charlotte put her hand on Anne's, and Anne began to weep. Charlotte knew Anne wasn't talking about Lot and his wife, but about Mr. Antony and the sisters' pact, made so many years ago.

"Perhaps God wanted to protect her from dwelling on the past," Charlotte said. "But, of course, any woman would have done the same." The stars began winking to life as the ferry moved between Cowes and East Cowes and into the strait. It was here that the worlds of the Medina River and the sea parted ways and that the past of the Isle and the present of London struggled in Charlotte to do the same.

"Look, Anne. It's a new moon. Can you see the slender crescent?"

Anne sniffed, looked to the sky, and then laughed. "Aunt Fanny always said new moons bring luck."

"And Nurse Goodman said Aunt would be happier if she read more of the good book and talked less of fairies," Charlotte said.

The sisters descended into the hull for the crossing, but before they did, Charlotte looked once more to the sky.

Below deck, Anne rested next to her while Charlotte thought of ships lost at sea, hung up on rocks off the coast, so near yet so far from land, going down into the sea's depths and the unknown, the running lights extinguished one by one as the ships pitched forward and then sank.

Ma had Henry, the Mews' first born, when she was twenty-eight. She had Freda, the Mews' last born, at forty-two. When Charlotte was twenty-four and Anne twenty-one, first Henry and then Freda faded before vanishing from 9 Gordon Street. Freda's and Henry's were blows one couldn't pass on knowingly to a child, and when there was a union between a man and a woman, when didn't children follow? So the sisters had made their pact never to marry, and they had kept their pact for fifteen years.

Charlotte couldn't tell Anne, as she longed to tell her, to forget the past and the sisters' pact and follow her heart to Mr. Antony. But neither would she tell Anne of Freda erasing the charcoals drawings as if they were sketches of number 9. Before the ferry docked at Southampton, Anne's head found rest on Charlotte's shoulder. That much I can do, Charlotte decided.

CHAPTER 12

In the Gordon Square garden, Charlotte found solace in the simple facts of grass and trees, birds and sky. In London, the garden was where she felt closest to the enchantment of the Isle of Wight and the magic realm of childhood, where she, Anne, Freda, and Henry still ranged about in the tall grass, the murmur of insects sown by sea breezes in the freshly cut hay. When birds chirruped or sang, they drew her into the language she had spoken as a child, the language she tried, mostly in vain, to speak in her poems.

But what about the other language that she had learned as a child, the language of Christ's sacrifice of the velvet skies of this world for the abstract heaven of his Father? She heard that language in St. Mary's with the company of Sunday parishioners. But in the chapel of Christ the King, whose single entrance she could see past the iron fence and plane trees from her most frequent seat in the Gordon Square garden, Charlotte might try to speak to God, not in the language of a child or of a Sunday parishioner, but in the language of her heart.

On the afternoon following their return, Charlotte found herself at the entrance to the chapel. She passed through the door, as if to a netherworld apart from her life with Anne and Ma. In the chapel, she felt like she was elsewhere and otherwise, and nowhere in particular, as though she were a seagull piggybacking the wind by spreading its wings and trusting the sky.

The chapel's stone walls and timbered ceiling created a heavy, damp atmosphere. Standing in the center, Charlotte could almost hear the start and stop of traffic on Gordon Street and the labors of a motorized omnibus.

Each of the north and south walls of the chapel embraced six stained-glass panels. The panels of the south wall depicted Christ in various walks of His life, such as His baptism by John, and read, "God so | loved the | world that | He gave | His only | begotten son." The north wall's panels read, "In the | beginning | God | created the | Heaven and | the Earth."

The chapel contained no pews or aisles, only niche seating beneath the north and south walls of stained glass. Charlotte sat beneath the stained-glass panel depicting Mary with the Christ child, but she faced the stained-glass panels telling the story of creation. The sea and sky, a spouting whale, and brown and white birds in flight represented Heaven; Adam and Eve, naked, the earth. The act of creation was represented by an orange sun rising on a purple earth, and the beginning, by an open hand and the sun's rays.

But it was the depiction of God that was Charlotte's favorite panel, and the one she gazed at now. Her hands clutched her umbrella as it lay lengthwise in her lap, and the damp and shifting light of the chapel buoyed her. It was a world she could hear but not see, sense but not articulate. God was a grove of trees of various shapes and shades of green.

Today, however, she saw not a grove of trees, but a forest, and not just any forest, but the terrifying forest of fairytales. In the morning post, she had received a letter from Nunhead Cemetery. The trustees asked her forgiveness for their belated reply, explaining that the head caretaker had been ill, and his records misplaced. The tree Charlotte inquired about was diseased, the letter said, and so it was cut down.

Charlotte couldn't find the right words for prayer. Instead, she remembered the woman in the Gordon Square garden, her skirt swaying as she walked, and below the bow at the back of her dress, the red stain, fanning outward and crimson, under a new moon.

Charlotte stared at the stained-glass forest. What might she have done to have her very own child, as she had so long thought of Freda? Her little sister had been lost to them before she had the chance to grow up. At least, Charlotte thought, Freda would never lose her innocence.

THE CHANGELING (1912)

CHAPTER 13

She appeared to address either the Greek bust to the right on the oak sideboard or the open book on a stand to the left. But Charlotte saw neither Hippocrates, the huge volume, nor the women seated before her with teacups in hand, their eager faces turned toward hers. She stood among them as though a mother of five, intuiting their presence while listening intently for a distant voice on the wind.

Charlotte began to read aloud, intoning the voice of the speaker of "The Farmer's Bride," her own hoarse voice wavering between octaves like that of a boy on the cusp of adolescence.

> *Three Summers since I chose a maid —*
> *Too young, maybe — but more's to do*
> *At harvest-time than bide and woo.*
> *When us was wed she turned afraid*
> *Of love and me and all things human;*
> *Like the shut of a winter's day*
> *Her smile went out, and 'twasn't a woman —*
> *More like a little frightened fay.*
> *One night, in the Fall, she runned away.*

She recited the poem as it had come to her, without straining for its rhythm or rhyme, and in fits and starts and a tumble of emotion. She knew the farmer's predicament as well as his bride's, and she hadn't questioned why her imagination chose to dramatize their situation.

> *'Out 'mong the sheep, her be,' they said,*
> *Should properly have been abed;*
> *But sure enough she wasn't there*
> *Lying awake with her wide brown stare.*
> *So over seven-acre field and up-along across the down*
> *We chased her, flying like a hare*
> *Before our lanterns. To Church-Town*
> *All in a shiver and a scare*
> *We caught her, fetched her home at last,*
> *And turned the key upon her, fast.*

She does the work about the house
As well as most, but like a mouse:
> *Happy enough to chat and play*
> *With birds and rabbits and such as they,*
> *So long as men-folk keep away.*
'Not near, not near!' her eyes beseech
When one of us comes within reach.
> *The women say that beast in stall*
> *Look round like children at her call.*
> *I've hardly heard her speak at all.*

Shy as a leveret, swift as he,
Straight and slight as a young larch tree,
Sweet as the first wild violets, she,
To her wild self. But what to me?

The short days shorten and the oaks are brown,
> *The blue smoke rises to the low grey sky,*
One leaf in the still air falls slowly down,
> *A magpie's spotted feathers lie*
On the black earth spread white with rime,
The berries redden up to Christmas-time.
> *What's Christmas-time without there be*
> *Some other in the house than we!*

She sleeps up in the attic there
> *Alone, poor maid. 'Tis but a stair*
Betwixt us. Oh! my God! the down,
The soft young down of her, the brown,
The brown of her — her eyes, her hair, her hair!

Though the women clapped enthusiastically, Charlotte ignored their applause. She closed her eyes and gathered herself to recite "In Nunhead Cemetery." The poem was spoken by a clerk standing alone in a graveyard, having just buried his intended. Like "The Farmer's Bride," "In Nunhead Cemetery" came to her as the pulse of a voice that Charlotte heard and transcribed, first as she wrote the poem, second as she read it to her audience.

When she finished reading, she continued to look beyond the women, as though a medium waiting to be certain that the message of the departed had been received by the living. Another moment passed before she tossed her head, as if to break the spell so she might reclaim her body, and then she took a seat unceremoniously among the women. She picked up a teacup in hands that were her own, yet foreign to her. She heard the women's questions as the clatter of cups in saucers. At Mrs. Scott's suggestion, the women turned politely away and talked among themselves until Charlotte regained her senses.

Mrs. Dawson Scott, hostess of the salon, had insisted by letter that Charlotte read her poems to a small gathering of women at her home in Southall. Charlotte, though honored, was hesitant, fearing she would disappoint Mrs. Scott and her guests. But Anne encouraged her to accept, arguing that only Charlotte could do her poems justice.

Though married to a doctor and mother to three children, Mrs. Scott (or Sappho, as her friends called her, not because she was lesbian, but because of her support of women writers) was less a housewife than a force of nature. Once in a parlor game of Truth or Dare she was asked what she might do with 100,000 pounds. She answered without hesitation. "Found a colony in which poor and wealthy artists alike could live and work without having to lose themselves making a meager living or cower in a genteel country house without conversation or self-respect." Her declaration disappointed feminists and like-minded social reformers at the party, who believed the strength of society was the family, not the arts. Shouldn't impoverished children and husbands given to drink (or worse) receive charity first? But Mrs. Scott was firm. Cultivating the arts by freeing its practitioners would do more good for society than one more committee of women running door to door with pamphlets preaching the virtues of solid family values.

She may not have 100,000 pounds, but she possessed the confidence, the vision, and, most important, the persistence to bring artists together, and thus end the greatest crippler of creativity — loneliness. An idea was born, and she convinced Dr. Scott to live nearer to London. They moved their household and his surgery to King Street in Southall, in the borough of Ealing, only a stone's throw from the city center via Paddington Station. Her tea parties included society women, but only if they were disposed (at Mrs. Scott's cajoling) to promote the arts through either their social position or their financial generosity. Thus, the fashionable set who appreciated Tennyson and Swinburne were to become familiar with Charlotte Mew, a poetess who seemed to have burst onto the literary scene with her publication of "The Farmer's Bride" in the February 1912 issue of *The Nation*.

Charlotte was at last drawn into their conversation. Mrs. Scott asked, "Why have you written a poem about such a contrary couple as the farmer and his bride?" Charlotte looked from one expectant face to another. She set her teacup in its saucer on the end table beside the love seat. "I didn't write it so much as transcribe it," she said, striving to be honest.

"My dear, you're much too modest," said Mrs. Scott, looking to the others for reinforcement.

Charlotte feared she stood accused of false humility and awaited their judgment.

"Whatever your method, the poem is brilliant," said Kathy Miles, an accomplished painter.

"I've never been able to write the Browning monologue myself," said Evelyn Underhill, a poet herself. "One must have an ear for an individual speaker's voice, and you have it, Miss Mew."

Mary Anne Bonneville, a second cousin of Mrs. Scott, said, "The similarity of the farmer and the clerk, despite their different worlds, is what strikes me. Both are in anguish from wanting and not getting. The farmer separated from his beloved by a stair; the clerk, a grave."

"And each poem captures an entire emotional life in a handful of stanzas," added Florence May Parsons. "I thought my heart would burst."

Charlotte felt her face flush with pleasure and embarrassment. "You're too kind," she said. She longed for her writing to be praised, but when the longing was fulfilled, it overwhelmed her.

"Have you studied Freud?" Mrs. Bonneville asked.

Charlotte could only shake her head.

"Well, don't," Mrs. Scott counseled. "It will ruin your natural insight into the human heart. You'll be left with a dissection of the mind — motivations and thought processes — and lose the true essence of humanity."

"I wouldn't say that about May Sinclair's work. Would you?" asked Mrs. Parsons.

Mrs. Scott explained, "That's different. May's a novelist, not a poet. Her characters are case studies. They're analytic and clinical, albeit brilliant. May sees each individual against the background of humanity. Charlotte sees the humanity of each individual."

"I still wonder how you know the farmer and the clerk so well," Mrs. Bonneville said. "Who was it that inspired you to write so hauntingly of their situations?"

Charlotte felt accused of insincerity or plagiarism.

"You're much too literal, Mary Anne," Mrs. Scott said. "Poets have better developed imaginations is all. Isn't that so, Charlotte? Wasn't your imagination, even as a child, more acute than other children's?"

Thankful for Mrs. Scott's interference, Charlotte recalled the attic rooms of Doughty Street and the farm at Newfairlee. "Yes," she said, "though as a child it was the world itself that was enchanted, not the imagination that enchanted the world. Perhaps poets better remember the world as they experienced it as children."

"But fairytales are the stuff of romance. Charlotte's poems are the world unvarnished," Miss Miles protested.

"My good woman," Mrs. Scott declared, "Not even the daily news is as macabre and sinister as a fairytale."

"The dark and the light in balance," Mrs. Underhill added, nodding over her teacup.

"And we know, as children and as adults, that the dark often triumphs," Mrs. Scott said.

"Yes, who hasn't lost a sibling in the nursery, for instance," Mrs. Parsons said.

Charlotte thought of Frederick, Richard, and Christopher. Frederick died before Charlotte was born. Charlotte was six when Christopher, like Frederick, died at two months. And Richard, two years younger than Charlotte, died at five of scarlet fever, while she and Henry and Anne had been spared.

"Too true," conceded Mrs. Bonneville.

"Whether in the nursery or at sea, and as children or as adults, any loss of life is tragic," Miss Miles said.

The women spoke of the *Titanic*, still on everyone's mind two months following the tragedy. "So much for modern progress," Mrs. Bonneville said, "when a ship deemed unsinkable is scuttled by a block of ice."

"The hubris of christening a ship *Titanic* was sure to bring about a tragedy," answered Mrs. Parsons.

Equally sensitive to the power of language, they all agreed.

"Nothing is sadder than a ship going down with all its lights," Charlotte thought, sipping her tea.

"War, perhaps," Mrs. Scott said.

With a rising panic, Charlotte realized she had spoken out loud. It was one thing to answer a direct question, another to volunteer an idle comment.

"Have you lost loved ones at sea?" Miss Miles asked.

"The Mew family goes back to the Isle of Wight," Charlotte said hurriedly, unsure, somehow, what might be demanded of her. "But they were innkeepers, brewers, and farmers, not seamen. Imagine a brewer lost at sea in a gale," she faltered, making no sense, she knew.

The women politely conceded, murmuring, "Yes, I see."

Charlotte would have liked to crawl beneath the love seat. She might have done if Mrs. Scott hadn't suddenly exclaimed, "Marjorie, Christopher, and Toby, what *are* you doing?"

Charlotte and the other women followed Mrs. Scott's gaze. Three disembodied heads peered from around the doorframe of the parlor.

"Come here," Mrs. Scott ordered. The three children materialized and crept obediently into the room. Marjorie was a schoolgirl of about thirteen, Christopher, in short pants and suspenders, about ten, and Toby, towheaded and barefoot, five or six. They might have been the Darling children from *Peter Pan*. "How long were you spying?" their mother asked.

Marjorie, sounding every bit as if she carried the weight of the world on her shoulders, said, "Only a minute. Honest."

"Weren't you to look after your brothers in the nursery?" her mother asked. Marjorie took a deep breath as if to argue or explain but bit her lip instead. "Yes, mother," she said, then looked down.

"Run along then," Mrs. Scott said. The boys raced off, and seconds later their feet were heard on the stairs. Marjorie looked up at her mother. "I'm sorry," she said.

"You're fine, child. Now go," said Mrs. Scott.

Marjorie caught Charlotte's eye as she turned to leave, and Charlotte winked. Did Charlotte imagine it, or did Marjorie smile shyly in reply?

CHAPTER 14

On the train from Southall to Paddington Station, Charlotte watched the engine's smoky breath roll past her window, its shade at half-mast. She longed for a cigarette to steady her nerves, but she economized to pay her fare to Southall. It was hell going without a cigarette for three hours and it had been two days since she last smoked. The reading itself came easily to her. Performing her poems was the same to Charlotte as parodying King George or doing the can-can for the Gower Street girls. Polite conversation over tea with society women was another matter.

Rather than observe the passing countryside, she imagined the open volume on its stand in Mrs. Scott's parlor. As she was leaving, she recognized it as an ordinary dictionary, though voluminous. The headword on its opened pages was *humility*. Nurse Goodman, seeing it, would unfold a cautionary tale. But Charlotte could only turn over again what Mary Anne Bonneville said as the women discussed novelist May Sinclair's study of Freud.

"He has a theory of what he calls the unconscious. We're driven to act out desires the unconscious has repressed, most of which are perverse. But we can unlock the unconscious by studying our dreams. Dreams, Freud claims, reveal our darkest secrets. And because stories and poems are like dreams, they reveal the writers' repressed desires to readers."

"You're saying that May, even as she uses Freudian psychology to reveal her characters, reveals as much about herself?" asked Miss Miles.

"Pshaw," Mrs. Scott exclaimed. "Mary Anne, you're talking nonsense."

"I didn't say it. Freud did," said Mrs. Bonneville.

"But you're sharing it as if it were small-town gossip," Mrs. Scott scolded.

The women had laughed uncomfortably. Mrs. Bonneville excused herself and said her goodbyes. After escorting her cousin to the door, Mrs. Scott returned and said, "She means well, perhaps, but she can't resist being the old wife with a tall tale. Children and dogs see right through her."

Charlotte, Nurse Goodman would conclude, had gotten too big for her britches, puffed up with pride by an invitation to a ladies' salon, and was paying the price, worrying she'd been caught out for being nothing more than who she really was.

"Humility," Charlotte said out loud, though there was no one to hear in the attic rooms of Gordon Street, where she had escaped to when she arrived home to smoke her last tobacco, hidden in case of emergency. She had climbed the height of the backstairs, and just off its third-floor landing, stood on tiptoe to grasp and then pull on a rope, releasing the narrow stairs to unfold like an accordion. She had climbed the stairs into the attic rooms, as a house wren flies into the canopy of an umbrella tree. When she screwed open the skylight with a pole long enough to pilot a gondola, the attic rooms, despite the sunlight, felt less like a tree house than the hull of an ocean frigate.

She sat on a chair whose rocker had broken and whose seat was too long for Charlotte to do anything but perch on its edge, sitting forward so her feet touched the uncarpeted floorboards. She wore the maroon smoking jacket, a castoff of Fred Mew, which hung on Miss Bolt's dress form during Charlotte's absence. From its pocket, Charlotte took a pouch of tobacco, cigarette papers, and matches.

She rolled the last of the tobacco in a paper, licked its edge and lighted it, then smoked her cigarette while the future lay at bay down the stairs and the jetsam of the past bobbed around her like souls lost at sea. The attic rooms held used household goods, all those furnishings displaced by tenants' individual tastes and needs, such as Mr. Boynton's tuba and its stand, Charlotte thought, surveying the Mews' past surrounding her. Her eyes rested on the dollhouse built by Fred Mew for Charlotte, Anne, and Freda. It stood abandoned beside the dress form as its roof gathered dust, the curtains of its tiny windows shut against the attic's thin light.

The attic rooms of Gordon Street merely suggested those of Doughty Street, where she and Henry, Anne and Freda, had lived enthralled by the magical spell of childhood, cudgeled and coddled in turns by Nurse Goodman. Each morning the Mew children had clamored single file up the attic stairs, Nurse Goodman pulling up the ladder behind them as if a gangplank, Henry going first because he was a boy and the eldest, then Charlotte and Anne, and later, Freda. All day they did their lessons and played their games, unaware that a day would come when none of the Mew children would mount the stairs to their own secret land beneath the blue skies and fairy dust of stars, having left the rooms and skies and stars instead for the generations of children sure to follow them.

CHAPTER 15

Charlotte stood outside the entrance gates of the London Zoo and watched nervously for the appearance of Mrs. Scott's children. It was the height of summer and unseasonably cool — not hot and heavy as late July more often is. But her walk to Regent's Park caused her to perspire (a lady, Nurse Goodman said, never sweats) as did her anxiety and fear of missing the children and their nanny.

The personae of her poems, whether or not they revealed Charlotte's deepest secrets, had not put off Mrs. Scott, for she had asked Charlotte to accompany her children to the zoo. Mrs. Scott was to attend a women writers' function with May Sinclair, Mr. Scott was occupied in his Southall office by a spate of new patients, and Mrs. Rose, the nanny, was expected at her niece's wedding in London.

Mrs. Rose must have felt certain of Charlotte's identity because she introduced herself in a declarative voice. "Miss Mew, I'm Mrs. Rose," she said without offering her hand. Mrs. Rose and the three children had approached from Charlotte's right, just as she was looking to her left. "It's very nice to meet you," Charlotte said. Mrs. Rose frowned, and Charlotte wondered if it was the gruffness of her own voice that displeased her. She also wondered how Mrs. Scott had described Charlotte to Mrs. Rose. Then again, Mrs. Scott wouldn't have needed to describe Charlotte because the children would recognize her, having seen her at their mother's salon on three occasions.

Marjorie looked down at her button-up shoes and her hands rested on her skirt, which fell to her knees. She wore her hair, the same rich brunette as Mrs. Scott's, down around her shoulders, except for what was pulled up in a yellow ribbon. The boys wore short pants and waistcoats over their suspenders and white shirts, whose collars sported matching bow ties. Towheaded Toby peeked at Charlotte from behind his sister's skirt, and Christopher stood apart from his siblings, an air of boredom permeating his countenance.

"I've told Marjorie she's responsible for her brothers, so you needn't worry about them." Mrs. Rose spoke as if the children were onerous charges she did yet didn't want to release into Charlotte's care.

"I understand," Charlotte said.

"I'll meet you at the Tottenham Court Station at 5 o'clock," Mrs. Rose said to Marjorie. To Charlotte, she said, "Don't be late or I'll have to tell Mrs. Scott." Charlotte could only smile to herself because Mrs. Rose's devotion to her occupation reminded her of Nurse Goodman's.

A uniformed man at the gate demanded a shilling each before letting them pass. When Charlotte offered her admittance fee, Marjorie rested her hand lightly on Charlotte's arm, and said, "No, Mrs. Mew. Mother says I'm to pay your entrance fee as well as ours." And from a petite curlicue matching her pale-yellow dress, she took four shillings in a gloved hand and gave them to the man.

Inside the gates, Charlotte said, "You mustn't call me Mrs. Mew. That's my mother's name."

"Then what should we call you," Christopher asked suspiciously, doubt crossing his face at the idea that Charlotte might have a mother, as old as she must be.

"Just Charlotte will do, I should think," she said.

But Marjorie shook her head. "We aren't allowed to address grown-ups by their Christian names."

Of course, Charlotte thought. "Then Miss Lotti. It's what our maid calls me."

None of the children objected or asked where "Lotti" came from. Afraid that if Marjorie discovered it was short for Charlotte, she would protest, Charlotte asked quickly, "And what should I call you?" She smiled at Toby, who shrieked and shouted, "To-by," before jumping up and down and clapping his hands in glee.

Christopher, his hands in his pockets, walked ahead. Charlotte and Marjorie followed five paces behind, Toby holding their hands as he walked between them, skipping every other step to keep up.

Christopher led them to the monkey house, and the four of them stood outside an expansive wire enclosure admiring the monkeys' highflying antics and complete lack of self-consciousness. Charlotte thought about how liberating it would be to live with nothing but a fur coat on your back and to swing from tree branches the entire day.

"When I was your age, my nanny told all the Mew children that when we sat, we mustn't let our legs dangle like a monkey's," Charlotte said, pointing toward a monkey who sat with one leg stretched across the high pole where he sat and the other hanging down as if a second tail. The monkey deftly balanced himself on the pole while peeling and then eating a banana with both his hands.

"Where were you to put them," Christopher asked, curious despite himself.

Charlotte laughed. "That's a good question." She thought a moment. "Where could we put them?" she asked Christopher.

"You could sit on them," Christopher said.

"Or cross them at the ankles," Marjorie added.

"That must be what we did," Charlotte said.

"Who's 'we'?" Marjorie asked. "Have you brothers and sisters?"

No one except the Mew family and their oldest friends knew of Henry and Freda. "A sister," Charlotte answered, "who you'll meet today when she has us for tea at her very own studio."

"If I had a tail, I could live in the trees and fly like a bird," Toby said.

"Don't be ridiculous," Christopher said, breaking the moment's spell. "Little boys don't live in trees and they can't fly."

Toby was even more taken by the elephants' trunks than by the monkeys' tails. "Is that his nose," he asked, pointing out an elephant whose trunk pulled leaves from a tree, then carried the green crumbs to his mouth.

"It's like having a hand that's a spoon," said Marjorie. "How nice that would be at picnics."

Charlotte admired its long tusks and wondered at the unlikely congregation of an elephant, an ebony tree, and an iron mine in a Victorian parlor. The key tops of the Mews' piano had been genuine ivory, whether that of an elephant or a rhinoceros she didn't know. But there was a hairline crack joining the front and the back of the keys as proof of their authenticity.

"Elephants mate for life," Christopher said. "I bet you didn't know that."

"You mustn't say 'mate,'" Marjorie said and blushed.

Christopher ignored Marjorie. "And when they're about to die, they leave their families and go off by themselves."

Toby asked if the elephant he pointed out was going to die.

"Of course, silly," Christopher said. "We all die. You'll die too."

Toby sat down on the ground where he had stood and sobbed.

Marjorie scolded Christopher. "Must you torment him? He's your brother. You should look after him."

"Death is a fact of life. He should know the truth," Christopher said with a shrug.

Marjorie picked Toby off the ground and dusted off his short trousers. Charlotte felt she should say something, but she was at a loss for words. At 9 Gordon Street, she smoothed Ma's ruffled feathers and comforted Anne and Jane. But as a child, headstrong and petulant, she had been guilty of ruffling everyone else's feathers.

They had even less luck at the petting zoo. The pony bit Christopher's hand when he fed it a carrot because he ignored Charlotte's advice to hold his palm flat. When Toby admired the piglets' translucent pink ears and fine white hair, Christopher told him that their breakfast sausage was the piglets' mother.

"Their mother is right there," Toby insisted, pointing out a sow and silencing Christopher.

At the rabbit hutches Charlotte told the children how to tell a fake rabbit's foot from a real one, just as Uncle Richard had told her, and Marjorie grew faint and excused herself, explaining politely that she hadn't known about the custom of carrying a rabbit's foot in one's pocket for good luck.

"What about the rabbit," Christopher argued, "wouldn't it be luckier for him to keep his foot?" It wasn't a question, but an indictment of Charlotte's ineptitude as their guardian.

"Can we leave now?" Toby asked. "I'm sleepy." Marjorie nodded at Charlotte in consent and Christopher walked back toward the entrance gates ahead of them. Charlotte willed herself not to cry in front of Marjorie and Toby, who walked two steps behind her, newly ashamed, perhaps, by her company.

"Why, Miss Mew, I hope I haven't missed your visit." A man in uniform, complete with epaulets and billed cap, stood between the quartet and their exit.

"Mr. Alden, good afternoon," Charlotte said. She barely recognized the assistant keeper outside the parrot house. "I'm not here regarding Wek's health, but to accompany my friends on their visit to the zoo."

"I see," said Mr. Alden, scratching his chin. "I was over at the penguin exhibit helping out. A lot of keepers vacation in July, the zoo's busiest time of year. But tell me, who have we here?" He smiled at Christopher and Toby, who were too impressed by Mr. Alden's uniform and official manner to be bored or tired.

"Marjorie, Christopher, and Toby, this is Mr. Alden, one of the keepers of the parrot house."

"How do you do, Mr. Alden," Marjorie said and made a small curtsy. Mr. Alden nodded at Marjorie, tapping the bill of his hat with a large gloved hand, and said, "How do you do, miss."

Toby took his place behind Marjorie's skirt, and Christopher kicked his toe into the pavement, his curiosity waning.

Mr. Alden smiled at Toby. "A blue macaw just arrived at the parrot house. Would you like to meet him?"

Wide-eyed, Toby shyly nodded.

"That is if you're not set to leave," Mr. Alden said to Charlotte. Charlotte looked at Christopher, whose eyes begged her to say they must go. She didn't want the day to end on an even worse note. She was ready to comply with Christopher's silent request and answer to Toby's pleas, when Marjorie said, "I've always wanted to meet a parrot." And they were decided.

The aviary was a geometric dome of glass encapsulating London's atmosphere as its own. Inside, young families and nannies with prams, small children in pinafores toddling beside them, looked into the exhibits of exotic and domestic birds. The haunting *eee-aahs* of peacocks floated in the tall air and visitors looked up and around as though expecting the chilling cries to rain down on their heads.

The quartet followed Mr. Alden, his hand-size ring of keys jangling from his belt. Both men and women turned to look as they whisked authoritatively past, and Charlotte felt as if she were the lead float in a royal parade.

They reached the black iron gate of the parrot enclosure and Mr. Alden turned toward them just as a master conductor gathers himself to direct errant voices in concert. The children huddled close to Charlotte, and she could feel their excitement.

"All I ask," Mr. Alden said, looking at one child and then the next, his face as solemn as Moses' on Mt. Sinai, "is that you tell no one of the secrets kept in the parrot house." Charlotte's heart raced as if she herself were a child, and she almost wished Mr. Alden would ask them to cross their hearts and hope to die if they betrayed his trust. Mr. Alden turned toward the gate and fitted its lock with a huge key from the ring on his belt. He turned the key in the lock, and then stepped aside and bade them to enter.

CHAPTER 16

"Your mother suggested that we walk down Harley Street, so you could see where your father's colleagues practice medicine," Charlotte said.

"How far is the studio?" Christopher asked.

"I used to walk much farther to and from school each day," Charlotte said as they walked.

"That must have been a long time ago," Christopher insisted.

"Sometimes it seems like only yesterday," Charlotte said.

"Is Mr. Wek your father?" Marjorie asked.

"Heavens, no, though sometimes he acts as if he might be," Charlotte said.

"Well, who is he?" Toby asked.

"He's my mother's parrot," Charlotte said.

"Your mother keeps a parrot?" Christopher asked.

Christopher, Charlotte gathered, chose to waive his doubts of Ma's and Wek's existence — at least for now — having heard Mr. Alden ask after Mr. Wek.

"Sometimes," Charlotte said, "I think Wek keeps her."

"Can we meet Wek and your mother?" Marjorie asked.

Charlotte thought of Ma on her invalid's sofa interrogating the Scott children. "Perhaps someday," she said.

"Is your mother a pirate?" Toby asked excitedly.

"Of course, she's not," Christopher said. "Why did Mr. Alden call you Aunt Lotti? He's too old to be your nephew."

"It's how he refers to me when he talks to the parrots. For instance, 'Aunt Lotti has come to see that you're not misbehaving,' " said Charlotte.

By the time they walked halfway to the studio, the children's energy and excitement had given way to a drowsy contentment. Christopher walked on ahead, not to escape them as before, but as if the proud captain of a distinguished regiment. Margaret and Charlotte held Toby's hands, which were sticky with perspiration and the day's journey.

"Would you like to be a doctor like your father? Or perhaps a nurse?" Charlotte asked Marjorie.

"No one's ever asked me what I'd like to be," Marjorie said.

"So you've never thought about it," Charlotte said, knowing Marjorie had.

"I don't want to marry and have children. I want to see the world and write about it. And I want a menagerie. Horses and dogs and cats and pigs and goats," said Marjorie.

"And a parrot?" Charlotte asked.

"And a parrot," Marjorie said. "Did you always want to be a poet?"

When she was Marjorie's age, all Charlotte wanted was to have her own house and children. "Not always," Charlotte said and smiled at Marjorie, who smiled back.

Suddenly Toby sat down on the pavement, rubbed his eyes with both fists, and said he wanted his nap.

"Later," Marjorie said, pulling on his arm to rouse him.

"No," he said, retrieving his arm and shaking his head.

They were blocking the sidewalk, and men and women stared at them, their heads turning as they walked around the threesome. Christopher stood apart in his command, having determined this was women's work.

"Then I'll have to carry you," Marjorie said, stooping down to stand her brother on his feet before taking him in her arms to pick him up. But as soon as she stood, Toby twisted around in her arms and said, holding his arms out to Charlotte, "I want Miss Lotti to carry me."

They walked on, Christopher again taking up the head of his regiment, Toby's arms wrapped around Charlotte's neck, his head on her shoulder, and his legs dangling at her sides as he slept.

"Is he too heavy?" Marjorie asked worriedly. Charlotte had exchanged her umbrella for Toby, and Marjorie carried it like a shepherd carries his staff.

"Not at all," Charlotte said. Sleeping, Toby was as heavy as a burlap feed sack, but Charlotte felt as light as a molted feather on the breeze.

Around the corner from Charlotte Street and Hogarth Studios, Toby woke and asked to be let down. They had walked seven blocks, and Charlotte shifted her joyous burden to his feet.

"Look," Marjorie said. She pointed above her head and laughed to Charlotte. "You've your own street sign." Charlotte Mews, the stables off Charlotte Street, invited carriages to enter under an arch from which the sign hung.

"Yes, I guess I have," Charlotte said, and thought it was true that there were at least three of her: sister to Anne and Freda, daughter to Ma, and since her recent publication of poems, scribbler of jingles.

Christopher stood on the corner and beckoned them to quit dawdling. Toby ran to his brother, and Charlotte and Marjorie, the rearguard, advanced.

The children were delighted to be indoors after their long walk through London's streets and galloped up the flight of stairs, stomping and screaming like wild horses corralled. Charlotte took the stairs slowly. When she reached the first-floor landing, the children were enveloped in the small studio, having been greeted by Anne, who introduced herself, in jest, as "Miss Mew, the Younger."

Just as they had grown solemn in the aviary's tall dome, the children stood arrested by the intense afternoon sun admitted by the studio's tall windows. They looked up and around at the canvases without moving or speaking.

"Who would like tea and gingerbread?" Anne asked. Though Anne smiled at the children, Charlotte could see that she was anxious and tired.

"I would, I would," Christopher said.

"Me, too," Toby added.

Marjorie said, "May I help serve?" Anne nodded, the small favor a welcome penny in an almost empty wishing well.

The boys sat up at the small table, their hands folded in polite anticipation. Anne lighted the gas ring and put on the tea kettle. Marjorie took the box of gingerbread and arranged it on the tray lined with linen doilies tatted by Aunt Mary Kendall.

As she sat with the boys, Charlotte saw a blank canvas on the easel, the same blank canvas she had seen for weeks. Charlotte and Anne had learned that "safe as houses" was an idle expression. In the last three years, the investment property left to them by Aunt Mary had failed to turn a profit. Anne, determined to keep the studio's lease, took a job in a shop that restored antique furniture. She worked four hours a day, six days a week, stripping finish from sofa tables, bed frames, and sideboards, and then sanding, staining, and varnishing them to the shop owner's exacting specifications. If she made a mistake, her wages were docked, and the work was given to another laborer. When Charlotte insisted they lease the first-floor rooms of number 9 so that Anne could quit, Anne protested. Where would the three women sleep? And how could she justify leasing her studio at the cost of subletting another floor when she hadn't painted anything in months?

Anne offered the boys the tray of gingerbread. Marjorie stood with the teapot in her hand and asked Charlotte and Anne if she might pour out their tea.

"Yes, please," Charlotte said, and Marjorie poured out a cup of tea for her and then a cup for Anne.

"And what will you have to drink," Anne asked Marjorie.

"Milk, please," Marjorie said, and Charlotte was suddenly glad that Marjorie wasn't too old to prefer milk to tea.

Between gulps of milk poured from a blue pitcher, the boys bit the legs and heads off their gingerbread men.

"Tell me about your visit to the zoo," Anne said, finally taking a seat.

None of the children mentioned the monkeys, the elephants, or even the silver pony in the petting zoo.

"We saw a real pirate's parrot," Christopher said.

"And a cockatoo and her chicks," Marjorie said.

Anne looked at Charlotte. "Not Lulu."

Charlotte nodded.

"But I thought...." She looked at Marjorie and then at Charlotte. "She's never had a brood."

Charlotte explained. "Mr. Alden claimed it was nothing short of a miracle, but I think she just hadn't met a male cockatoo she could tolerate."

"We got to watch as she regurgitated her supper into her chicks' mouths," Christopher said.

"Not at tea," Marjorie scolded Christopher.

"It's true," Toby said and bit the leg off another gingerbread man.

"Mr. Alden was proud as a new parent," Charlotte said.

"And the pirate's parrot called us 'mateys' and told us 'Land Ahoy' when we left," Marjorie said.

"But the best part of all," Christopher said without humility, "was passing through the parrot-house gates while all the other children and their nannies stood outside, green with envy."

"Oh no!" Marjorie said suddenly. "We promised Mr. Alden we wouldn't tell anyone the secrets we learned in the parrot house. And we've told Miss Mew, the younger." Marjorie looked fearfully at Charlotte and then at Anne.

The sisters laughed at Marjorie's reference to Anne as "the younger," even though it was Anne herself who had planted the seed.

"What's so funny?" Christopher demanded.

"Miss Mew, the younger," Charlotte said, "isn't just anyone. She's a painter who's exhibited at the Royal Academy. Mr. Alden has attended her show, and he even bought one of her paintings."

"Though years ago," Anne said, but smiled in thanks at Charlotte's pride in her sister's art.

At the Tottenham Court Station, Charlotte transferred her charges to Mrs. Rose, who held a nosegay of pink roses in her hands.

"How was the wedding, Nurse Rose?" Marjorie asked politely.

Mrs. Rose looked at Charlotte and said, "My niece left the groom standing at the altar. I want to know what women and the world are coming to these days."

"I'm very sorry to hear it," Charlotte said, unsure what to say. "It" was her niece's betrayal of her intended, the state of women, and whatever else Mrs. Rose found wanting.

"I'm surprised you didn't say, as Mrs. Scott's other Bohemian friends would, that at least my niece's betrayal was a refreshing twist to an old story." She sniffed and turned toward the track as if expecting God's kingdom to come, confident that neither her niece nor Charlotte would be invited aboard.

But when the train arrived, Marjorie turned and smiled, Christopher said, "thank you" and shook her hand, and Toby yawned and said, "Good night, Aunt Lotti."

CHAPTER 17

At home, delighted to have been called both Aunt Lotti and a Bohemian within a day's span, Charlotte listened in the entry for Wek's chatter or Ma calling from the dining room, asking if Charlotte planned to be late for dinner from here on out. The grandfather clock said it was nearly six.

She heard Jane's steps on the stairs before seeing her come around the first-floor banister and slowly descend the stairs toward Charlotte.

"You look tired," Charlotte said.

"I am," Jane said resignedly. No retort. No refinement of terms. Charlotte knew Jane must be truly exhausted.

"Mrs. Mew is in bed and says she doesn't want dinner, and that you and Miss Anne are to eat without her."

"Is she ill? Should I go to her?"

Jane chose the second question to answer. "I wouldn't if I were you. If you'll excuse my language, I'll describe her mood as most foul." Jane pronounced 'foul' as 'fow-all,' suggesting a disagreeable hen. Charlotte thought the expression fitting, for she had often seen Ma in that temper.

"What happened? Did Mrs. Kiplinger stand up Ma's invitation to tea?" Charlotte asked.

"She was here all right. It was after she left that Mrs. Mew insisted I help her to bed. But she didn't say a thing to me about it, only sulked as if Christ had come again and gone and left her behind. Then she took that latchkey and Mrs. Kiplinger's calling card," Jane pointed to the salver on the entry table, "and told me to deposit them in the dust bin."

Jane read Charlotte's mind. "I put them there because I thought you should know about it." "It," Charlotte deduced, being the cause of Ma's foul mood. "There's also a telegram addressed to you. It was delivered late this afternoon."

"Thank you, Jane," Charlotte said.

"I am tired, Miss. Would you mind if I left a cold plate for you and Anne and then took the night off?"

"Of course not," Charlotte said. She was eager to read the telegram in private.

She retreated to her room and sat at her vanity. The telegram was straightforward: "Miss Freda Mew has been taken ill. Please telephone at your earliest convenience to discuss her condition." It was signed: "Sister Lockhart, Head Matron, Whitecroft Hospital, Carisbrooke, Isle of Wight."

The last telegram Charlotte received was from Peckham Hospital in London, where Henry had been institutionalized for the entirety of his adult life. Its message had been equally straightforward: "We regret to inform you that Henry Herne Mew died yesterday after his cold turned suddenly to pneumonia. Please accept our condolences and notify us regarding instructions for his remains."

The term "remains" reminded Charlotte of Miss Harrison's lessons in long division. If a number couldn't be divided evenly by another number, the resulting quotient would consist of another number plus a decimal fraction. But it had required only simple division to understand that when Fred Mew gave Charlotte a dollhouse on her eighth birthday and said she must share it with Anne, Charlotte hadn't been given a dollhouse, but half a dollhouse. Opened on its hinge, the dollhouse revealed three floors, like their house on Doughty Street.

When Freda was born two years later, her father didn't have to tell Charlotte and Anne that their sublease now consisted of just one floor each. Before Charlotte held Freda, she understood that Freda was Ma's daughter, the same as she and Anne. But in Charlotte's arms, Freda was entirely hers, a baby doll brought to life by wishing on a star. That moment, when she was ten years old, was the happiest moment of Charlotte's life because she learned anything was possible.

That night, after she dressed in her nightgown and combed out her hair, Charlotte lay in bed and imagined the stars as they had shown through the skylight of the attic rooms of Doughty Street. No amount of climbing over country stiles in her imagination, Charlotte knew, could deliver her to the land of sleep tonight. So she told herself she would just lie there and rest without trying to sleep. She had tried to reach Whitecroft that evening, thankful for the first time since the telephone was installed at 9 Gordon Street that she had conceded to Mrs. Caroline McHardy's dogged request for what Charlotte saw as an extravagance. But she couldn't get through, and the operator suggested she try again the next day.

She rose at 6:30 and sat on the side of her bed. Her feet, lower back, and arms ached, reminding her of carrying Toby so joyously only the day before, but which now seemed like a lifetime ago. Without dressing or smoking a cigarette, she tried ringing Whitecroft until she was able to get through.

At 9 o'clock, she knocked on Anne's bedroom door.

"Is Ma installed on her sofa?" Anne asked of Charlotte's reflection as Charlotte stood in the doorway. Anne was dressing in front of a full-length mirror, an addition to the room culled from the attic when the studio absorbed her easel. She worked at the shop from 10 to 2 on Wednesdays, so she wore an old dress over her camisole and slip.

Anne studied Charlotte's reflection. "What is it?" she asked, turning to Charlotte, who sat in the chair next to Anne's bed. Anne sat down on the bed catty-corner from Charlotte.

Charlotte related the news she had gathered that morning from the head matron. Freda's menses had grown heavier over the past three months, and in the last week, she began flowing before her menses was due. The resident doctor said there was a growth. He recommended surgery immediately by the best surgeon the Mews could afford. He said a colleague on Harley Street was uniquely qualified because of his experience with these cases.

"We must tell Ma," Anne said, "as soon as possible. At tea today if it can wait that long."

Charlotte nodded, though she suspected Anne meant "you," not "we."

Neither Charlotte nor Anne shared their worry that the growth was cancerous.

"I'll need to go there," Charlotte said, "when they operate. One of us must be there."

"Harley Street?" Anne asked.

"No, Carisbrooke. The surgeon will operate at Whitecroft for his regular fee and traveling expenses."

"However will we afford it?" Anne asked, a question for which Charlotte had no answer.

That afternoon she sat on her throne in the morning room, studying the household accounts. Of the 300 pounds from Ma's annuity, 130 pounds went toward Freda's care at Whitecroft. The surgery, she thought, would cost at least half that. There was the fifty pounds Fred Mew had left Charlotte for dire emergencies and that she had squirreled away, thinking she would need it for Ma's medical care. The only relative left who might be able to lend them money was Ma's brother, Edward Hearne Kendall. But Charlotte knew Ma would never hear of asking her brother for anything, even if it meant their starving on the streets. Doing so would require a degree of humility that Ma simply didn't possess.

Later that afternoon, Charlotte would scavenge the attic rooms for any castoff that could be sold. She might sell the Chippendale chairs or the mahogany sideboard from the dining room and parlor, but Ma would notice their absence and blindly insist that such measures were nonsense. The thought of arguing with Ma and then consoling her exhausted Charlotte, and she feared Ma would exercise the same blind eye when she learned of Freda's illness. If worse came to worst, Charlotte could pawn Aunt Fanny's wedding band and engagement ring, bequeathed to Charlotte on her aunt's death.

Charlotte was deep in her meditation on the vagaries of fate and family dynamics when Mr. Boynton rapped on the frame of the morning room's open door. "Good day, Miss Mew," he began. "Do you have a moment?"

For a second, seeing his silhouette in the doorway's frame, Charlotte imagined Fred Mew, his hand in his hair, having come to her rescue.

"Of course, Mr. Boynton," she said, turning in her chair to face him, "but I'm afraid I've no chair to offer you. If you like, we could move to the parlor."

A few months before, she ran into Mr. Boynton on the backstairs en route to the attic rooms, but he hurried past her without a word. His monthly rent check was left on his tea tray, so Charlotte had rarely seen Mr. Boynton after she and Jane returned his teeth.

Mr. Boynton waived her offer and took a long envelope from his suit coat's pocket and held it.

"My sister lost her husband recently," he said, turning the envelope around in his hands, "and she's asked me to live with her in Cornwall." Mr. Boynton studied the envelope. "My wife's been gone ten years, and neither my sister nor I was blessed with children, so we're all that's left of the family. It's only fitting that we pass our last years in each other's company."

Charlotte waited, as did Mr. Boynton, and then they both spoke at once.

"You go ahead, please," Charlotte said.

Mr. Boynton looked up. "This is the month's notice for my rooms." But still he clung to the envelope.

"I understand," Charlotte said, thinking about having to let the rooms to another tenant and how trouble did come in lots.

"I've been very happy in my rooms," he said. "It's not every landlord who will tolerate a tuba player." He handed his notice to her at last, and Charlotte knew she would miss the rumblings above her head at night like distant foghorns at sea.

"There's something else," he said and pulled a piece of rumpled white cloth from his pants pocket. "You left your handkerchief with me when you returned my teeth. I meant to leave it on the tea tray with my rent check, but somehow it found its way into a drawer. I only discovered it yesterday, clearing some things in anticipation of my leaving Gordon Street."

"Thank you, Mr. Boynton," Charlotte said, and she stood and took the balled-up handkerchief from him lest his discomfort continue. Watching him walk away, with his hand in his hair and scuttling sideways like a crab, she again imagined Fred Mew before he himself departed 9 Gordon Street and left its responsibilities on Charlotte's shoulders.

CHAPTER 18

That morning, Anne suggested to Charlotte that they take their afternoon tea in the back garden and tell Ma about Freda then.

But Ma wouldn't hear of taking her tea out of doors. "I won't subject myself to leavings of birds feeding off the mulberry bushes and I certainly don't want to look at the old crab apple tree that should've been taken out years ago." It was yet another indictment of Fred Mew's neglect before his ultimate abandonment of his family in death. Ma insisted tea be served in her bedroom, and if Charlotte and Anne cared to join her, they may. If they didn't, they needn't bother.

Charlotte helped Jane prepare tea below stairs and wondered how she could tell Ma the news from Whitecroft on this of all days. Pouring milk into the pitcher, Jane said, "This is what I meant yesterday about Mrs. Mew's mood being foul. But I thought a morning in bed might cure it."

Charlotte placed spice biscuits, Ma's favorite, on the tray without comment.

"I wonder what Mrs. Kiplinger might've said or done to agitate Mrs. Mew so that she's even more disagreeable than usual," Jane said, but then caught herself. "Oh, Miss, I'm sorry. I didn't mean to speak ill of your mother, especially when she's been good to me in her own way."

"It's all right, Jane," Charlotte said.

But, of course, nothing was all right that day, and Charlotte herself felt disagreeable. She was anxious about Freda's health and irritated that she would have to placate Ma once she had shared the news, adding to the day's burdens. In principle, Charlotte agreed with Anne: as Freda's mother, Ma had a right to know. But as Charlotte carried the tea service up two flights of stairs, having told Jane she could manage on her own, she remembered Ma's relationship with Freda as that of a doting stage mother. The family and all their friends had assumed Freda's breathtaking beauty and precocious talent as a singer destined her for great things. To Ma, Freda was the means to reclaim her birthright as a distinguished member of society and the matriarch of a family worthy of the Kendall name.

Ma's bedroom was marked by years of stasis. Its organization, if there was any, consisted of shifting piles — newspapers and magazines on the writing table, clothes draped over a pair of chairs and on pegs inside the wardrobe, its left door hanging perpetually open. Medicines stood on the nightstand by her bed. The shades were pulled, and the curtains drawn, and bright crevices of light shone out from where the shades had aged and torn in the room's southern exposure.

Charlotte looked for Ma propped up in bed as if on her invalid's sofa, but Anna Maria sat on a chair in a corner behind the door. The overhead and bedside lamps were switched off, but even in the dark room, Charlotte could see her mother was dressed in a corset, shirtwaist, full skirt, and crinoline she hadn't worn for years.

"Put the tray on the bed," she told Charlotte. The bed was unmade, its linens and counterpane in bunches on top of the feather mattress, which itself was lumpy and misshapen. Charlotte moved the linens and counterpane aside as she maneuvered and leveled the tray.

"Where is your sister," Ma demanded before Charlotte had turned with a teacup in her hand. She handed the cup to Ma, who took it without thanking or looking at Charlotte.

"I thought she was here with you," Charlotte said. She held the sugar bowl for Ma, who ladled three teaspoons into her cup. Charlotte drew the stool of the vanity to the foot of the bed and sat facing Ma.

Anna Maria looked like a schoolgirl sent to sit alone in the corner as punishment for a heinous act, and Charlotte felt as if she were the friend who dared talk with her during recess. But when she looked more closely, Charlotte saw in Ma's dejected expression less defiance than confusion and pain. She forgot about her own news. "Ma, what is it? What's the matter?"

Ma pulled herself up and set her tea on the nightstand. "I don't know what the world is coming to when old family friends call after years of silence only to peddle what they couldn't sell to strangers." Ma spoke with a tone of indignation, but the pain in her voice caused it to waver. Charlotte suddenly ached for her mother, and her own pain in the small of her back subsided.

"What did Mrs. Kiplinger want to sell to you?" Charlotte asked, unable to imagine her mother's old friend from Brunswick Square selling anything, given that she was five years older than Mrs. Mew.

"Votes for women," Ma whispered. "Can you imagine asking my support for something so ridiculous?"

Charlotte couldn't imagine Mrs. Kiplinger supporting the vote for women, let alone petitioning for friends' support. But she felt relieved to hear a note of intrigue in Ma's voice threaded with the pain.

Ma sat back, warming to her subject, and Charlotte, feeling a sneeze coming on, reached into her own pocket for a handkerchief. "They wanted me to hang a placard in our front room's window. I told them Bloomsbury might be guilty of social liberalism, but 9 Gordon Street would never stoop to political agitation. If Parliament won't hear their case, they might as well hawk their ideas on Speakers' Corner."

"You said they wanted to hang their placard. Who's 'they'?" Charlotte asked. She held the handkerchief Mr. Boynton had handed to her that morning.

"That's the worst part," Ma sniffed. "It wasn't Mrs. Kiplinger who called, but her daughter Doris and one of her granddaughters. You know, Doris, the daughter who's your age?"

Charlotte nodded. Doris was married and had three daughters. Charlotte unfolded the balled-up handkerchief. In its folds, she saw burnt red flecks.

"When the granddaughter began quoting Mrs. Pankhurst and talking about how the vote for women was all the more important given the inevitability of war in Europe, I said I wouldn't hear any more nonsense."

What in the world, thought Charlotte, before realizing that the red flakes were the ashes of the rose petal she had retrieved from Henry's grave.

"Are you listening to me, Charlotte?"

"I'm sorry, Ma. I felt a sneeze coming on." She wondered how the ashes had found a home in her handkerchief while in Mr. Boynton's care.

Ma continued, "To think Kaiser Wilhelm, cousin to King George, would declare war on his mother's homeland, is unthinkable." Ma's voice had grown bitter.

Charlotte began to understand the situation. Ma's confusion and pain were rooted in Mrs. Kiplinger's pretense of calling on Ma in friendship and her betrayal of Ma's trust in sending her daughter to seek her own ends.

"It's flattering, though, isn't it, that the Kiplingers felt your social position might be a useful influence?"

"Useful," Ma snorted. "Useful. That's the last thing any of us is." Charlotte didn't know whether Ma referred to women in general or the women of the Mew household in particular.

"Do you want to know how *useful* I am?" Ma asked. The hurt had returned to her voice, accompanied by a note of helplessness. "Before leaving, Doris said she had something from her mother to return to me. And you know exactly what that was, don't you, my clever girl, because Jane saved the latchkey to show you, even though I expressly told her to throw it out. I've no authority any longer, I know," Ma said, "but that doesn't mean I'm without feelings."

"You're hurt because Jane didn't follow your instructions," Charlotte said. It was a statement, not a question. She had thought she understood the root of Ma's pain, but realized now she hadn't. She faintly recalled picking up the rose petal at Henry's grave more than three years ago. She clearly remembered putting the handkerchief with Mr. Boynton's teeth in her pocket. But she still couldn't imagine how the rose petal found its way inside the handkerchief.

"The latchkey," Ma said, "was to the Kendall house on Brunswick Square. A house that's only a memory now that my sister's left this vale of tears and my brother's living on his own." Ma spoke as if Charlotte had never met her Aunt and Uncle Kendall.

"But why would Mrs. Kiplinger have a duplicate key?" Charlotte asked, puzzled.

"If we were inadvertently locked out," Ma explained, "we could go to their house and ask for the copy."

Charlotte saw the latchkey's significance in Ma's mind. It symbolized a world that she was no longer part of, as well as the grandchildren that she would never have.

"And then," Ma said and stopped, her voice cracking. She gripped the arms of her chair. "Doris asked me to return the latchkey of their house, where Mrs. Kiplinger still lives." Ma didn't check her tears with her own handkerchief but let them run down her cheeks.

"It was if," Charlotte said, believing Ma's thought had to be spoken to silence it, "your standing and your name were being taken from you. In asking for their latchkey and returning ours, they were officially excluding us." Ma broke down and sobbed into her hands. When Charlotte said "us," she meant Mrs. Anna Maria Kendall Mew and her two spinster daughters.

Before Charlotte could comfort her, Ma gathered herself to say, "Besides, who holds onto old latchkeys? Only folks with nothing better to do." Ma sniffed and wiped her cheek with her hand. "So I told them in no uncertain terms that I couldn't remember ever having a latchkey to the Kiplinger house, let alone having kept it all these years." Ma looked at Charlotte, her eyes narrowed. "But I'd rather cut off my right hand than shake a Kiplinger's hand again."

That evening, Charlotte rubbed linseed oil on her sister's shoulders and lower back. Anne had stayed past the end of her shift, missing afternoon tea and arriving late for supper.

"If we leased the first-floor rooms," Charlotte said, "we would still have the ground-floor rooms and below stairs to live."

"But where would we sleep?" Anne asked.

"Ma could take the front room, and you and I, the parlor and the morning room."

"Where would you put your bed? The morning room is half the size of the parlor and the front room, even without father's old desk."

"A cot would serve me, and then we could sell my bed," Charlotte said.

"You'd have no place to write," Anne argued.

"Father's old desk could double as a place for me to keep the household accounts and a place to write."

Anne frowned. "There must be a better solution. For instance, I could work more hours. After all, I was able to work two additional hours today."

"Mr. Sands all but made you," Charlotte said. "It's already difficult for you to find the time and energy for your own painting. And your back wouldn't thank you."

"It wouldn't be forever," Anne said.

Despite what else they might do to raise money for Freda's surgery, they might still need to lease the first-floor rooms to make ends meet. But Charlotte said nothing. They had avoided the one subject even touchier than money: telling Ma about Freda.

"Ma seemed fine at dinner," Anne ventured.

"You didn't see her at tea," Charlotte said.

"I don't understand why Mrs. Kiplinger not wanting Ma to have a latchkey should keep us from telling her about Freda."

Charlotte thought Anne, hounded by Ma for the last three years about "her young man," should be the first to understand that a granddaughter of Mrs. Kiplinger's on their front doorstep would make Ma volatile.

Anne sat up and looked at Charlotte. "Ma didn't even ask about Freda and September as she usually does at Saturday supper."

"All the more reason, I think, that we shouldn't tell her just now."

"Then when should we tell her?" Anne asked. Charlotte studied the weariness and fear in her sister's eyes. She understood the subtext of Anne's question: what would they tell Ma if Freda didn't live through the surgery, and how could Ma ever forgive them?

Charlotte shook her head and said, "I don't know."

CHAPTER 19

The forecast for Friday, when Charlotte would travel to Whitecroft Hospital, was hot and windy. The sun would shine blindingly white off the choppy waves in the strait, and Charlotte would shade her eyes with one hand, her hat in the other, as the wind's fingers combed the shining waves of her hair. The ferry would fall and rise on the swells, and as the Isle rose on the back of the horizon like a woman raising herself to stand on a cantering horse, Charlotte would gain and then lose sight of the chalk cliffs of Cowes.

Alone on the Isle, she could imagine she was still twelve years old and that Freda, almost two, was her sole responsibility. The Mew children would walk from the farm at Newfairlee to St. Paul's Church on a dirt road, alongside cow pastures and alfalfa fields swelling with the August heat. Spatters of rain from dark, swollen clouds would stir the dust, and drops would pool on the packed earth like dew on grass. In the gentle rain, the dust, the alfalfa, and the clover would blossom together in a phantasmagoria of scents. Freda would beg to be picked up and carried so her shoes wouldn't get muddy, and Charlotte would show her how to catch the raindrops on her tongue while Anne and Henry walked ahead of them.

When a milk cart came along and asked if they wanted a lift, Henry would sit on the buckboard with the driver, and Anne, Charlotte, and Freda would crawl into the cart under the tarpaulin and sit with the milk cans while listening to the gathering rain pelt the canvas roof of their moving house. From the tall grass beside the road, a meadowlark would pipe its liquid flute, and Freda would ask, "What's that?" pointing her finger in the darkness of the cart. "God is singing," Anne would say, and the cart's wheels would creak, the milk cans clank together, and the harness and riggings jangle. The meadowlark, having taken flight and cast itself beyond them, would trill and chortle its honeyed scale again, its yellow and black suit hidden behind a green veil.

On Thursday evening, Charlotte opened the door of her wardrobe and took out a cigar box from the recess of its floor. She switched on the nightstand's lamp and sat sideways on the bed as if she were going to play solitaire, like Aunt Fanny used to do. She opened the box and shifted its contents to the counterpane, trinket by trinket, reveling in the long-buried treasure: a small thimble, a rabbit's foot, and the gift, years ago, of ruby-colored rosary beads from her cousin Ellen, now an Anglican nun. Charlotte called these her worry beads and fingered one and then another until she completed the circle.

The thimble was a gift from Miss Bolt, the itinerant sewing woman of the Mews and other Bloomsbury families, "with the hope she might never have use of it." It was the traditional gift for young ladies who were to marry rather than work as governesses, fine seamstresses, or ladies' companions. Miss Bolt wrapped the thimble in a tiny drawstring pouch of black velvet, which had been lost down the years. Now Charlotte donned the silver thimble on the middle finger of her right hand and studied it.

Along with the thimble, Miss Bolt shared a cautionary tale. Young girls who grow up too fast, she said, come to no good. Charlotte, just seven years old, held Anne in her lap. When Miss Bolt leaned toward them, as if to take a bite, Charlotte pulled Anne toward her and covered her sister's ears. Never had Miss Bolt, her narrow mouth and two buck teeth like those of a rabbit, looked more like a wicked witch. "My very own niece, Fanny," Miss Bolt continued, "fell low as the gutter of a mean street."

"Where is she now?" Charlotte asked, not understanding what Miss Bolt meant.

"Living on the same street, wearing the same red dress, scraping her breakfast, dinner, and supper from the same gutter."

"Why doesn't her mother find her and take her home?"

"Once the dark of the forest claims you," Miss Bolt said with a distant look in her pale brown eyes, "there's no finding your way back to the light. Let this thimble be a constant reminder of a fate worse than death." She put the thimble in its tiny pouch and pulled the golden drawstring closed, as though a noose around a neck, before handing the black velvet sachet to Charlotte.

Pulling Anne closer, Charlotte said, "I don't want it." Anne began to cry and struggle against her, and Charlotte let her go. Only then did Miss Bolt look around and ask where Richard had got to.

Standing up, her head held high, and her hands pressed against the starched cotton of her pinafore, Charlotte looked evenly at Miss Bolt, who was seated on the sewing stool she carried over her arm as she traveled from house to house. "Richard's gone straight to the devil, just like your niece, Fanny," Charlotte said.

Miss Bolt's eyes grew wide and her expression horror-stricken.

"He caught fire in the night and burnt up 'just like that,' " Charlotte said, snapping her fingers as she had seen her father do.

It was the last time Charlotte saw Miss Bolt, who left the thimble in its pouch for Charlotte and a pin cushion made from half a seashell for Anne, both in the care of Nurse Goodman. Richard, at the age of five, had died suddenly of scarlet fever. Father told Henry, Charlotte, and Anne that Richard had gone to live in heaven with their brothers Frederick and Christopher. Until Richard's death, Charlotte believed Nurse Goodman named each star as she pointed them out one by one through the skylight of the nursery. Charlotte said Nurse should name three of the stars after Richard, Frederick, and Christopher. That's when Nurse told her the stars weren't hers to name. She only called them by the names they had been given by someone else.

As Charlotte looked at Richard's long dark lashes resting against cheeks flushed even in death, she thought she herself hadn't been spared, only that the hand of God or the hand of Satan hadn't yet snatched her from the attic rooms, either to live in the sky with the stars or in a dark forest all alone, the devil behind every tree. With Miss Bolt's abrupt departure, those attic rooms, once only enchanted, became haunted as well.

Charlotte returned the thimble to its place in the cigar box. Telling Ma about Freda's illness and surgery was the right thing to do, Charlotte reminded herself. But in the last week, she hadn't found the right time. Ma refused to take her place on her invalid's sofa. Instead, she and Wek remained in Ma's bedroom, where they took their meals and tea. Wek was molting, and he preened and picked at his feathers in disgrace. Ma pointed to him. "I feel just like Wek looks." Half of Wek's feathers had fallen to the bottom of his cage and the new feathers growing in their place were as wispy as the seeds of a cottonwood tree in spring.

When Anne arrived home late Wednesday afternoon, smelling of paint thinner and as bedraggled as Ma and Wek from her sweated labor, Charlotte confessed that she hadn't been able to tell Ma. Anne grew sullen, and, feeling bedraggled herself, Charlotte told Anne she could tell Ma herself if she liked. "But you're the eldest," Anne said. "It should come from you."

Now she picked up Aunt Fanny's engagement ring and wedding band, welded together before she and Uncle Richard honeymooned at Cowes, refusing to leave the Isle even for a long weekend. When Charlotte returned to London from the Isle, she would pawn the set and place an advertisement for a tenant to replace Mr. Boynton. For a moment, she imagined Mr. Boynton in Cornwall, playing his tuba in concert with the crescending waves, his faithful sister turning the sheet music on its stand.

Charlotte didn't see Freda before or after her surgery.

"She's sedated," the matron said.

"I'd like to see her," Charlotte insisted.

"It's better this way," the matron assured her.

Charlotte couldn't understand how it was better not to see Freda. But because there was nothing else she could do, Charlotte waited nervously, fingering the worry beads she had taken from the cigar box and carried in her pocket. She had also taken May Sinclair's literary biography of the Brontë sisters, published earlier that year, but the day was too bright and too windy to read with a clear head. When Charlotte opened the book, she concentrated only long enough to read Miss Sinclair's description of Emily Brontë as a "virile adolescent." She tried not to remember Freda's last day at 9 Gordon Street, but when she began thinking it might be better for Freda to die in surgery, she gave herself body and soul to the memory she had revisited only a handful of times during the past twenty years. She wasn't ready to lose Freda to death as she had Henry, or the hope, however faint, that one day Freda might return home.

Henry had been institutionalized at Peckham Hospital in London for two years when Freda began displaying similar behavior. Six months later, when Fred insisted Freda be sent to Whitecroft Hospital on the Isle because the family could no longer care for her, Freda had been dazed and incoherent for weeks, mumbling to herself as she rocked back and forth in bed, her legs drawn up to her chest. When she became violent, shrieking and striking out at anyone who came near her, then began hitting herself again and again with a hairbrush, drawing purple bruises on her face and legs and arms, Fred contacted Whitecroft to arrange for Freda's care.

But the morning three men came for her with a straitjacket and a padded van, Freda grew lucid and remorseful, confessing that she'd been a bad girl, saying again and again how sorry she was, and begging them not to send her away like they had sent away Henry. "I'll be a good girl, like Lotti, I promise," Freda cried. Charlotte was beside herself. "Look, she's back with us. She needn't go away," she pleaded with their father. But Fred only shook his head, refusing to meet Charlotte's eyes.

Fred, Ma, Charlotte, and Anne waited in the entry hall as the men ascended to Freda's room. The men unlocked the door, and Charlotte heard Freda's screams of terror as the men restrained her. Ma turned and walked unsteadily to the morning room, while Charlotte and Anne held each other and Fred stood by the stair, his hand resting authoritatively on the newel post as though he were in control. Suddenly, Freda's screams were silenced, and the sisters and their father waited for whatever was to come. Two of the men walked on either side of Freda, leading her down the stairs, while the third man followed closely behind. None of the men met the family's gaze. But Freda did.

They had warned the family about the straitjacket, but they hadn't told them Freda would be gagged. She didn't look at Anne or Fred, only at Charlotte. Freda's dark eyes, wild with terror, knifed through Charlotte. At the bottom of the stair, Freda turned her head to hold Charlotte's gaze, and Charlotte, intuitively, reached out for her baby sister. Freda squirmed and bucked in her straitjacket, trying to break the men's hold, and let out the guttural moan of a cornered animal. But the men hustled her forward and Fred and Anne restrained Charlotte, as she cried out Freda's name again and again.

AT WHITECROFT HOSPITAL, the matron and Charlotte stood inside the doorway of the matron's office.

"The surgery was a complete success," the doctor told Charlotte. He sat behind the matron's desk. "Please, sit down," he said to them. He pointed out two chairs in front of the desk.

"The growth wasn't cancerous?" Charlotte asked.

"We'll run a few tests, but I'm quite certain they will confirm that the tumor was benign."

Charlotte breathed out and felt faint. "And she'll be fine?" she asked.

"She'll be sore while the muscles of her abdomen heal, but she'll be kept sedated. She probably won't even notice anything is different." The doctor sat back in the matron's chair. "This might even be a blessing in disguise," he said smiling.

Charlotte looked questioningly at the matron, who looked down at her hands.

The doctor sat forward and folded his hands on the desk in front of him. "Without the hormonal fluctuation driven by her ovaries, a woman is often much calmer. You must appreciate in your sister's case that such a benefit is particularly desirable."

Charlotte didn't understand, except the fact that the surgery was not the success the doctor had claimed. "Matron?" Charlotte asked.

Matron looked squarely at Charlotte. "The doctor performed a hysterectomy when he removed the tumor ..."

"It's a new procedure," the doctor interrupted, but the matron held up her hand to silence him.

"A hysterectomy is the removal of a woman's uterus and ovaries. Freda will no longer menstruate." The matron paused. "And she will no longer be able to bear children."

Charlotte heard the surgeon say, "The tumor was inoperable otherwise," as the chair moved out from beneath her.

She woke on the floor of the matron's office, unsure where she was or what time it was. Matron knelt over her with smelling salts and the doctor with a stethoscope, which he held to her chest.

"Nothing to worry about," he said, taking the stethoscope from his ears. "I'm surprised all three of us didn't faint given the hot day and the tight confines of this room." He stood and loomed above Charlotte like a white-coated giant. "I'll check on Miss Mew today and tomorrow, and she'll be in excellent hands with Whitecroft's resident physicians. But I'm sure she'll be just fine." For a brief moment, Charlotte wasn't sure if "Miss Mew" referred to Freda or to herself.

"Your bill," Charlotte asked, sitting up.

"There will be plenty of time for settling accounts," he said, winking at Charlotte as if they were conspirators. In what enterprise, however, she refused to fathom.

CHAPTER 20

It wasn't until early September that Charlotte found time to take the Scott children to see the Peter Pan statue. "We'd rather meet your mother and Wek," said Marjorie with such politeness it pained Charlotte to say no. "Perhaps someday," she repeated.

Anne refused Charlotte's invitation to join them, replying without emotion that she was beginning a new canvas. But when Charlotte asked excitedly what it was, Anne said she wasn't sure. In Anne's voice, Charlotte heard the distance that had grown between them since Freda's surgery.

"Where is Christopher?" Charlotte asked. They stood at Lancaster Gate of Kensington Gardens, where they had met. In two short months, Toby had grown taller and Marjorie prettier.

"He's gone off with father," Marjorie said. "To race go-carts," Toby added.

"Weren't you invited?" Charlotte asked.

"We said we'd rather see you," Marjorie said.

Toby nodded, then said, "And Peter Pan."

Charlotte suspected it was Peter Pan's company and not her own that the children craved. But she said, "I'm honored."

They walked south along Lancaster Walk and looked to either side at the trees, whose green shades were shifting slowly to yellow in late summer's changing light. To their left lay Round Pond, and beyond Round Pond and the Broad Walk lay Kensington Palace. But their destination wasn't the pond or the palace, but the patchwork clearing beside the Long Water, where Peter Pan's reed pipe joined the chorus of honking geese and quacking ducks who made their home in the marshland of the river's banks.

Charlotte led Marjorie and Toby onto one of the narrower paths crisscrossing the gardens. Since the three had entered the gate, the many trees had put their heads together, and now the trees' canopy and trunks shut out the view of where they had come from. They had shared the wide path with perambulators and nannies, but on the narrower paths, they walked alone.

"Are you sure you know the way?" asked Marjorie.

"I'm certain unless Peter Pan's flown away," Charlotte said. "Why? Would you prefer to become lost?"

Just then, they came upon the clearing. "It's Peter Pan!" Toby cried out. He ran toward the statue and Marjorie asked Charlotte if she might join him. "Of course," Charlotte said, laughing, and Marjorie skipped off as though she were six years old, not twelve.

Charlotte followed slowly so the children could see Peter Pan on their own first, just as she had in May when the statue was unveiled. The children ran around the statue, pausing on one side and then another to point out a rabbit, a bird, or a fairy perched in the nooks of the bronze tree on which Peter Pan marched, caught mid-stride with his reed pipe to his lips. Charlotte was reminded of Peter's talent for mimicry, whether of the clock the crocodile swallowed or the voice of Captain Hook, and she wondered what tune he played.

"You must see this," Marjorie said, beckoning Charlotte to her side. The statue rose above them and Marjorie reached toward Peter Pan's big toe. "It's even bigger than father's," she said. "You don't suppose Peter Pan is really that big," Toby asked as he came around the other side and stood looking up at Peter.

"He's not real at all," Marjorie said. "Don't be ridiculous!"

"I meant in the story," Toby answered sheepishly. He reached out to pet the rabbits in a niche, so lifelike that Charlotte thought she could see the one's nose twitch.

"In the story, he's a boy, so of course he's not that big," Marjorie explained. She put the tip of her index finger on one of the fairy's wings. "They look so real," she said.

"But they're not real, silly," Toby chided her, and Marjorie blushed.

Charlotte looked toward the path, where she heard shoes on the loose gravel and the babbling of a child. Its mother or nannie held the child, not more than a toddler, by the hand. The child's arm was too short to reach the woman's hand with its own, and the woman made no concession, so the child walked off-balance as it tottered alongside her and babbled happily to itself. The woman stopped suddenly and, stooping down just long enough to slap the child across its mouth, said, "Quit your babbling or I'll give you something to cry about." The child's face expressed only surprise, and the guardian pulled the child along again, its happy babbling silenced.

"Why did she do that?" Marjorie asked Charlotte.

They stood watching as the woman and the child walked up the path and out of sight. Toby sat in the grass across the path by the banks of the Long Water, having discovered teenaged goslings feeding on insects apart from their mother.

"I don't know," Charlotte said. "Perhaps she doesn't feel well or she worked hard this morning and is tired. And maybe she hoped to have the afternoon to herself."

"It was cruel," Marjorie said. "Anyone who's that cruel shouldn't have children, whether a mother or a nanny."

"The Darling children had a Newfoundland dog for a nanny. Would you like that?" Charlotte asked. They watched as the goslings darted from Toby each time he tried to come nearer to them. Charlotte wondered if she should warn Toby about the mother goose sure to be nearby. Uncle Richard had warned the Mew children, but it hadn't done any good.

"Miss Rose is kind to us," Marjorie said, "though sometimes she can be a sourpuss."

Charlotte laughed. "That's exactly how I would have described our nurse growing up. She treated us as though we were her own children."

"What about your mother?" Marjorie asked. "Was she kind to you?"

Instead of Ma, Charlotte thought of Mrs. Darling, whose husband was well-intentioned but simple-minded, and who kept a kiss in the corner of her mouth that Mr. Darling couldn't quite capture. Despite being unevenly yoked in her marriage, however, Mrs. Darling kept vigilant watch for the Darling children, leaving the window open and their beds turned down, sure they would return one day.

"Yes, my mother was very kind," Charlotte said, "though her life hasn't been easy and the past years have hardened her."

"What do you mean?" Marjorie asked.

"She's grown moody and somewhat obsessive about keeping up appearances, a little like Captain Hook," Charlotte said and shook her head.

"She doesn't have a hook for a hand, does she?" Marjorie asked, and Charlotte heard in Marjorie's voice the hope that Mrs. Mew, indeed, had only one real hand.

"Good heavens, no," Charlotte chortled. "But she does keep a pet crocodile in the scullery." She winked at Marjorie, and this time Marjorie laughed.

Marjorie watched Toby gallivant in the tall grass as she spoke. "Wendy was a mother to her brothers and to the lost boys in Neverland, and when they returned to their house in Bloomsbury, Wendy grew up so she could have her own children. If I have children someday, I hope that I'll be a good mother like Wendy, and my mother, and your mother."

"You will. I'm sure of it," Charlotte told her. She thought about how only a month earlier Marjorie had said she never wanted a husband or children. Youth was truly wonderful in its fits and starts, its wide kaleidoscope of dreams.

"But how can you know?" Marjorie asked, her voice pensive.

The raucous honking and hissing of a goose arrested their conversation. They looked over to see Toby running from a huge goose, its wings outstretched and its beak nipping at his heels.

"That's how I know," said Charlotte. "It's instinctual to protect and nurture one's children. You'll see." And she smiled at Marjorie and at the delicate hope that youth held in its hands.

CHAPTER 21

"Why not use the advertisement you used to lease the rooms to Mr. Boynton?" Anne asked.

Charlotte sat in Anne's room on the chair beside her bed, while Anne dressed her hair in the long mirror.

Anne added, "I should think you might write a poem instead of another advertisement." She pulled a hat onto her head and stuck it emphatically with a long hat pin.

The advertisement Charlotte placed had run three weeks and garnered a single inquiry from Mrs. Netty, who wondered if the rooms came with a companion. "I am lonely," the letter began. The handwriting was cramped and careful. It ended: "In hope, always."

Charlotte's reply, which went out in the next day's post, took her the entire day to compose. She struggled to sound a professional note that also conveyed her sympathy, but since she was afraid to encourage a personal correspondence, her final draft said only that the rooms would accommodate a companion, but the leaseholder was unable to provide one. She signed the note in what Anne had described as a confident, artistic hand: Sincerely, C. M. M. She received no other word from Mrs. Netty.

Dressed for a day of "faking" old furniture, as she called it, Anne stood at her bedroom door. "I am sorry, Charlotte, but I mustn't be late."

Charlotte found her feet. "Of course, not," she said. The sisters stood a yard apart, but there was a country between them.

The house agent's fee was dear, but Mr. Sommes produced six potential tenants. The third week in September, he received Charlotte in his office to review the applicants.

The agent's office was a model of efficiency. Ninety-degree angles determined the relationship of objects, from the inkwell stand and blotter on his oversized executive desk to the maps of London (populated with pushpins, their beaded heads in a rainbow of colors) on each wall. Even the oversized chair in which Charlotte took a seat (feeling even smaller than usual) was positioned just so in its relationship to his desk. When she signaled her intention to move the chair closer to his desk, Mr. Sommes shook his head. Charlotte sat and crossed her ankles.

Once he had systematically presented each prospective tenant, Charlotte said, "I think Mrs. Elizabeth Houghton-Smith ..."

"I know," interrupted Mr. Sommes, "that Mr. and Mrs. Clayton Campbell will be ideal."

In time, they would prove to be just that, and Charlotte only wished that Mr. Sommes, for a fee, could set the entirety of the Mews' household affairs right.

When she had installed Mr. and Mrs. Campbell in what Charlotte continued to think of as Mr. Boynton's rooms, she began drafting the poem suggested to her by Toby and Marjorie when they visited Peter Pan's statue. "Did Mr. Barrie make up the fairies?" Toby had asked. They each sat on one of the bronze tree's gnarled roots, and Toby sucked on the stem of a long blade of grass.

"My Aunt Fanny talked about fairies when I was just a little girl," Charlotte said. "And the changeling has always been part of folklore."

"What's a changeling?" Marjorie asked.

"A changeling is the fairy child left in place of a human child, who the fairies take to live with them in the woods," said Charlotte. "But a changeling can also refer to the human child who is stolen."

"So Peter is a changeling," said Marjorie.

"But which is he," asked Toby, "the human child or the fairy child?"

"I think," Charlotte said, "Peter Pan is the human child lured by the fairies to live in Neverland."

"And the fairy child left in his place is the one Peter Pan sees when he returns to his house in Bloomsbury and finds that the nursery window is barred," said Marjorie.

"But why are there changelings at all?" asked Toby.

"That's a good question," Charlotte answered. "Parents who have a child they can't understand or who doesn't meet their expectations of what a child should be will sometimes refer to their child as a changeling. It's as though their human child has been stolen by the fairies, and in its place, the fairies have left a fairy child who confounds them."

"That's sad," said Toby.

"I feel especially sad for the fairy child who's deserted by his fairy parents and whose human parents don't want him," said Marjorie.

"Why don't you write a story about the fairy child," Toby asked Charlotte. "The changeling no one wants?"

"You want me to write a sad story?" Charlotte asked.

"Maybe you could make it happy," Marjorie said.

"Or just not quite as sad," Toby said.

Charlotte's draft of most poems need only please her, but "The Changeling" must please Toby and Marjorie as well. Autumn and winter lay before spring, and Charlotte would work off and on for months before daring to share the poem with the Scott children or Mrs. Scott and her ladies' salon. Deciding to write from the perspective of a changeling left by the fairies wasn't difficult. But it wasn't until the fourth draft of crossed out phrases and lines that Charlotte determined the changeling should address his thoughts to his adoptive human parents in way of apology for preferring the fairy wood to their fireside.

After all, Charlotte mused, who hasn't felt more at home in nature than beside a fire contained by a hearth and screen? As a child, she remembered feeling like she was a tall blade of grass on the hill behind Uncle's and Aunt's house on the Isle. Another time she was the red ant who crawled up its stem, as if Elijah making his ascent to heaven. And still other times she was a bluebell, a squirrel or a redstart, or even a pebble in the stream, still and aware of everything except herself, because she just was, without self-consciousness.

But then a breeze would come up and turn down the sun's bed, the sun would lay its yellow head obligingly on the far horizon, and Charlotte would remember herself and know that she was alone. Then she would long for her mother, a world away in Brighton, or for her father in London, sitting in the parlor in the armchair with its Holland shroud after another day at his drafting table, wondering as he sat by himself in the late August heat if the commercial bank whose plans he had drafted would finally please its owners.

And at one time or another, what child doesn't feel out of place in the nursery with his siblings, who seem contented and at home in a way he never will, even though he's happy when playing jacks or learning to write a large Q next to a small q in cursive letters. His displacement is sensed first like the beginning of a cold is felt at the back of one's throat. The more one tries to ignore it, the more deliberately it comes on.

Then one hour in late afternoon, when the children are down for naps in cots with white linen sheets, comfortably stiff and smelling almost of the mown flax fields of which they're woven, and Nurse has fallen asleep over her knitting (the second of a pair of booties, though the nursery's youngest is five), a rapping on the pane or a bluebird on the sill calls you out. No one else hears, only you, and so you must go. You wake beside your sister, whose bed and sheet are undisturbed, while your sheet is twisted and damp with sweat. Or is it dew from the wood where you were reunited with your fairy siblings in your dream?

THE FETE (1913-1914)

CHAPTER 22

Fall blurred seamlessly into winter, and winter passed as quickly as a summer squall. It was an early spring day, with the soil smelling as if it had been freshly turned, and the birds flitting and chattering in the bushes. The wind, brisk in its enthusiasm, pushed Charlotte along the pavements and whipped her hair from its chignon. She ducked for cover under the Scotts' portico and hurriedly pinned up her hair before pulling the bell.

"You, Charlotte, are a warm personality. May is cool," Mrs. Scott had declared. "You'll bring each other around." Charlotte read *The Combined Maze* and admitted to being impressed, yet she was leery of meeting May Sinclair, who everyone said was clever, and whom Charlotte could never forgive for her characterization of Emily as a "virile adolescent."

Mrs. Scott insisted, however, so it was pointless for her to resist. Charlotte only wished Mrs. Scott's children would be there to bolster her confidence. But Mrs. Scott said Dr. Scott had escaped his surgery and planned an outing for the children.

May had already arrived. When Charlotte entered the parlor, she sensed that May hadn't expected her. May looked to Mrs. Scott, who introduced them. "So you're the poetess Sappho's so fond of," May said, while looking Charlotte up and down.

"I feel a bit more like a paper bag the wind blew in," Charlotte said wryly. May smiled demurely but made no comment. She was small in stature and plump, Charlotte noticed, like a bobwhite hen, and her hair was an unusual and striking chestnut.

"Sit down," Mrs. Scott said, "next to May, on the love seat." Charlotte took her seat but sat forward so that her feet touched the ground. She could feel May's eyes on the nape of her neck.

"I was just about to tell May about your reading of "The Pedlar" to the children and how thrilled they were." Charlotte had written "The Pedlar," a short children's poem, while working on "The Changeling."

"Where are those precious bits?" May asked. "I hadn't even noticed they were missing."

"Their father's taken them on an outing," Mrs. Scott said, "to fly kites."

"I didn't realize Mr. Scott was interested in aerodynamics," May said.

"I don't believe he is," Mrs. Scott said. "I think he was fond of flying kites with his father as a child, but whether or not he remembers how to fly a kite is an entirely different matter."

Charlotte said, "Boys seem to remember what their fathers have forgot."

"Charlotte, that doesn't make any sense," Mrs. Scott said. "Did you mean to say that boys remember what their fathers forget?"

Charlotte could only shake her head.

"It's one thing to be illogical and another thing to be blind to one's own sex," May declared. "What about girls?" she asked Charlotte. "Do they remember what their mothers have forgot?"

Charlotte heard the scorn in May's voice and wondered if this was a trick question.

Mrs. Scott interceded. "Marjorie is wise beyond her years. I only hope that she doesn't grow up too quickly."

"For my part, independence couldn't come soon enough," May answered. "But I didn't have the luxury of living on King Street with brothers who minded what I said."

"Childhood should be the best years of one's life," Charlotte heard herself argue.

"Yes, if only one is so lucky," May said coolly.

They sat in silence.

Suddenly, Mrs. Scott said with forced gaiety, "Charlotte, you must read us 'The Farmer's Bride.' "

"If you like," Charlotte said, happy to step outside of her own skin, especially at this moment.

She stood up, manuscript in hand, but paused. In the women's silence, she could hear the wind in the courtyard rattle the French doors. She closed her eyes and began, rendering the manuscript useless.

Her performance was effective, she thought, and when she finished, May broke into applause. For a terrifying instant, Charlotte believed May clapped in ironic jest.

"It's altogether ruthless," May gushed. "The restrained fury is simply marvelous. But the most brilliant touch is the spotted feathers of the magpie." May turned to Sappho. "Why didn't you tell me that Charlotte is a genius?"

The praise was a warm bath of sunshine, and Charlotte's face flushed. She took her seat.

"Charlotte is a bird lover," Sappho said. "She even keeps a parrot."

"Wek is less a parrot than an institution," Charlotte said, "and he's not mine, but my mother's."

"Feathers are just invitations to lunch for my cats, Tommy and Jerry," May said. "I had an uncle who claimed to be a bird lover. But everyone knew he watched birds to escape his wife. He would spend whole days out of doors tramping the woods near his home. He once spent an entire afternoon whistling back and forth to a bird perched at the top of a pine tree. He said it was more rewarding than trying to talk to his wife."

"Does your uncle live in New England?" Charlotte asked.

"He did. Both he and his wife are deceased," May said. "They emigrated just after they married and settled in Vermont. However did you guess?"

"Hermit thrushes are indigenous to North America," Charlotte said. "They nest in coniferous forests and like to sing from the tops of trees. Even though they're quite small, their voices are voluminous."

"Why that sounds like a description of you, my dear Charlotte," May said.

Charlotte didn't know how to reply, so she said, "Did you know that all songbirds are omnivorous?"

May threw back her head to laugh, then said, "Sappho, would you care if Charlotte and I take a turn in your courtyard?" Sappho just smiled. May held out her arm to Charlotte, and they walked out together through the French doors into the four winds.

In bed that night, Charlotte remembered the sensation of flying a kite as a child. For moments on end, the kite rose upward on the wind's back, higher and higher, until it felt as though the kite weren't on a string at all. But suddenly the wind bucked and the kite tugged her hand and her entire body felt as if it were aloft. She forgave May for what she had written about Emily Brontë.

CHAPTER 23

"I can't see," Nurse Rose said, speaking through her nose, "how leaving paper baskets on stoops will do anything other than confuse our neighbors."

"What Nurse Rose means," Mrs. Scott translated for Charlotte, "is that the first of May is a pagan holy day."

The three women stood in the kitchen around the table the cook used to stage the Scott family meals.

"It's hardly a holy day," Nurse Rose insisted, staring at Charlotte. "And encouraging children to celebrate it by trespassing on good neighbors who've never done us any harm isn't Christian."

Mrs. Scott spoke calmly. "It's a beautiful day. Couldn't we view it as a celebration of spring, nothing more or less?" She smiled at Nurse Rose.

Nurse Rose glowered back. "Isn't that the purpose of Easter?"

"On Easter," Mrs. Scott said brightly, "we observe the resurrection of Christ."

Tricked by Mrs. Scott's word play, Nurse Rose put her chin in the air to say, "I'll leave you to your folly, as you can't make me a party to it."

She left the kitchen to make her way up the stairs to ground level. On the stairs, she turned and called back, "I'll offer to spend my afternoon off in the park with the children, in case they know better than to spend it here. If you don't mind, that is, Mrs. Scott."

"Do as you please," Mrs. Scott called. And with that, Nurse Rose left the two women below stairs.

"Had I thought I'd stir up controversy ..." Charlotte began. But Mrs. Scott only shook her head and laughed.

"You do realize," she said to Charlotte, "that Nurse Rose is green with envy of you."

"Of me!" Charlotte exclaimed. The idea was ridiculous.

"Of your relationship with the children, particularly Marjorie. You're Aunt Lotti to the children. Nurse Rose is only Nurse or Miss Rose." Mrs. Scott chuckled, obviously pleased.

Charlotte demurred. "I have the luxury of coming and going and doing only fun things with the children."

"Leave it to you, Charlotte, to downplay your talents." Mrs. Scott shook her head. "Humility is one thing. Self-deprecation is another. You must own your talents."

At that, Marjorie, Christopher, and Toby barreled down the stairs and into the kitchen.

"I was first," Christopher claimed.

"It wasn't a race," Marjorie argued.

"No fighting," Mrs. Scott gently chided them, "or Aunt Lotti won't show you how to make May baskets."

None of them, Charlotte observed, had preferred Nurse Rose's offer of an afternoon in the park.

Marjorie looked shyly at Charlotte. "I hoped Anne would come, too."

"She would've liked to very much," Charlotte said. It was a fib only in that Charlotte was still struggling to find her way back into Anne's good graces.

"Then why didn't she?" Christopher demanded.

"Be polite," Sappho said.

"I'm only asking a rhetorical question," Christopher said.

"An honest question," corrected Marjorie. "A rhetorical question is one for which the speaker has the answer."

"Then why ask the question?" Christopher said. "Adults are so confusing. I hope I never grow up."

Charlotte showed the three children how to weave baskets from strips of colored construction paper before filling them with popcorn and soft candy wrapped in waxed paper.

"What are we to do with the baskets," Marjorie asked, "once they're finished?"

"Leave each basket on a neighbor's doorstep, preferably a neighbor with children your age, then pull the bell," Charlotte explained. "When the neighbor answers the door, run toward home. If the neighbor catches you before you reach home, you must kiss him or her on the cheek."

"*Bleck*!" Christopher shrieked. "Who'd want to kiss anyone, especially a dumb neighbor?"

"That was a rhetorical question," Marjorie explained to Christopher.

"Marjorie would!" Toby shouted gleefully.

"Marjorie would what?" Sappho asked Toby.

Toby looked guiltily at Marjorie, whose face was lit by red splotches.

Before Toby could answer, Christopher began chanting in sing-song fashion, "Marjorie's got a sweetheart. Marjorie's got a sweetheart."

Marjorie cried, "Mother, make them stop teasing me!"

"What's his name?" Christopher asked. "You have to tell!"

"No, I don't!" Marjorie cried.

"You admit it!" Christopher said. "You have a sweetheart!"

"Stop it this instant," Mrs. Scott demanded. "The baskets are finished. Off you go."

Dutifully, the children gathered up the baskets and marched together toward the stairs. Mrs. Scott called after them. "Marjorie, put on your cape, and Toby, your woolen blazer. And don't be long. Aunt Lotti has a surprise for you when you return home."

Mrs. Scott laughed, then sighed. "They've grown up so quickly. It's astonishing, really. Oh, I know it's clichéd. Only yesterday Marjorie was pushing her dolls in their cart. Soon it'll be a perambulator. And I'll be a grandmother."

"How wonderful that you have grandchildren to look forward to," Charlotte said.

"Yes, isn't it?" Mrs. Scott replied. "I only hope Marjorie finds a husband who respects her."

"I know she will," Charlotte said. "She must."

Charlotte's thoughts returned to May Sinclair, as they had done repeatedly ever since they met two months ago.

"Have you heard from May lately?" she asked Mrs. Scott. May's name hung in the air like the sound of a bell.

"The last I heard, she's hard at work with the Medico-Psychological Society. She's up to her chin in bureaucratic red tape. But if anyone can move mountains, it's May."

"Has she always been so industrious?" asked Charlotte.

"As long as I've known her," said Mrs. Scott. "Of course, it's much easier to write books at will and run a handful of organizations if you haven't three children and a husband."

"I'm unmarried, but not half as accomplished," Charlotte admitted.

"But you've a mother and a sister, and a house and a maid, all who depend on you. May has only her cats."

"I've just finished rereading *The Combined Maze*, and I thought it was even more beautiful the second time. The characters' emotions are so intense and heartfelt."

"May's insights are keen, I'll grant you. But she's more dispassionate than you imagine. She writes about men and women in relationship to remind herself not to condemn herself to one."

"A man or a relationship?" Charlotte asked, then bit her tongue.

Mrs. Scott looked at her appreciatively. "I believe you have a writer's crush on our dear May."

Charlotte's heart raced.

"I introduced you to each other," Mrs. Scott said carefully, "and that's why I feel I can say this." She looked directly at Charlotte and held her gaze. Charlotte felt her face flush and hid behind her teacup and saucer.

"May will do anything for a friend. But her causes and her cats come first." Mrs. Scott looked away. "I suppose a few boats are bound to be left in her wake at the speed she captains her ship." Mrs. Scott sighed. "I don't know," she said abstractedly. "Perhaps I'm only jealous and want you and May all to myself."

The front door opened, then slowly closed. Mrs. Scott said, "The children are home."

But it was only Marjorie and Toby. They entered the kitchen as if it were the sanctuary of a church. Marjorie cradled one of the baskets. "I found a baby bird in Mrs. Hitchens' flowerbed. It must've fallen from its nest." She gazed into the basket.

"And you've brought it into our home?" her mother asked.

Toby said, "We didn't know what else to do, and we thought Aunt Lotti could save it."

Marjorie brought Charlotte the basket. Charlotte took it and looked in at a fledgling with only fuzz for feathers. It lay on its side gasping for breath. Its reptilian eye winked halfway open and then shut.

"Well?" Toby asked. Both Marjorie and Toby hung over Charlotte.

"It's a house wren," said Charlotte.

"What can we do?" Marjorie asked. Charlotte felt as though she were being addressed as an all-powerful god. She knew of only one bird outside of the zoo that had survived captivity, and that was a hawk, nearly full grown and with only a broken wing.

"The wren has a good chance of survival if we return it to its nest," Charlotte said as softly as she could.

"But the mother will reject it, won't she?" asked Mrs. Scott.

"An old wives' tale, I'm afraid," Charlotte replied. "Unlike rabbits, whose smell is keen, most birds can't distinguish a human's scent from a flower's."

"We didn't see a nest, honest," said Toby. Marjorie took the basket from Charlotte.

"Why don't we have a second look, just in case you missed it," Charlotte said.

"But what if we can't find it?" Marjorie asked.

"Or we can't reach it?" Toby argued.

"Then you will have to keep our feathered friend warm and feed it," said Charlotte.

"Don't worry. I'll help you," Mrs. Scott said, surprising the children. However, Charlotte wasn't surprised. She smiled at Mrs. Scott.

But before they could look for its nest, the baby bird's labored breathing slowed, then stopped.

"It never had a chance," Marjorie said.

"It's not fair," Toby said.

"No," agreed Mrs. Scott and Charlotte in unison.

After tea, which no one drank, Charlotte tried to read "The Changeling" to the children, as Mrs. Scott listened in. But even as Charlotte began to read, she knew the poem wouldn't engage their imaginations or lift their spirits. When she reached the bird's "tweet tweet" in the second stanza, she stopped.

"We're sorry, Aunt Lotti," Marjorie said.

"Yes, we're sorry," Toby echoed.

Just then, the doorbell rang.

Marjorie and Toby looked at each other and then at Charlotte. "Perhaps it's a May Day-er," said Mrs. Scott. She excused herself to Charlotte and rose to answer the door. Marjorie and Toby jumped up to follow her.

Charlotte sat in her usual place on the love seat, sad about the fledgling, and sad about how "The Changeling" had no effect on the children's spirits.

Mrs. Scott returned with Marjorie, Toby, and Christopher behind her.

"It wasn't a May Day-er," said Toby, "only Christopher pretending to be one."

"I only meant it as a joke," said Christopher. "How was I to know a stupid bird died?"

Mrs. Scott looked at Charlotte, and Charlotte returned her gaze. The meaning of their exchange was clear. In the final tally, innocence always seemed to lose out to experience.

CHAPTER 24

Charlotte needed a summer holiday, however brief, to clear the cobwebs of her mind. The journey from London to the village of Dieppe in northern France freed Charlotte from the preoccupations that made up her life in London. If the range acted up or the boiler's pilot light went out, Jane or Anne must see to it, for Charlotte was no longer the housewife of 9 Gordon Street but a gypsying bird.

At the Hotel du Commerce, meals were provided and her bed made each morning and turned down each night by a maid. The hotel's matron, Madame Binoche, wore a sleeveless dress of red velvet and a shawl of either black or white lace, depending on the time of day. Her English was the equivalent of Charlotte's French, so their conversations were successful if sometimes stilted and accompanied by much smiling and head nodding. To Charlotte's delight, Madame Binoche called her *"ma petite poupée chinoise."*

Charlotte's room on the ground floor afforded a view of wash hung on lines over a cobblestone alley, but as she planned to spend her days wandering the town's narrow streets or at the quays watching the fishermen, she didn't mind. And anyway, there was something decadent about looking out one's French window at red and blue underclothes luffing in the breeze between homey, white-washed buildings.

Charlotte sat on the edge of her bed. For an entire week, this room was to be her home, and no strings were attached (i.e., ten more rooms demanding her attention for one thing and still another). She needn't worry about the bicycle in the hallway propped against the wall, thinking Ma and it would sooner or later be at odds. She could merely wonder about its owner and whether or not he wore a goatee.

She imagined that her room was a caravan escorted by a kindly gray mare and that they might travel anywhere in the world or stay exactly where they found themselves. Her clothes were unpacked in the chest of drawers, her brush, hand mirror, and toiletries were set out on the vanity, and her shoes, which she had unlaced and removed, were placed under the bed beside her case. She lay down on the crisp white sheet, fell fast asleep, and slept without dreaming.

When his health no longer permitted his staying in London, Henry Harland, editor of *The Yellow Book*, retired to a villa in Dieppe. Irrepressible, courageous, and charitable, Harland (first "Mr. Harland" and then just "Harland" to Charlotte) possessed the talent of instilling confidence in young writers at critical junctures. He had done so for

Charlotte, who submitted "Passed," one of her first short stories, immediately after she had written it. Harland accepted "Passed," quibbling over a few small details but praising it, and of almost secondary importance, publishing it.

However, Charlotte couldn't afford to remember those heady *Yellow Book* days, when in her early 20's the wider world seemed to open its arms to welcome her just as Henry and Freda were shut away from the world's embrace. It was no wonder Charlotte couldn't be like Ella D'Arcy, a fiction writer and Harland's editorial assistant. Ella, with her devil-may-care and take-it-or-leave-it attitude, was a typical New Woman of the 90's. But her ability to recognize and as easily accept her weaknesses as well as her strengths was what most set her apart from other late Victorian women.

Simply, Harland and Ella knew how to make a good time of life, whereas Charlotte had to will herself to learn. Charlotte wore her hair down like a schoolgirl's, and acquired a taste for cigarettes, slang, and swear words. If only, Harland said, Charlotte would fully commit herself to a writer's life, she might get somewhere. A writer himself, he meant Charlotte's life might be better served with a richer and less conventional storyline.

Charlotte woke sometime after midnight and wondered where she was. The moon's white light shone through the French window and lay on the floor. A sea breeze salted the room, and waves crashed on the shore in the near distance. For a moment, Charlotte forgot herself. She was a child in the attic rooms of Doughty Street unafraid of the shadow of the chest of drawers lurking like a bear in the corner. For a moment, she lost her self-consciousness and existed without fear or desire. Just as suddenly, the moment passed, and she was conscious of herself in a strange room with moonlight for its carpet.

In the morning, she walked down to the quays and watched the gulls scavenge for food in the surf. Seaweed and kelp, hung up by high tide, were strewn along the shore. A gull walked toward a tide pool. As the waves eddied out, the gull sped toward it. Before the gull could satisfy its curiosity regarding the pool's contents, the waves crashed on the shore and rushed forward, chasing the gull away. If Charlotte were a gull, she wouldn't think, she would merely exist, without the knowledge that she and the sky were separate. She wondered, watching another seagull fuss over a crust of bread, if the enchantment of childhood isn't transformed into desire during adolescence. Are we awakened to our separateness and to desire by seeing our reflection in a beloved's face? But why should desire make the senses and the soul seem like they are one and the same?

"You must attend the circus," Madame Binoche said that afternoon when Charlotte claimed the key to her room.

"The circus," Charlotte repeated.

"It goes around each year. For three days, it's here." Madame Binoche pointed to the register on the desk in front of her. "Just southwest of town. Everyone goes there, even the bear who skips."

Charlotte nodded. "*Merci beaucoup*," she said, and took the room key from Madame Binoche's elegant hands. That afternoon she smelled of lavender toilet water. Charlotte felt Madame Binoche size her up, before nodding her approval. "*Ma petite poupée chinoise*," she said, then turned away.

Charlotte, her umbrella over her shoulder, walked the dusty road where the circus performers had pitched tents, set up stalls, and parked their string of caravans. Perspiration gathered on her upper lip. Tall leaves of grass fronting the woodlands beyond the road slumped in the humid air. On the roadside, sparrows hopped along in the short grass feeding on gnats, but they didn't startle as Charlotte passed by, as if their wings were too heavy to lift. She looked to her right and left at the deserted booths. An occasional huckster glanced up as she passed but ignored her just as the sparrows had. The hucksters resumed what they were doing: polishing a harness, unloading bottles for a ring toss, or lying in the shade of a tree with a blade of long grass between their teeth. Horses stood on three legs, resting the fourth, and swatted flies with their tails. They slowly blinked as she passed or they blew out their breath through their nostrils and shook their manes. A lion roared, or she imagined one had. She stopped in her tracks, confused by the inactivity.

"Show doesn't start 'til late," a disembodied voice called out. Charlotte looked around.

"Over here."

Charlotte turned to see a curl of smoke rise from inside a stall. Charlotte sidled toward the stall as the gull had the tide pool. A woman sat on a short stool picking through a mongrel's coat. She looked up at Charlotte. "Fleas," she said, after taking a brown cigarette from her mouth. "But better fleas than mange or louses," she reasoned. The stall's walls were green canvas, its floor was matted grass. Two wooden crates, whose contents Charlotte couldn't see, waited in a corner.

"How did...." Charlotte began.

"I know you walked there?" the woman asked.

"You couldn't have seen me from where you're seated," Charlotte volunteered.

The woman stood. She was much taller than she appeared when seated. "Psychic," the woman said, pointing to her head, wrapped in a scarlet kerchief from which black hair spilled out in waves. "It's a gift." She shrugged and laughed. "Or a curse."

Charlotte looked over her shoulder. "Where is everyone?"

"That I can tell you without my gift," she said. "The villagers don't come 'til late, after supper. Unless it's Saturday. Until they come, we sleep, or we feed the lions." The woman threw her head back and laughed again.

"Come." The woman motioned to Charlotte. She turned and escaped the stall through a door Charlotte hadn't noticed. Charlotte walked around the stall and followed the woman, who strode across the clearing to a string of caravans.

They came to the back of a dull yellow one, where a gray horse tethered to a stake looked up from grazing and nickered to the woman. The caravan's hitching gear lay idle at its head. The woman opened the small door of the caravan and let down a short ladder, reminding Charlotte of the attic stairs of Doughty Street. "Follow me," she said, and climbed through the small doorway into the darkness. Charlotte obeyed.

She stood in what seemed like a nether region until her eyes adjusted to the pale light. Pots and pans hung on one wall, and a narrow bunk with a horsehair blanket stood along another. Chests of drawers were tucked below the bunk, and Charlotte imagined the woman kept her clothes there. Above the bunk hung a cross made of a dark metal. Charlotte looked at the woman.

"What? You think Christ never came to Hungary?" the woman asked. Charlotte looked down, embarrassed. "Don't feel bad," the woman continued. "A horseshoe once hung there."

Opposite the bunk, tarot cards and a crystal ball rested on a small round table, behind which the woman seated herself.

"Tell your fortune?" the woman asked, looking up at Charlotte while shuffling the deck of cards in a waterfall, beaded bracelets jangling on her wrists. The woman set the cards aside and cracked her knuckles. Nurse Goodman warned Charlotte of fortune tellers when one offered to reveal her fate at a Saturday Market on the Isle.

"Sit down," the woman said, waving her hand toward a stool beside the table. "You pay me only if you like what I see, huh? Give me your hand."

The fatalism appealed to Charlotte. She sat down on the stool and offered her hand. The woman took it and turned it over several times before examining its palm. The woman's hands were warm and surprisingly soft.

"I see you've met a dark and handsome stranger, not so tall maybe, named Bill or Ned." She gazed into Charlotte's face as though it were the crystal ball.

"My father's name was Fred," Charlotte offered, "and once upon a time he was a stranger to me."

The woman threw her head back and laughed a third time. "Good. A sense of humor helps." She studied Charlotte's palm a second time. "You're famous," she said, looking up in disbelief.

"Not exactly," Charlotte said.

"You will be," she said, shrugging her shoulders before again studying Charlotte's palm. "Your past is tragical." She looked up. "I'm sorry," she said, then looked down. "Your future is tragical also. I'm more so sorry," she said without looking up. "But too it is magical, enchanted. Also like your past." The woman continued studying the hand, turning it over in her own. Finally, she returned Charlotte's hand and sniffed. "That's all. The gift it comes, it goes," she said.

Charlotte examined her own hand but saw only its resemblance to her father's. The woman's eyes met Charlotte's. "And love, you wonder about romance, yes?" Charlotte felt blood throb in her head as an image of May's chestnut hair came vividly to her mind. "That," the woman said, "is up to chance, not fate. You may have one great love or you may have many lesser ones. Who's to say but the four winds?" she concluded and folded her hands.

"What can I pay you?" Charlotte asked.

"You like your fortune then?" the woman asked. Charlotte herself shrugged, as the woman had, and the woman laughed.

"Go now," she said to Charlotte. "But watch for me. We met before, and we will meet again."

Charlotte had imagined a woman on horseback cantering into the circus tent's center ring. When she returned to the clearing that night, however, she saw a drunken clown with a monkey who refused to come down from his perch and a lion who would do nothing but roll over in the dirt, beat the broom of its tail into dust clouds, and open its mouth as if to roar, only to yawn and fall asleep. When the crowd began to boo, the lion tamer merely shook his head as if to say, *"C'est la vie."* A clown on a tricycle diverted the crowd's attention with his horn and got a few rounds of laughter. But when a distinct odor sifted through the tent and someone yelled, "Look out, a skunk," the crowd became angry and jeered, and the management had no choice but to refund the crowd's money. The circus, which was to stay in Dieppe three nights, was shut down before its first performance had ended. By the following afternoon, the troupe's tents, stalls, caravans, and horses had vanished.

The following morning, Madame Binoche said to Charlotte, "It is too bad." Charlotte dropped off her key at the desk, planning to return to the clearing out of curiosity, but it began raining and then pouring before she had walked half a mile. She collected her key from Madame Binoche, who said again, "It is too bad," this time, Charlotte assumed, referring to the rain-soaked day, and she returned to her room. The French window had to be closed to keep out the rain, so Charlotte lay in the semi-darkness and imagined what the circus might have been.

It began with a parade on Dieppe's main street. A dwarf led a dancing bear on a chain and several performers did cartwheels and backflips. At night, the villagers gathered in a clearing surrounded by a black forest and lighted by the whiteness of a full moon. A line of booths with games and sweets led the villagers to the Big Top, a huge tent made of red canvas. The air smelled of dust and the sea, and the breeze echoed with music and hoof beats. Though the night air was cool, the Big Top held the heat of the day.

In the rush lighting of the tent, clowns teased the crowd before a woman standing on horseback entered the center ring. She was as ephemeral as a dream. Her silver headdress, sequined leotard, and pink stockings called to mind the damsel in distress of medieval romances, yet she was as self-possessed as she was vulnerable. She looked to someone in the crowd. Her eyes met Charlotte's and held her gaze. Charlotte saw in the woman's reflection her own restlessness and desire.

Because Charlotte's vision was so intense, she wondered if she hadn't fallen asleep and dreamt what she imagined. She rose and took stationery from the vanity's drawer. She wrote "Fête" in the center of a sheet and spent the next three hours putting words, meter, and rhyme to what she had seen, but from the point of view of a sixteen-year-old boy rather than her own. It was rough, but she had sketched the heart of the poem and jotted down ideas and images that she still wanted to include. It was a beginning, and she was content. She lay on her bed and slept, missing dinner and afternoon tea, and woke only when the supper gong sounded.

In two days, she must return to number 9. She felt confident that this trip was exactly what she had needed. She thought of the fortuneteller and wondered if fate had destined their meeting. Even if chance did hold all the cards, might they meet again, as the fortuneteller predicted?

CHAPTER 25

When she was a child, Mr. Ainsley took Charlotte's right hand in his large ones and placed her right thumb sideways on an ivory key. He stood over her, his breath stale with pipe smoke. "This," he said deliberately, "is Middle C. It's in the center of the piano because it's the piano's heart. And its roots are like a tree's. They go down and down." Mr. Ainsley pointed to Charlotte's shoes. "Without Middle C, the piano cannot sing. It gathers other notes around it as a tree gathers birds in its branches before dawn. Without birdsong, the sun could not rise, and the light of the earth would go out. Now, you know how special is this note." He pressed her thumb on the key. And then again. And again.

"This week, at home, play only Middle C and listen to its truth. Play it out loud, hear it in your imagination, feel it sing here." Mr. Ainsley placed his right hand on his heart. "Next week I will show you what it looks like in our book. And you will be able to recognize it anywhere, even when you travel far away." He pointed at the book on the music rest, but his eyes looked at a photograph of his late wife on top of the piano, just beyond Charlotte's vision.

Home from Dieppe, Charlotte sat at her vanity and read May's letter. "Dear Miss Mew: I do so want to see you and know you better. I was more grieved than I can say at having to let you go the other evening. I was steward at that terrible dinner and had to leave to see that everything was in order. But I know you have forgiven me." Next, May asked (in what Charlotte thought of as a beautiful scrawl) if Charlotte might bring whatever poems she had to May's flat. Charlotte was thrilled by the invitation, but she hated being reminded of the dinner.

She had spent the first half hour peering out the window of the entry to the hall where the dinner was to commence. A placard on an easel read: Women Writers Society Dinner ~ Featuring Mrs. Sedgwick.

Women dressed in crisply ironed shirtwaists and suits chatted brightly among themselves while drinking punch from dainty cups of cut glass. Charlotte stood alone facing the large window while pretending to be eagerly waiting for someone to join her. In fact, she was waiting for May.

Charlotte wore an embroidered shirtwaist, a plain linen skirt, and a hat with a small crown and brim. Her reflection next to the other women's in the windowpane told Charlotte that she looked as out of place as she felt. She knew she should have worn her gray suit, but she had thought the shirtwaist and skirt were more feminine.

At half past five, a woman ceremoniously opened the doors to the dining hall and another woman ushered the chattering women in. Charlotte hung back, still hoping that May would appear. Finally, when she feared she would be left completely alone in the entry, she moved toward the hall and heard May's distinct laughter, demure and bell-like.

When May invited her to the dinner, Charlotte hadn't imagined May might be working. But May wore a purple banner across her white shirtwaist, and a name tag pinned below her collar. "Charlotte," she exclaimed, breaking away from a table where she was distributing what looked like fliers. "I'm so delighted you could make it." She looked into Charlotte's eyes, and Charlotte imagined that she could see herself in May's pupils. May put her arm in Charlotte's and escorted her to one of ten banquet tables. "I've put you next to Mrs. Endicott," May said, pulling out a chair for Charlotte, "because you both like Flaubert."

Mrs. Endicott did like Flaubert, but her stomach didn't care for the appetizer, an egg soufflé with endive, and when Mrs. Sedgwick took the podium, Mrs. Endicott excused herself, explaining to Charlotte from behind a handkerchief that she needed a bromide. Charlotte asked if she could be of help. Mrs. Endicott only shook her head before dashing off.

During Mrs. Sedgwick's lecture, Charlotte caught glimpses of May as she chatted familiarly with another woman. The two women stood at the back of the hall and half-listened and nodded toward the front as they spoke in asides to each other. When the lecture concluded, no one clapped more enthusiastically than May. Charlotte stood for an ovation and clapped herself. When she looked again to where May stood, May was gone.

Charlotte had imagined herself and May seated together, at May's insistence, May commanding the maître d' as she so ably did everything else.

Now Charlotte looked at her own reflection in her vanity and thought what an appropriate term for a mirror. Well, this time she would assume nothing. But she was unsure, even in that moment, of her resolve. May was self-possessed and self-sufficient. Why couldn't Charlotte be as well? Because May didn't need anyone, it seemed. And Charlotte did.

She folded the letter into the small rectangle it had come as. She moved to the bed where her treasure chest lay, deposited May's letter with its objects, and closed the lid on all the "what ifs" and "if onlys" of her past.

Her second piano lesson with Mr. Ainsley intimidated Charlotte as much as the first. She walked slowly along Doughty Street, her piano book under her arm, two shillings in her right palm, and her stockings slipping down into her new shoes. The lace bow of her pinafore's collar caught at her throat.

The afternoon was warm with the honeyed light of early autumn. The leaves, newly turned from green to flame red, were still supple with summer's rain. Time hung suspended in the branches as Charlotte passed below them. She struck Middle C with her mind's thumb but heard only the chatter of a squirrel somewhere above her and the hollering of children playing hopscotch across the street.

Mr. Ainsley answered the door in a black velvet smoking jacket over a waistcoat and with a bow tie at his neck. He nodded at Charlotte, grunted, and then stood aside. Charlotte squeezed past him into the entry and waited. Suddenly, she knew how much she wanted to please him, more than she had ever wanted to please anyone.

He led her into the parlor and sat next to her on the bench. He opened the book on the music rest. "Now," he said, "I want you to read Middle C." He pointed to a note that hovered below a number of parallel lines, which he called the treble clef. "But you must remember. That isn't Middle C. It's only the way Middle C appears in the book. Middle C is here," he said," pointing to the piano, "and here," he said, pointing to his forehead.

The four-story Georgian building on Edwardes Square in Kensington was grander than Mr. Ainsley's small terrace house, and the dark green foliage of July's trees threw long shadows on the pavements. But Charlotte felt the same giddy excitement mixed with terror that she had felt stepping onto the stoop of Mr. Ainsley's residence.

When Charlotte rang May's doorbell, a girl not much older than Marjorie answered.

"Yes," she said mildly, her eyebrows raised. "Have you come about the drains?"

"I'm sorry. I must have the wrong flat," Charlotte said, backing away.

"Who's that you're looking for?" asked the girl. "Perhaps I can direct you."

"Miss May Sinclair." Charlotte's voice trembled as she said May's name.

"Oh, but I'm her maid," said the girl, putting her hand to her heart. "At least on Saturdays. It's when I straighten things 'round, dust, and turn the mattress if need be. I don't live in. I'm not quite old enough, my ma says."

"Is Miss Sinclair at home?" asked Charlotte cautiously.

"Why, yes," the girl said and shook her head, "but I don't expect she's receiving callers. You see, she's in her bedroom, catching up her correspondences. I might pass along your calling card, if you care to leave one."

"Sally," May called, "show Miss Mew in, please. You've kept her standing in the hall long enough."

The maid smiled sheepishly and stood aside to let Charlotte pass, then led her to the front room. Standing in profile by a window whose curtains were drawn, May wore a flowing red peignoir and house slippers, and her hair was pulled back in a silk headscarf.

May held her pose long enough to say, "The third floor affords the privacy a first floor flat can't boast." She swept toward Charlotte. To Sally, she said, "You may go."

"I could make your tea if you like, Miss." The eagerness in Sally's voice lightened the dark mahogany of the room.

"That's quite all right, Sally," said May firmly.

"Yes, Miss." She made a slight curtsy and left May and Charlotte alone.

"I'm not interrupting your work, I hope," Charlotte said, confused by May's reception.

"You have, in fact," May said and smiled. "But it concerns you." The lights of May's brown eyes flashed, and Charlotte's pulse raced.

"I've been copying out the poems you sent to Sappho. Now don't be cross," May continued, her voice unusually conciliatory. "After all, you and I met because Mrs. Scott introduced us, and you did promise to share everything with me that you shared with her." No one except Anne and the girls had been so familiar with Charlotte.

"Come here," May implored, "and make yourself at home." May led Charlotte across the room, where they stood beside her writing table. There was a chair drawn up to the walnut leaf on which "Fête" in Charlotte's large and distinctive handwriting lay. Beside it was a copy written in May's equally distinctive handwriting. "See?" May said in response to Charlotte's silence.

May sat down and continued copying the poem, working as if a practiced scribe. "It's all right," she cooed, without looking at Charlotte. "My handwriting is legible to Ezra Pound, and he must see your poems and tell us where to submit them. They deserve a wider, more discerning audience than that of *The Nation* and *The English Woman*."

Mesmerized by May's ability to talk and write about two entirely different things at the same time, Charlotte ignored the contradiction in terms.

"Tell me," May said, without looking up, "what you imagined when Sally said I was in my boudoir." Charlotte thought of Ella D'Arcy in Paris, propped up by pillows in an overstuffed feather bed and surrounded by books. In her right hand was a glass of red table wine, its bottle on the nightstand, and her left hand, which held a book or a fountain pen, bore the ink stains of the writer Charlotte had longed to become herself.

May looked up, and Charlotte smiled cautiously. "I saw you writing away on your latest novel with Tommy and Jerry sleeping in their bed beside you, twitching in delight as they dreamt of eating Wek, feathers and all."

Abruptly, May said, "I do apologize. I forgot to ask after your mother and sister. Your sister's name. It's on the tip of my tongue."

It was if they were at the women writers' dinner and Charlotte was no longer an intimate friend, but a guest, and May was her host. "Both Anne and my mother are well," Charlotte said, "as is Wek."

May laughed. "When I listen to myself, I hear a pompous bore. You must forgive my lapses in the social graces. I've been remonstrated countless times for being less a human being than a detached observer of human behavior. As a novelist, I can't help myself."

Charlotte was unsure. Had May apologized for her earlier familiarity or for being an ungracious host? The clock chimed the hour, and May said, "We must have tea." Without excusing herself, May deserted Charlotte, who stood dazed.

Before May returned with the tea tray, Charlotte decided that she didn't want to be either May's charity or her pupil. She wanted to be her equal.

After May poured out their tea, Charlotte asked, "Do you have siblings?"

May sipped her tea. "Only brothers. Five of them, in fact."

"Are you close to them?" Charlotte asked, her confidence rising.

"Not unless you count dependency as closeness. None of them was physically strong. The same congenital heart condition, I'm afraid," May said frankly.

"What about your father and your mother?" Charlotte asked, truly curious.

"I supported my mother until she died. My father never supported anyone but the corner pub's barkeep. And so I was decided at twelve years old never to be dependent on anyone for anything." May shook her head.

"I understand," Charlotte said. "I don't support my mother. But I care for her. And my father worked so much that we rarely saw him."

"And what about you, Charlotte, have you always wanted to be a poet?" May asked.

Charlotte hesitated a moment. "When I was much younger, I wanted to be a musician. I learned how to play the piano, but I wasn't a talented student. Then I discovered the stillness and music of language."

"Being a poet is a truer calling than that of a writer, I think. But as a writer, in any case, I've been able to channel my energy into my books and my causes," May replied.

"Like the Medico-Psychological," said Charlotte.

"Psychology has freed me from a life of social convention. Introspection is as important as the vote to women's political freedom and economic equality. A woman can't expect to make sound decisions without self-knowledge. Only if we know what drives our behavior can we change it." May paused. "You know, I could imagine you taking vows and living a contemplative life — if you weren't a sensualist, that is." May smiled.

Charlotte felt the familiar tingle along her spine.

"'Fête,' for instance, has such vitality," May continued. "The boy's passion is stirred as much by his own sense impressions as by the eroticism of the woman on horseback. What I'm trying to say, though without any art, Charlotte, is that you mustn't worry over the poem's metrical imprecisions, lest you silence its pulse."

Charlotte felt dismissed as a promising pupil, and her heart sank. "It's Anne who has the faith and patience of a saint," Charlotte said. Her eyes met May's. "I once thought of living in Paris," she added. Charlotte looked down, unable to hold May's gaze.

"That I can imagine. You mustn't let family ties keep you," May spoke confidentially. "When you do get to Paris, you'll live in the Latin Quarter as a Bohemian, I suppose. And you'll have me to your flat, where your boudoir will be red." It wasn't a question. When Charlotte looked up, May winked and Charlotte's face flushed, the hot flame of possession rising in her throat.

Mr. Ainsley had to return suddenly to "the old country," to help a brother in need. While he was away, Charlotte was to practice just as if Mr. Ainsley were seated on the bench beside her. She was to read the key and the time signature, to play the notes indicated, and to hold the notes the correct count. But when she played for Mr. Ainsley one last time, he only shook his head and said, "Maybe someday."

He talked again of her needing to listen for the notes here (he pointed to his forehead) while playing them here (he patted her hands). "This is not the instrument," he said, stroking the sill of the music rest, "this is" and he pointed at her heart. "Do you understand?" Charlotte didn't want to disappoint Mr. Ainsley, who was so patient with her, but she didn't understand, and she couldn't lie. "Maybe someday," he said again. But he sounded less hopeful than resigned.

CHAPTER 26

August moved into Bloomsbury as if its own season. Flowers burst into bloom and hung suspended in eternity. Birdsong — the ensemble of August with wind as its breath — enacted a symphony. Six notes repeated themselves in stunning variation. Though Charlotte couldn't discern the key or the time signature, she felt the melody move through her hands to her heart and then catch in her throat as she fondled the deep red petals of a geranium.

May Sinclair had escaped to Yorkshire to write her latest novel. But Charlotte saw May everywhere in London's streets, the Gordon Square garden, and number 9's rooms. When she dressed, she saw May in the wardrobe's mirror and her own face wearing May's slim, ironic smile. As Charlotte's own hand wrote, she saw May's hand.

But when she read what she'd written out loud, she heard only the sentiment and forced rhymes of a schoolgirl, and Mr. Ainsley's voice saying, "Maybe someday." Just as a schoolgirl might gaze out an open window at the sky and daydream, so Charlotte set aside her paper and pen, closed her eyes, and listened for the whistle of a mourning dove's wings as it flies up into the purple beech tree to perch by its mate's side or the mourning dove's sonorous lament: *oo—oo—oo—oo*.

Another day, intoxicated by the slow motion of late summer and its haze of cascading moments, Charlotte watched a rabbit sprint across the gardens, its white tail flashing. The wind stirred the twigs and limbs of the purple beech tree, jiggling them as if mute castanets, and spoke just under its breath. Another day, the wind played the chimes in the back garden the same way an unschooled child, present to the moment, sure it was eternity, plucks the petals of a daisy. The next day, the wind picked up its pace and rushed to the end of the line of plane trees and finished out of breath and voiceless.

In Yorkshire, May was writing another novel. May could tell herself: sit, write. Make your living.

Charlotte knew the imagery of the senses. She knew the music of words. She floated in the black velvet of the earth's night sky, closed to heaven's view, except its bright white pinpricks. Every other thought was the silken image of May's hair, unstrung and free, except from the wind's hands. Every other word was "May." The name of a month. Another word for "yes." You "may." And then its undertow. You "mayn't." Or "you mustn't," as Nurse Goodman said, slapping her hand when Charlotte reached for a currant bun on Easter Sunday. Before the Mews ate breakfast,

Christ must rise during the sunrise service, Father Cecil rolling away the stone of his grave, as he said, "The Christ is risen indeed."

The body and blood of Christ was distributed during Holy Communion. But his blood wasn't the blood of Mary at his conception or his birth. And when Christ wept, his tears weren't those of Mary Magdalene as she washed his feet before wiping them with her brilliant, silken hair. When Christ cast out her demons, she repented her sins, and she followed him to his stone grave, and when he rose from the dead, she lived in his resurrection.

It wasn't enough to repent. To follow Christ into eternity, to live in his resurrection, you must change your life. You must sacrifice not only your tears and your long shining hair, but also your own body and blood. You could no longer live out your days in darkness. You had to move into the bright white light of day before fellow Christians and before God.

Christ was that light. He was the road and the gate to God the Father. But how could Christ, God's only Son and therefore without sin, know what it cost to turn away from the flesh and blood of Mary Magdalene, a woman whose hair was sufficient to dry a lost soul's tears? Could he touch her face and say, "You are not wrong. You are who you are. God's adopted daughter, but also a woman made of flesh and blood"?

May was in Yorkshire, writing. Charlotte would do the same, writing through autumn and May's absence. She would tell the story of Mary Magdalene's sacrifice, but Mary Magdalene reborn in the twentieth century. "Madeleine" would confess her transgressions — her love of life's sensual pleasures — but she would not renounce her desire or her shame.

Charlotte's own desire was the love of one woman for another, even in the beloved's absence. It was indulgent, she knew, and unnatural. It was perhaps (say it) a kind of insanity. But the desire and the shame were who she was, a desire and a shame she believed that even Anne could not accept, acknowledge, or forgive her for, especially as it violated the spirit of the sisters' pact. And yet she embraced the desire and the shame because in them she felt alive.

Two weeks before Christmas, Charlotte slept well and woke rested. Ma descended the stairs on Charlotte's arm without complaint. Jane prepared poached eggs with toasted rye, while Charlotte laid the table with the best white linen cloth, lace-trimmed by hand, and the porcelain china, red and gold-trimmed — delicate teacups with matched saucers, dinner plates and chargers — and the silverware, with the heft and weight of pitchforks and spades. Below stairs, Jane sang, "O Come All Ye Faithful, Joyful and Triumphant," Charlotte humming along above stairs.

"Why the pomp and circumstance?" Ma asked. She stood, leaning heavily on her cane, in the doorframe. She moved unsteadily to her armchair at the table's head and rested her free hand on the armchair's back. Charlotte felt Ma's gaze as she laid Anne's plate and silverware and then stood back to survey the tableau she had created.

"Look at you, my girl," Ma said, "soft and bright as an angel of our Lord." Her tone of voice was at once astonished and appreciative, a voice she reserved for Freda.

Self-conscious and fearful of Ma's meddling, Charlotte busied her hands, straightening the knives of each of three settings before turning from Ma toward the sideboard. From one of its cupboards, she withdrew two silver candlesticks, and from the center drawer, two fresh taper candles and a box of wooden matches. She looked up and met her own gray eyes in the sideboard's mirror, its silver worn by time's persistent march forward.

"We've no parsley for garnish," Jane said, passing through the doorway to the sideboard with a platter of poached eggs. Charlotte moved aside, leaving the portrait, edged in silver and illuminated by winter's pale light, of a woman dressed in a blue-gray scarf draped artfully over a white shirtwaist and whose face reflected the season's peace and joy.

Anne took her seat across from Charlotte's, her tired eyes like the faded violets of a distant field. Hope for an impossible future had stolen the season's peace and joy for Anne. She kept a tyrant's hours on weekdays and sat in the Mew family's pew on Sundays, while Mr. Antony sat across the aisle on the right, in keeping with the custom and memory of his Italian homeland.

So much was left unspoken, and the chasm of silence between the sisters had only widened since they had fallen out over telling Ma about Freda's surgery.

In the front room, a single mistletoe sprig hung from the doorframe. The silver tinsel and the fir boughs laid on the fireplace mantel were Mew family traditions, as was the nativity scene placed in the bay window. Because Christ wasn't born until Christmas Day, the set lay tucked away in yellow packing straw in the attic rooms. Then, from Christmas Day until the Feast of the Epiphany, the shepherds would watch over Mary, Joseph, and Jesus as they awaited the wise men's arrival from the East.

In the meantime, Charlotte and Jane tidied and scrubbed the house to a silver shimmer. Together they exchanged the women's bedding for taut new sheets. Stripping her own bed, Charlotte imagined, for just a moment, that she and Jane were Lucy Harrison and Amy Greener, retired headmistress and teacher, keeping their cottage in Cupples Field. When making the bed with fresh linens, she imagined May's chestnut hair floating around her head, which lay just so on Charlotte's best feather pillow.

Her anticipation of May's return in January thrilled Charlotte the same way as running headlong with Henry into the surf at Brighton Beach had when they were children. The waves tripped up Charlotte only to catch her in their embrace. Then, as she floated or swam, the waves threw her toward the faint blue sky before carrying her back to shore. Henry's and Charlotte's antics were accompanied by the rough call of seagulls and the rumblings of the surf, which gathered like distant thunder over the sea and then erupted in one giant roar after another as each wave met the shore.

But the Mew children were never to trust *la mer*. Uncle Richard would suck air through his teeth and shake his head. "The sea has a mind of her own," he warned them, "whether on the Isle or at Brighton." Anne preferred gathering shells or making sand castles with exquisite details. Just like Henry, Anne had inherited their father's gift for imagining three-dimensional objects and rendering them in models or line drawings. The castles' ramparts, breeched by high tide, tumbled and the entire castle fell to ruins. But Anne never minded. "I'll just make another castle," she would say.

This year, Anne had spent more and more of December as an elf in Mr. Sands' workshop. His clients had begun requesting Anne's unique handiwork by name, and in particular, the floral bouquets that she painted on the drawers of dressers. She hadn't a stencil or pattern, yet she could reproduce each bouquet in the exact shape and scale necessary, quickly and unerringly.

"Aren't you a clever girl," Ma said without irony.

"The commissions mean nothing without the pay raise and Christmas bonus," Anne said.

"You can be pleased with both," Charlotte said, beaming with pride at her little sister's success.

In return, Anne smiled at Charlotte for the first time in a long while, the same smile that made her violet eyes glimmer.

While Anne worked at the shop completing the Christmas commissions flooding in, Ma worked her crossword or stared out into the gray day while waiting on the season's first snowflake. The mild winter had brought rain, even sleet, but not snow, not yet.

"What do you see," asked Jane good-naturedly when she tucked Ma into her afghan on the sofa.

"Nothing yet," Ma said, "but the snow is near. I can smell it."

Once she and Charlotte had painstakingly cleaned, blackened, and laid a fresh fire in the kitchen range, Jane made gingerbread and cooked cranberries. When Charlotte heard carolers on Gordon Street coming near number 9, she opened the door so they would stop. After the carolers sang "O Holy Night," Charlotte put a shilling in their charity cup, and Jane handed them frosted gingerbread in waxed paper. The men doffed stocking hats or bowlers, the women curtsied, and then the carolers continued along the pavements, singing or ringing hand bells as they disappeared into a winter night that promised snow and so much more.

CHAPTER 27

Three days before Christmas Eve, Charlotte journeyed to Southall, bringing oranges and peppermint sticks for the children's stockings and a glass scent bottle, powder pink and faceted, for Mrs. Scott, whom Charlotte had begun calling Sappho, just as May did. In addition, she had copied out, in her best handwriting, "The Pedlar" and "The Changeling" for Marjorie, Christopher, and Toby to share (or to fight over) once the holidays had passed.

"You're too good to us," Sappho said, taking the packages Charlotte offered. Though the two women stood in the Scotts' entry, Sappho seemed lost. "Where are my manners?" she suddenly asked. "Give me your coat, my dear Charlotte, and take a seat in the parlor."

But when Charlotte passed her coat to Sappho, she only stared at it.

Instinctively, Charlotte put her hand on Sappho's arm. "What is it," Charlotte asked, "and how can I help?"

"You're too good to me, and I'm no good for anyone," Sappho said before sharing with Charlotte what had happened earlier that day, shaking her head at intervals in disbelief.

Christopher saw Marjorie in the parlor on the love seat, holding hands with her sweetheart. By the time the story reached Mr. Scott, who was in his surgery until noon, handholding had been stretched by Christopher to kissing while in a passionate embrace.

Sappho had arrived home from having her hair set in a permanent wave to find three suitcases in the hall, the children crying on the stair, and Mr. Scott scribbling Mrs. Scott a note to say the family had gone to his mother's for the weekend, where chastity and decency were still fashionable.

"He called me an unfit mother who chased after her literary friends while her children ran wild. I'd be angry if I were certain that I'm right and he's wrong." Sappho blew her nose into a handkerchief.

"Fathers tend to be overprotective of their daughters, as you know," Charlotte said, feeling her way. "Perhaps he's afraid his little girl is growing up too quickly, before he has the chance to really know her. He's probably angrier at himself for not noticing that Marjorie is becoming a woman than he is angry at you for not being here to chaperone."

Winter's stillness hung itself comfortably around the women's shoulders.

"Marjorie, a woman," Sappho said, as if its inevitability had escaped her until that very moment. "Yes," she said, smiling shyly at Charlotte. "You must be right." Sappho released her coat as Charlotte gently took it, before letting herself out and returning to her place in her own family saga.

The wise men's thoughtfulness nearly two millennia before ensured that London's shop bells would ring out until the last goose was sold on Christmas Eve. Anne's recent success meant that she must work to complete a rash of last-minute orders, not the least of which was a serving tray decorated with poinsettias for Mr. Sands' wife.

Before Jane left number 9 to join her mother and brother for Christmas, she shopped for the Mews' Christmas dinner. Charlotte retrieved the nativity set from the attic rooms, and Ma sifted through greeting cards from distant cousins even Ma had difficulty remembering.

Below stairs, the street entrance door slammed shut, and in a minute, Jane stood in the doorway of the front room under the mistletoe. She wore a long wool coat, and a red knit hat and matching scarf. "Beg your pardon," she said, "but I've set the oysters and the duck in the icebox and the day-old bread, onion, and currants in the pantry."

"Thank you," Charlotte said. She was standing on a step stool polishing the mirror above the mantel. She stepped down. "Wait a minute. I have gifts for your family."

"You shouldn't have," Jane insisted.

"She shouldn't have, but she did," Ma said from her sofa. Wek woke from his nap, stretched one wing, then the other, bobbed his head and squawked, "Too bad."

Charlotte followed Jane into the hallway. But before Charlotte could pass her the string bag with gifts, Jane said in her most conspiratorial whisper, "I should warn you. The duck may not be Mr. Antony's best."

Charlotte's thoughts flew to Ma, who could smell an ill-fed or too-old (and thus tough) duck better than a dishonest butcher.

Jane continued, "Mr. Antony has been out sick for three days. The son of an old family friend is helping out at his shop." Here Jane shook her head. "And he doesn't know a calf liver from an old boot shoe. Mark my word," and she put her finger to the side of her nose. Jane turned on her heel and hurried down the stairs with the string bag. "Merry Christmas to you," she called over her shoulder.

On Christmas Day, the sky over Bloomsbury hung heavily with the promise of snow. Even the rooms of number 9, anticipating the first solitary snowflake, held their breath and reflected the taupe and slate shadows of the day's arrival on Gordon Street.

Charlotte rose at six, removed her bed jacket and nightgown, and, before donning her gray suit, stood before the wardrobe's mirror in the dawn's light and saw herself as Ma had, her pale face and waves of shining hair as luminous as a full moon and its halo. Her hand reached out to touch the face in the mirror but was stopped by another hand reaching out to touch hers. Who was she? God's daughter, adopted through Christ's miraculous birth and sacrificial death. A woman in love with another woman, who may or may not love her in return. Charlotte closed the door of the wardrobe and descended below stairs.

By the time Anne and Ma rose, Charlotte had prepared dinner. They ate duck and poached eggs with fried potatoes, hollandaise sauce, and sweet bread. Charlotte served and waited for Ma's verdict on the duck, while wondering if Anne knew of Mr. Antony's illness. Anne's face was both tired and bright. Charlotte saw no sign of worry or distraction, only relief for a day of rest.

"This is very good, Charlotte," Anne said. "Thank you."

"Truly good duck requires a skilled hand, but this duck is very satisfactory," Ma conceded.

Had Jane cooked, Ma might have blamed Mr. Antony. Instead, Charlotte could be thankful for Ma's faint praise.

A half hour later, the three sat among opened gifts and overturned stockings. The Gower Street girls sent pen wipers and scent bottles for the sisters and Mrs. Mew. Charlotte gave Ma a set of red pencils and a pencil sharpener for her crosswords, and Anne a set of horsehair brushes for her oil paints. Anne gave both Ma and Charlotte miniature paintings of flowers — for Ma, vibrant buttercups, and for Charlotte, violets. Ma gave her daughters exquisite kid leather gloves, the nicest pair either Anne or Charlotte had owned. "You deserve more," Ma replied, "than I could ever give you." That was Ma, one minute arrogant and dismissive, the next minute self-effacing and kind.

In the late afternoon, the sky heavy with snow it refused the earth, the three women gathered together in the front room under the portraits of Ma and the Shining City. They removed the figurines of the manger scene one by one from their resting place in the straw-lined box. Anne placed the stable in the center of the bay window, and near it, Mary and Joseph. Charlotte added the shepherds and their sheep, and Ma, as was tradition, placed the manger with the baby Jesus in Mary and Joseph's care. Anne set the three wise men and their camels at the edge of the tableau, and Charlotte hung the cardboard star above the stable, its tin foil shell reflecting the Gordon Street lamplight in anticipation of the three wise men's arrival in Bethlehem.

CHAPTER 28

May returned to London at last, arriving on the twelfth day of Christmas. The weather report said it snowed overnight. But because the snow melted like dew with the coming of day, Ma refused to believe it. "I haven't seen the first snowflake," she said that morning, "so it hasn't snowed." She tucked herself into her afghan, refusing Charlotte's help, and stared out the window, her gaze directed just above the manger scene with its tinfoil star, daring the first flake to fall.

Anne was sleeping in after a long work day, and Jane was below stairs cleaning up the breakfast dishes. When the post arrived with news of May's arrival, Charlotte felt the same way Ma did about the weather report. A week before, May wrote from Yorkshire to say that she would be returning very soon after the new year, but Charlotte had difficulty believing May had finally arrived after having been away so long. In the note, May asked Charlotte to her flat in Edwardes Square to talk about Charlotte's poems.

Charlotte spent the morning deciding what to wear, though she hadn't many choices. She wanted to ask Anne her opinion, but that didn't seem possible. Though Mr. Antony had returned to his shop in good health, Anne was as preoccupied as ever. Frustrated by her own indecision, Charlotte at last decided on a red silk scarf left to her by Aunt Fanny, because it was beautiful but also because Aunt Fanny had considered it lucky.

Charlotte had missed May without once imagining their reunion. It was if May would stay away indefinitely, like the specter of adulthood when one is a child. You anticipate it because you know one day you will meet it. But you can't imagine yourself as an adult. Then one day you recognize the adult in the mirror as yourself, and you must accept that you're no longer a child.

Before Charlotte left for May's flat, she looked in on Ma, who was on her sofa, staring out the window, just as she had been all week. "There's every sign of snow, but not one snowflake," Ma said for the third time that day. The sky was gray and swollen. "Perhaps someday," Charlotte said.

May answered the door, primly dressed in a white embroidered shirtwaist and brown crepe skirt, her hair immaculate in its customary pompadour. Her greeting was no more familiar or foreign than if the two women had seen each other weekly during the last four months, instead of only exchanging letters. But Charlotte felt the same shyness she did when Uncle Richard pulled her braid and teased her about "the boys." It was as if May had ceased to exist in reality and had become a phantom of her imagination, a phantom constantly present yet always exceeding Charlotte's grasp.

"Where is your maid?" Charlotte asked timidly.

"Taking care of her mother, I'm afraid," May said. "I could certainly use her help." May led Charlotte into the front room, where Charlotte tripped over a packing crate. "You're not moving," she cried out, despite her reserve.

"I'm afraid I've no choice. A band of musicians has moved into the floor below mine, and though I like their music well enough, it muddies my thoughts while I'm trying to work."

May sat down at her writing desk and motioned for Charlotte to sit beside her. May crossed her hands on the desk, Charlotte's unfinished manuscript of "Madeleine in Church" beneath them. Charlotte knew she needed to bring the poem to a close, but she couldn't imagine its resolution no matter how long she sat at her own desk, sweating over the manuscript. She needed May's guidance and encouragement.

"Where will you go? Not Yorkshire?" Charlotte asked, her voice filling with a tinny-sounding desperation she prayed May wouldn't hear.

"Heavens, no. I can't be so far from London indefinitely, not with all the functions I'm expected to attend. But I do need a quiet neighborhood where writers and musicians co-exist in peace." May's face was radiant and as white as the collar of her shirtwaist. Her brown eyes flashed, and Charlotte felt dizzy gazing into their shifting light. May was no longer the abstraction of Charlotte's reveries but a sensual presence.

"Even Tommy," May continued, "doesn't care for the musicians. When they play, he sulks in his basket. I've already asked all my friends for help. I simply must find a flat in London that's quiet, so that I can write. Since my return, I've fallen behind schedule. The problem is I haven't much money."

Charlotte nodded, concluding that May counted Charlotte as a hanger-on, not a friend, because she hadn't asked Charlotte for her help in finding a flat.

"And Jerry," Charlotte asked, disappointed by May's breezy demeanor after her long absence, "do the musicians play any music that he likes?"

"Jerry has the enviable talent of taking life as it comes, asking neither more nor less than whatever life offers. Tell me, are the rents in Bloomsbury reasonable? I hear there aren't any musicians there."

Ignoring May's question, Charlotte answered, "Some of us share Jerry's philosophy but not the ability to act on it, especially when taking action matters most."

"Why Charlotte, I don't remember your being interested in philosophy."

Charlotte continued, daring to meet May's eyes, "What do you ask of life? Is there something life has refused you?"

For a moment, May looked as if she were pondering Charlotte's question. She rested her hand on her chin, her beautiful chestnut hair beckoning Charlotte to reach out and touch it. But May replied with a cavalier laugh and toss of her head, "It's what convention has tried to press upon me and I've refused to accept that matters most."

Charlotte, too, felt life's conventions pressing upon her, and she wanted to break free of them if only for one afternoon. "That's hardly a straightforward answer," she replied.

"Then let me give you an example," May said, meeting Charlotte's gaze. "I wouldn't know what to do with your lease on Gordon Street, your mother, and, least of all, her parrot. They'd fill my head with distractions, and I'd never write a thing. I admire you tremendously for what you've been able to accomplish, given your circumstances. For instance," May said as she pulled an envelope from a cubbyhole in her desk, "Mr. Pound has taken 'Fête' for *The Egoist*. And it will be published alongside James Joyce's *A Portrait of the Artist as a Young Man*." May handed Charlotte the envelope. "Forgive Ezra for not writing to you directly, but I wanted the pleasure of telling you myself."

Charlotte was thrilled. Aside from love, there was nothing she wanted more than recognition for her poetry. "If it hadn't been for your help, Mr. Pound wouldn't have accepted 'Fête,' " Charlotte said.

"Don't let me take the credit. It was you who wrote the poem," May said emphatically. She paused, then continued her previous thought. "Still, a house and a mother, as difficult as they must be to keep, are preferable to a husband and child. A woman might as well wear a straitjacket as marry." May paused dramatically. "What do you ask of life, my dear Charlotte? Is there something life has refused *you*?"

Charlotte wasn't sure which flustered her more: May's question or her seeming dismissal of Charlotte as a poet ensnared by domestic entanglements. She answered, "What I ask of life isn't as obvious as some might think. There's so much I've always wanted, including my own home," she said, her voice trembling, "someone to share it with, and children."

May shook her head. "To be truly independent, a woman must support herself and live alone. She simply cannot have a man hovering over her all day and then hanging onto a bar stool at night, expecting her to care for the children while he's painting the town or laid up in bed, sleeping off yet another hangover. Your courtesan, Madeleine, understands the stultifying effects of marriage and Christian dogma on women," May said, holding up the manuscript.

"You think that Christianity encourages women to sacrifice themselves to husbands and children?" Charlotte asked.

"Freudian psychology and German idealism are more helpful to women than Christian mythology." May paused and looked directly at Charlotte. Her dark eyes sparkled. "As Madeleine's creator, it follows that you understand Madeleine's position."

Charlotte longed to ask May if two women in a relationship might escape the pattern of men and women. But she couldn't ask without revealing her own hand, and she couldn't bear May's judgment if she were wrong about May's feelings for her. If only May would make her position clear to her, Charlotte might do more than hope.

"Madeleine has had a number of disappointing relationships with men," Charlotte ventured, "and she refuses to sacrifice the sensual life she's so familiar with for a spiritual world beyond her own understanding. But she doesn't speak for every woman, and she certainly doesn't speak for me, or not for all of me, at least," she said, her voice trailing off.

May cocked her head and frowned. "Charlotte, you fascinate me. Just when I think I understand you finally, you surprise me. I imagine you even surprise yourself on occasion." May sounded truly confounded.

"It's having to read between the lines to get at the essence of someone that evokes surprises," Charlotte offered. She was satisfied, at least, by being as much a puzzle to May as May was to her.

"One thing I do know about you," May said. "You simply must finish 'Madeleine in Church.' I know that the ending will come to you, just like the beginning. You only need to step aside and let it unfold. Trust me," May said.

CHAPTER 29

Despite her initial misgivings at May's flat, Charlotte realized that May's absence had only fueled Charlotte's admiration and affection for her. Every time she thought of May during her absence, Charlotte had believed her heart would burst. Seeing May again confirmed those feelings, and yet Charlotte still had no clear sense of May's feelings toward her. Even in her uncertainty, Charlotte longed to take May's hand in hers and for May to return the gesture.

Until she knew how May felt, Charlotte couldn't reveal her own feelings, but she could help May find a flat at a reasonable cost. Charlotte thought immediately of Mr. Sommes. He could find a flat for May, surely. Unfortunately, as Charlotte soon learned, Mr. Sommes was not inclined to broker flats on the cheap. When Charlotte conveyed May's limited budget, Mr. Sommes snickered, then quickly begged her pardon, appalled, evidently, by his own lack of professionalism.

And so Charlotte took it upon herself in February and March to read the advertisements for flats for let in Bloomsbury. A number of flats were promising while Charlotte stood on the pavement admiring their buildings. But as soon as she opened the outer door to the entry, her heart would begin to grow faint. By the time she reached the flat itself (down a dim corridor smelling of overcooked greens), she knew her hope had been in vain. The flats themselves made Charlotte thankful for number 9, even if the Mews themselves must sublet half of their rooms to make ends meet.

Charlotte dreamt of May taking up residence in the rooms of number 9, though she knew it was impossible. Even if the rooms weren't occupied, their rent was higher than May's limit. One afternoon after weeks of running from one disappointing flat to another, Charlotte sat over the Mews' accounts and imagined giving May a reduced rate if only the Campbells or Mrs. McHardy would give notice and the Mews didn't have to pay an additional twenty pounds per annum for Freda's care at Whitecroft. But she knew it was impossible, especially when she admitted to herself the ultimate hurdle: Ma and Anne. Living under the same roof with May would make it impossible for Charlotte to contain her feelings. And she couldn't reveal her hand, whether to Ma, or Anne, or even May. Not unless May revealed hers first.

In late March, when Charlotte presented May with a short list of available flats in Bloomsbury, May was aghast. "And all my days I shall be haunted by a vision of you, small, and too fragile by far for the hideous task, going up and down those infernal houses." These words weren't tempered by May's praise: "Of course I know you were angelic enough too — perhaps — but can't you see that your time ought to be given to poems, and not to lazy friends?"

Charlotte was mortified. She had meant to be helpful. She had meant to be indispensable as May's friend and equal. But she had only made a fool of herself.

To escape her embarrassment as well as May, Charlotte decided she must get away from London, and she immediately thought of Dieppe.

But Jane's mother became ill, and Jane needed to return home to take care of her. Anne was still working five days a week at the shop, and Ma couldn't be left alone.

What could Charlotte do?

Scouring the ads for flats at last proved helpful. Charlotte recalled seeing a section dedicated to cleaning women for hire. After only one inquiry, Charlotte secured the services of Mrs. Andrews, who was willing to look after Mrs. Mew and Miss Mew, by cooking meals and washing up dishes, as well as keep number 9 "tidy." Charlotte didn't mention the tenants, afraid Mrs. Andrews would balk, but she did tell her of Wek, and, thankfully, Mrs. Andrews didn't object.

When Charlotte told Anne and Ma of her plans to vacation at Dieppe and the arrangements she had made with Mrs. Andrews, Anne shrugged her shoulders and Ma said, "Do what you like. Your sister and I can't stop you." Charlotte refused to be swayed; she would escape to Dieppe until her limited funds ran dry or Ma called her back to number 9, because she or Wek had fallen out with Mrs. Andrews.

The Hotel du Commerce was booked with vacationing Londoners. Madame Binoche was vacationing herself, and the soft-spoken receptionist who had taken her place refused to speak with Charlotte in French, despite her persistence in speaking French with him when asking for or returning her key. His responses were always in English, indicating that he understood Charlotte but had no interest in sharing his mother tongue with her.

She was given a room on the top floor, and though she loved the view of the shore from her French windows, she missed the red and blue underclothes strung over the alley. When she visited the quays, she hoped to watch the fishermen's wives mend nets. But the first day she walked down to the shore, an auction was being held, and the fisherwomen held their arms behind their backs and shook their heads as they witnessed the used household goods of one of the fishermen sold by an auctioneer.

Among the baskets of clothing and the assorted pots and pans stood an upright piano. Rather than being auctioned separately, it was being sold as part of a lot, which included the rusted anchor of a skiff and three wooden crates of musical scores. Charlotte wondered who had played the piano: the fisherman, his wife, or one or more of his children. She looked around the crowd to identify the family whose life lay out in the open for passersby to pick through, but she saw no one except the fisherwomen huddled together, looking at once indignant and forlorn. Charlotte understood their dismay: it was as if someone's home were being sold out from underneath him.

When the piano was at last pushed up to the auction block by three young men in shirtsleeves and newsboy caps, Charlotte wanted to leave, but she stood and watched as a few men, encouraged by the auctioneer, bid halfheartedly on the lot. While the auctioneer continued to cajole the crowd, claiming the piano had been played by Chopin, a barefoot child in disheveled clothing broke from her mother and, reaching the piano, banged on the keys with both hands. The piano cried out, and Charlotte thought her heart would burst. To put everyone out of their misery, the auctioneer finally accepted the highest bid, placed by a man in a suit coat, who held a sign in English reading, "Cameret Bros. Antiques."

Charlotte couldn't bring herself to watch the gulls ogle the tide pools, so she returned to the hotel, hoping that if she couldn't stop thinking about the sale of the piano, she could at least stop thinking about May. When she reached the receptionist to collect her key, he handed a telegram to her from Mrs. Andrews. Charlotte knew instantly that Mrs. Andrews was writing to be relieved of her duties, tired of contending with Ma or Wek. Charlotte was thoroughly defeated. She retired to her room, even as the dinner gong sounded.

But it wasn't Ma or Wek or even Mrs. Andrews who was the problem. It was Anne. After working a ten-hour day, she came home ill with a fever. Mrs. Andrews helped her to bed. When her fever refused to break, Mrs. Andrews telegrammed Charlotte, advising her to return home at once.

Charlotte caught the next ferry and was home at number 9 within half a day. Anne was indeed ill, and Charlotte hated herself for ignoring Anne before leaving for Dieppe. But just before Charlotte left, she had learned that *New Weekly* would publish two of her poems: "Fame" and "Pêcheresse." There was no one else Charlotte would rather share the news with than Anne. But the longer Anne's canvases in her studio remained blank, the less Charlotte felt she could share her own successes with her sister.

In a delirious state somewhere between waking and sleeping, Anne called out that she was late for work and must get up or she would be fired.

"It's quite simple," Charlotte instructed Anne, pressing a cold compress on her forehead. "You cannot work in your present condition. I've contacted Mr. Sands, and he's agreed that you must rest." Charlotte wasn't sure if Anne understood what she had said, but Anne ceased calling out.

The doctor diagnosed a bad case of flu and told Charlotte the best medicine was rest. Charlotte sat at Anne's bedside, refusing to leave even to sleep herself, and Mrs. Andrews stayed on to look after Ma and Wek.

In three days, Anne was better, and Jane had returned. Anne's fever had broken, and she stayed awake for longer and longer periods. But she was still weak and drawn, and Charlotte knew that Anne could no longer work for Mr. Sands, regardless of how much she protested.

"It's quite simple," Charlotte said again. "You cannot work for Mr. Sands in his sweat shop." Anne was propped up on her pillows, and Charlotte sat on the mattress beside her. "I want you to quit this afternoon."

"However will I pay rent on the studio?" Anne asked.

Just then, Charlotte had a brainstorm. "Why don't you give lessons?" she asked excitedly. "After all, you've taken lessons, so you know how to be a student. And you certainly know how to paint. Surely, giving lessons couldn't be that difficult."

Relief flooded Anne's face and Charlotte wondered why one of them hadn't thought of this very solution before.

Anne took Charlotte's hand. "Thank you, Charlotte. I'll never forget this as long as we're sisters." They smiled at each other a moment and then laughed, and Charlotte felt as relieved as Anne looked.

Now, if only they could resolve the impasse over Mr. Antony, May, and their pact. But Charlotte knew that was impossible, even if paying for the studio wasn't.

When she went to bed that night after not having slept for several days, it occurred to Charlotte that the auction of the piano and the other household goods wasn't just the loss of a home but the disbanding of a family.

CHAPTER 30

It was Anne's idea to ask Sappho and May to tea at the studio. Anne was grateful for her liberation from Mr. Sands' sweatshop, a liberation she credited to Charlotte. She had begun giving lessons in both oil paints and watercolors, and she had three regular students, including a singer who wore ermine and called everyone "darling." Anne could show her gratitude by hosting a tea for Charlotte's friends.

Charlotte didn't see how she could refuse Anne's offer.

"You'll be there, of course," Charlotte said.

"As hostess, I ought to be. Would you prefer I wasn't?" Anne asked. "You're welcome to use the studio anytime you like, whether or not I'm there." It was an offer Anne wouldn't have advanced a few short months ago, though she would have said yes, Charlotte knew, had Charlotte asked. The sisters were finally mending their falling out over Ma's knowledge of Freda's surgery, but the wound was slow to heal.

Before answering Anne, Charlotte thought of May. A month ago, she wouldn't have wanted to share May with Anne, preferring instead to keep the worlds of number 9 and her heart's deepest desire as far apart as possible. Now she was thankful for the protection from May that Anne offered. May would finally see Charlotte as an independent woman who didn't need to follow after May, whether to seek advice about her poetry or to chase down vacant flats on the cheap. She could invite May to a casual tea with no expectations or strings attached.

"Thank you, Anne," Charlotte said, "I would like you to attend the tea."

Charlotte's resolve weakened when she received May's reply. "I'd ever so much rather see you by yourself (though I like Mrs. Dawson Scott very much)," May wrote. She didn't mention Anne. Charlotte's heart fluttered, and for a delicious moment she felt just like she had before May cast her as an object of pity. Perhaps I was wrong, Charlotte thought, or perhaps I'm wrong now. But she wasn't sure which of her selves she referred to in either moment. She refolded May's letter and vowed not to think about May until she could think more clearly.

Tea with Sappho and May did little to clarify Charlotte's thoughts. While Sappho complimented Anne on her studio, May hung back, seemingly unimpressed either with the studio or with Anne being a painter. When she sat down at the table, May perched on the edge of her seat, as if she planned to leave any minute. Moreover, she didn't wear her slim, ironic smile; instead she pursed her lips as if preoccupied. Finally, Sappho, seated across from Charlotte, said, "You'll have to forgive our May. She lost her Tommy." May only looked up and nodded.

Charlotte said, "Oh, May, I'm so sorry. Not Tommy."

"That's your cat, yes?" Anne asked politely. She poured out tea for the women and offered them milk and sugar.

"Forgive my rudeness, Anne. I'm often distracted by my writing or charities, but Tommy's death has left me altogether beside myself. I never understood that expression. But I do now."

Charlotte's heart ached for May. She couldn't imagine losing Wek, even as contrary as he was, without feeling she had lost part of herself. "How is Jerry?" Charlotte asked.

"Oh, thank heavens for Jerry," May exclaimed. "Tommy and Jerry were never the best of friends, but even he seems forlorn. I wouldn't know what I'd do if there were no one to greet me when I woke each morning."

"You gave Tommy the best life a cat could ask for," Sappho said, "but I know that doesn't take the sting out of your loss."

"Yes, he did live a good and long life for a cat," May said abstractedly. She sipped her tea and gazed into space. Charlotte wished she were alone with May so that she could comfort her, yet she wasn't sure how she would do so.

"Tell me about your children," Anne said to Sappho.

"Toby has discovered astronomy, Christopher has discovered cricket, and Marjorie has discovered boys. It seems like only yesterday that Marjorie was Toby's age. What will I do when they've all grown up and left me?"

"They sound delightful," Anne said.

"Charlotte has told me that she would have liked to have children. What about you, Anne, would you have liked to have children?" May asked.

Anne looked at Charlotte. Did Anne fear Charlotte had told May about their pact? "Had things been different," Charlotte said, more to Anne than to May and Sappho, "I would have liked to have as many children as the old lady in her shoe. That's what I told May."

Sappho said, "It seems a man is needed for the most mundane of tasks, including bearing and raising children. But don't get May started on marriage," Sappho cautioned Anne, "It's her pet subject."

"You're too hard on me, Mrs. Scott," May said. "Men are fine. And marriage is fine. It's the two together that don't mix." May winked at Charlotte.

"Whatever do you mean?" Sappho asked. "How can one exist without the other?"

"That's my point exactly," May said. "And women who remain single understand that better than anyone. Don't you agree, Anne?" May turned to gaze directly at Anne.

"I ... I don't know," Anne said. "I suppose you must be right."

"Have you ever had a beau you were smart enough to resist?" May asked. "You look intelligent. I bet you have."

Anne looked at Charlotte, confused whether or not May's was a rhetorical question.

Silence hung in the studio. Charlotte could hear foot traffic below the studio's windows.

Anne broke the silence. "No, no I haven't." She again looked at Charlotte. "But I did care for someone."

"I'm glad to hear it," May said. "If taken lightly, affairs of the heart help build women's willpower."

"You're so clinical, May!" Sappho exclaimed.

"Wouldn't you like Marjorie to be clinical?" May asked. "She would have a better chance of finding a good man to marry."

"Even a good man doesn't guarantee a happy marriage," Charlotte said, employing May's logic.

"I don't know," Anne said. "Objectivity doesn't guarantee that a woman will find a suitable husband, or that she will be able to marry him even if she does."

"Are you speaking of the man you alluded to before?" Sappho asked pointedly.

Anne's face reddened. "I had a friend at church. But he's left London and returned to Italy. He says there's going to be a war, and he can't remain here and leave his mother to care for his seven younger siblings."

It was the most Anne had ever spoken of Mr. Antony to Charlotte or to anyone else, despite Ma's constant nagging.

"You poor thing," Sappho said.

"Leave it to me to say exactly the wrong thing at exactly the wrong time," May said. "I'm so very sorry, Anne."

"But surely there won't be a war," Sappho said. "That's just gossip to sell newspapers."

"I wish that were true," May said. "But I fear war, like marriage, is as inevitable as it is undesirable."

On leaving, May took Charlotte aside while Sappho talked to Anne. "Your sister is darling, Charlotte, but I do wish we had spent the afternoon alone." Charlotte's heart leapt. "I would've liked to talk with you about Tommy. No one has been as loyal a friend to me, not even Sappho." Charlotte wondered, if that were true, why had May told Sappho about Tommy's death before she had told Charlotte?

"It's not that I dislike May," Anne said when the sisters were clearing the tea service. "It's just that ..."

"You don't know how to read her," Charlotte said.

Anne took Charlotte's arm. "Please don't take this wrong, Charlotte. May's just so different, and you're different when you're with her."

"Meaning?" Charlotte asked, feeling irritated.

"Unsure of yourself, I guess," Anne finished. "You're not angry with me, are you?" Anne asked.

"If you're not angry with me," Charlotte replied. She wanted to say more about Mr. Antony, but without May and Sappho there, she didn't feel she could. Or was she afraid that if Anne confessed to loving Mr. Antony, she would have to confess to loving May?

A day later, when Charlotte could no longer stopper her thoughts of May, she resolved to take life as it came, just as May said Jerry had. She would no longer fantasize about a non-existent relationship with a woman who could never love her. Her desire for May had blinded Charlotte to reality. To see clearly again, she must sacrifice her desire, no matter how difficult doing so proved to be.

But even as she counseled herself to think and act reasonably, her intuition told Charlotte she had been right all along. May did care. She just didn't act on her feelings because she was a moral coward. She preferred her books to reality. After all, it was easier to write about other people's lives than to live one's own.

The other explanations for May's behavior were too disturbing to fully consider. May was either callous to the subtext of her remarks to Charlotte or (Charlotte shuddered to think) May was malicious and had purposely played Charlotte's emotions for sport.

At bottom, Charlotte decided, May's opinion of her mattered, whether May loved her in return or May was callous, even malicious, toward her. Charlotte despised herself for caring what May thought.

Her own heart seemed to have betrayed Charlotte, but there was no return.

CHAPTER 31

The late afternoon was hot and humid. The shadow play between the sun and plane trees cast dark green patterns on the pavements. Charlotte had to dispense with her gray suit and wore only a shirtwaist with short sleeves. Her skirt fell to the top of her shoes, which she polished twice as long as usual the evening before. There was also no excuse for her umbrella. Making her way to May's new flat in St. John's Wood, Charlotte felt like she was lacking her usual social armor.

Passersby on the pavements appeared weighed down by the heat. Women patted their foreheads or pressed their lips with handkerchiefs. Men stumbled forward, their shirtsleeves rolled up over their elbows and their suit coats slung over a shoulder, anchored there by a thumb. An electrical current buzzed in the sodden air, as if a summer squall waited on the horizon. At sea, the current would demand action, a battening down of hatches. But Londoners, unlike seamen, waded through the waves of oppressive heat caught up in surviving the moment.

The charged atmosphere reminded Charlotte of the way she felt as a child on the night before the Mew children left London to spend summer on the Isle. Charlotte found herself on May's doorstep as if she were dreaming, yet she felt acutely aware of every vibration around her.

May greeted her in apology. "The flat's simply a mess," she said, escorting Charlotte through a short hallway that led to a sitting room on the right, a dinette set and china cabinet directly ahead, and a small kitchen on the left. The flat's one bedroom was off the sitting room, up a stair. Gone was all the heavy mahogany furniture of Edwardes Square. The flat was immaculate, as was May's attire.

When Charlotte removed her hat, May placed it on a side table in the entry. "Please, sit. You must be exhausted after wandering around in the heat." May motioned to one of the dinette set's chairs and Charlotte took it. "I'll put on the kettle."

Charlotte unbuttoned her collar to more easily breathe and watched as May bustled around her kitchen, crisp and unflappable despite the heat. "Where is Jerry?" Charlotte asked.

"Still distraught, poor thing, I'm afraid," May said, having misheard Charlotte's question. "I can quite understand, feeling the same way myself. Tommy was the rock of our existence in Edwardes Square.

"Charlotte," May asked, appearing in the doorway between the kitchen and dining room. "You don't think I killed Tommy by moving him here. They say cats feel the same way about homes that people feel about loved ones." May looked imploringly at Charlotte, and Charlotte felt her face flush.

"I wouldn't think so," Charlotte said, trying her best to sound reassuring. When May spoke of her cats, she seemed almost like Anne and herself. "You explained to Tommy and Jerry why you were moving, and Tommy understood how important it was for you to work at home."

May laughed. "Listening to us," she said, "people might think we're insane, talking about cats as if they were people." May smiled at her, and Charlotte caught her breath. "But we know birds and cats are better than people. That's the difference between the two of us and everyone else. I'm so thankful to have one person who understands me. Sappho must roll her eyes when she tells me the latest antics of her ragamuffins, then I report on Tommy and Jerry in kind." May stopped and looked away. "Well, just Jerry now." The kettle whistled. May turned to silence it, and Charlotte breathed more easily.

May returned with the tea service. She took two new taper candles, already trimmed, from the china cabinet and set them on the table before lighting each one with a match. She then drew the curtains and sat down. May offered Charlotte a fancy cake, and the tea itself was Charlotte's favorite. Everything about the afternoon felt like a special occasion, yet Charlotte could call none to mind.

"You mustn't think, Charlotte, that I've an ulterior motive in inviting you to tea," May said, "but I do, in fact, have a surprise for you." May walked to her writing desk in the sitting room and took a slip of paper from its center drawer. She returned and placed the paper on the table, then drew her chair next to Charlotte's. When May sat beside her, Charlotte felt the roots of her hair stand on end.

"It's a poem," Charlotte said, "written in French." She looked at May.

"Yes," May said, looking directly at Charlotte, "and I wrote it." May's brown eyes glinted like a mischievous child's. "Let me read it to you," May said, "and then you can help me correct its grammar."

May began, reading the poem in halting French, but investing the lines with the sensation of a heartfelt experience transmuted into language.

The Dead Woman

My dear, what have you done with the best days of your life, the days which are past and gone, and what have you done with your harsh and bitter joys?

What have you done with your little body, so tender, so sensitive to the cold, your writhing arms, your wicked little heart, and those eyes which shed so many tears?

What have you done with that wild soul, which is twisting and breaking itself, my poor beloved, that little, fleeting, fragile, exquisite soul?

Oh my child, you will never understand how much you have suffered, and as for me, I wouldn't give up my share of hell to be what you are now.

An electrical charge ran from Charlotte's hair to her toes, suffusing her body with energy, so she felt exhilarated and dizzy at once. May's hand lay on the table beside hers, and Charlotte removed her own hand, afraid of what it might do.

"Charlotte," May called from far away, "Charlotte."

Charlotte knew instinctively that she dare not look at May. She felt herself rise and knock her chair to the floor. "I must go," she said, refusing to look at May, though she could feel herself drawn to May against her will as if by a magnetic force. "I'm afraid the heat's gotten to me."

May placed her hand on Charlotte's arm. "Surely, you would rather lie down on the bed." Charlotte longed to take May's hand and hold its palm to her lips.

"Oh no," she heard herself say, "I must leave at once." But Charlotte stood frozen, afraid if she moved, she might throw herself at May's feet.

"You must at least say goodbye to Jerry. He'll feel forsaken if you don't."

Charlotte looked sideways at May, whose eyes beseeched her. Thankful for the distraction, Charlotte felt her composure return. "Of course," she said.

"He's in the bedroom, on his rug. As you'll remember, he always naps this time of day."

May retrieved Charlotte's hat from the side table, as though Charlotte could leave through the bedroom. With the hat in one hand, and the other hand outstretched to Charlotte, May said, "Come with me."

Charlotte refused her hand but followed May. They climbed the short stair to the bedroom.

"Look. There's my baby." In May's bed, on his rug, lay Jerry, curled up and obviously asleep.

"He'll hardly know I was here," Charlotte said, suddenly angry that May insisted she stop to say goodbye to Jerry before leaving.

"Charlotte," May said, taking Charlotte's hand in her own, "the world isn't against you. You only fear it's so."

And what could Charlotte do, when someone told her she wasn't wrong? She brought May's hand to her lips and kissed it, before murmuring, "I love you."

May pulled her hand away. In a voice Charlotte had never heard before, May said, "Get hold of yourself. You must be mad. I can't imagine what gave you the idea that I was something so horrid." May turned away from Charlotte, and Charlotte fled May's flat, leaving her hat behind.

CHAPTER 32

The skies were as gray and uniform as the pavements, and they had come to stay, as if London were a vast room, the skies its gray ceiling, and its lodgers too dull to imagine a house that might just as well be yellow and lovely.

Charlotte stayed in at number 9 and spent her free time in the attic rooms beneath the gray skylight. She didn't care to smoke or to write, and like the dull skies over London, July seemed suspended and eternal. She perched on the broken rocking chair and stared at the blank picture frames or closed her eyes and saw nothing. Oblivion, she thought, must feel like this stasis. She was thankful for the wide berth given to her by Jane and Anne, and for Ma's ignorance of anything beyond the contours of her invalid's sofa. She was thankful not to think or to feel or to remember when she could help it.

In the attic rooms surrounded by the effects of childhood or busily attending household chores with Jane, she could forget. But as she lay in bed during those stale July nights, she relived moment by moment, as slow torture, her last time at May's flat and felt again how ridiculous she had made herself. She had confessed her next-to-last secret to May, and May, because she knew Charlotte was wrong, had corrected and dismissed her, just as Nurse Goodman might have done.

Her stomach churned and her head spun. She tossed back and forth, trying to forget and take back everything she said and was. Oh God, she prayed, Oh God, please let it not be true. But what she had done and what May had said — and how she had said it — replayed themselves again and again in Charlotte's head.

How many languorous days had she been afforded the year before, days spent arrested by her senses in the Gordon Square garden, furiously writing in her room, or walking the pavements in May's absence, yet feeling the intoxicating depth of her presence in every delicious waking moment? Was all that erased, or could Charlotte keep those days in the deep hollow of a maze of Chinese boxes, apart from her confession and May's dismissal?

The worst nights were those when she imagined May and Sappho's tête–à–tête — the why-I-never series of exclamations and the to-think's — a tête–à–tête she was convinced had transpired, as she hadn't heard from Sappho. She would wake suddenly to the sounds of their shared laughter, Sappho's guffaws and May's titters. Almost worst of all was thinking of Marjorie and Christopher and Toby.

What might Sappho have told them when asked why Charlotte hadn't come to take them to a matinee of *Peter Pan*, as she had promised?

At night, Marjorie's soulful eyes incriminated Charlotte as she lay in the dark and prayed earnestly to die. Some days Marjorie appeared in the entry's mirror and rested her chin on Charlotte's shoulder, just as Freda liked to do before she was sent away to Whitecroft.

Worst of all, the very worst of everything, was that Charlotte believed she had betrayed Anne by breaking their pact. Charlotte hadn't married. But she had loved someone as if she were married. And how could she have betrayed dear, sweet Anne, the closest person to her in the world? For desire? For fame? She knew asking Anne's forgiveness would be selfish. No, Charlotte had learned she must never confess, not to anyone, ever again. Charlotte had never felt so utterly alone.

THE FARMER'S BRIDE (1915-1920)

CHAPTER 33

Charlotte sat on a wooden folding chair. Other audience members milled and conversed around her. In another place and time, she might expect an oboe to sound its eerie voice and violins to join in as an orchestra tuned its instruments before the houselights dropped. But the skylight of the attic rooms on Devonshire Street was blackened by a tarpaulin, and the lights were only bright enough for readers to register the glow of a white page and just make out its script and for audience members like Charlotte to anticipate the offerings of poetry the penny-sheet program listed. This evening those offerings included James Joyce, D. H. Lawrence, and John Masefield.

Outside the war was on. King Edward had failed to tame his nephew, Kaiser Wilhelm, so now it was up to Edward's son, King George, to defeat his cousin. Defeat. England must prevail. Throughout London, from Russell Square to Paddington Station, troops readied for mobilization to France. The Continent grew closer by the day following nights of aerial bombardment by German Zeppelins. But despite privations and casualties, life, somehow, went on. Londoners rallied to the cause of freedom, doing whatever they might for the war effort. Even a smile or a nod from a civilian, the newspapers stressed, could fortify a soldier's heart for the front.

A round woman with a mass of chestnut hair took a seat in the front row. Charlotte's heart leapt in her throat. She studied the back of the woman, willing her to turn around while hoping she wouldn't. If it was May, Charlotte could rise quietly and leave down the steep attic stairs and exit into the autumn fog. Before she could see and make a move, a different woman, with beautiful dark hair and much younger than Charlotte, took her place behind a desk in the corner of the room, dimly illuminated by an oil lamp. Freda, thought Charlotte.

Anything was possible on a night such as this and in a place so out of the way it was more a stumbling point than a destination. The attic rooms in which Charlotte sat were those of a Georgian house hiding along the street by trick of the house's drabness. But Devonshire was less a city street than an alleyway, and its buildings huddled together, blocking out the night sky and its faint stars. Charlotte had expected no more than a room emptied of furniture and a barrel fire upon entering the building a half hour before. But inside she had found a different world altogether.

There was a fire, but it burned calmly in a fieldstone hearth with a huge mouth and tall andirons standing sentinel. The furniture, though worn, was outsized and heavy, like that of a castle. It was as if Charlotte had stepped into a lair on the Scottish Highlands, and the drabness of the exterior and the fog were entirely extinguished on her entry. What she noticed first weren't the substantial chairs or even the hearth, however, but the poetry books, in bookshelves lining all the walls as well as set out in stacks on long tables.

As the war and fog rolled on outside, the dark-haired woman behind the desk introduced herself as Alida Klementaski. She welcomed the audience to The Poetry Bookshop and expressed her wish that everyone might enjoy that evening's program of poems. In case of an air raid, they were to make their way single file (as if there were another way) down the attic rooms' stairs and take cover on the ground floor.

Charlotte forgot about May, whom she hadn't seen for more than a year, and the woman who might be her in the front row not ten feet from Charlotte. She forgot about number 9 and the aging boiler and her forty-sixth birthday only days away. She heard only the music of poetry, and when Miss Klementaski read "The Changeling" and "The Farmer's Bride" in her rich alto voice, Charlotte listened to them as if they were written by someone else. She was transported.

The woman in the front row wasn't May, Charlotte soon discovered. Shortly after she had finished reading, Miss Klementaski approached Charlotte and asked hopefully, "Are you Miss Mew?"

"I am sorry to say I am," Charlotte said, feeling suddenly self-conscious in the warmth of Miss Klementaski's simple charm. "But please call me Charlotte."

"I'm so glad you were able to come, Charlotte," Alida said, and Charlotte knew she meant it. Alida took Charlotte's arm, saying, "You must meet a few people."

Last of these people was Mrs. Kemp, who Charlotte saw now looked nothing like May except for her chestnut hair. Alida left Charlotte in care of Mrs. Kemp's circle. Among them was a young man in uniform (to Charlotte, anyone under forty looked young), an older, mustached man in tweed smoking a pipe, and Mrs. Kemp's friend, Miss Green, who, Charlotte was humored to see, wore a green suit.

The circle nodded to Charlotte, then freely discussed her poems as if she weren't there. The penny-sheet program, which she had wrung in her hands while thinking of May, dropped from Charlotte's hands as she listened.

"The point is," said the mustached man, "the poet has compassion for both the bride and the farmer. No one's at fault altogether."

"But certainly, you can agree he's more sinned against than sinning," insisted Mrs. Kemp.

"I don't know. It's unfair that the whole town joined forces against the girl," said the soldier.

Miss Green chimed in. "But what's a woman to do but marry and submit to her husband?"

"Vote, for starters," said the soldier. "My mother's a suffragist, and my father's proud of her."

"The Kaiser has his war, the suffragists and suffragettes have theirs," the mustached man offered and sucked on his pipe. He looked at Charlotte, but not as if he expected Charlotte to explain herself or her poems, she was relieved to see.

"Marriage and war. Part and parcel of the same thing," said Mrs. Kemp and sniffed.

"It's not the theme of the poem that finally matters but its beauty and its music," said Miss Green.

"I quite agree," Alida said, joining them. "By the way, what did I agree with?"

"Art is what finally matters," said Charlotte.

The mustached man raised his glass of punch and said, "Here, here."

Alida smiled at Charlotte and winked, and Charlotte better understood the ability of a smile to steel soldiers' courage for the trenches.

Over Alida's shoulder, just out of focus, stood a man Charlotte almost recognized but couldn't place.

"The laird of the castle," Alida said to Charlotte, "and the proprietor of The Bookshop, Harold Monro."

CHAPTER 34

Like many poets at the turn of the century, Harold Monro believed that poetry's role was essential to the modern age and that poetry was on the verge of a revolution. Poetry wasn't a frivolity or idle pastime, as many opponents held, but a serious, even sacred, endeavor. But for poetry to affect the future, it must be brought to the forefront of public attention, where it could influence society for the better. To that end, Harold Monro conceived of The Poetry Bookshop, a haven for poets and poetry lovers alike and a place to bring poets and the public together.

In January 1913, when Monro was thirty-three years old, The Poetry Bookshop opened, and he brought out the first issue of *Poetry & Drama*, a quarterly chapbook of selected poetry, drama, and criticism by contemporary writers. The Bookshop's mission included weekly poetry readings and sales of contemporary poetry books, many published by The Bookshop itself. Visitors could browse the books on the shelves and tables and read from them while seated in an armchair beside the fire. Harold Monro occupied an office at the front of The Bookshop, where he often sat behind his typewriter and numerous manuscripts and nodded diffidently to visitors.

In January 1916, more than a month after Alida's reading of Charlotte's poems, Alida invited Charlotte to her flat in Red Lion Square, a stone's throw from The Bookshop. She was Harold's right-hand man and didn't dare leave the shop until late afternoon. She asked that Charlotte meet her there.

Charlotte was leery of Alida's apparent offer of friendship, largely because Alida was no more than twenty years old and Charlotte was forty-five. What might they have in common besides a love of poetry? But because Alida had asked or because Alida's dark features reminded Charlotte so much of Freda, Charlotte accepted Alida's invitation.

Charlotte arrived at 4 o'clock. There was just enough time before the wartime curfew and blackout for a walk to Alida's flat and back to The Bookshop, as well as a cup of tea. Alida was at the back of the shop helping a customer. Harold was in his office. He nodded at Charlotte and then bent over his typewriter, which held no paper. He impressed Charlotte as furtive. But perhaps, she thought, he was only shy. He wore a mustache like Fred Mew's, and his dark hair was parted slightly to one side. As Alida caught Charlotte's eye and waved, Charlotte listened for sounds of the typewriter but heard nothing. Alida greeted her at the entrance.

She took Charlotte's arm and put it gently in hers, as though Charlotte were a maiden aunt, and they walked together into the afternoon. Before they had gone ten feet, Alida said, "My flat isn't much. But it's home." As powdery snow drifted to the ground, enlisted men in khaki uniforms walked by them with purposeful strides and strained expressions on their faces. The snow disappeared as it dusted their uniforms, and Charlotte wondered how life would ever return to normal.

Alida's flat was, as she had claimed, tiny and sparsely furnished. Orange crates functioned as end tables and two straight-back chairs as seating. Alida hung her red wool coat on a peg behind the door, then she took Charlotte's topcoat and hung it on the same peg over her own coat. Charlotte sat on one of the chairs at Alida's invitation and wondered what to do with her hands. Alida, busy in the kitchenette just off the living room, quickly produced a solution by handing Charlotte a glass of red wine.

"What should we toast?" she asked without preamble. She held up her glass.

"To The Poetry Bookshop," Charlotte said and held up her own glass.

"Here, here," said Alida. She took a drink, then laughed. "The wine's simply awful, I know. But it's the best I can afford, especially these days."

Charlotte looked at Alida and saw Freda, or rather Freda as she might have been at twenty if only.... Alida was handsome rather than pretty, and her manner was open, engaging, and altogether guileless.

"Tell me about your admirers," Alida insisted. "Harold and I can't be your only fans." She sat comfortably back in her chair, lounging in it as if the uncomfortable chair were a settee.

Charlotte thought about Sappho and May but said, "I'm afraid you and Harold are in a minority." Charlotte looked around Alida's flat and admired its economy.

"I'm certain that you'll have more admirers in a short while," Alida said. "I've memorized 'The Farmer's Bride.' Aren't you impressed?"

"I'm pleased you thought it was worth committing to memory," Charlotte said. She longed to know about Alida and Harold's relationship, though she knew it was none of her business. Charlotte imagined they had met when Alida applied for a position at The Bookshop. But she sensed their relationship went beyond that of boss and employee.

"Harold is more knowledgeable about the traditions of poetry," Alida admitted, sipping her wine. "But I'm just as passionate."

Charlotte saw her opening. "How did you and Harold meet?"

"Just as you might expect," Alida said, leaning forward. "I was reading at a poets' club dinner in the spring of 1913, shortly after Harold opened The Bookshop. We hit it off immediately. He asked if I liked Byron or Keats better. "When I replied, 'Shelley,' I had no idea he was Harold's favorite poet. I began working at The Bookshop the very next day."

Charlotte asked shamelessly, "Is there a Mrs. Monro?" After all, a maiden aunt should do no less than protect the younger generation as best as she can.

"Two, in fact," said Alida, sitting back. "His estranged wife, Dorothy, and his mother, neither of whom is pleasant. His mother, though I hardly know her, has chastised me for preferring butter over the seven-penny margarine, 'used by all women who love their country.' Not to my face, mind you. But through Harold."

Charlotte wondered why Harold would pass along such an unpleasant message.

Alida paused and Charlotte waited. "Interestingly, Harold is still very good friends with Dorothy's brother, Maurice. In fact, it was through Maurice that Harold and Dorothy met. I'm glad Harold has such a close friend," Alida finished. But she suddenly seemed preoccupied.

She collected herself and said, "We have just enough time for a cigarette. Would you like one?" Alida stood and proffered a cigarette box that she had produced from an orange crate. When Charlotte smiled and took one, Alida appeared surprised. Alida took one herself and quickly produced matches and an ashtray. "To new friends," she said, lighting Charlotte's cigarette, then her own.

"To new friends," Charlotte agreed.

They returned to The Bookshop along Devonshire Street as snowflakes continued falling in the early dusk. Alida wore the hood of her coat up, and Charlotte donned her felt hat. At the entrance to The Bookshop, Alida thanked Charlotte for her company and asked her to drop by her flat any evening. Just inside the entrance stood Harold, striking Charlotte suddenly as a hungry wolf. He nodded through the glass at Charlotte, and she felt as if he were challenging her. But to what, Charlotte couldn't say.

CHAPTER 35

Evening blackouts might as well have extended into day. London's streets were shrouded by the war effort. If it wasn't men in uniform en route to their garrisons who monopolized the pavements, it was young women on their way to the munitions factories. Every industry was subjugated to the war effort and each citizen felt obligated to do his or her part.

The Mew women had "no men to give," yet Ma wouldn't hear of either Anne or Charlotte laboring at a factory job, whatever the contribution to the war effort. So the sisters made home visits to war widows and attended teas sponsored by the War Department. They couldn't eliminate the women's grief, but they could lighten its burden, if only for an hour or two.

At the war's beginning, it wasn't widows whom the sisters visited but wives. However, as soon as the casualty lists began rolling in, the widows grew in numbers. Charlotte and Anne vowed to eschew all platitudes when counseling the widows, platitudes centering on the heroic status conferred on each dead solider, regardless of the nature of his death. But as the war widows multiplied, the platitudes came to the sisters' aid in stilted conversations where loss was so omnipresent it seemed to take its place at the head of the table each time tea was served.

For many of the widows, loss gave nothing and took everything, even hope. The older widows were often more tragic than the young, even though they had lost less of their future. Charlotte, sitting in the Edwardian parlor of one such widow in late January, understood the many ways in which age could complicate grief. The parlor itself struck Charlotte as a relic of a civilization that had thought itself worldly at the turn of the century but was forced now to admit its own naïveté in the face of trench warfare, long range artillery, and mustard gas. Moreover, the aerial bombing of not only munitions factories but also civilian populations miles away from industry made any claim to civilized behavior absurd.

The parlor of Mrs. Muller, whose husband had been a third-generation immigrant to England, was a time capsule of a lost age, an age ripe less than three years ago when "human progress" was still the watchword of the modern era. Charlotte saw the tatted antimacassars on the backs of the armchairs and imagined Mr. Muller sitting in the larger of the two, holding a skein of yarn while Mrs. Muller scolded him to hold his arms up while she parceled out the skein into three balls.

Mrs. Muller had answered Charlotte's knock with a knitting needle in her hand. When Charlotte explained who she was, Mrs. Muller protested, claiming she had asked the War Department to discontinue its calls to her home. But she asked Charlotte in, and Charlotte, sure loneliness only worsened the despair that loss triggered, was glad to be let in for Mrs. Muller's sake, and for her own.

During her visit, Mrs. Muller asked Charlotte if she had lost a husband in the war. When Charlotte was mute, she continued, "And a son? Have you lost a husband and a son in the war? Or perhaps a brother?" Charlotte could only shake her head. "No matter," Mrs. Muller said. "It's no consolation for me to know that other women's losses have been as great. I'm as happy for you as anyone can be during wartime."

On her way home from Mrs. Muller's, Charlotte passed a bombed-out building, the contents of its inhabitants' lives on display for passersby to see. It was as if a dollhouse had been turned inside-out and left open on its hinge for all the world to witness its unkempt state. In the rubble next to a doll with one arm missing was a china teapot, apparently undamaged.

When Charlotte arrived home, number 9 was as she had left it. She knew, however, that by tomorrow it could be in ruins. Occasionally evening air raids by German Zeppelins hurried the Mew women and the tenants below stairs, where the windows facing Gordon Street were blacked out and the occupants saw each other by candlelight. Now, on the entry's table, Charlotte found a letter from the matron at Whitecroft Hospital and a letter from May. She wasn't surprised. May had continued to write Charlotte as if nothing had happened between them, though May did confine her comments to writing and literature. Charlotte's replies were noncommittal and lighthearted. She simply refused to let May think that her rebuff of Charlotte had gone any further than skin-deep. The letter from Whitecroft was as perfunctory as Charlotte's replies to May. The matron assured the Mew family that Freda was as safe as if she were in London. It was a slim comfort, but a comfort nonetheless.

There had been no letters from Italy, either before or after the war began, and Anne, of course, said nothing to Charlotte about Mr. Antony. Despite the war, Miss Carr, the singer who wore ermine, continued her painting lessons with Anne, providing a diversion and some much-needed income. But Anne's solace came from her church — a solace Charlotte shared even less with Anne since the advent of the war.

Charlotte looked at her gray self in the entry's mirror. The world had grown more and more absurd, and no one could make sense of the mounting chaos, least of all Reverend Cecil, who claimed that the war was God's along with everything else. No one could believe that the world might return to normalcy if the war ended. All anyone could do, Charlotte believed, was endure.

CHAPTER 36

"You trust May as well as Harold," said Anne. It was a question rather than a statement.

The sisters sat in the February light of Hogarth Studios, Anne at her easel and Charlotte, who was molding plasticine figurines, at the wooden table. They focused on their projects and talked sporadically without any expectation of thoughtful or timely responses. For Charlotte, the plasticine worked like worry beads under the pressure of her fingertips.

"I trust Harold's devotion to poetry," Charlotte said.

Harold Monro had proposed that The Poetry Bookshop publish a book of Charlotte's poems. Charlotte sent off seventeen poems, with an admittedly diffident note: "No one will want to read them." But despite Charlotte's lack of encouragement and the constraints of wartime London, Harold Monroe thought a book of Charlotte's poems must come out.

Charlotte, modeling the ear of a rabbit, said, "Trust the tides to the moon and the cows to green pastures."

Anne laughed. "Uncle's maxims for country living."

The ear of the rabbit drooped, and Charlotte mashed the plasticine into a ball and began again. No one who knew that a rabbit's paws were tufts of fur, without pads like a dog's or cat's paws, would accept a fake rabbit's foot for good luck. It was yet another maxim from Uncle, to help guarantee the good life, he said. The moon and the tides, rabbits, pastures and cows. If only human nature were as reliable as Mother Nature, Charlotte might rest assured. Alida and Anne, because they were guileless themselves, expected nothing but goodness from others as a matter of course. Charlotte wasn't as certain.

Today the winter sun appeared as white as a full moon. Jane was sitting with Ma, and Parliament had recently passed the Military Service Act, which meant compulsory military service for all able-bodied men aged eighteen to forty-one, except those men in reserved occupations. Only a few weeks earlier, the Allied forces had been defeated at Gallipoli following a yearlong campaign. Charlotte and Alida talked yesterday of their inability to recall the war's early days when it was predicted to last weeks, not years.

Alida feared Harold would be called up, as was Harold himself. He could claim to be a conscientious objector, avoid the front, and instead do war-related work at home. Until then, Alida told Charlotte, he was dedicating himself, as always, to the cause of poetry. "It's needed more than ever," Harold proclaimed. But he refused to profit from the public's hunger for patriotic poetry. Instead, he continued to publish the anthologies of

Georgian poetry co-edited by Eddie Marsh, private secretary to Winston Churchill, and single volumes by individual poets. The previous December, Harold brought out F. S. Flint's *Cadences* and Richard Aldington's *Images*.

"Is it a kangaroo?" Anne asked. She had left her canvas and stood over Charlotte's shoulder.

"It could be," Charlotte replied noncommittally.

"Or perhaps a rabbit," said Anne doubtfully. She took off her smock and sat across from Charlotte. "May is very knowledgeable about book publishing, you've said. If she says advances are rare for poetry books and royalties are the normal payment, it must be so."

Charlotte again collapsed the rabbit (or the kangaroo) into a ball and massaged the plasticine with her fingertips. Perhaps May's letter advising Charlotte to accept The Bookshop's contract was a fake rabbit's foot. True, May had never failed to encourage Charlotte as a writer. But how could she separate May, an experienced author with good advice, from May, the malevolent woman who had broken Charlotte's confidence by playing her for a fool?

Harold, Charlotte suspected, wasn't altogether as he appeared either. His family ran a private asylum, similar to the one on the Isle where Freda lived, and its profits supported Harold and helped fund The Bookshop. One could argue that the Monro family provided a service, nothing more and nothing less. But the idea of profiting from those like Freda who couldn't help their own condition still galled Charlotte. Neither she nor Anne would ever tell Alida of Freda, or of Henry, or of the sisters' pact, however true a friend Alida proved to be. If she and Anne never spoke of their pact with each other, why would they share its existence with anyone else?

But there was more to Charlotte's distrust of Harold than his family's business. She saw him in her mind's eye looking back at her from the entryway mirror of number 9. She felt certain that Harold's affection for Alida could lead to nothing more than friendship. And she feared Alida was in love with Harold.

Anne asked, "Are you afraid the book won't sell?"

Charlotte looked up from the plasticine. "I'm more afraid of how much its success means to me."

Anne nodded. It was less an understanding between sisters than an understanding between artists trying to make good in the world.

"I miss the yellow light of summer," Anne said, "but at least the white light of winter reminds me of Uncle's moon." Charlotte nodded as she thought of the calendar with its daily tidal charts in the farm house's kitchen. But first she remembered *The Yellow Book*, its decadent beauty, and how much fame had meant to her when she was younger.

Trust the tides to the moon. But could she trust the siren call of a book with her own name?

Her *Yellow Book* days had been heady. In 1894, when she was twenty-four years old, Charlotte, desperate for its acceptance, submitted a short story to Henry Harland, the editor of *The Yellow Book*.

No one could have guessed that "Passed" was inspired by Miss Bolt's story of her niece's fall from grace, a story which had haunted Charlotte's imagination ever since she was a little girl. Despite its original inspiration, "Passed" used the standard tropes of popular literature of the 1890's, including a fallen woman who meets a tragic end, and with whom readers sympathize, even as they feel obligated to judge her. The male narrator meets the fallen woman in a church, follows her home, and sits at her deathbed along with the woman's sister. Later, returning to the scene, he witnesses the sister walking the same streets her sister had. He does nothing to intervene in either sister's fate, and he acts bewildered by their behavior and his own. The plot might have been maudlin and predictable, but Henry Harland saw something in the story that was original. Perhaps it was the narrator's confusion and disbelief. Perhaps it was the writer's passion. At any rate, Mr. Harland wrote to Charlotte, inviting her to his flat at 144 Cromwell Road.

Later, she would attend Harland's "Saturday evenings" at his flat, dressed in a felt hat and men's overcoat, with her cigarettes and umbrella newly in hand. It was the age of Art for Art's Sake and the New Woman. Both the aesthete and the New Woman were poses that suited Charlotte in her early 20's, when the world had closed its doors to Henry's and Freda's futures while promising to open its doors to her own. But the day she met Henry Harland in his flat for the first time, the future she longed for hadn't arrived, and she prayed that "Passed" would earn her an appreciative audience, even fame. Though he couldn't pay first-time contributors, Mr. Harland assured Charlotte that her story would be in good company.

In July, "Passed" appeared in the pages of *The Yellow Book*, alongside John Davidson's "Thirty Bob a Week," Henry James' play *The Coxon Fund*, and six illustrations by Aubrey Beardsley. Charlotte was well on her way to recognition, even minor celebrity. But the promise of fame meant so much more to Charlotte than it did to other hopeful young writers. It represented nothing short of redemption.

That evening, Charlotte sat on her mattress with her cigar box of mementos. Though it was May who had encouraged Charlotte to finish "Madeleine in Church," the poem was Charlotte's achievement, not May's. And though May had advised Charlotte to publish the manuscript, the book itself would be Charlotte's, not May's. Charlotte would possess the book as she herself wanted to be possessed. She touched the tuft of fur on the underside of the rabbit's foot. "For good luck," she said out loud. As a child, she had loved the rabbit's foot. Now she found it macabre. But in these times, she would take luck wherever she might find it.

CHAPTER 37

A month later, Ma, Anne, and Charlotte took their tea as the sisters talked of Harold Monro's latest plans for the publication of *The Farmer's Bride*.

"A green cover might be just as nice as the grey you had wanted, and the illustration matters less than the poems themselves," Anne reassured Charlotte.

"But now it's not even to be a bound volume, only a chapbook," argued Charlotte.

Every day during the last month, she had imagined the dark gray volume of poems with a careful line drawing by James Guthrie as the cover's illustration. Now the cover's illustration, by Lovat Fraser, was to be a thatched cottage with a tiny window that no one inside could possibly see out of.

"With the war on, everything's more expensive, and as Alida says, chapbooks are selling better than regular volumes," Anne said.

"I can't understand you girls," said Ma. "You're like men and their wars, but with you, it's art. How can any of it matter?"

It did matter to Charlotte. With Alida's help, she had convinced Harold to honor the original line lengths rather than break "Madeleine in Church" into ugly bits. But as a result, the book was to be nearly square. And if its cover was to be green rather than dark grey, as she had imagined, and the cover's illustration was to be a cottage having nothing to do with the poems, the book was quickly becoming less and less a reflection of Charlotte's vision.

Once Ma had retired, Anne comforted Charlotte. "Ma means well. She just doesn't understand."

"She's right about both the war and art," said Charlotte. "The more offensive our military leaders are, the less satisfactory their results. The more I attempt to shape the book, the more absurd the result promises to be." But Charlotte decided she could tolerate no more gravity that evening. "Ma is a Philistine, through and through," Charlotte said, and smiled at Anne.

"She is predictable, at least," Anne said, and laughed, but grew serious once more. "She's wrong about art. It does matter. Your book matters, Charlotte, and it will turn out brilliantly."

But things were to get worse before they got better.

In the fall of 1894, on the heels of her recent success, Charlotte had worked incessantly on a play she titled *The China Bowl*, feeling confident that

Henry Harland would publish it in *The Yellow Book*. The play's tragedy was no less maudlin than that of "Passed." Set in Cornwall, it told the story of a fisherman, his wife, and his mother. To assert her independence, the fisherman's wife, Susannah, sells a china bowl — an heirloom of the family. The fisherman strikes her, Susannah leaves their home, and the fisherman takes his boat out to sea and is drowned.

When Charlotte was working on the play, Freda and Henry had been taken from number 9, and Fred and Anna Maria seemed to watch Charlotte and Anne for any sign that they, too, might succumb to madness. Ma took to her invalid's sofa, and Fred forbade anyone to wind the grandfather clock in the entry, so time stood still as Ma lay on her invalid's sofa and her father worked at his drafting table, with Henry's table still by its side.

Proud of all her hard work and desperate for recognition, Charlotte sent *The China Bowl* to Henry Harland in January of 1895. He praised it, telling Charlotte her play had "supreme emotion and a true tragic sense." But he claimed it was too long to publish in *The Yellow Book*. Might she let him publish her play in another collection? *The China Bowl* was the same length as *The Coxon Fund*, which had appeared alongside "Passed" the previous July. Charlotte wouldn't be put off. She had her heart set on seeing *The China Bowl* published in *The Yellow Book*. She threw the manuscript in a drawer and her umbrella in a trash bin.

"It's nothing," Harold Monro reassured Charlotte, "but one compositor's opinion."

"And his opinion is wrong," Alida insisted.

"We'll simply find another printer," Harold said.

Charlotte could have died on the spot. All she could see in that moment was the trouble her moral high ground (regarding art, not religion) had brought upon The Bookshop.

"I'm so sorry," she said to Harold, and meant it.

"There's nothing to be sorry about," Harold said. "Good poems demand risks."

The compositor, who happened to be a pious Methodist, had read "Madeleine in Church" while setting its type.

"It's blasphemous. Pure and simple," the printer, taking the compositor's side, reported to Harold. "And I won't do any of the devil's work for him, despite the lost wages."

After conveying the news to Alida and Charlotte, Harold asked, "I wonder whose side he's on in the war?"

"I wonder how his wife tolerates his narrowmindedness?" Alida replied.

"Perhaps," Charlotte said, "they're a matched set."

CHARLOTTE DISCOVERED HER UMBRELLA in the corner of her bedroom and assumed that either her father or Anne had rescued it from the trash bin. She was thankful because the sisters had been invited to St. James Theatre by Evelyn Millard. After a series of tryouts, Evelyn had been cast as Cecily in Oscar Wilde's *The Importance of Being Earnest*. Later, Evelyn would say that it was just her luck to earn a plum role in a play destined to end its run after only two months because of scandal. Charlotte, recovered from Henry Harland's rejection of *The China Bowl*, was disappointed to learn that *The Yellow Book*, by dint of association with the aesthete movement and thus Oscar Wilde, had ceased publication.

It was clear in the laws of the state as well as the laws of moral propriety that homosexuality was not only wrong but also punishable by imprisonment and hard labor. Charlotte's crush on Miss Lucy Harrison had been only that, a crush. Many schoolgirls had innocent infatuations with their school's headmistress. In fact, all of Charlotte and Anne's friends from the Gower Street days had admitted, at one time or another, to being smitten by Miss Harrison. But Charlotte suspected that she was different from her friends. When she met Ella D'Arcy at one of Henry Harland's "Saturday evenings," Charlotte knew she was different because she fell in love with Ella.

That evening Charlotte reread "Madeleine in Church" through the eyes of the compositor. Was Charlotte a modernist artist who believed art might replace religion as an ultimate value system? Or were Madeleine's doubts about God, about love and marriage, and about loyalty to one's heart merely Madeleine's own personal creed, not a secular one?

No, she reasoned. Madeleine spoke from her heart just as Charlotte had when she wrote the poem. And she spoke only for herself and her desire to believe in the sacrifice of Christ benefitting all of humankind, including the sinner whose sin seemed unforgivable.

But what was that dream of forgiveness — the bloodless life of the spirit — in comparison to the human touch, or the trees of Eden and Calvary in comparison to the plane trees of the Gordon Square garden? How could Christ ask Mary Magdalene to forsake the life of the flesh, when the sensual world, its joy and its pain, were so exquisite? *Tell me there will be someone.* Someone who might understand and accept Charlotte without asking her to renounce the very clay of which she was made.

CHAPTER 38

The war was still on, and when it would end was anyone's guess. The news reports of Allied military offenses struck Charlotte as less and less real. Anne would only say, "Of course, they can't tell us everything or they would jeopardize our defense." But she admitted to painting a country lane with red roses strewn along the path, then covering the entire canvas in black paint.

"All I could do today," she told Charlotte, "was to paint layer after layer of black paint onto the same canvas."

"What have you titled the canvas," asked Charlotte, for whom names mattered. "Just today's date," Anne replied. "January 20, 1917." Six months earlier, in an Allied offensive on the Somme deemed certain to bring the war to an end, 19,000 British troops were killed in one day.

The disastrous offensive coincided with Charlotte's admission that *The Farmer's Bride* was a failure. Of the large run of 1,000 copies Charlotte herself had insisted upon, 850 sat unwanted on The Bookshop's shelves or in storage.

"I won't remainder them, and I'll leave the book in standing type," Harold Monro told her. "We mustn't lose faith."

Charlotte recognized that her loss of fame — or her dream of fame — was nothing compared to the loss of so many lives and the grief the dead soldiers left behind.

But Harold kept his word. The book remained for sale on the table of new releases, he hadn't remaindered the excess copies, and he'd arranged with the printer to keep the book in standing type. In short, Harold's faith was greater than Charlotte's.

In early afternoon, Charlotte climbed the back staircase of number 9. She pulled down the stairs leading to the attic rooms and ascended to the top of the steps. She looked around at the castoff goods. The dollhouse was shut tight on its hinge, reminding Charlotte of the line drawing of the cottage on the cover of *The Farmer's Bride*. Just like the line drawing of the cottage, the silhouette of the dollhouse outlined a home long abandoned by family members who lived diminished lives elsewhere.

Charlotte took Fred Mew's smoking jacket from its place on Miss Bolt's dress form and pulled it onto her petite frame, even smaller in size since the War Department had introduced voluntary rationing of all but basic staples. The less food eaten by civilians, the more food that was available to the troops. "Soon we'll have to queue for bread and milk," Ma said. Jane tested the recipes for "patriotic meals" published in the newspapers, and Charlotte couldn't distinguish one dish from the next. But if pressed by Jane, Charlotte would say that the day's meal was better than last night's. It wasn't much of a lie, as all the food tasted equally bland. Ma, of course, complained. But Jane, smartly, ignored her.

Charlotte perched on the broken rocker as she studied the empty picture frames on the wall. They reminded her of the line drawings she had purchased in Paris from a street vendor who had set up shop in front of the Musee d'Orsey. More than ten years ago, Charlotte had journeyed to Paris to see Ella D'Arcy, who was living there in the smallest of rooms. Charlotte stayed at a hotel a few arrondissements away and spent a couple heady days walking the streets of Paris in anticipation of calling on Ella, who was expecting her.

On one of those days, she stumbled over the street vendor and discovered the line drawings. There were two sets, and each set consisted of three drawings. One set was of a giraffe transformed frame by frame into the Eiffel Tower, and the other set was of the Eiffel Tower transformed frame by frame into a schoolgirl with a solitary balloon floating high above her head. The transformations were futuristic. Madcap. The street vendor had a wide grin, with a space between his two front teeth. He wore a shabby coat and thin, gray trousers, in which he shivered visibly in the brisk March wind.

Now France, the site of so many useless deaths, lay in ruins, and Charlotte's time in Paris was a distant memory, a hazy outline of days gone by.

Charlotte had purchased the line drawings and celebrated having found them over a lunch of spaghetti Bolognese and red wine. As she smiled and ate, the cylindrical tube containing the drawings sat by her side on the bench. Charlotte daydreamed of Ella's reception, hoping she might detect in Ella's manner the same feelings Charlotte felt for Ella. Daydreaming over a second glass of wine, she remembered seeing Lucy Harrison and Amy Greener together in the classroom. The class was at recess and Charlotte had hidden in the cloakroom, where she looked through the keyhole to see Miss Harrison kiss Miss Greener. Charlotte's heart had raced, not from fear but the excitement of what a relationship between two women might be. She had never seen her own parents embrace, let alone kiss, and here were two women obviously in love with each other, unlike Charlotte's parents.

When Charlotte returned to her Paris hotel room, she realized with a growing panic that she no longer carried the cylindrical tube of drawings. Realizing she must have left them on the bench, she retraced her steps to the restaurant. The maître d' could only say *"Je suis désolée"* when he reported to Charlotte that the tube was gone, and Charlotte's waiter hadn't seen it when he cleared her table.

Loss. Once Charlotte stirred up her courage to visit Ella in her rooms, Ella greeted her warmly. She was dressed simply in a peignoir and motioned to Charlotte to take a seat in the chair next to the bed. Ella resumed her position, climbing into the bed amidst manuscript and books. On her bedside table, she kept pen and ink, and a glass and a bottle of red wine. Ella had been writing, what Charlotte might have done instead of walking the streets of Paris thinking about Ella.

"It's nothing much," Ella said, pointing to the manuscript. "It's only a translation, none of my own work."

"It's admirable that your French allows you to write translations," Charlotte said. Her feet hurt from all the walking she had been doing, and her topcoat was too warm for the small room and its coal fire.

"Would you like a glass of wine?" Ella asked, though there was only one glass that Charlotte could see.

"I'm fine," Charlotte assured Ella. Before she could stop herself, Charlotte blurted out the story of the line drawings — how she had found and then lost them, all in an afternoon.

"I've found and lost entire relationships in an afternoon," Ella said. "You shouldn't feel embarrassed over a few line drawings." Charlotte knew Ella meant well. But Charlotte only felt chagrin.

"Listen," Ella said, sitting up in her bed. "I'm going to be direct, so correct me if I take a misstep and, more important, forgive me."

Charlotte held her breath.

"I sense that you like me as more than just a friend. But I'm afraid I like men. Otherwise, I'd be charmed to be your sweetheart."

Charlotte had laughed and shook her head. She continued to laugh so she wouldn't have to talk.

"Well, I see I've put my foot in it," Ella said good-naturedly. "I can be obtuse at the most awkward moments." She laughed at herself and winked at Charlotte, and Charlotte felt her heart break.

Now, more than ten years later, she thought if she were Miss Harrison or Miss Greener, perhaps she wouldn't feel so wrong. Instead of believing that she deserved Ella's and May's rejections because her attraction to women was a disgrace in God's eyes, she might believe that God's Word was open to interpretation. But like her persona, Madeleine, Charlotte knew she was a sinner and a social outcast. She wanted to believe as Anne believed, simply and without question. But Charlotte couldn't change who she was, and how could God, despite his great mercy, forgive her when she couldn't repent her sins because they were who she was?

When Charlotte was fourteen, she attended Saturday Market in Newfairlee with Uncle Henry. The market was full of huckster's stalls and wares and baubles. While Uncle Henry went off to do the week's shopping, Charlotte stood mesmerized as a cooper bent the staves of a barrel and shaped them to the barrel's metal rings. She was so mesmerized by his skill that she lost track of time. When she realized how late it was, she hurried off to meet Uncle at the miller's stall. In her haste, she ran into a young man, who took Charlotte in his arms and whirled her around, before he hastily said he was sorry and bounded off. Charlotte longed to feel again what she had felt when she was in the man's arms: safe, cared for, and wanted, if only for a fleeting moment.

Sitting in the attic on her broken rocker, remembering Ella and May and the man at Saturday Market, Charlotte imagined and drafted a narrative poem. She used the imperative voice and began

> *Bury your heart in some deep green hollow*
> *Or hide it up in a kind old tree*
> *Better still, give it the swallow*
> *When she goes over the sea*

In the second stanza, the narrator describes the Saturday Market, including

> *Grey old gaffers and boys of twenty —*
> *Girls and women of the town —*
> *Pitchers and sugar-sticks, ribbons and laces ...*

In the third stanza, the narrator asks

> *What were you showing in Saturday Market*
> *That set it grinning from end to end*
> *Girls and gaffers and boys of twenty — ?*

before he advises the woman to

> *Cover it close with your shawl, my friend — ...*

In the fourth stanza, when the woman arrives home, the narrator instructs her

> *See, you, the shawl is wet, take out from under*
> *The red dead thing — . In the white of the moon*
> *On the flags does it stir again? Well, and no wonder —*
> *Best make an end of it; bury it soon.*
> *If there is blood on the hearth who'll know it?*

In the last stanza, the narrator says

Think no more of the swallow,
Forget, you, the sea,
Never again remember the deep green hollow
Or the top of the kind old tree!

It was as bleak, perhaps, as Anne's black canvas. But it captured Charlotte's sense of exposure and betrayal, and, in its shadings of grief, what might have been.

CHAPTER 39

In early June, when it struck Charlotte for the third year that it wasn't possible to appreciate summer with a war on, she received a letter from Sappho requesting that Charlotte read for her newest venture, the Tomorrow Club.

Sappho hadn't contacted Charlotte since Charlotte's falling out with May. Specifically, she hadn't kept her promise to let Charlotte take the Scott children to a matinee of *Peter Pan*. That was three years ago. Perhaps Sappho wanted to make amends. But if that's what Sappho wanted, she could apologize directly to Charlotte, not invite her to read at a women's gathering as a pretense for letting bygones be bygones. If May hadn't told Sappho what happened between May and Charlotte, Sappho would have been in touch with Charlotte long before now. No, Sappho had chosen to spurn Charlotte just as May had.

The only way to retain her dignity was to reply to Sappho's letter, without giving her room to wheedle her way back into Charlotte's life and further humiliate her. Like her replies to May, her reply to Sappho was formal, yet polite. She told Sappho that she was "snowed under" with managing number 9 and with her war work. (Charlotte didn't tell Sappho what her war work consisted of because it was none of her business.)

In mid-June, Sappho sent Charlotte a second letter insisting that Charlotte read for her club. In her letter, Sappho reminded Charlotte of her sacred duty to the arts and reassured her that she could manage this one other obligation among her many important tasks. Charlotte bristled. She placed the letter in a drawer of her vanity and swore to herself that she wouldn't answer it unless she could do so coolly and civilly.

Even for June, the day was sunny and unseasonably hot. The plane trees of Gordon Square garden had fully leafed out in the nurturing rains and heat of early summer. Dappled light played with shadows on the pavements as Anne came home from her studio for tea. A few minutes later, Alida arrived at number 9.

Alida had become a fixture at Gordon Street, dropping in on Charlotte and Anne just as Charlotte dropped in on Alida at her apartment in Red Lion Square. Alida had met Ma and Wek, and she hadn't backed down when Ma questioned Alida on her marital status and her political views. Most important, Alida and Anne had become as close friends as Alida and Charlotte.

The friendships were all the more important to Alida because Harold had been drafted and was serving at Newton Heath as a second lieutenant. Mercifully, he hadn't been called up to the front. In their frequent letters, Alida and Harold exchanged news of their days. Knowing that Alida opened The Bookshop each morning kept Harold going. Indeed, Alida not only opened The Bookshop but singlehandedly ran it, serving as clerk, stock boy, bookkeeper, and copyeditor. But occasionally she would escape her duties for a visit to number 9.

The three women gathered in the parlor. Anne sat in a corner armchair and Alida perched on a footstool nearby as Charlotte served tea.

"I've been wondering," said Alida, "about something that Harold wrote the other day that's been niggling me ever since."

"What is it?" Anne asked politely.

"A newspaper editorial claimed that Germany's guilt was not its people's but Kaiser Wilhelm's alone. Harold staunchly disagreed, saying that the German people must share Kaiser Wilhelm's shame. I wrote back to Harold, asking if there wasn't a difference between guilt and shame," Alida said, "but I haven't received a letter from him in return."

"Surely, guilt and shame aren't synonymous," Anne agreed.

"As a poet, Harold would know the difference between one word and another." Alida turned to Charlotte. "You're number 9's resident poet. What's your view?"

Charlotte twisted the ring on her right hand and looked from Anne to Alida. "I defer to Anne's opinion. Tell us, Anne, what you see is the difference."

"Well," Anne began tentatively, "The two words are related, of course. For example, some people claim that the Kaiser is willful. He has done horrible things against God and man. He should feel shame, not just guilt. Guilt is too light a word."

Alida replied calmly, "Yes, guilt implies that if one confesses his sin, he can be forgiven. Whereas the Kaiser's sins, if one can use that word, are much too grave for atonement." Alida turned to Charlotte once again. "Do you agree?"

Charlotte hesitated. "Perhaps guilt, for those with a conscience, is for things we've done, whereas shame is about who we are at heart."

Alida grew animated. "Yes, that's what I mean. Shame goes deeper than guilt, though I don't suppose Kaiser Wilhelm has a conscience. Do you think he might be insane? If he's insane, he wouldn't feel either guilt or shame, would he?"

Charlotte felt Anne staring at her. Though Alida was a welcome guest at number 9 and even knew about its tenants, Charlotte and Anne could never tell her about Henry or Freda.

The grandfather clock struck 4:30. Anne said, "I must get back to the studio. Alida, forgive me."

"I must go, too," said Alida. "The Bookshop won't wait forever. But before I leave, I'd like to hear Charlotte read one of the war poems she's been working on."

"Only if you read one first," Charlotte insisted, relieved to escape the subjects of guilt and shame and of sanity and insanity.

"With pleasure," Alida said. Charlotte retrieved the two poems from the mantel where she had placed them earlier that day. She handed one to Alida.

Alida read slowly.

June, 1915

Who thinks of June's first rose to-day?
    Only some child, perhaps, with shining eyes and rough
      bright hair will reach it down
In a green sunny lane, to us almost as far away
    As are the fearless stars from these veiled lamps of town.
    What's little June to the great broken world with eyes gone
      dim
    From too much looking on the face of grief, the face of
      dread?
      Or what's the broken world to June and him
    Of the small eager hand, the shining eyes, the rough bright
      head?

"It's beautiful," Alida said. "And powerful."

Wek's squawking erupted from the front room and then Ma's voice reprimanding him.

"I apologize," Charlotte said, "but the second poem will have to wait until another day. Perhaps in your rooms."

"Of course," said Alida. "I'll show myself out."

That evening, Charlotte sat at her vanity and reread Sappho's second letter. How dare she, having snubbed Charlotte years ago, order her to do anything? A month before the incident with May, Charlotte had revealed to Sappho that the one attitude in people she couldn't understand was hardness toward individual differences. Obviously, Sappho hadn't heard Charlotte, and she hadn't bothered about Charlotte after May tattled on her. Perhaps Charlotte shouldn't expect anyone else to accept her differences when she had such difficulty accepting them herself. But she was hurt and angry.

She took out a piece of stationery and her pen, and she addressed a letter to "Mrs. Scott." In the first paragraph, she admitted her own deafness to the sacred call of the arts, but she refused to apologize for being "snowed under" with responsibilities. In the second and last paragraph she wrote: "People are only 'disappointing' when one makes a wrong diagnosis." (After all, Sappho had dismissed Charlotte out of hand.) Then Charlotte questioned why an organization named the "Tomorrow Club" would be interested in the "green field of yesterdays"? For surely, Sappho's and Charlotte's friendship was history.

It was hardly a cool or civil letter. But when Charlotte posted it the next day, she felt vindicated.

CHAPTER 40

"Eventually they'll run out of men to kill," Ma said. "Then the war will have to end."

"Don't say that, Ma. It's tasteless," Anne said.

"Just like this food," Ma insisted. They were sharing a meal of beans and rice.

"Jane does well with what very little she has to work with," Charlotte argued.

It was October of 1917. The War Department had instituted queues across the nation to ration milk and sugar. (Charlotte and Anne began taking their tea black, to save the milk and sugar for Ma.) It also began drafting men in reserved occupations, which meant more women than ever were needed on the home front.

But what really upset Ma, both sisters knew, was Charlotte's news that they could no longer afford to keep their rooms on the first floor of number 9, and they would need to let them furnished. That meant they would have only the rooms of the ground level and below stairs to eat and sleep.

It fell on Charlotte's shoulders not only to find suitable tenants but also to rearrange the rooms on the ground level to accommodate cots for the three women to sleep on. Ma's cot would go in the morning room with Fred Mew's desk. The sisters would sleep in the parlor, and the dining room would have to accommodate a wardrobe so the women would have some place to put their clothes. Charlotte's writing desk would be included in the furnishings for the new tenants, as would Ma's feather bed. The attic rooms would receive the personal possessions that the ground level rooms could not.

"You're welcome to write at the studio," Anne told Charlotte. (Charlotte had insisted they keep the lease to the studio in case "worse came to worst," which neither she nor Anne dared fathom.)

Ma and Wek had the front room to sit in during daylight hours, as they had always done. But as soon as Charlotte relayed the news to Ma, Wek began to molt and Ma to sulk. "This is my punishment for having married your father," Ma said. Neither Charlotte nor Anne pointed out to Ma that without Fred Mew the sisters wouldn't exist.

"Pretty soon you won't need my services," Jane said to Charlotte, "at which point I'll move in with my mother. God help us both!" Charlotte couldn't disagree with Jane's assessment. She simply put her hand on Jane's arm and smiled.

Jane said, "I'm most sorry about your writing table and your steamer trunks, Miss. I know how much you love them."

"There's the desk in the morning room," Charlotte said, "and Ma will be there only during the night. I'll have all day to write if I wish."

Jane gave her a knowing look. They both realized that Charlotte would have difficulty writing at the same desk she kept the Mews' accounts. The steamer trunks, which contained all of Charlotte's manuscripts, would have to be moved to the attic rooms. But Charlotte could visit them when she climbed the attic stairs, donned Fred Mew's jacket, and smoked the few cigarettes she still allowed herself.

"It could be much worse," Anne told Ma when tenants had been secured through Mr. Sommes' agency and the date of their move was set. Mr. Sommes was serving the army in an administrative post, and Mrs. Sommes and their daughter were running the agency. Anne continued, "Our house could be one of the many that has been bombed."

Anne was right, of course. But Ma refused to be comforted. "The day I'm content sleeping on a cot at the back of a house I was once mistress of is the day I'll die."

But they *were* lucky. Ma still had the front room and her invalid's sofa, Charlotte still had the attic rooms and the Gordon Square garden, and Anne still had her studio. Nonetheless, on the day of their move, Charlotte was melancholy. She looked at her reflection in the wardrobe's mirror one last time. She searched for a shadow of her younger self, the self who was certain that recognition and fame would compensate for a family curse of insanity, as well as atone for her individual sins. But she saw a forty-eight-year-old spinster, graying and dressed in a shabby shirtwaist and skirt, who had experienced two short brushes with fame, neither of which had redeemed Charlotte in her own eyes.

CHAPTER 41

Later, the sisters were to see Sidney Cockerell as the kindest and most doting of men. When Charlotte sent Mr. Cockerell a copy of *The Farmer's Bride* at Alida's insistence, however, they saw him only as the imposing director of the most important concern in Cambridge outside of the University, the Fitzwilliam Museum.

It was Sidney Cockerell's pleasure to acquire precious artifacts, whatever the cost in museum funds, in courting of patrons, or in his own vast store of energy and meticulous attention to the finest of details. Whether obtaining an *objet d'art* or celebrating the great men of culture such as John Ruskin or William Morris, Sidney Cockerell was indefatigable.

Mr. Cockerell, Alida informed Charlotte when she dropped in at number 9, was in attendance at a reading last Tuesday when two of Charlotte's poems were on the program. Interested in writers and poets alike (among its treasures the Fitzwilliam curated Emily Brontë's letters), Mr. Cockerell told Alida that Charlotte's poems were a delight. Charlotte replied, "It was surely your reading, Alida, that interested him."

Alida's introduction notwithstanding, Charlotte felt as if she were asking for a handout in sending out one of the many unsold copies of her book. "You've nothing to lose," Alida said, and so with that sentiment as her guide, Charlotte posted her meek package to "Mr. Sidney Cockerell, Director of the Fitzwilliam Museum, Cambridge" with a note apologizing for the book, even as she gave it in offering.

When Mr. Cockerell replied a short time later expressing his gratitude for the book and offering in turn "a few suggestions" for revisions, Charlotte feared he meant to collect her for the Fitzwilliam but only if he could be sure she wasn't found wanting. Was he like Harland, or even May, who while championing Charlotte's writing thought they might improve her character through their ostensibly well-meaning advice?

Charlotte sat at Fred Mew's desk and gently rebuffed him in her distinctive handwriting. She wouldn't, she explained, be willing or capable of altering "The Farmer's Bride" or any other poem from the collection (they were published, after all), but she thanked him for his suggestions.

After the morning post had gone out, she sat on Anne's cot and predicted that was the end of her short-lived correspondence with the man who spent his days seeing to things and not to ideas or to people. "Perhaps," Anne said, "he'll prove us wrong."

"Perhaps," Charlotte said doubtfully.

But in another letter from Mr. Cockerell arriving a few posts later, he recanted. "Of course, you are wholly right. Once I posted my letter, I realized my impertinence." Whatever his character proves to be, thought Charlotte, he's certainly not May.

Three weeks later, Charlotte asked Anne and Alida,"How does he find the time to attend exhibits and auctions, correspond with famous men, and still keep a social calendar?" Sidney, for the sisters and for Alida, had become a curiosity.

"He doesn't sleep, or he has a hundred footmen or a wife as tireless as he is to keep the home fires burning," Alida speculated.

But his wife, Anne explained, was an invalid and unable to help at home or attend social gatherings. Mrs. Cockerell insists, Anne continued, her face altogether deadpan, Mr. Cockerell see portrait artist Dorothy Hawksley and other female friends so as not to grow inward and resent her. Anne smiled, then confessed. "Katharine Righton told me the last time we had tea."

"He's not up to our late King Edward's old tricks, I should hope," said Charlotte.

"He'll squire you around London, I hear, as if it's his city and not yours," Alida warned.

"We'll be caution itself," said Charlotte.

They must have him for tea, the sisters decided. "Tell me everything," Alida said, giving them her blessing.

"Of course," Charlotte promised. Then added, "That he's our friend is your fault, after all."

As the day of their tea approached, Charlotte put off worrying about having to take on additional boarders, further reducing their already cramped quarters at number 9. They couldn't, it was clear, invite Sidney to their home. When they had let the first-floor rooms only a short while ago, Ma had complained they would be living below stairs before long. "We might as well be servants," she complained, ignoring Jane who was removing the soup tureen from the sideboard. (Ma hated the soup tureen because she thought it might be confused with a chamber pot.)

Sidney was punctual, tapping on the studio door at one minute 'til the assigned hour. When Anne greeted him and moved aside to let him in, Charlotte, standing behind Anne, was delighted to observe that he was nervous, even the slightest bit flustered. "I'm so very pleased to meet my correspondent," he said to Anne, taking her hand. Anne looked at him quizzically, and Sidney blushed, realizing his error.

"Mr. Cockerell," Charlotte said, stepping forward.

He took her hand. "You must be Miss Charlotte Mew," Sidney said.

"The eldest Mew," Charlotte replied, bowing slightly. "And this is my sister, Anne."

But Mr. Cockerell soon found his social bearings, and as Charlotte laid the table and readied the tea and biscuits, Sidney let Anne lead him around the small studio while he stopped to admire (honestly, Charlotte thought appreciatively) this or that canvas.

"Two sisters of the arts," Sidney said when they had gathered around the small table used to serve tea, "May you always reign," and held up his teacup in a toast.

When he had gone, departing graciously but with haste because he had yet another social event that day, the sisters laughed at recounting the exact precision with which Sidney, having taken a bite of biscuit, dabbed the corners of his mouth with his napkin.

"I'd describe him as avuncular," Charlotte said, and Anne added, "not to mention altogether delightful."

And so as 1918 wound down and the war promised to end soon, Charlotte, and very often Anne as well, were fitted into Sidney's bustling social calendar. But Charlotte refused his invitation for a weekend in Cambridge, however gracious and sincere. She simply couldn't, she knew, return the invitation in kind because the Mews had let the ground floor and moved to "the dungeon" of number 9.

Just that year, women over thirty had been given the right to vote, and "liberty for all" was the watchword on every newsstand. Like freedom, liberty was just one more seven-letter word, Charlotte thought. In the kitchen below stairs, she looked up through the windows and saw the railings as the iron bars of a jail.

CHAPTER 42

Max Gate was as gloomy as rumored, even foreboding, thought Charlotte. "It's the country house of a Victorian gentleman," a guidebook might generously claim. But its being hemmed in by bush and tree suggested the gentleman valued privacy more than impressing passersby, the country set, or even the infrequent invited guest.

The villa lay in Dorchester, three hours southwest of London by train. The red brick facade was mottled by lichen, and its mortared seams needed repointing. Though the roof revealed dormer windows for the house's attic rooms, these small windows were overwhelmed by the house's imposing size and looked like tiny spectacles on the face of a fat (though not jolly) man.

Inside, the villa resembled an old shoe, molded by years of daily wear to the owner's foot — bunions, flat feet, and all. But there were a pair of feet fitted to this one house, those of Thomas Hardy himself and his second wife, Florence.

It was Florence Hardy who had summoned Charlotte at Thomas Hardy's request. Though the summons came months ago by post, it was only this weekend in early December that she was able to comply. Sidney (still Mr. Cockerell to Charlotte in letter and in person) was as mirthful as a child when he learned of the invitation.

"He only feigned surprise," Charlotte told Anne, "because it allowed him freer rein in expressing his delight." But Charlotte was happy that Sidney was happy. It was Sidney, after all, who sent Mr. Hardy *The Farmer's Bride*.

"He's Ma's age. We might not have anything to talk about," Charlotte told Anne, then Alida. It was just one bead on the long string of worries she fingered in anticipation of meeting the Hardys.

"You could wear the Chinese scarf and pearl brooch," Anne said as if they were Charlotte's. The scarf was a rich crimson and one of Anne's most cherished possessions, as was the brooch.

Charlotte said, "But do you think dressed in crimson I'll appear to be a painted lady?"

Anne laughed. "All the better if you're mistaken for his Tess Durbeyfield or your Madeleine in Church."

But it wasn't Fred Mew's trade as a builder that Thomas Hardy wished to speak about with Charlotte (though it was once Hardy's own trade), nor did he care to hear Charlotte compliment Hardy's deft portrait of

Jude's dire heartache in the book that ended Hardy's career as a novelist because of the public's rejection of it.

"It's my poems I want people to remember me for if anything," Mr. Hardy told Charlotte, "not the novels or an architect's idle dreams. Poetry is what matters. It's what lives on."

And so they read their poems to one another, Hardy, his face like that of a King Charles spaniel, gray and lined but its warm brown eyes like beacons of the soul, and bundled under layers of quilts Charlotte suspected accompanied Hardy in summer as well as winter months.

Surprisingly, it wasn't Madeleine who captivated Hardy but the nameless woman of "Saturday Market," whom the nameless narrator speaks for as she hides her forsaken heart under her shawl lest anyone at the market witness her shame. Though the two spoke easily and confidentially to one another as poets, when Hardy excused himself, saying he must sleep, Charlotte wondered if she should have spoken only in the voice of the nameless narrator of her poem.

Florence Hardy, on the other hand, wanted to keep Charlotte up. Florence's eyes were heavily shadowed, like those of a person who had never slept, and in her voice, Charlotte thought she heard the anxiety and longing of a child who has a roomful of toys but no friend or sibling his own age to play with. Following Charlotte's visit, it was to be Florence, and not Hardy, who sought out Charlotte as a friend and confidant. She wanted, Charlotte learned, to write herself but hadn't known how to go about it, so she had married a writer instead.

When Charlotte returned to London, she described the Hardys to Anne as two left feet wanting to wear the same shoe, like the converging of the twain, and the sisters laughed.

"Is it possible she envies you?" Anne asked.

"Just possible," Charlotte said wryly, "though it's hard to imagine." Charlotte was an old maid, living below stairs, with only a few immortal jingles to her name. Florence had married, for better or for worse, as Ma and society said every woman ought to do, even now when women's suffrage and world peace had been won at such great costs.

CHAPTER 43

Anne stood at her easel and Charlotte sat at the small table in the center of the studio. The morning before, on the second anniversary of Armistice Day, The Cenotaph was unveiled in a ceremony commemorating those who had perished in the Great War. Designed by Edwin Lutyens, the memorial was erected in the carriageway of Whitehall Street. The stone column was rectangular and stood thirty-five feet. THE GLORIOUS DEAD was etched on each of the two shorter sides of the column. At the top of the column lay a stone casket, symbolizing the resting place of the soldiers whose graves were in foreign fields.

Anne sketched the statue from memory, using a charcoal pencil and a large canvas. Though she usually sketched and painted flowers, not buildings or statues, she and Charlotte had attended the dedication, along with thousands of other Londoners, and Anne was moved by all the people who brought wreaths of roses, violets, and laurel to rest at the base of the statue.

Charlotte scribbled on a blackboard. She wanted to write a poem titled "The Cenotaph," but so far, she had only the title and the image of the statue in Anne's sketch. The casket itself reminded Charlotte of the upper half of a piano. She sketched a piano (or what looked like a piano to her) on the blackboard, then a column beneath it as if a stand.

"The Cenotaph memorializes the dead," Anne mused, stepping back from her sketch, "but it's all those loved ones left behind who are truly pitiful."

"I couldn't have said that better myself," Charlotte said. The sisters hadn't lost any family in the war, and as a non-combatant, Charlotte wasn't sure she was entitled to write a poem about the war. But she had met and talked to hundreds of war wives and widows, and it was for them as much as anyone that The Cenotaph had been built, erected and unveiled.

She erased her drawing of a piano with her fingertips. In three days, she would turn fifty years old. "I don't understand how anyone can go on, except that he has no choice," Charlotte said.

"It's ironic, isn't it? The statue reminds us of what we can't forget," Anne replied. She was sketching wreath after wreath at the foot of The Cenotaph.

"Governments roll on, commerce continues, families eat their suppers at 5 o'clock sharp following table grace. None of it makes sense. Shouldn't the world have ended?" said Charlotte. She wrote "lonely hearths" on the chalkboard.

"Yes, after so many people have died, living seems unconscionable," Anne agreed.

"Years from now, do you suppose people will remember The Cenotaph's designer?" Charlotte asked.

"Are you asking why we create art in the face of so much destruction?" Anne replied.

"Honestly? I was thinking of Father. Remember in those last years his attempting in vain to make sure he was credited for the buildings he had designed?" Charlotte asked.

"He was obsessed," Anne said, "even on his deathbed."

Charlotte remembered the days and nights spent at her father's bedside while he wasted away from cancer and, with the little strength he had, raved about how his name had been left off this or that building.

"Have you forgiven him?" Anne asked, sitting down across from Charlotte, the charcoal pencil still in her hand.

"For dying?" asked Charlotte. She wrote *DEATH* on the chalkboard.

"For selling your piano," Anne said.

"Technically, it was his," Charlotte said, writing over *DEATH* in bigger and bigger letters. "And I know we needed the money after Henry and then Freda went into the hospital."

"But he'd given the piano to you. It was *yours*. He might have asked you," Anne replied.

"I was never any good at piano," Charlotte said. "I learned the notes, but I never had any passion for them."

"But you liked to play," Anne said.

"I wasn't any good, so playing was easy," Charlotte explained.

"And writing?" Anne asked.

Charlotte laughed. "Let's say that I enjoy having written something worth reading. And I do have a passion for the sound of language."

"That's how I feel about painting," Anne said, and stood. "I love the moment after hours of working on a canvas when the painting suddenly appears to me and then it's just a matter of finishing it." She looked at her easel. The Cenotaph was perfectly executed, so that Charlotte thought she was looking at a photograph. The statue looked like a broadsword, whose hilt was at the point of the sword and formed the casket, rather than forming part of the handle at the sword's base.

Charlotte ran the chalk sideways across the blackboard. *DEATH* disappeared under a haze of white chalk. But Charlotte still felt its presence everywhere. Despite the beauty and sentiment of The Cenotaph, she believed the dead lay unrequited in their graves and that those left behind to live bled to death slowly from the thrust of an inward sword.

CHAPTER 44

Harold and his estranged wife had divorced, and Alida, who had wanted to marry Harold since they first met, finally convinced him to marry her.

"You must feel so very sorry for Alida," Sidney said, "knowing that her new husband balked at the prospect of their honeymoon." Sidney and Charlotte were dining at Les Gobelins, Sidney's favorite London restaurant.

"Anything worth having typically proves illusory or fleeting," said Charlotte. She admired a tapestry (beautiful, but imitation) on the wall, in which a long-haired maiden fed a unicorn from her hand. "Then again," Charlotte continued, "Alida knows both Harold's virtues and his vices. She might have been disappointed, but she couldn't have been surprised." Though she knows some of his vices, Charlotte thought, his dependency on Scotch, for instance, Alida couldn't possibly know who Harold really was or she wouldn't have married him.

The fighting had ceased in November of 1918, but the official end to the war hadn't come until the first meeting of the League of Nations, held in London that January in 1920. Like the marriage contract between couples, the League promised to bind the great nations in a union, and, in doing so, prevent another world war. Mutual interests will shield the world against further bloodshed, the League prophesied.

"But wasn't it alliances among nations that caused the war?" Charlotte asked Sidney.

"Nationalism is a delicate balance," said Sidney, "between the identity and power of a given political state and the identity and power of other political states." Sidney paused. "At least so my friends who understand these things tell me."

Sidney continued. "I understand it best when I think of it in terms of the holdings of various museums."

Charlotte smiled. Sidney was in his element.

"Though individual museums who share specializations compete with one another to acquire artifacts, they depend on one another to buttress the overarching culture of holdings and to promote its appreciation by patrons, investors, and, of course, lay visitors to the museums."

"I see," Charlotte said. But she didn't see. Civilization had nearly met its end, and no alliance or delegation or treaty had prevented it, only a final pecking order of conquered and conqueror.

Marriage, like nationalism, was a delicate balance, thought Charlotte. She walked that April day by Red Lion Square and Alida's small but dear flat, where Charlotte might drop in at odd hours. "But not on this day or at this hour," Charlotte said to the gray squirrel monkeying above her on a telephone wire strung between the modest building of flats facing the square. Progress, thought Charlotte, at the cost of an unhampered view of London's skies.

She kept walking without a particular destination in mind. She had believed Alida and Harold might content themselves as devoted companions without adopting the monikers of Mr. and Mrs. They had married without religious ceremony, pomp, or even guests at the Clerkenwell register office, and at the news, Charlotte had sent Alida her best wishes: "Dear Alida, with all my heart I wish you happiness, and if it is not fatally bad for you, your heart's desire."

What desire of Charlotte's hadn't been fatal to her? Yet, at the same time, her desires had been life itself, and she had known, truly *known*, "everlastin' as the sea."

Alida might love Harold, but she would never know Harold. Not all of him. Maybe the same could be said of any couple. Harold must keep certain secrets, hidden deep in his heart, to curate his part of the social institution of marriage, not to mention Alida's peace of mind.

Alida was in Sussex at the Monros' honeymoon cottage. When the crockery was laid in, Harold would appear, sheepish and apologetic, and more ashamed, Charlotte foresaw, than Alida, guileless and unsuspecting, could possibly imagine. The two might be as happy together as they'd always been, sharing their days, and nights, as one.

She stood before the Mews' old house on Doughty Street, not remembering the route she took in getting there. Fred's and Anna Maria's marriage had been an uneven yoking. Early on, Charlotte imagined, looking up at the dormer windows of the attic rooms, they had declared a truce for the children's sake. She thought of Florence and Hardy, another couple of Victorian propriety. Still, they were a couple, whether a well-matched or ill-matched set.

She walked around the railings of Mecklenburgh Square, next to Doughty Street. How Ma had hated being so close yet so far from a good address. Now, as when they were children, the square's garden was restricted to those tenants who lived in the properties on the square. She hadn't understood, nor had Henry, Anne, or Freda, why they couldn't roll in the manicured grass in spring like the other children they saw behind the bars.

"Think of them in prison," Nurse Goodman advised, "and yourself on the outside, free as birds, looking in." If she were a bird, Charlotte had imagined, she could fly in and out of the garden, lighting on this or that tree as she chose. But she had bitten her tongue, knowing Nurse Goodman would scold her if she said anything.

Nurse Goodman's advice was a cold comfort, but she had embraced it, as had Anne. There were compensations, after all, such as the paints and glue, the poster board and writing tablets, up above the square in the attic rooms, where they could look through the skylight on cloudless nights and count the stars. The magic of childhood had been the mutual passion of the Mew children. They had slept under covers and waited together year-round for Christmas morning, until they discovered Father Christmas was only the make-believe of adults.

Because of her parents' unhappy marriage, not entering that adult world of marriage and its half-truths hadn't seemed like a loss to Charlotte when she and Anne made their pact, even though Charlotte had desperately wanted her own children. Yet Alida and Harold had entered it. Harold and Alida had found a way, their own way, to be a couple. Theirs had been an unconventional relationship, and theirs would be an unconventional marriage, Charlotte knew. But they could keep a house and talk about poetry over breakfast, and perhaps even share a marriage bed.

Charlotte hadn't believed the war would continue without end, yet when the armistice came, she had been surprised. She knew Alida and Harold cared for one another, and she had imagined they'd run The Bookshop, side by side, as Alida Klementaski and Harold Monro even after the war. But that Alida and Harold would marry, that they *were* married, was outside of her comprehension of how things might be for those such as herself and Harold.

CHAPTER 45

Charlotte was released from behind number 9's prison bars when she could no longer refuse Sidney's invitation for a weekend in Cambridge. He cajoled her ever so gently by reminding Charlotte that she had, after all, taken the train all the way to Dorchester to visit Thomas and Florence Hardy. While she couldn't return Sidney's invitation in kind, she and Anne might have him again for tea at Hogarth Studios. Plus, Anne prodded Charlotte, wasn't she curious to see the domestic front of Sidney's Cambridge enterprise?

Kate Cockerell loomed large in Charlotte's imagination. Sidney, of course, spoke often of his wife, but Charlotte felt a tremor of fear at the near prospect of meeting her face to face. She didn't expect Kate Cockerell to be threatened or in turn territorial with Sidney, so why did Charlotte sense she was an interloper on a foreign land?

On the train, she pulled the shade of her carriage's window and shut her eyes against the light and her fears. *Thump thump, thump thump, thump thump* went the train over the tracks, or was it her apprehensive heart? She heard the rustle of a fellow passenger's daily newspaper and thought of Ma's crossword puzzles. Cross word, *thump thump*, cross word, *thump thump*.

Sidney's greeting at the Cambridge station buttressed her resolve. He took her small case and placed his hand on her elbow to guide her. "Kate says I must bring you straight home," he said as they walked to a taxi stand. Here I am, thought Charlotte, with toothbrush and change of clothes. If I'm turned out because I'm found wanting, I'll take a cab to the nearest hotel and say nothing to Anne or Ma.

Cambridge's streets, dressed in autumn's finest foliage, turned Charlotte's head in their grandeur. "It's a miniature London," Charlotte told Sidney as their cab wended its way through the narrow streets.

"Better," said Sidney, and Charlotte laughed. But as the cab slowed near a curb certain to be that of the Cockerells' home, Charlotte again felt the now familiar butterflies in her stomach and chest.

She and Henry as children had thought the little summer moths on the Isle were fairies because they fluttered rather than flew and because their wings were made of fine gold dust. Charlotte remembered catching one in her hand and her surprise at how strong its tiny body felt beating its wings against the confines of her fist, trying to escape. When she opened her hand, the fairy was only an insect, nothing but a dainty fly in a golden robe.

To match the season outside, the Cockerells' home was ablaze in rich golds, crimson reds, and browns. "Opulent" was the first word to Charlotte's mind. It wasn't an opulence bought for show, however, but one of exquisite taste effected through a patient diligence. The furniture, like that of The Poetry Bookshop, was at once substantial and spartan, but unlike The Bookshop's, the Cockerells' chairs and divans weren't shabbily worn but painstakingly upholstered and preserved in brocades and velvets.

A grandfather clock chimed the hour with great solemnity. "Your home is beautiful," said Charlotte, "simply beautiful." Beaming with pride in all things well made, Sidney blushed and smiled.

"Now," he said, following the tour of public rooms, "you must meet Kate and begin your lifelong friendship." Charlotte's pulse sang in her ear as Sidney led her to the back of the house and a room in its corner. He rapped on the threshold's dark trim, just as he had rapped on the door of Anne's studio the day they first met, and said, "Kate, I have someone special for you to meet."

A middle-aged woman with red hair gone almost gray rose gingerly from an armchair and made her way toward them, walking stiffly with a cane. "You must be Miss Charlotte Mew," Kate said before reaching Charlotte and Sidney, still standing in the doorway. "Welcome," Kate said, holding out her free hand to Charlotte, and with that gesture, all of Charlotte's butterflies folded their wings up over their backs and vanished.

Kate and Charlotte sat together in the back room, Sidney leaving them so he might catch up on a few things at the museum, and talked as if old friends. "I'm so pleased you've taken an interest in Sidney and his work," Kate said, as though Sidney were a charity case. But Kate, Charlotte felt, meant it as a compliment. "He works too hard and I'm no good any longer at socializing, not that I ever was, honestly." Kate gripped the head of her cane and Charlotte was reminded of her own horn-handled umbrella, forgotten at number 9 in Charlotte's anxious preparations only a few hours ago.

Kate was soft-spoken and, Charlotte realized, more painfully shy than even Charlotte herself. Her eyes were a clear blue and her luminous face, as if the moon itself, reflected the autumn light flooding the room through the tall windows. Kate didn't query Charlotte about anything other than Anne and Ma, their home in London (Charlotte did not mention the dungeon), and the time Charlotte spent as a child on the Isle of Wight, once Kate learned of it.

Their conversation was straightforward and unhurried, yet without a hint of idle small talk. Even speaking of the weather or the sky and its clouds with Kate, Charlotte quickly learned, was a simple pleasure, with rich undertones of having discovered the essence of living. Undoubtedly, Kate's sclerosis had limited her activities, but it had also clarified what was important to her, as well as having revealed the hidden heart of things. She is a kind, gentle soul, Charlotte later told Anne, and the better part of Sidney, despite his greatness.

"You will have to meet our children next time you visit," Kate said. "Today they're with friends who help out with them from time to time. The children, I know, will adore you." Kate reached out her hand to Charlotte a second time that day, and Charlotte took it with even greater gratitude. Kate expected nothing from Charlotte other than she be herself and asked only that she be allowed to do the same.

The next day, Sidney let Kate lead their conversation over tea, but he did cajole her into showing Charlotte one of her illuminations. "I feel like a fraud," Kate told Charlotte as if in apology as Sidney unveiled an illumination. Charlotte marveled at its colors and craftsmanship. "It's beautiful," she said, echoing her praise of Cambridge to Sidney only the day before, which now seemed weeks ago.

"I can't do the work any longer," Kate said, "and what is an artist without work at hand?" Charlotte looked at the head of Kate's cane and her hand, twisted as a plane tree's roots.

"I often feel a fraud myself," Charlotte confessed to Kate. Sidney had left the women to their conversation and to safely store one of the last works Kate was to create.

"You mustn't feel like a fraud," Kate exclaimed. "Look at all you've accomplished!" For some reason Kate's compliment struck Charlotte as absurdly funny, and she laughed. Kate, catching Charlotte's hilarity, joined her, and they both laughed until Charlotte hiccoughed. Soon Sidney stood in the doorway, asking what on earth they found so funny. "Life," Kate replied, and Charlotte hiccoughed again, then smiled because she and Kate were of one mind. And so the weekend Charlotte had so feared passed as if the pleasantest of dreams.

Charlotte meant to see Sidney off in the morning before taking a cab herself to the Cambridge train station. She woke late, however, and Sidney told her later that he hadn't wanted to disturb "the rest of the vanquished." She rose and dressed, then crept down the stairs to see if Kate was up. The front rooms were empty as was the back room where Charlotte met Kate. But the middle room, whose open door she peered in now, glowed with the morning light and its rich tapestries and wallpaper.

Sidney's study. A fire burned in the grate and laid out on his desk were stationery and a choice array of writing implements, left for Charlotte to exercise her craft should she choose. She took a seat on Sidney's throne, trying it on for size, and selected a scepter. She decided to wield her power for good and not evil, and wrote a letter feeling very regal indeed. But the sense of grandeur was ephemeral. Who was she, Charlotte Mew, to pretend she was anything but a middle-aged spinster lucky that a few of her jingles had drawn to her a circle of dear friends such as Sidney and now Kate?

She laid down her scepter, only a fountain pen, and looked to the grate and its coal fire. Kate hadn't needed to find her wanting, for Charlotte had found herself wanting. Her heart was as black as the hearth's andirons. She was wrong, a fraud, thinking a pen could be her scepter, and a moth a fairy, and with that thought, the spell of her magical weekend was broken.

She left Kate at the door of the Cockerells' home, wishing her well and thanking her for the lovely stay. Charlotte meant everything she said, and the warmth in Kate's eyes as she leaned on her cane and bade Charlotte farewell was a grace bestowed on her that Charlotte knew she could never deserve.

The train ride home gave Charlotte time for reflection. The truth was, despite Kate's hardships, Charlotte was envious of her. Not of Sidney, of course, not exactly, but of her marriage, her home, and her children. Kate had lived as an artist and as a wife and a mother, and it was only a physical ailment that had outwitted her. Charlotte felt a stab through her black heart. How small she was, and mean, to envy Kate absolutely anything, when she was so kind and so gentle?

Charlotte let herself in the back door of number 9. The dungeon was pea green, not gray, as she had always thought, and for the first time Charlotte saw below stairs for what it was: the reduced circumstances of three women alone in the world.

Ma and Anne were in the pantry-turned-sitting room, just as Charlotte had left them, Ma doing her crossword and Anne fussing over a needlepoint. She stood in the doorway of the pantry unnoticed, her case still in hand, and saw herself as square and useless as a third wheel — whether with Sidney and Kate, Alida and Harold, Florence and Hardy, or, in this moment, Ma and Anne, who continued to work their crossword and needlepoint in companionable silence, ignorant of Charlotte's presence just over their shoulders.

Standing there alone, Charlotte realized she had lived neither a life of love nor the life of an independent artist. She had been on a long journey, and she had returned, but she no longer recognized what she thought of for so very long and so fondly as home.

FAME (1921–1927)

CHAPTER 46

The spring of 1921, like the year before, found the Mews living below stairs with Jane, Charlotte having sublet the ground floor to a demobilized army sergeant, his wife, and their growing family of children. Ma still refused to acknowledge their living in the basement of a house whose five floors she had once been mistress of. Her invalid's sofa was installed in what had been the pantry, and she and Wek took up their daily residence within its windowless walls as if it were the front room on the ground floor above them. In the evening, Jane and Anne assisted Ma to a cot set up in one of two back rooms.

Anne and Charlotte slept in the second back room on cots like Ma's. These rooms had been the wine cellar and scullery and were as dreary as their names portended, despite their being made over by Anne with yellow paint and her best canvases of pansies. Jane, as she had for years, slept on her own cot in the front room beside the range, and during the day shared the kitchen with the sisters, who often sat at its dining table within reach of the light filtering down from the street.

For the Mews, entering or leaving number 9 meant using the backstairs or the servant's entrance in front, climbing up to the railings and street level as if "a mole from its hole," Ma complained. The sisters fostered the illusion for Ma's sake that they hadn't been shunted by dire straits into a basement that might just as well serve as a morgue as it had a servant's hall.

"It's like," Anne said to Charlotte, "the most interior chamber of a nautilus shell."

"Or," Charlotte added, "a Chinese box within a series of boxes, each smaller and more cramped."

"But the final box is the least cramped," Anne insisted, "because the boxes outside it house other boxes."

Charlotte smiled at Anne's persistent optimism. "We are fortunate," Charlotte admitted, "that you still have your studio."

"And you, the Gordon Square garden."

The new spring day held the last of winter in its roots, so the damp and cold of the earth rose through the pavements and soles of Londoners' shoes. It misted throughout the early morning hours while the sun kept its light to itself, and low cloud banks, like shorn wool in rippling heaps, massed above the pavements. But by late morning the clouds disappeared, themselves like sheep, straying over the distant horizon. Londoners slowed their gait to an amble as they turned their faces like daisies to absorb the spring sun's feather-light caress.

Below stairs, Charlotte and Anne watched the legs and hips of passersby. "Less is more" was fashion's cry. The waists of dresses had dropped, their skirts had risen, and the silhouette, though fuller, was made of less and lighter fabric.

"It's unsettling," Sidney remarked the week before, "to know women have legs the same as men."

"But not like men's," Charlotte joked, and Sidney, bless him, blushed.

Anne, looking pensive, sat at the dining table abstractedly shelling peas while Charlotte paced the length of the kitchen. Outside in Gordon Street, the decade yawned before London. It was a new era in which anything might happen, for better or for worse, and it struck Charlotte as she paced toward the light of the street, tinted by a green gauze curtain, that this decade's atmosphere mimicked the decade of her own 20's. Her young life was just beginning when Henry's and Freda's lives became unfurnished rooms, whose window shades were drawn against the too-bright light of the decadent 90's and the new century. But this new decade was not hers or Anne's or even Alida's, but a post-war generation's whose own youth may or may not uphold the decade's delicate promise in the face of all that had been lost.

Just as Charlotte turned from the green light of Gordon Street, Alida entered the kitchen from the passageway. Anne ceased shelling peas and reached out for Charlotte. Charlotte rested her hand on Anne's shoulder and looked in askance at Alida, who hesitated a moment before nodding.

"He didn't suffer, did he?" Anne asked.

"Not in the least. I'm certain," Alida said.

"Thank God," Anne said, letting out her breath. "He's at peace."

"Thank you," Charlotte told Alida. "We couldn't have managed things by ourselves."

"I've placed him in the box," Alida said. "If you'd like to see him one last time ..."

"You go, Charlotte," Anne said, looking up at Charlotte and patting the hand on her shoulder. "I couldn't bear to see him." Anne choked up but recovered herself. "Call me when you're ready."

Charlotte followed Alida to the back room where Anne's and her cot stood perpendicular to one another, so that the sisters slept with their heads together. Inside the door on a small table, Wek's cage stood empty. Beside the cage, a cardboard box rested, its lid ajar. A candle sputtered in the dampness of the room, striking Charlotte as a failed token of respect for Wek's passing. Alida gathered a sponge from the cage and the can of chloroform from a chair beside the table. She wrapped these in a thick towel as if contraband and left Charlotte alone.

Charlotte lifted the lid of the box. Inside, on a bed of blue silk prepared by Anne, lay Wek. His fragile form and stillness were so unfamiliar that she wondered if Alida hadn't replaced Wek's corpse with another bird's. But then she recognized the one lime-green feather on his chest, then his scaly beak and rheumatic claws, stiff even in life. "Wek," Charlotte said, gently ruffling the feathers of his head, "how will we know ourselves without you?"

She had believed, along with Anne and Ma, that Wek would outlive them all, staying on at number 9 through its flow of tenants, of which Anne and Charlotte and Ma were only three. The chloroform had been got from the corner chemist, along with the sponge. On her mission to gather the necessary supplies, Charlotte felt the eyes of the world on her.

"It's the damp of this dungeon," Ma said when Wek's rheumatism worsened and made it impossible for him to grasp onto his perch. Rather than sit on his long-held throne, Wek sat at the bottom of his cage. "A Kendall in disgrace," Ma said, "for the world to see. If it weren't for your father stealing me away from Brunswick Square," Ma continued, as if this had happened only yesterday, "none of us would have fallen so far." By this, Charlotte knew, Ma meant Wek to the floor of his cage, Ma to the basement of number 9, Anne and Charlotte, husbandless and childless, with her.

Charlotte looked to Wek one last time. His feathers were bedraggled and dull, and without his surly manner animating it, the corpse was just that, and no longer Wek. Charlotte closed the lid of Wek's coffin before snuffing out the candle.

Ma asked to sit in the back garden while Wek's "execution" took place. She never trusted the advice of the parrot keepers at the zoo, and their sentencing Wek to death as the only humane act convinced her finally of their utter incompetence.

Charlotte called to Anne and Alida, who followed her up the backstairs to the garden, where Charlotte had dug a grave for Wek beneath the crab apple tree that morning. Ma sat facing away on a chair ten feet from the shallow hole. Standing over the grave, Wek's coffin in her hands, Charlotte thought of Henry and of her father. Henry had been dead for twenty years and her father nearly twenty-five. Though Wek never liked Henry or Fred or any man, for that matter, Henry had admired all birds, including Wek, for their ability to fly.

Charlotte stooped and placed Wek's coffin in the grave. She said, "Dust to dust, and ashes to ashes," before shoveling the waiting mound of earth over the coffin. Anne began to weep, and Charlotte stood, the shovel at her side.

"Say a prayer," Ma commanded, still refusing to face Wek's grave.

Charlotte looked to Anne. Anne wiped her eyes, folded her hands in front of her waist, and bowed her head. "May God keep us all, especially Father and Henry and you, William Ernest Kendall. Amen."

"Amen," Ma said and sniffed into a handkerchief.

The funeral procession, led by Charlotte, returned to the house, entrusting Wek to God and Mother Nature.

"Do you suppose there is a heaven for parrots," Anne asked Charlotte that night as they lay in their cots.

"Maybe not for parrots," Charlotte said, "but certainly for Wek."

An hour later, unable to sleep, Charlotte stared at the empty cage in the distilled light of the moon. In the shadows, she saw Wek as he looked when they were young. He perched on top of the cage with one claw, stretched his wings to his sides with the grace of a clown on the high wire, and squawked, "Isn't Wek a handsome boy?"

Charlotte asked the ghost of Wek, "Who will keep us in our place?" Hearing nothing but Anne's breathing, and suddenly missing Wek's irritating little voice, Charlotte cried out, "Nothing will be the same again," and she wept until she fell into a restless sleep.

CHAPTER 47

Why should the world that once held Charlotte's offering of *The Farmer's Bride* only long enough to flip through a page or two, close it triumphantly as proof that Charlotte Mew, like most scribblers of poems, said nothing of importance to them, then rest her book again on the stack, ask for another edition five years later?

Charlotte suspected that Harold Monro had convinced the editors at Macmillan in New York City that readers were nostalgic for an older, saner world, the world they remembered existing before the inexplicable horror of the war. Hence, Harold wanted to publish a new edition of *The Farmer's Bride* in England and Macmillan wanted to publish a separate edition, titled *Saturday Market*, in America. Both the British and the American editions were to include the original seventeen poems and eleven new ones.

She held out no hope for positive reviews or sales, and any bid for recognition, let alone fame, had died with the last decade. Like love, Charlotte thought, fame had passed her door, knocked and even wished her a good day, but neither love nor fame had stopped and acknowledged Charlotte by name.

The new editions would prove to be short-lived shooting stars, Charlotte imagined, just as the poem "The Farmer's Bride" and the first edition of the book had been. After all, that her little poems, whose hope was as thin as the lines making up a life (or trying to make up for a life half-lived through a heart's experiments in verse), should outlive the dead — those killed outright in the war and those who survived only to scavenge in the margins of half-lives — was, she knew now, just as she had known then (whether or not she had admitted it to herself), ridiculous.

She looked around at the attic's contents. Soon, very soon, the Mews must find another home and live within its rooms. No place they leased would house the attic's remains. They could store all of it, but for what purpose? To leave in their wills? For whom? They could find the castoffs homes elsewhere. They could, if necessary, sell everything at auction, used household goods set out on a lawn for bored strangers to wend their way through as if so much flotsam cast by the sea onto the shore.

Suddenly, Charlotte imagined the tide rise beneath her feet. She saw the sea nip the legs of the dressers and bedsteads, then lift a felt hat onto its shoulders. Wek's cage bobbled and fell when a wave upended its stand. Charlotte heard a trunk housing her manuscripts groan as the fingers of the swirling waters fumbled with the leather straps and picked its lock. A cry escaped the trunk, and Anne's head bobbed up just beyond it.

"Charlotte," the severed head said, "Charlotte?" Anne's voice echoed from where she stood on the attic stair.

"Yes, Charlotte said," relieved that her dear sister hadn't drowned at sea, even in Charlotte's imagination. Anne finished her climb and wended her way toward Charlotte.

"I thought you'd taken up with gypsies," Anne said, "packed it in and run away. Then I remembered it was in the attic rooms that you most liked to think."

"I've decided," Charlotte said, her voice as rough as always, yet clear above the retreating surf, "to fight Poseidon for the lives of eleven more of my poems."

Anne, missing the allusion but understanding the gist, smiled.

Charlotte couldn't, she knew, save the family's household goods from dispersion, but she could gather eleven more of her poems along with those published originally in *The Farmer's Bride* and give them a new home in the world. Like the poems published before them, the new poems would be silently jilted, but in that silence, they might rest safe and sound, entombed and forgotten, as the new decade, its generation's songs composed in an altogether different meter than the last generation's, bounded ahead to meet the dizzying future.

CHAPTER 48

In late July 1921, four months following the publication of *The Farmer's Bride*, Charlotte received a letter postmarked New York City. Inside, the letterhead read: LOUIS UNTERMEYER. He wrote: "I reproach myself because of my ignorance of your work, an awareness that was only made conscious a year ago.... Now that Macmillan have brought out *Saturday Market*, we experience a wave of relief not unmixed with triumph." He thanked her for "the really great feelings — pleasure is too thin a word — you have given us" and called her poetry "rich emotional communication."

He enclosed a clipping of a review he had written, in which he argued that her poetry had been overlooked by the editors of the *Georgian Poetry* anthologies. In part, the review read: "... but what makes the Georgian anthologies so misleading and actually misrepresentative is not the vapidity of their inclusions but the number — and the quality — of their damning omissions. One looks vainly ... for the burning penetrations of Charlotte Mew ..." Before closing his letter, Mr. Untermeyer asked that Charlotte send him three poems for the anthology *Modern British Poetry*, which he was editing.

Charlotte knew that Louis Untermeyer was a renowned anthologist, critic, and editor, not to mention a poet himself. His anthologies introduced American and British schoolchildren alike to the best thought and said in English letters and poetry. To have one's poems anthologized by Untermeyer, the prestigious tastemaker, was to have truly arrived. Charlotte reread his letter a number of times before its reality sunk in and she was ready to share the news with Anne and Sidney, as well as Alida and Harold, all who were elated for Charlotte and congratulatory but "hardly surprised," as Alida said.

Charlotte was glad for the confidence that Mr. Untermeyer's letter instilled in her, especially when a month later a parody of Charlotte's poetry appeared in *Punch*, a longstanding weekly magazine with a circulation of over 100,000 copies that featured humor and satire. Titled "The Circus Clown," the parody lampooned "Fête," "The Quiet House," and "The Forest Road," among other poems of Charlotte's. Charlotte was mortified. She sat at the Mews' kitchen table with Anne, the magazine between them.

> *The moonlight drips on the parlour floor;*
> *I shall go mad if no one wipes it up.*
> *When I was one year old Nurse used to say,*
> *"It's no more use to cry when milk is spilt*
> *Than cry about the moon.*

The poem continued across fifty-nine lines, poking fun at her poems' use of the color red and her love of French phrases.

Anne peeled potatoes for their supper. "The second edition of *The Farmer's Bride* has attracted a lot more attention than the first, and it has sold remarkably well. Perhaps you could think of the parody as the price of success," Anne suggested.

Charlotte cut the potatoes in half, then into quarters. "You mean 'the punishment' for success."

"I don't know," Anne said. "You might even sell more books. After all, everyone reads *Punch*."

Charlotte groaned. "I'll be the laughingstock among the Gower Street girls."

"I imagine so. But isn't laughter the point?" Anne asked.

"Not at my expense," Charlotte said, loading the potatoes into a stew pot. "At least Ma will never need to see it."

"Oh, she already has," Anne said, looking up from the potato peelings. "She thought the parody was even cleverer than your poems."

Charlotte laughed nervously. "I can't imagine her reading my poems, let alone appreciating them."

"Ma is full of secrets," was all Anne would say.

Three days later, Charlotte sought out Sidney's opinion. "My dear Charlotte," he said, smiling, "next to imitation, parody is the sincerest form of flattery. Like it or not, you're a minor celebrity, and with Louis Untermeyer's endorsement, even a household name."

By the time she received a second letter from Louis Untermeyer, just a week after the parody appeared in *Punch*, she was willing to view the episode with a sense of humor. After all, Thomas Hardy and Alfred Noyes had been parodied the month before in a poem titled "The Two Shepherds." In short, Charlotte admitted that she was in the best possible company.

In his letter, Mr. Untermeyer thanked Charlotte for her own letter and the poems she had sent to him and informed her that *Modern British Poetry* would be published in a year. He also said that he and his wife, Jean Starr, would be spending "1923 abroad ... unless God, my associates and the seamen interfere." He closed his letter by opening the doors to his home should Charlotte ever visit New York City, "these not inhospitable shores," and by calling himself and his wife "ardent admirers of Charlotte Mew."

As she had so many times before, Charlotte marveled at the many friends that her "immortal jingles" had brought into her life. How could a parody of her poetry, or even fame, outweigh those kind friendships?

CHAPTER 49

Having survived the length of their Gordon Street lease, the Mews admitted, finally, that they must leave number 9, and all of its rooms, for good. The house fit them like a second skin, molding itself to their lives over thirty years just as Charlotte's doll-sized boots had done her feet.

In these shoes, Charlotte walked the pavements, competing with like-situated Londoners living in the waning weeks of an outgrown lease. A woman in her 50's, Charlotte was invisible to the youth who made their restless home in the new decade. For once, she was thankful for her invisibility because it worked to halve her self-consciousness and its accompanying voice telling her, again, that she was altogether wrong. But her invisibility also afforded Charlotte the opportunity to observe the bright young women of this new world and see them as reflections of her twenty-something self in the 90's.

Today women walked London's streets unchaperoned. Their smart cloche hats were the envy of Anne, Charlotte knew, as were their heels and stockings, which Edwardian skirts, more fitted but also heavier and longer, had refused to reveal. These women linked arms on their lunch hour from secretarial and nursing jobs, looking for flats with rooms enough for two women, while Charlotte searched by herself for a flat with rooms enough for three women, two sisters and their mother, all fading souvenirs of another generation.

Indeed, if they looked at Charlotte as a mirror of the past, they saw a fading silvered complexion easily mistaken for a ghost or a woman out of time. They would not see her as a New Woman of the 90's, her latchkey and cigarettes in hand, as she boldly strode the pavements, bound for a life, she was sure, entirely different from her mother's, or any other Kendall woman's, except in its propriety. Then and now, she was liberal in her attitude and hopes for women as professionals outside the home, but she was also a Kendall, at heart, and so a good address mattered. And so it fell on Charlotte to find rooms for the Mew women, rooms, however shabby otherwise, that passed as a good address in a polite society that was quickly disappearing.

It was only when Charlotte felt near defeat that she stumbled upon the rooms on Delancey Street, next to Regent's Park and her old haunt, the zoo. And shabby they were. The flat roosted on top of a house. There were two proper rooms, two attic rooms, and a makeshift kitchen in miniature. The whole of the Mews' new home, in fact, was like the upper stories of a doll's house, opened on its hinge.

The next day Anne asked, "Is it too dear?" They stood on the threshold, peering into their future.

"Yes," Charlotte said, "I'm afraid it's here or the streets, however, so I'm counting us lucky."

"Ma won't like the stairs," Anne said.

"No," Charlotte agreed. They stood in the main rooms at the foot of the stairs to the attic. She could sleep here," Anne offered, "if necessary."

"And Wek?" Charlotte asked. Before Anne could gently remind her of Wek's passing, Charlotte added, "Would he approve, I wonder?"

It was Anne's turn to say no. "Ma and he would be in agreement that no address besides Buckingham Palace would suit a Kendall. Still, the king might envy this view," Anne said honestly. They stood at the windows overlooking Regent's Park. The green canopies of trees in the afternoon light appeared as lacework sewn by the sun. Charlotte looked instead at the shuttered windows of the house across the street, just below where they stood.

"Charlotte?" Anne asked, breaking the elder sister's reverie.

"Yes, Anne," she replied, which meant neither Wek nor his king might prefer the Gordon dungeon and its view from below stairs of London's ever burgeoning foot and automobile traffic, but which Charlotte and Anne still thought of as home.

Strange men went in and out of Gordon Street, empty-handed one way, encumbered the other. Watching two men shoulder Ma's sofa from her vantage point at the curb, Charlotte saw the weight of the Mews' past in the familiar possessions. Some, like Ma's sofa and Wek's cage, the women had lived with day-in and day-out for thirty years; others, like the dollhouse built by Fred Mew, had traveled from the Doughty Street nursery in its attics to the attics in Gordon Street, where Charlotte presided over them in her vagabond travels under the skylight. And, indeed, it was as if the contents of a time-traveling caravan had been swept out onto London's pavements, looking displaced in the open air.

The five men from the removal company argued what should go where in the lorry, so finally, ending a skit comical to anyone but the Mew women themselves, the smallest of the men, his cap askew as he scratched his head, decided they should deposit all the goods on the walks before loading the lorry. Anne, bemused or dismayed, came to Charlotte on the curb to relay the news. Having decided there wasn't any farther they might climb down, given they had lived in the dungeon the last few years, Charlotte only said that she was glad Ma was in the back garden waiting for their sentence to be executed.

The men grouped the items according to the labels the Mews had affixed over the preceding weeks, often deliberating longer than was worthwhile over what should move with them to Delancey Street, what they might afford to store (for what future, they dared not discuss), and what they must leave to the auction block.

The day was overcast, and it was unusually warm for late spring, without even the slightest breeze. But it wasn't humid, and the sky held no threat of more than a fine mist. So that Gordon Street's traffic wasn't hindered, the two removal lorries pulled onto the curb and waited for the Mews' household goods. As the three groupings of the Mews' possessions gathered, Charlotte and Anne could only watch as passersby wended their way through London's quaintest labyrinth.

An older gentleman, in a black bowler hat, poked at an armchair with his cane. "What you give for this," he asked a woman he mistook for the possession's mistress, and she said to him, her nose in the air, "Why, I never." The bowler-hatted man looked amused as he continued to pick his way through the Mews' possessions, stopping to poke one thing or another as if a standing ashtray and a dress form were daisies along a country lane.

Charlotte and Anne watched and laughed, invisible to the man from their lookout behind a china hutch, whose left door had "auction" posted on it, as did the armchair that the older gentleman had queried the indignant woman about.

The day, despite the movers' confusion and the unplanned airing of all their worldly possessions outside Gordon Street, was anticlimactic given the emotional cost exacted from sorting their past the preceding weeks. At the center of the tribunal was Ma, sure everything must be stored and nothing surrendered to the auction house, whose proprietor couldn't know this vase's historical value or that damask curtain's original cost.

"Ma," Anne said gently, "think how much joy the young marrieds will get from the lazy Susan."

Less diplomatic, Charlotte said, "What we take or we store must be offset by what we auction. Storage is dear and our four rooms on Delancey will hold us and what we need, no more."

But each woman was guilty of finding herself inseparable from this or that cherished item. For Ma, it was Wek's cage. For Anne and Charlotte together, it was the dollhouse Fred Mew had made and which had kept itself in the attic rooms at Gordon Street year-in and year-out, without having been so much as peeked in. Yet, like Gordon Street's itself, the dolls' furniture had fallen into disrepair (through fairies' use?) or was lost to time.

As the Mew tribunal held court regarding the fate of moth-eaten umbrellas and handmade doilies, Wek's old haunt and Fred Mew's only work as a builder-in-miniature stood daring the women to forsake them. They were nearly the same dimensions, suggesting to Ma that one be kept with them or stored and the other auctioned.

"Ma," Anne said, now less diplomatic than reasonable, "Wek's new home is heaven. He wouldn't expect us to take this old cage with us. He would understand, of course, that we've only so much room in our own new home."

Charlotte always disliked Wek's cage, just as she disliked all bird cages. Birds, whether or not they were domesticated parrots, should be free to fly. But she said obligingly, "Perhaps Wek has a distant cousin," meaning another parrot living out his days in London, "who needs this cage as his new home."

Ma guffawed. "Don't patronize me, girls. Charlotte, you'd give Wek's cage to the zoo's parrot house, and I won't have it. Anne, you'd use the cage for an art project, and I won't have that. Wek is not in heaven. He's buried in the back garden under the tree with those rotten crab apples. I can't take Wek with me. But I won't leave what I have left of him behind."

Ma's demand was ridiculous, and despite her age and status as their mother, Charlotte was determined that Wek's cage, though it might be stored, would not accompany them to Delancey Street when so much else must be sacrificed.

But then something happened that made Charlotte and Anne happy they could concede to Ma's impractical demand.

It was the morning after their failed tribunal on the fate of Wek's cage and Fred Mew's dollhouse. "Charlotte," Ma asked, "could you collect a box from on top of Grandma Kendall's china hutch in the attic? It has some things in it that I'd like to keep."

Charlotte discovered the red box Ma described on top of two floral hat boxes. But even by stepping up on a stray dining room chair, its wood squeaking under Charlotte's slight weight, the red box exceeded her reach.

Anne, a head taller and with longer arms, reached the red box after Charlotte found a step stool, built by Henry, sturdier than the stray squeaking chair. Charlotte took the box, which was as light as the hat boxes Anne handed her in turn. They set the red box on the tired chair, which accepted it without complaint.

The sisters each lifted the lid of a hatbox to discover, of all things, hats.

"Look at this one," Anne squealed. She removed the hat pin and placed the hat on her head, but not until she had examined it, turning the oversized purple object in her hands, its ostrich feather as ostentatious as it was intended forty years ago.

"Just the style, yes?" Anne asked Charlotte, giggling.

"Especially the worn brocade and moth-eaten brim," Charlotte replied, as if she knew or cared for fashion.

"Try yours on," Anne excited, demanded.

The blue hat's brim was shorter than Anne's, but its bonnet was taller.

"It's almost as if the milliner fashioned a bowler for women," Anne exclaimed, admiring the smart pleats and the designer's restraint. "It must be from the 90's or later," Anne explained. "It looks almost smart on you, Charlotte!"

There was no mirror in the attic to be uncovered, so Charlotte took Anne's word. "Whose hats do you suppose these were?" Anne asked, taking hers off to turn it in her hands.

"They must have been Ma's, I should think," Charlotte said.

"I can't recall Ma ever wearing hats like these," Anne said, "especially not the blue hat."

That afternoon, they asked Anna Maria about the owner of the hats, but she waved them off as she took the red box and opened it on her lap. "Go now," she said, as simply as that. She was on her invalid's sofa in the old pantry, so the girls left her.

The next day Charlotte remembered the hats, then the red box and Ma's eagerness to examine its contents in private. Ma had been somewhat listless that morning when Charlotte got her up, but by late afternoon she was more irritable than usual.

Over tea, she asked Charlotte, "You didn't take anything from the box, did you?" Her voice was both menacing and hopeful.

"No, Ma, of course not," Charlotte said.

"Unless you mean the hats from the other boxes. But we returned them," Anne said.

Ma sat back, despondent.

"What is it, Ma?" Anne asked. The sisters looked at one another in curiosity and concern.

Ma waved the question away like she had their questions the day before, but this time without the same intensity.

It wasn't until that evening that Ma confessed to them in a small voice they had never heard her use. "All these years I thought it was there, under the lid of the red box, waiting."

"What," Anne asked, "what was there?"

They sat with Ma after dinner. Jane was washing up the dishes on the sideboard, since the scullery was now the sisters' room.

There was a third wave of the hand. But this time she went on, talking to them or to herself, they weren't sure.

"It's not important. It was only everything for a while, and, you see," she looked at them, "I thought I'd like to remember it one last time before I was to leave."

"Before you were to leave, from Gordon Street?" Anne asked quietly.

Ma said nothing.

"We could help you look for it if we knew what it was," Charlotte offered.

But Ma only shut her eyes, and the subject, the sisters knew, was closed.

And that is how Wek's cage traveled with the Mews to Delancey Street. "We mustn't," Anne said, "deny her the comfort of Wek's cage." Charlotte nodded. She understood the nature of disappointment and of secrets, as well as the sanity that compensations, however inadequate, might restore.

CHAPTER 50

Whereas Gordon Street faced east, Delancey Street faced west. Ma said she preferred the gentler light of "our old home," but she didn't complain. Their rooms on Delancey Street were decidedly warm and bright, in the afternoon because of the setting sun, in the morning because their rooms, at the top of the house, reached into the sky as if they were Charlotte's beloved plane trees. Despite the cheeriness of their new home, Charlotte missed the garden of Gordon Square, no longer her second room, though not that far of a walk from Delancey Street.

"I feel," Anne told Charlotte, "as if we're floating in the sky."

They were having tea in the round yellow light of a July afternoon. Ma was upstairs in her bedroom, choosing a nap over tea. Jane, as she promised, had moved home to care for her own mother, now that the Mews no longer needed her services.

Charlotte replied, "It does seem like we've moved from a mouse's hole to an eagle's nest. You like it, don't you?"

"I do," Anne said brightly, "though of course it's a bit farther from the studio and even smaller than our dungeon at number 9. And you, Charlotte, do you like it?"

"Yes," Charlotte said. But she knew they were paying too much for rent and that other things, though what she didn't know, would have to be sacrificed sooner or later to make ends meet.

"If Ma hadn't had us, what might she have done, do you think?" Anne asked. It was another way around their conversation about Ma's secret treasure, lost for good, after years of her believing it was safe in the attic rooms of number 9.

"I wonder," Charlotte said, and stirred her tea.

The sisters sat in companionable silence, Charlotte musing on what might have been, just like she had done in the weeks before their move, as she sifted through possessions and memories at number 9. With chagrin, she remembered what she would have given for fame when she was twenty and believed she might escape Ma, and even Anne, to venture out into the world as Henry Harland told her she must if she hoped to be a success as an author. She had lived between worlds — Harland's flat and offices, where she thought of herself as "going places," and number 9, where she half expected to succumb to Henry's and Freda's fate.

"Remember," Anne said, gently interrupting Charlotte's musings, "to spend more time remembering good times than bad." Anne caught her eye, and Charlotte smiled. It was the advice Charlotte had offered to Anne when they were sorting a sheaf of Henry's drawings, which they came across in number 9's attic rooms. Most weren't of buildings, but of flying machines. Anne had saved the drawings and taken them to her studio.

"Good advice," Charlotte said, then returned to her musings. She was unable to find a place for all the memories stirred up by their move, both good memories and bad, so that one memory and then another surfaced. She feared that she had let Ma and Anne down all these years, having spent too much of her emotion on art for want of fame and then money. Yet Charlotte did enjoy the light of Delancey Street, and she hoped, floating here in the sky with Anne, that her memories from Gordon Street, which she had carried on her shoulders all these long years, might be laid to rest by the Mews' flight.

"I only wish," Anne said, pulling on a cloche hat that she had fashioned from knit remnants, "Ma was happier here." Anne left for the studio, the afternoon still her best time to paint, and Charlotte, content to sit in the sun and listen should Ma want help down the stairs, wondered if she would ever write another poem.

The next day, buoyed by hope and in uncommonly good spirits, Charlotte thought it was time she visit her old room on Gordon Square. Anne was up early and sitting in the Delancey Street's morning light. Ma, still as subdued as she had been since their move, worked the crossword puzzle on her invalid's sofa.

Change, thought Charlotte, as she walked west on Delancey, could be heartening. She made her way down Hampstead Road toward North Gower Street. Near Euston Road, she began to appreciate the breezy day, the summer fashions of her fellow pedestrians, and the darkening foliage of the trees.

In the shifting breeze, Charlotte heard what sounded like Uncle's handsaw as he cut lumber into logs for firewood. But today Uncle's handsaw didn't compete with the yard hens clucking and squawking as Aunt scattered their feed but rose above the motors and horns of automobiles on Euston Road.

Charlotte looked up to see a limb from the upper boughs of a plane tree swinging unnaturally from a rope, as if the broken arm of a man. Her heart pounded in her chest as she walked faster toward the scene and was nearly run over by a lorry at a crossroads.

Growing nearer, she saw men on the ground yelling to other men at the top of the trees. Charlotte asked a passerby what was happening. The man stared at Charlotte through his monocle before walking on, the look in his eye reflecting the absurdity of her question.

She joined a group of onlookers who watched as the tallest of the plane trees was dismantled. The limbs and boughs and then portions of the trunk were lowered in jerking motions to the ground, where men wrestled with branches in full leaf to drag them to other men who reduced them to smaller and smaller bits. Over the drone of the back and forth of the saws, the men whooped and hollered as the great tree was felled.

"A jolly good system that is," the man standing to Charlotte's right said to no one.

A woman asked, "Why are they felling the trees?"

A young girl, presumably the woman's daughter, said what Charlotte herself was thinking. "It seems so sad to kill them when all their leaves are green."

The man to Charlotte's right said finally, in answer to the woman and her daughter, "Progress comes in flats these days. Of course, if Londoners could live in trees," the man added, "we wouldn't have to fell them."

"Stuff and nonsense," a second man snorted. "Any tree in London is living on borrowed time. They should have been removed long ago. Every last one of them."

Charlotte grew weaker as she continued watching the trees come down, feeling altogether pathetic in her powerlessness to end the slaughter. She turned her face. Half afraid that the plane trees of Gordon Square were meeting the same fate, Charlotte hurried south on Gordon Street, the sawing accompanying her as if it were her own body the men trespassed.

Three days later, on a Saturday morning, Charlotte sat in Christ the King Chapel across from the stained glass of "God," a grove of trees in various shades of green dress. Her trees, the plane trees of Gordon Square, just across from the chapel, stood untouched, while half a mile to the north, the fate of the plane trees of Euston Road had been executed. In the trees' stead lay a bare plain, except for countless stumps and a growing number of construction materials and men.

The last few nights, she had dreamt of men, on scaffolds the height of Big Ben or the Tower of Babel, sawing apart the sky. Birds, unable to fly in the sky or roost in the trees, took to walking the pavements with other Londoners, their wings idle appendages.

This morning, she woke before dawn and lay in her cot listening. She felt something gathering in her chest, like a flock of displaced rooks congregating in a stand of trees. Rooks caw to one another in their colonies. A rook alone, however, will chatter to itself, sounding notes a passerby might mistake for words.

Just as she was powerless to save the plane trees of Euston Square, Charlotte was powerless to stop the chattering words from gathering themselves into a poem as she sat in the chapel. And just as the men had disassembled the plane trees with their whoops and grating saws, the poem assembled itself from the words coming to her unbidden.

"They are cutting the plane trees at the end of the gardens" introduced itself as the first line of a poem. Charlotte heard again the branches swish as they fell, the crash of the trunks, the rustle of trodden leaves, and the men as they *whooped* and *whoa'd*.

She closed her eyes and remembered the dead rat they saw one June day when Nurse Goodman, Charlotte, Henry and Anne arrived at Uncle's and Aunt's farm before Freda was born. "How's that for a greeting," was all Nurse Goodman said, until Charlotte reached down to pet the rat, and then Nurse added, cuffing Charlotte's hand, "A rat's not God's work, alive or dead."

How many years had Charlotte spent on the Isle of Wight or in her room at the Gordon Square garden or anywhere on the pavements of London lifted up whenever she looked to the top of a plane tree, particularly when it took a great gale blowing in from the sea, like a child catches a ball.

Charlotte opened her eyes and looked again to the grove of trees in the stained glass and felt her pulse beat with the heart of the planes and remembered the verse from Revelation: " — and he cried with a loud voice / Hurt not the earth, neither the sea, nor the trees —."

"The Trees are Down" was written and lay in the trunk in her and Anne's attic room. Though Charlotte didn't speak of the poem to Anne (or, of course, Ma), Anne had tiptoed around Charlotte the last few days, obviously sensing that she was living in the breath of a poem.

Anne was with Katherine Righton for a day at the galleries, followed by tea at Anne's studio. After her tea, Ma lost interest in the newspaper, and it lay on her chest as she dozed fitfully on her invalid's sofa. She slept most of her days now, but only off and on, so that she might wake suddenly and cry out in a soft voice, which Charlotte and Anne barely recognized as their mother's.

Charlotte sat by a window looking out at the tops of Regent Park's trees and the convent windows across the street. She mused over whether or not a poem was adequate compensation for its emotional cost. So much of life is loss, she thought. She looked to the shuttered windows of the convent, so like those she had thrown open on an overcast day in Paris, but an overcast day imbued with bright promise because Ella D'Arcy might look out onto the same day from her own Paris window.

CHAPTER 51

The easy days of The Bookshop were rarer and rarer, due partly to growing competition in the neighborhood and partly to Harold and Alida absenting The Bookshop at the same time. From February to April 1922, Harold checked himself into a clinic for the treatment of alcoholism and Alida went to France to get away from it all. She had been working sixteen-hour days at The Bookshop fulfilling every role from clerking to bookkeeping, and she was exhausted.

Before Alida and Harold left, Charlotte helped out when she could get away from Delancey Street. In spare moments, Alida confided in Charlotte, telling her how difficult it was to live with a complex personality like Harold's. "I'm never sure from one day to the next whether he'll be gloomy because the sky is falling or relentless because he views poetry as the only solution to the world's disillusionment. Though he and I talk and talk I'll never understand all of his personal demons."

Charlotte consoled her, assuring Alida that she wouldn't have it any other way. "I imagine," said Charlotte one late afternoon when they were closing The Bookshop together, "Anne could say the same thing about living with me, as I certainly can be difficult."

Alida looked at Charlotte in complete surprise. "But you're so protective of Anne. You always put her concerns first."

Charlotte patted Alida's arm. "Thank you for saying so. But even you must admit that I can be exasperating."

"You, Charlotte? Never." And they both laughed.

The last customer came up to the till to inquire about a book of poems. "Can you tell me," the man said, "whether or not you'd recommend this book? I read Edith Sitwell's positive review of it, but I'm still unsure." The man held *The Farmer's Bride* in his left hand.

"That depends," Alida said, "whether or not you prefer really good poetry."

Charlotte felt herself blush.

"Well, of course," the man answered as he put *The Farmer's Bride* on the counter to be rung up. Alida took the man's shillings as Charlotte packaged the book in brown paper and string. After the man left, Alida confessed that she was tempted to introduce the man to the book's author. "But I knew you would die of chagrin."

"Thank you for that," Charlotte said. "Though I appreciate the recognition *The Farmer's Bride* has brought me, I don't think I'll ever get used to the personal attention of strangers."

Charlotte caught an omnibus to Delancey Street. As the bus started and stopped to pick up or leave off passengers, Charlotte thought about how indebted she was to Harold for publishing and championing her poetry. But she worried about his influence on Alida. Though Charlotte believed Harold loved Alida, she no longer envied Harold's decision to live in a world of propriety and rules, a world he could never really be part of.

CHAPTER 52

Ma never regained her spirit after the contents of the red box were lost and their move to 86 Delancey Street was final. She slept or dozed in her bed up the attic stairs until midmorning when Anne or Charlotte helped her down them. At eighty-six, Anna Maria Kendall was nearly the age of Queen Victoria on her Diamond Jubilee, but there was no pageantry as Charlotte assisted Ma down the stairs this day or any other.

Anna Maria inched her way from the stair to her sofa, where she sat until she retired as early as late afternoon, refusing anything more for her evening meal than a cup of tea and half a biscuit, most of whose crumbs remained on the plate.

In between her morning crossword (usually left more than half incomplete) and late afternoon tea and biscuit, Ma lay on the sofa in her dressing gown, shawl, and slippers, where she gazed into the middle distance of the Mews' close living quarters, squinting her eyes shut like a cat. If Anne or Charlotte spoke to her, either she didn't hear or she ignored them.

Summer and autumn passed as Anna Maria faded with the seasons. By November's end, when the dim white light of winter crept nearer, Ma was a shrunken shade of her old self, and the sisters feared she was so slight and frail she might break. So they were alarmed but not surprised when on a blustery day at the beginning of December, with Old Man Winter shaking the panes as if to break in, Ma fell as Charlotte helped her up the stairs late in the afternoon. They were on the top stair, so Charlotte was able to grasp Anna Maria by the shoulders and carry her three feet to the cot, where Anna Maria quickly collapsed, moaning and grabbing at her leg. Anne was at her studio, so it was Charlotte who called Ma's doctor to Delancey Street, where he calmly diagnosed Ma's pain as a broken femur.

Bedridden, Ma needed constant care. A nurse in a starched uniform and white cap was engaged to help out during the day, urging Anna Maria to eat, administering her medicine, giving her sponge baths, and reading Dickens' *Great Expectations* to her whether Ma was awake or sleeping. The nurse read in the singsong voice one might use to read bedtime stories or nursery rhymes to a child and spoke in a much louder voice than Ma's hearing required. But in the sitting room by the window in the thin light of a January day, Charlotte enjoyed eavesdropping on Pip's adventures.

During the evenings, nights, and weekends, Anne and Charlotte kept watch, vigilant at making Anna Maria as comfortable as possible. This task was most difficult when Ma began mumbling and rambling in her sleep.

Charlotte would listen as she looked on Ma in her bed, her heavy covers pulled to her ears, her form under the covers looking like a lump in a poorly made bed. Charlotte tried to make out what her mother said, but understood only when she said "Freda" quite distinctly. Once Ma had settled in, Charlotte took herself down the stairs and sat at the window writing letters and sometimes scribbling stray phrases or lines of poems, often until 1 o'clock in the morning.

It was during one of these sessions after midnight that Charlotte wrote "Fin de Fête." It was a simple poem with three stanzas of four lines each. Staring at the shadowy moon, she thought of Ma, Anne, and Freda in their beds, each alone, and of how hard it was as a child to fall asleep, especially after the excitement of one's birthday or a day at the fair. The night, Charlotte decided, must be payment for the day, but even so, one mustn't grudge the score. It was something Nurse Goodman might have said after showing the children a picture book in the attic nursery of Doughty Street, the skylight revealing a full moon as it peeked at the Mew children saying their prayers before bed.

Charlotte once thought of Ma as a killdeer, its shrill call and low flight distracting passersby from its nest of young, hidden nearby in the hollow of a field or an outcropping of trees. Ma wanted Anne and Charlotte to remember that they were Kendalls. Fred Mew might have been that passerby, or the passerby might be anyone or anything that might steal Anne and Charlotte away from Ma, as Henry and Freda had been stolen. If Ma died, Charlotte thought now, she and Anne, no longer young and no longer daughters, would be left all alone in the world, vulnerable without their mother to protect them and to remind them who they were with her persistent, shrieking, and galling cries.

Ma regained some strength as her health improved, but the doctor remained only cautiously optimistic. "Her leg will never wholly mend and being bedridden makes her susceptible to flu and pneumonia, not to mention blood clots. Exercise her as much as possible, letting her balance herself on you and her cane," he instructed the sisters.

But early one morning in late spring, Ma's breathing grew labored and she complained of heaviness in her chest. "Pneumonia," the doctor said after listening to Ma's chest with a stethoscope. "I'm afraid the hospital is the only place for her now as she'll need constant care. You two," he said looking at Anne, then Charlotte, "have done your best."

In the hospital, Ma brightened for several days, enjoying, her daughters and nurses agreed, the attention. Sitting at her bedside, Charlotte watched as Ma dozed. In Charlotte's lap lay *Great Expectations*, brought to the hospital at Ma's request, so that Charlotte might finish reading it to her. But she had waved it away when Charlotte sat down. "Not today," she said. "I must talk to you."

A nurse came in to take Ma's temperature and give her medicine, and under the strain of these activities, still weak, Ma dozed off. Charlotte wondered if Ma wanted to talk about the red box. Charlotte saw Anna Maria then, wrapped in the shroud of white sheets except for the lace shawl about her small shoulders, her face as heavily lined and yellow as Miss Havisham's. Ma, however, had not been left at the altar. She had a proposal that she, an old maid in her late twenties, couldn't refuse. And so she had married beneath her station and never forgiven Fred Mew his effrontery. Had there been someone else Ma had loved, Charlotte wondered (but would never ask).

When Ma woke, she reached for Charlotte's hand but did not look at her. "Anne tells me," she began, "that your poetry book has done well, both in England and in America." Charlotte felt her pulse quicken, because her mother never spoke of her daughters' lives as professional women. "I want you to know I am proud." Ma squeezed her hand, and Charlotte realized just how weak Ma was. Charlotte's eyes filled with tears and burned. "I only wish," Ma continued, almost out of breath, "your book had the Kendall name."

Days later, her breathing labored, Ma lapsed in and out of consciousness before passing away in her sleep. Both Anne and Charlotte were at her side.

At home again on Delancey Street, where Ma's invalid sofa stood like a cenotaph in the sitting room, Anne cried and Charlotte fought off weeping so that she could comfort her sister. "We can't think only of her death. We must keep in sight the whole of her life," Charlotte said.

"You're right, of course," Anne said, then blew her nose in her handkerchief.

They didn't speak of the red box, which Anne found under Ma's bed after she had been taken to the hospital. Most things go unspoken, Charlotte knew. Whatever Ma's secrets, she had taken them to her grave, unshared and unforgiven. Charlotte wanted to tell Anne what Ma had said to her at the last, but she was afraid it would hurt her if Ma hadn't told Anne she was proud of her paintings.

Anne took Charlotte's hand. "Let's think of her with Wek and Henry, and with her own mother and sister."

"Yes," agreed Charlotte. In acknowledging Charlotte as a writer, Ma had reminded Charlotte one last time that she was a Kendall. But Charlotte thought, as she squeezed Anne's hand, of Anne and herself as the "Sisters Mew," together, but also alone.

CHAPTER 53

It was a celebratory lunch for a project that had been in the works for months. Though the project was Sidney's doing, Charlotte was to be the guest of honor. In attendance were Sidney, Anne, Florence Hardy, and Walter de la Mare. The December day was still, and a fine layer of hoarfrost lay on every surface. Charlotte worried less about slipping on London's pavements than embarrassing herself in front of Sidney. Though Sidney didn't know it, Walter de la Mare had turned down Charlotte's poems for inclusion in the bestselling *Georgian Poetry* anthologies, not once but twice, though years ago now.

Les Gobelins was busy with its faithful lunch crowd. But Sidney, who knew the owner, had reserved a table weeks earlier. Charlotte and Anne arrived at the restaurant before Mr. de la Mare or Florence. But Sidney was waiting anxiously for them in the front entrance. He asked the maître d' to seat Charlotte and Anne, insisting that he wait alone for the remaining guests.

Les Gobelins was stunning in its elegance. The place settings consisted of three white plates, each smaller than the next and nested one inside the other, a white cloth napkin folded in the shape of a swan, three forks, a knife and spoon, and two glasses. Charlotte and Anne took their seats. Though Charlotte had been to Les Gobelins a number of times with Sidney, this visit was Anne's first.

"I feel somewhat underdressed," she whispered to Charlotte.

"We can take comfort in the knowledge that no one dining at Les Gobelins will care enough to notice our clothes," Charlotte said, adjusting her scarf just so at Anne's words.

Sidney and Mr. de la Mare will notice," Anne said, "and so will Florence."

"Florence, bless her, won't judge us, nor will Sidney. Mr. de la Mare will have to take us as he finds us, in dated fashions the worse for wear."

As if on cue, the maître d' escorted Florence, Mr. de la Mare, and Sidney to their table. Mr. de la Mare bowed first to Charlotte, then to Anne, as Sidney introduced them.

Charlotte's nervousness fell away as the five chatted easily. When they both ordered the oyster stew, Charlotte complimented Mr. de la Mare on his good taste. "Likewise," he laughed. By the time they had finished their entrees, it felt to Charlotte as if all five of them were lifelong friends.

Over dessert, Charlotte told Mr. de la Mare and the others about a sight she had seen near Paddington Station during the war. "Four little boys were playing prisoner of war. One boy was placed in a gunny sack, which was drawn shut and dragged over the pavements by the other three boys. Once the first boy was let out of the gunny sack, the other three boys begged for a turn playing the German prisoner." Walter de la Mare laughed, and Sidney flashed a conspiratorial grin at Charlotte and winked.

Before the party broke up, Charlotte proposed a toast. "To Sidney, who is entirely to blame for his wonderfully madcap scheme, and to Mr. de la Mare for writing his kind letter of support. Cheers."

"Please call me Walter," Mr. de la Mare said to Charlotte and Anne as they were leaving the restaurant, and Anne squeezed Charlotte's arm.

The luncheon really began six months earlier when Sidney went to the Prime Minister's office to speak with the Prime Minister's secretary. Sidney requested that Charlotte be granted a Civil List Pension of 75 pounds a year, based on her contribution to British letters as well as financial need. He enlisted Thomas Hardy, John Masefield, and Walter de la Mare to write letters of support on her behalf.

There was no question of financial need. Upon her death, most of Ma's annuity had reverted to her brother, Edward Hearne Kendall. Charlotte and Anne were left to eke out their survival on 225 pounds a year. Though 300 pounds still wasn't much money to support Charlotte, Anne, and Freda, Charlotte and Anne welcomed the relief that the extra 75 pounds would bring. Moreover, Charlotte felt honored by the national tribute to her poetry, though she feared her days of poetic inspiration were through. "You never know," Sidney said, "when the muse might visit, and it won't serve anyone if you're starving when the muse arrives."

At the end of December, the Civil List Pension of 75 pounds per annum became official, and Charlotte and Anne were to spend two happy years in relative ease at Delancey Street, while still maintaining Anne's studio.

CHAPTER 54

Lady Otterline Morrell was not only an aristocrat but also a patron of the arts. Her activities were documented in the society pages of various newspapers, and there were rumors that she and her husband had an open marriage, of which Lady Otterline took ample advantage. Between affairs, she took a number of writers and artists under her wing, including T. S. Eliot, D. H. Lawrence, and Dora Carrington. She and her husband, MP Philip Morrell, kept two residences, a row house in Bloomsbury and a manor house near Oxford. She opened these residences to writers, artists, and intellectuals. During the Great War, the couple invited conscientious objectors such as Lytton Strachey and Clive Bell to lodge at their country manor because the couple were pacifists themselves.

Of course, Charlotte knew who Lady Otterline was, which only made her more surprised that Lady Otterline would leave her calling card for Charlotte at Anne's studio.

"You've yet another admirer," Anne said when she delivered the card to Charlotte.

Flattered but wary, Charlotte said, "She probably wants to collect me along with her other poets."

But because she was curious, Charlotte contacted Lady Otterline and arranged to have tea with her at the studio. "You don't mind?" Charlotte asked Anne.

"Not in the least," Anne said, "as long as you turn all my canvases toward the wall, lest she judge them."

Struck by a sudden inspiration, Charlotte said, "Maybe she wants to talk with me about your paintings."

Anne demurred. "If the society pages are correct, Lady Otterline is nothing short of direct. If she had wanted to see me, she would have left me a calling card."

"She did call at your studio," Charlotte countered.

"But her calling card was addressed to you," Anne said. "Have her to tea at the studio but please don't show her my paintings unless she asks."

Because of her long nose and face, Lady Otterline resembled a dachshund. But she struck Charlotte as the subject of a Pre-Raphaelite painting. Her eyebrows were strong and determined, and her dark blue eyes were deep set and drooped downward ever so slightly at their edges.

Her manner was polite yet single-minded. "I'd like to have you as part of my literary salon," Lady Otterline told Charlotte without preamble.

They sat at the small table in the center of the studio. Charlotte poured out their tea, and Lady Otterline stirred hers as they talked. She wore a long flowing dress, but she sat with her legs crossed.

Though Charlotte appreciated Lady Otterline's frankness, she refused to acquiesce. She tried to turn Lady Otterline down lightly. "I've had some disappointing experiences with lady salons," she confided in Lady Otterline.

"This isn't a salon for ladies," Lady Otterline insisted. "It's for writers and poets."

"I'd be asked to read my poems?" Charlotte asked.

"Yes, and talk about your own and other poets' work. The salon would make your poetry visible to the highest echelons of society, or at least the echelons that don't frown on the Bohemian lifestyle. I'm saying that you'd never be expected to censor yourself, reading only the poems of yours that polite society is willing to appreciate."

Sensing that Lady Otterline wasn't likely to be put off, Charlotte told her she would have to think about it.

"Think all you like," Lady Otterline insisted, but don't say 'no.' I'll be in contact with you again." Lady Otterline left another card for Charlotte, and abruptly departed, her long skirt rustling over the studio's floors.

Charlotte looked around the studio. Lady Otterline hadn't asked about Anne's paintings, which were perched along the perimeter, their faces turned toward the studio's walls. She had promised Anne she would say nothing.

It would be less difficult to say 'no' to Lady Otterline in a letter, and so Charlotte wrote to Lady Otterline at her Bedford Square address in Bloomsbury. She thanked Lady Otterline for thinking of her, but she flatly refused to be part of a literary salon.

Lady Otterline wouldn't be put off — in person or in a letter — and she continued to court Charlotte with her entreaties. At Christmas, she sent Charlotte a copy of Emily Brontë's poems. It was a thoughtful gift, but Charlotte had a copy already. Charlotte sent a thank you note, but she refused to back down. She didn't want to be collected.

CHAPTER 55

"But why would I sit for Dorothy?" Charlotte asked, looking to Anne, then Alida. They sat in the sitting room of Delaney Street.

"Like it or not," Alida said, "You're a poet of note."

"And poets of note," Anne said, "have their portraits painted."

"Who knows," Alida added. "The National Portrait Gallery might want it."

"Only because Dorothy painted it," Charlotte demurred.

Sensing Charlotte's hesitation, Anne said, "Dorothy isn't Lady Otterline. She won't try to collect you."

Alida and Anne chatted over their tea and biscuits while Charlotte stirred her tea absentmindedly and considered Dorothy's proposal. Dorothy, whom Charlotte, Anne, and Alida knew through Sidney, was a careful portrait artist. If she painted Charlotte's portrait, Dorothy would be faithful to her vision of Charlotte, and Charlotte felt apprehensive about what that vision might reveal. Charlotte was fifty-six years old, with grey hair and a perpetually surprised expression on her face because of her highly arched eyebrows. Seeing herself through Dorothy's eyes might be even more difficult for Charlotte than looking at herself in a mirror.

Despite that difficulty, however, Charlotte was curious to know how an artist might envision her. Perhaps Dorothy would see something in Charlotte's countenance that Charlotte herself had missed all these years. On the other hand, once she sat for Dorothy, Charlotte's likeness became Dorothy's painting and possession. Was Charlotte willing to give herself over to someone else's vision of who she had become?

A week later, Charlotte's curiosity won over her trepidation. She agreed to sit for Dorothy on the condition that Charlotte approve Dorothy's rendering of Charlotte in her painting, and that all studies done in preparation for the portrait be destroyed.

Anne protested. "You can't handcuff an artist, especially not Dorothy Hawksley, our friend. Would you let one of your personae dictate the poem you wrote?"

"That's different," Charlotte argued. "My personae are imaginary."

"Then would you let a publisher dictate the edits of a poem you wrote?" Anne countered.

"If I wanted the poem to appear in his magazine, I might," Charlotte said.

"You know as well as I know, Charlotte, that you would never compromise your vision, not even for a prominent editor of a prestigious magazine. And you can't ask Dorothy to compromise hers."

Charlotte knew Anne was right, and so she conceded and agreed to have her portrait painted — no strings attached.

But the week in May that Charlotte was to sit for Dorothy at Dorothy's studio, a general strike broke out across England. One hundred twenty trade unions and nearly two million workers united in support of coal miners striking for better pay and working conditions. The front pages of London's newspapers were dominated by photos of demonstrations on London's streets and news of tense negotiations between labor and management.

"Ma would say it was the beginning of the end of civilization," Anne said to Charlotte as they read *The Times*, "when workers insist on biting the hand that feeds them because they've forgotten their place."

"Yes," Charlotte said, "because Ma had the good fortune of an annuity, so she didn't have to work for wages."

Because it was so close to Tottenham Court Road, even Delancey Street wasn't immune to picketers, walking the pavements and blocking traffic while carrying placards that read: "Not a penny tax on workers' wages. Not a penny tax on food." Bobbies on foot and on horseback attempted to manage the protesters, while volunteers ran the trams, subway, and omnibuses, and traffic backed up.

Charlotte told Dorothy they must postpone her sitting as Charlotte couldn't possibly make it to Dorothy's studio. "Let me come to you," Dorothy said, "I happen to own a magic carpet."

And so Charlotte sat for Dorothy's preliminary sketches in the front room of Delancey Street while the angry voices of strikers echoed in the streets below. Each morning for three days, Dorothy appeared at the Mews' door with her tiny folding chair, portable easel, sketch pad, and an array of pencils. Unusually beautiful, Dorothy's olive skin set off dark brown hair and mesmerizing grey eyes.

The first day, Charlotte was embarrassed to be the center of attention, but by the second and third day, she was numb to it. Dorothy worked quickly, sketching Charlotte in one pose, then another, asking her to smile or not, to look down or up. Charlotte complied, while Anne looked on.

The strike ended after nine days, the unions and workers deflated and defeated. But Charlotte was able to travel easily to Dorothy's studio, where she was to have her final sitting. While Dorothy sketched and painted, Charlotte thought about how much sitting for a portrait would have meant to her when she was younger. Wasn't this the fame she had always imagined for herself? The second edition of *The Farmer's Bride* had sold well in England, and *Saturday Market* had sold well in America. Both books had been very favorably reviewed, and Louis Untermeyer had anthologized eight of Charlotte's poems in *Modern British Poetry*. She had been parodied in *Punch* magazine, and she had been granted a Civil List Pension. In August, Alida's reading of Charlotte's short lyric "Sea Love" would be broadcast on the BBC and heard by thousands of listeners. And now, a poet of note, she was having her portrait painted.

When Dorothy showed Charlotte the finished painting, Charlotte recognized the woman in the portrait. She looked thoughtful, even a bit pensive, and she appeared pleased with herself, as if she had journeyed a long way and had finally arrived at her destination. But what lay beyond that destination, Charlotte couldn't fathom.

CHAPTER 56

From the floor-to-ceiling windows of Anne's studio, Charlotte watched as white beds of clouds scuttled across the sky as quickly as crabs at the seashore. A week before, Charlotte had suggested Anne invite Katherine Righton to tea. Anne, of course, knew Charlotte's ulterior motive. They had been sisters if not always confidantes for too many years for each other's behavior to be less than transparent.

But Katherine accepted, and so on this spring afternoon in 1926, the three chatted about the miners' strike, the current fashions, and finally the breezy weather and late daffodils before Anne herself called forth the elephant, gray as the spring sky, from its corner in the studio. Propped against the studio's walls were a jumble of canvases, three whose frames and hollow backs were turned toward the tea party of three.

"I thought this year would be different," Anne said, her own back to the canvases as she sat on a milk crate. "But it seems flowers, or at least my flowers, are out of season again this year." Charlotte heard the undertow of sadness in Anne's voice, despite her breezy tone and obvious effort to be cavalier.

"The academy judges are blind," Katherine averred and snorted. "Even Kenneth Williams was given a spot only as an alternate."

Charlotte bit her lower lip, feeling the pain that crossed Anne's face. She knew that earning a place even as an alternate would thrill Anne.

Charlotte said, "You're right, of course, Katherine. There's always next year."

"Or the year after," Anne added ruefully. The bitterness in her comment revealed how much being part of the Royal Academy's exhibit meant to Anne — and more each passing year. Charlotte would give her right arm, all her publications, and any further experiences of being drawn out by a poem if only Anne could win acknowledgement for her paintings as Charlotte had these last years for her poetry.

"Fame in one's lifetime," Charlotte said, "often damns one's art to obscurity after the artist's death."

"Of course," Katherine said, "your proper audience is posterity. The academy's oversight will be the next generation's brilliant discovery."

Anne smiled at this. "What's important," she said, "is to have friends who believe in you when the world turns away." Charlotte received Anne's smile as if the warmth of a long absent sun. "Besides," Anne said, "there's always the work itself, which only death can steal from us."

"To the work," Katherine said, raising her teacup in a toast.

CHARLOTTE WROTE "SEA LOVE" AT NUMBER 9, when the Mews were residing in the dungeon. The poem was included in the second edition of *A Farmer's Bride*, and it was to be heard in homes over "the wireless," a technological invention that Charlotte marveled at without caring to understand.

"It's quite interesting," Sidney began, but Charlotte stopped him.

"Anything claiming to be interesting is inevitably complex," Charlotte said. "I will simply trust the radio waves not to harm Londoners' health."

Alida recorded the poem at the Savoy Hill Studio, although she offered the honor to Charlotte. "I'm sure you will do it justice," Charlotte had assured Alida. "And I'm not sure I'd like hearing my own voice over the wireless, knowing it had floated disembodied over the Thames."

On August 24, 1926, the recording was broadcast, and Charlotte and Anne listened along with Alida as her recorded voice read the poem.

> *Tide be runnin' the great world over:*
> *'Twas only last June month, I mind, that we*
> *Was thinkin' the toss and the call in the breast of the lover*
> *So everlastin' as the sea.*
>
> *Here's the same little fishes that splutter and swim,*
> *Wi' the moon's old glim on the grey, wet sand;*
> *An' him no more to me nor me to him*
> *Than the wind goin' over my hand.*

Charlotte held her breath until Anne clapped loudly and Alida declared, "Your poem has just been heard by thousands of listeners."

Charlotte answered, "Your reading was lovely. I couldn't have read it half as well. Thank you, Alida."

It was to be the last happy moment Charlotte and Anne shared for a long while.

By September, Anne's uncharacteristic depression hadn't lifted, and she had grown listless. Charlotte, seriously worried, knew they must have a change of scenery from London's ever-increasing pace so that Anne might have a rest cure.

The difficulty was lodgings. They couldn't afford two residences, even for a brief respite, so Charlotte, determined to help Anne any way she could, gave up the lease on Delancey Street and secured rooms for them in Sussex, at St. George's House in Chichester. The rest of their furniture joined that already in storage, and the sisters said goodbye to Delancey Street and London to winter at the seashore.

The weight of the past held in a family wardrobe disappeared entirely at Chichester. Their rooms were freeing in their spartan simplicity. Charlotte's room, a soft pink, reminded her of the inside of a shell, and she wondered if she hadn't finally achieved her life as a gypsy or vagabond — home nowhere and everywhere at once. From her window, she saw the turning leaves of autumn in trees breathed to life by sea air and heard the cry of gulls and the steady crash of waves against the rocky shore.

Looking out to sea their first night, the sisters marveled that they could see all the way to the Isle of Wight. So near, it was, Anne said, she could hear the feeders on the farm clanking as the pigs nosed them open with their snouts. But neither sister mentioned Freda.

Though the weather was charitable, the sun shining every day in the slanting yellow light so true to October, and the autumn and sea air were bracing, Anne was less and less able to get comfortable, whether she was lying in bed or seated in her room. Worse, she said, was the persistent bad taste in her mouth.

"It's as though I've been sucking on a copper coin," Anne said, trying to explain. "And it's especially bad when I lie down at night or wake in the morning."

Charlotte felt the bed must be to blame, and when she investigated Anne's bedding, she noticed with disgust that the sheets smelled stale.

"We changed them before you came," the head maid insisted," but a few of the linens had been in storage for some time."

"Then why didn't you launder them," asked Charlotte, feeling irritable and impatient.

"We were shorthanded a week ago. Our laundress was off because her sister was sick in childbirth, their mother had passed away only a month before, and the baby's father, a fisherman, was lost at sea during a summer squall."

A chill went through Charlotte, and she turned from the head maid without another word, only to turn back, the maid looking at her as if Charlotte were now a ghost, to say, "I'm so sorry."

So many people are lost at sea, Charlotte thought, yet I bring my sister who's ill to the seashore to recover. Though her thought process was illogical, it pointed to the helplessness and guilt she felt.

Despite the freshly laundered sheets dried outdoors and smelling of the sun and the sea, Anne's health grew worse, so that she no longer drank her hot cocoa in the evening, claiming even the acrid smell gave her indigestion.

Charlotte asked Anne what she would like to do.

Without hesitation, Anne said, "Go home."

CHAPTER 57

But where was *home* for the sisters? London, yes. But where in London?

Anne suggested they stay in her studio until they could make more permanent arrangements. Charlotte's trunks and manuscripts were there as were Anne's canvases and painting supplies. True, there wasn't any way to cook; they might only boil water got from the landing for tea, but they ate so little anyway, and they could send out for what food they needed. So they took their cots out of storage and set up housekeeping on Charlotte Street among paint boxes and trunks of manuscripts.

Just as it was impossible to accept Lady Otterline's advances (which came even in Chichester because Charlotte had left a forwarding address), it was impossible to refuse Maggie Browne's invitation for Christmas. Charlotte feared being an interloper or a charity case, but she feared most being a hanger-on. Maggie, however, as true and good as all the sisters' friends from their Gower Street days, could be trusted to welcome them honestly as cherished guests who brought the very spirit of Christmas into the Browne home. Holding the invitation in hand, Charlotte told Anne she was ashamed of ever faulting Maggie for being commonplace.

Anne, for whom the doctor refused to prescribe anything but traditional medicines, explaining that she was quite ill, but he didn't know exactly why, was up to travel, he said, so they graciously accepted Maggie's invitation. So, with their toothbrushes, nightgowns, change of clothes and Anne's medicines in cases, they arrived by train at Berkhamsted in Hertfordshire.

The Brownes' house was large, and the sisters were given separate rooms. Like them, Maggie had never married, and she lived with her mother and father. While Charlotte would have liked the company of children at Christmastime, she was glad for Anne's sake that there would be no reminders of what might have been.

On Christmas Eve, the sisters accompanied the Brownes to Christmas services before coming home for a late supper of oyster stew. The tranquility of the church and beauty of the nativity scene brought back memories of the Mews' Christmases on Doughty and Gordon Streets. As a child, Charlotte knew attending church was the price one paid for Christmas gifts, and so she, Henry, Anne, and Freda would sit side by side on the hard wooden pews through the service until Charlotte was sure she would burst. But as an adult, it was the stillness and solemnity of Christmas that moved her, and she took Anne's hand in hers as they listened to the rector read from Luke the story of Christ's birth.

The day after Christmas, Maggie asked Charlotte if she and Anne would speak alone with her father. In his study with its overflow of textbooks on marine biology, Professor Browne asked as straightforwardly as Aunt Fanny might what had been done for Anne.

And so it was out of his magnanimity that Mr. Browne arranged for Anne to see a specialist at a nursing home in Nottingham Place. Just as Charlotte had graciously accepted the Civil List Pension out of gratitude but more so from dire need, the sisters accepted Mr. Browne's offer to Anne.

The specialist's diagnosis of Anne's illness as cancer of the liver shook Charlotte, bringing back memories of Fred Mew's deathbed and his illness of cancer of the stomach. It was what Charlotte had most feared and struggled to deny. Now she felt defeated in a war whose many battles she had slowly lost one by one. She must be strong for Anne, but it was as though a final curtain had already fallen.

However, Anne seemed noticeably calmer following the doctor's prognosis: three months to live.

"It's her faith, her stalwart faith in God and goodness," Charlotte told Sidney, "that gives her strength."

"It's you who gives her strength," was all Sidney said after expressing his condolences, besides adding, "you and your faithfulness to her."

CHAPTER 58

It was Sidney who suggested Anne be moved elsewhere so that she and Charlotte might spend their last days together outside the confines of institutionalized care.

Thankful for his guidance, in early February, Charlotte found a room for Anne on Charlotte Street by Hogarth Studios above the Etoile, an Italian family restaurant. During the days of late winter, Charlotte sat by Anne's bed and the sisters listened to the murmurings of the restaurant's machinations a floor below them, imagining together what the family was really like.

"The father, I believe," Charlotte said, "isn't Italian at all, but a gypsy."

"He met his wife traveling through the small villages of northern Italy," Anne said slowly, catching her breath between phrases because she tired easily, "mending the pots and pans of Italian mothers ... who were sure any fault in their cooking could be blamed on a spot wearing away in their cookware."

Outside, February's trees climbed against the sky like vines against a palace wall. The day's light was both gray and the palest blue. Anne closed her eyes to doze. Charlotte sat still, letting Anne rest and her own thoughts wander as she gazed at the window. She saw the window as a picture frame. Within its black borders were the uppermost and cobwebbed branches of a family tree, its limbs and branches winnowed by time and countless storms. Night came on, blotting out the tracery of lines against the charcoal sky, a picture dimming and dimming until it was obscured by blackness, the only light left that of the street lamps below and the table lamp beside Anne's bed.

Then Charlotte saw the door to Anne's room reflected in the window, its hardwood and recessed panels, its doorknob and latch, placed now by trick of light in the blue-black sky of the picture's frame. She remembered the sketch Anne had made of the farm on the Isle of Wight, to which Charlotte added a doorknob and latch of gold. Now, in the window's reflection, Charlotte imagined a providential hand open the narrow door and then one by one Henry, Nurse Goodman, Fred Mew, Wek, and Ma pass through it into the dark of night.

Anne stirred, woke, and asked how long she had slept.

"It's seven o'clock," Charlotte said.

"I slept four hours, but it seems like only a moment or a whole ... lifetime," Anne replied.

While a nurse kept vigil beside Anne's bed at night, Charlotte retired to Hogarth Studios and its hodgepodge of hoarded possessions. Unlike Anne's room above the Etoile, the full strength of the street lamps flooded through the studio's floor-to-ceiling windows, casting its yellow light across the canvases, trunks, and tea set, which had traveled with them in their faithful taking up and putting down of houses and rooms to let. Charlotte took her tea alone, looking across the sea of flotsam as she had once looked across the flotsam of Gordon Street's attic rooms.

On Valentine's Day, after another morning and afternoon of waiting on Anne, Charlotte sat on a crate and had her late tea. She heard no one on the landing that evening, only the traffic below. Once back in Bloomsbury above the Etoile, Anne had asked that Charlotte accompany her to church on a Sunday when Anne felt well enough to go. This hadn't been possible, and Charlotte, selfishly, she knew, had been relieved.

Anne's acceptance of death was complete, and whereas Anne had faith, Charlotte had doubt. If there was a God, his taking Anne from Charlotte pointed to his cruel humor. That Anne should live only to middle age and suffer a hard death, when Ma had lived into her 80's, and Edward Hearne Kendall, their maternal uncle who had never done anything for anyone, still lived, was absurd.

And whereas Anne's life had been structured by confession and atonement, Charlotte's had been built on passion and renunciation. Charlotte remembered Anne at the farm on the buckboard of the pony cart, unwilling to step down and ruin her shoes. Henry tested the late spring mud in gum boots and walked around a tree to measure its circumference. Charlotte, angry because she had wanted to sit on the buckboard next to the driver, broke her umbrella across her knee. Nurse Goodman, frustrated with "the lot of 'em," told the driver "they were ungrateful snots." Charlotte, though she loved Nurse, refused to say she was sorry. Anne asked forgiveness from Nurse for "the lot of 'em," and Henry and Charlotte had no choice but let Nurse take them into her great bosom and kiss them.

Anne, obviously sensing a religious tack couldn't comfort Charlotte, tried a literary one. The day after the doctor's prognosis, Anne had told Charlotte it was like Victor Hugo said: we're all sentenced to death, but we've been given an indefinite reprieve. "It's just that now," Anne said, "I know when death will come."

Though she had never thought much of Valentine's Day before this year, knowing it was the last she and Anne might commiserate over their losses in silence shook Charlotte. "You and I," she counseled a sculpted head of a newborn, made from plaster of Paris by Anne and held in Charlotte's palm, "will have only each other this time next year."

CHAPTER 59

And so the sisters waited on death as if he were a vagrant suitor, listening for the sound of his boots on the entry step or the cough he used to clear his throat before tapping on the door of Anne's room.

March came in like a lamb, and time crept ahead. Charlotte watched the same moving picture framed by Anne's window as night came on, while during the day, when Anne wasn't sleeping (less and less now), they continued their Italian family saga. As the saga grew longer, Anne became frailer: her form yellowed and shriveled as if an autumn leaf, and Charlotte was reminded of Wek's last days as he struggled to hold on or finally let go of his perch. Yet each day Anne's inner light shone brighter, so that it seemed apparent to all her visitors, Charlotte was certain, that Anne's body and soul were a part of, yet apart from, each other.

While her soul won its release, Anne's slight form clung to life, as if there were only one page to conclude the heroine's journey and in that one page everything must be resolved. From this urgency, Anne spoke of things that she and Charlotte had let remain unspoken. In late March, she said it was because Charlotte was the strongest, truest, and best of the Mews that she would follow last into God's kingdom. Charlotte thought of Freda, but said nothing. That night, alone, Charlotte realized how terrified she was of losing Anne as her better half and the reflection of her own sanity.

Before she was to become much worse, Anne had a good Saturday, in which she sat up in a chair by the window for an hour, when usually she had strength to sit up only long enough to eat a half cup of broth. On Sunday, with the nurse to assist them, the sisters attended church off Gordon Square as they had as children and young adults, and on Henry's birthdays after his death.

In the vestibule of St. Mary's, Anne steadied by Charlotte and the nurse's arms, the gravity of the sanctuary struck Charlotte with its damp grayness. Father Cecil, shrunken by the years but recognizable by his thundering voice, greeted them as Charlotte led Anne and the nurse.

"Ah, if it's not the prodigal daughter returned to the flock," Father Cecil said, pointedly mixing his parables. He took Charlotte's free hand. "And where is your dear sister, Anne," he asked, still holding Charlotte's hand in his. "She's well, I hope." He looked to the two strangers standing beside Charlotte.

Anne remained silent, perhaps stunned not to be recognized by Father Cecil, whom she held so dear. Charlotte said, "This is Anne, Father Cecil, and her nurse, Miss Turner." Anne took her hand from the nurse's arm and held it out to Father Cecil. He took it in both of his as if a fine piece of Venetian glass. "Anne," he said, "my dear, dear child. Why didn't anyone tell me?"

It was a gross oversight not to inform Father Cecil of Anne's illness. But it was proof, Charlotte realized during Father Cecil's sermon on each disciple's martyrdom for Christ, that Charlotte had refused to believe that Anne would die.

The next few weeks, Anne grew much worse and it became impossible for her to get comfortable. "Anne," the doctor said, "needs a place where she'll receive constant medical attention." Their leaving Etoile was made all the more necessary by complaints from regular customers who had seen "a very sick woman" on the premises "last Sunday." Was it wise to house a sick person above a family restaurant?

A room was found in a nursing home in West Hampshire, and Charlotte was forced to take the underground home to the studio on nights she couldn't convince the staff to let her sleep over.

Charlotte received another letter from Lady Otterline asking her to a salon. With Anne sick, Charlotte didn't bother to be polite. She wrote to Lady Otterline: "As my sister is dangerously ill in a nursing home I spend all my time with her and consequently have none for seeing anyone else."

Charlotte had slept at the studio the night before. Today she emerged from the West Hampstead Underground station and walked to the nursing home on Priory Road. The day's clouds raced across the gray morning sky as if fueled by an ecstatic urgency, and the sun illuminated the pale clouds without showing its face.

Anne was awake. Her skin was yellow and waxen, but her countenance was serene. In a voice as hoarse as her sister's, she told Charlotte, "I feel much better today." It was a gracious lie between sisters. The clouds scudded by the window, its shade lifted, as Charlotte plumped Anne's pillow, then held a glass of water for her to drink from.

"Alida said she'll visit today if it doesn't storm," Charlotte said brightly.

"I hope she's able to," Anne said weakly. "I know how terribly busy she must be at The Bookshop."

Alida arrived just a half hour later, while Charlotte was reading aloud to Anne, though the racing clouds had swallowed up the gray sky and showers seemed inevitable. Charlotte could see in Alida's expression how startled she was by Anne's appearance. But Alida caught herself before Anne opened her eyes to smile at her.

"My dear Anne," Alida said, bending forward and kissing Anne on her cheek.

As she motioned toward the one chair next to her bed, Anne replied hoarsely, "Please sit down, Alida."

Alida took a seat while looking at Charlotte, who stood by the doorway, just inside the room. Charlotte watched as Anne took Alida's hand in hers and said how glad she was to see her. A gas fire exhausted its heat in the corner, and the room grew uncomfortably warm for everyone but Anne. Alida, prepared for a storm, had worn an overcoat, which she took off and placed on the back of the chair.

After several minutes, Anne turned her head and gazed at the fire. Several more minutes passed, and Charlotte thought Anne had fallen asleep. But then she heard her murmur, "I shan't want a fire soon."

"Don't say that," Alida said, petting Anne's hand. "You must look ahead to when you'll be well again."

Anne placed her other hand on top of Alida's hand, stilling it. "Don't be sad for me, Alida. Soon I'll be living in heaven with God and his angels, and with Mother, Father, and Henry."

Charlotte felt tears well up in her eyes and swell the back of her throat. She excused herself and made her way to the waiting room, where she took a seat and swallowed her tears. She had cried enough this last fortnight.

In a quarter of an hour, Alida joined her.

"Anne's asleep," Alida said, after taking a chair across from Charlotte. "How are you, Charlotte?"

"As well as can be expected," Charlotte said frankly. "But it's Anne I worry about, of course. The doctor says her death may come at any time. As much as I want her to escape this misery, I can't bear the thought of life without her. It's selfish, I know. But we've lived our entire lives together."

Alida said soothingly, "The love between sisters or brothers is truer than the love between husbands and wives, I think. And heaven knows there are fewer complications." Alida's gaze was preoccupied, and Charlotte knew she was thinking of her life with Harold.

"Once upon a time," Charlotte said, "I wanted fame more than anything else in life. At long last, I realize that the love of family and friends matters far more. It's so simple, really, the answer to happiness. And yet that answer eluded me most of my life."

"You might still covet fame if you hadn't gained recognition as a poet," Alida said philosophically.

"Then I feel very fortunate to have gained recognition as a poet so that I'm able to judge fame's relative worth," Charlotte replied, a wistful note in her voice.

Alida sighed. "More than anything else, besides Anne's health, that is, I want things between Harold and me to be simpler."

"Perhaps love isn't meant to be simple," Charlotte said honestly. "Truly knowing someone, for better and for worse, takes courage. And trusting that person to accept you, for better and for worse, takes that much more courage."

"You sound as if you speak from years and years of experience," Alida said quizzically. "But, then again, I suppose you do," she conceded.

Charlotte winked at Alida, and Alida smiled. She left Charlotte alone in the waiting room next to its one window, watching storm clouds slow and gather. Charlotte felt the storm clouds' urgency as though it were her own, without being able to say what that urgency was for.

CHAPTER 60

When Anne wasn't trying to get comfortable, taking medication, or sleeping, she wanted to talk to Charlotte. The rose left on Henry's grave, Ma's red box, father's uncredited buildings, and their own successes and failures as dutiful daughters and as artists hung above Anne's bed and Charlotte's chair ready to be plucked down and bitten into like apples, Charlotte feared, from the tree of knowledge. At the center was the sisters' pact made so long ago, but never mentioned since, which had bound them together, and which, Charlotte knew, had separated them just as it had silenced them. It was indeed ironic that the familiarity of years of living so near to one another had made them virtual strangers.

Charlotte, with her distrust of confession and atonement, felt she must discourage Anne's desire to walk into the light of truth, for Charlotte knew she couldn't follow. She was wrong, a sinner whose wrongdoing was the very fabric of herself, and she saw no possibility for the sanctity of truth, when forgiveness itself was impossible.

Worse, Charlotte was to be abandoned. Whatever was said or left unspoken, Anne was to die in spring as Henry had. The birds were to sing and to mate and to rejoice as they always had and always would, and Charlotte was to be left alone in the cold comfort of summer. Even now, it was as if the hottest days of summer were upon them, and the sisters' path was directed by the shade of trees where Charlotte sought refuge, but which Anne forsook to step ahead of Charlotte into the brilliant light of truth.

But at the end, it wasn't Anne but Charlotte who pulled down the fruit of knowledge and offered it to Anne. It was June, and Charlotte knew that if God had any mercy, Anne's vagrant suitor must arrive soon. Anne, though her inner light raged forth like the sun's lengthening rays to see her through her last days, was a dried husk of herself and nearly unrecognizable, even to Charlotte who had never been separated from Anne for more than a fortnight.

Outside, even in London, the summer insects had begun their singsong murmurings in late afternoons, and in early evenings and nights, miller and gypsy moths flung themselves at street lamps and the headlamps of motorcars. Shop windows, whose interiors remained lit to discourage loiterers, were accosted by the moths, and miles away in West Hampshire, where Anne Mew lay dying, Charlotte felt the presence and persistence of the moths even with the curtains drawn.

That day, escaping the underground into the early summer light of West Hampshire, Charlotte strolled on the tree-lined walks of this suburb of

London and was taken by the sight of a fledgling robin in a crab apple tree. I must describe him to Anne, Charlotte thought. On cue, the young robin, its breast a dull red and its wing and head feathers mottled, chortled its "cheerio." Then it hopped on its branch to get closer to this odd middle-aged woman, dressed in the fashion of the last decade, her wavy silver hair done up on her head like spun sugar at county fairs.

"It was as if," Charlotte told Anne, "he was inspecting me so as to describe me to his mother.

Anne, her eyes closed, smiled weakly, and she grasped Charlotte's hand. "Just like Ma always expected us to tell her everything," she said. Her voice had grown as raspy as Charlotte's, but it also reminded Charlotte of a child's.

"I looked down so as not to trip, and when I looked up, the robin was gone," Charlotte said.

Anne, still with a strained smile, said nothing, so that Charlotte supposed she was dozing, yet Anne's grasp of Charlotte's left hand was firm. Charlotte felt the gold band she wore on her middle finger bite into the bone.

"Did Ma know of our pact, I wonder?" Charlotte asked. Having spoken the words, she hoped Anne dozed.

Anne squeezed Charlotte's hand more tightly. "I suppose," Anne began, "Ma counted us incapable of securing husbands is all."

Charlotte took a deep breath and let it out. It was the relief of mentioning what hadn't been spoken of for thirty-five years.

Reading her thoughts, Anne said simply, "Why have we never talked about the pact we made so long ago?" Charlotte thought of Mr. Antony, of Ella, of May. Anne said, "Is it that by keeping the vow we needn't have spoken of it?"

"It's true neither of us married and thus had no children," Charlotte said. She spoke calmly, yet she felt the moths in her stomach, like butterflies, fluttering.

"Ma wouldn't have understood our reasons, although to anyone else who knew of Henry and Freda, our reasons would have been transparent," Anne said matter-of-factly.

"But who might we have told of Henry and Freda besides the Gower Street girls?" Charlotte asked. Even Alida and Sidney didn't know of Freda.

The sisters' conversation continued, so that it might have been Anne or Charlotte who said one thing or another, until Anne said abruptly, "Charlotte, forgive me Mr. Antony."

Charlotte, holding back tears, choked, "Oh my dear, dear sister, there's nothing whatsoever to forgive."

"Had he come back after the war," said Anne, fluttering toward the bright yellow light of the afternoon sun bursting through the invalid's window, "I might have gone to him. I might have broken our pact. Worse, I might have left Ma, and you, Charlotte."

Both sisters wept as they choked on words long stoppered by years of fear bred by the very familiarity that bound them.

"You might have, but you didn't, Anne. You didn't."

Anne breathed deeply, the air catching in her throat, until she coughed and coughed. Charlotte held a glass of water for her to drink from.

Anne lay back down. "Charlotte," Anne said, and the moths flew up into Charlotte's throat. She believed, even if Anne knew, that Anne couldn't understand and certainly not accept Ella and May, passions Charlotte herself had wanted to renounce. But only Ella's and May's rejections had saved her. Charlotte held her breath, willing the moths to fly away.

But Anne's inner light shone out, and the moths flew toward her jaundiced form, willing to sacrifice themselves to the truth, whatever the cost.

"I always thought moths were fairies," Anne said. Charlotte breathed out. "And when Miss Bolt insisted we kill them lest they 'sow holes in the woof and warp of things,' I couldn't believe fairies would do such a mischievous thing as eat my best wool jumper. But Aunt Fanny said moths and fairies were only distant cousins, and we mustn't fault either, the moths for liking clothes as much as Parisian women or the fairies for being mischievous, because both were being true to themselves."

So Anne did know, all along. How could Charlotte have doubted?

"You might have gone to Paris, Charlotte."

"I did," Charlotte confessed.

"But you didn't stay," Anne said. "You came home, to Ma and me, and the reasons why you did don't matter, especially now."

Charlotte, encouraged by Anne's frankness, asked, "And in me, you didn't see Henry and Freda?" What she asked, she knew, was whether or not Anne saw Charlotte as wrong, the way Charlotte always felt.

"Never," Anne said, "I only saw their goodness in you, and their light." Charlotte felt like she did as a child when Nurse Goodman, as fast to forgive as to anger, took the Mew children onto her lap and held them all together in her arms.

Anne slept as the June sun blazed in the sky and set its bright head on the earth to rest. Charlotte, sensing Anne's death was near, refused to leave at the end of visiting hours. When the sky blackened, Anne's vagrant suitor rapped on the door and let himself in without catching the latch behind him. As Charlotte held Anne's left hand, the familiar stranger took her right hand, and Charlotte watched as he escorted Anne through the narrow doorway into the night — the moths no longer fluttering within the frame of the room's picture window — leaving Charlotte alone in the dark.

CHAPTER 61

In late June and July, Charlotte sought whatever peace she could find at Ethel Oliver's home in Isleworth. Lady Otterline, however, persisted, leaving flowers and messages for Charlotte at the Olivers' home. Enough was enough. Charlotte wrote: "I hoped you would understand as everyone else has been good enough to do without my saying so that I am only seeing and writing to old friends. I came here for some quiet."

August was beautiful, yet its atmosphere reminded Charlotte less of Keats' "Ode to Autumn" than his "Ode on Melancholy." In September, the leaves flamed out in reds and yellows, and the air was cool with an undertow of warmth. But by mid-October, when Charlotte left Kate and Sydney, afraid to trespass on their home in Cambridge or her friends' gracious kindness any longer, the air had grown crisp, the colors muted and muddy, and the decay endemic of the season swelled up from the ground through the soles of Charlotte's small boots. She made her way from the underground with her carpet bag feeling every bit the vagabond she had become.

In London's streets the falling light of the late afternoon cast shadows on the pavements. Behind closed doors of the row houses and new flats erupting overnight like clover, the lights of homes came on. Around the corner from Hogarth Studios by Charlotte Mews, now converted from stables into garages, a young girl in braids, walking hand in hand with her mother, somehow recognized Charlotte, though Charlotte thought she must appear as only a ghost of herself.

"Are you Miss Charlotte Mew, the poetess?" the girl asked. Charlotte stopped. She remembered herself as a schoolgirl in the thrall of Emily Brontë's poems.

"I'm afraid I am," said Charlotte.

The mother said to her child, "You mustn't bother the lady," then turned to Charlotte and smiled in apology.

"Of course not, Mother. But may I ask for her autograph?"

Not allowing the mother to refuse her daughter, Charlotte, humored to comply, set her bag on the pavement. The child reached into her school bag to pull out a pen and folder. Charlotte signed the folder with her distinctive signature and handed it back to the girl, thinking how much she herself would have thrilled to meet Emily Brontë along Gower Street. But she could no longer feel the emotion she recalled as only a faint memory.

The schoolgirl looked at the signature, then handed it back to Charlotte as if, Charlotte suddenly thought, it was counterfeit and Charlotte, the ghost, had been found out.

"Could you add 'To Henry'? He's my grandfather, and your biggest fan."

Coincidences, thought Charlotte, as she turned the corner onto Charlotte Street, are the rule rather than the exception, and they required one to laugh, not cry.

The autumn twilight blurred the outline of objects — those hurrying home to a hearth fire and warm supper, the railings of Hogarth Studios, and its door and doorknob — and gave Charlotte Street a cast of otherworldliness, of things neither quite here nor there.

Charlotte set down her bag a second time to retrieve her latchkey, unused since just before Anne's funeral, and sensed a ghost step on her own grave. She started and looked down to see a white cat rubbing its muzzle against her stockinged leg. The cat looked up to meow at Charlotte, as if it were a long-lost friend, home after a journey to distant lands and impatient for news of the day.

Charlotte let them in, and the cat, which Charlotte saw in Hogarth Studios' half-light was white with gray markings on its back and head, followed her up the stairs to the first-floor landing where Charlotte stood, irresolute, before the door of Anne's studio.

She wondered later if she could have opened Anne's door without an escort. When she did, the cat (White Cat to Charlotte by then) ran in ahead of her and began scrounging among the crates (for mice, deduced Charlotte), and Charlotte set down her carpet bag for the last time and seated herself on one of her trunks of manuscripts. But before she had the chance to rest, White Cat, now at her feet, again meowed, plaintively this time.

"You must be hungry," Charlotte said, and was surprised to hear her own voice, as if she really were a ghost and couldn't speak.

White Cat bumped its head against her legs and purred, softly and wistfully, like a train's whistle at a distant crossing, thought Charlotte. In her carpet bag, Charlotte found a string sack of provisions, sent by Kate to see her through the next few days. She drew out a sardine tin and carton of saltines, dinner enough for a woman past her prime and her friend White Cat.

"We must be quite a sight," said Charlotte, as if passersby could see into the studio's tall windows now that the street lamps had come up. White Cat ignored her as it attended to its post-supper ritual of licking the sides of its front paws to use as washcloths for its muzzle and whiskers.

Charlotte dared to look around at the clutter of lives left hurriedly. "Disarray" suggested chaos was temporary and all one needed was a plan to turn things around so that living again made sense. The only items, in fact, that suggested order were the tea set with its single serving and the white cot set up in a corner, away from the encroaching light of the street lamps.

Behind her, at the door of the studio, White Cat meowed. Charlotte let it out before following it down to the ground floor, where Charlotte again opened the front door for it. White Cat sprinted into the cool night and its aroma of decay, evidently knowing exactly where it was going and impatient to get there.

Charlotte half woke in her cot just before dawn, her bedclothes as sodden as a drowning victim's. She gulped for air as the sheet tangled about her legs and pulled at her like seaweed as she struggled to escape the undertow. In her delirium and fatigue, she had disobeyed Uncle, she knew, and this was the consequence. "Never trust the sea," he had told the Mew children time and time again.

But it wasn't the seaweed or even the sea itself that pulled Charlotte under the water so that she couldn't breathe. When Charlotte opened her eyes, it was Anne, her long hair streaming out behind her face, who stared back unseeing at Charlotte. Charlotte let go then and fell back to sleep, allowing the undertow of sorrow to pull her downward in its long embrace.

THE SUNLIT HOUSE (1928)

CHAPTER 62

The new year found Charlotte much like the last half of the old. She would wake in the night listening for Anne's labored breathing and for a moment wonder at the silence. Then she would hear the street noise below or the comforting scrape of a tree bough on the pane. A street lamp half-lit the studio, so that familiar objects of the morning took on peculiar shapes and dimensions in the night.

However, she did not seek the oblivion of sleep as she had as late as Christmas, burying herself in a swath of blankets. But rather than rise, Charlotte would lie in her cot almost at home in this odd imaginative space, sensing her right leg and then the left, as if parts of herself she had just realized. She could see the peculiar shapes around her for what they were and not as their impersonations in the daylight as castoffs of Charlotte and Anne's past lives on Gordon and Doughty Streets. She began to wonder if she weren't the changeling brought back to her rightful place. But was that place the wood of the fairies or the hearth of the family home?

In the early mornings, she walked the streets of Bloomsbury with different eyes. Everything was distant and foreign. What before irritated or invigorated her took the cast of another world. It wasn't so much that she was above it all as that she was beyond it. Had the world changed with all its bright young things or had she changed since Anne's passing?

She didn't need to eat more than a few pieces of bread at breakfast and at dinner. She drank her tea diluted. And smoking, except a cigarette in the morning and a cigarette in the evening, no longer appealed to her. In mid-January, it occurred to her that she no longer desired or feared anything. She didn't even fear losing her mind. Hadn't she lost everything except her dearest friends? But all of them, Alida and Harold, Sidney and Kate, Florence and Hardy, had one another.

When she heard that Thomas Hardy had died, she thought first, the great author of *Jude the Obscure* is gone; then she thought of Florence, dear forbearing Florence; and last she thought of Sidney, necessarily caught up in a flurry of activity putting the great man's estate in order as only Sidney could do. So she was surprised when she received a note from Sidney. She had been out walking the streets, avoiding in the daylight of the studio the leavings of a lifetime, which weighed her down as she struggled to move among them. She preferred to weave between strangers on the pavements and think of herself as a wayfarer on the highways or a gypsy on country lanes, self-contained and light enough to fly to the moon.

She opened the note over a pot of tea. It contained a slip of paper from the British Museum, which on one side, in longhand, was her poem, she suddenly realized, "Fin de Fête."

> *Sweetheart, for such a day*
> > *One mustn't grudge the score;*
> *Here, then, it's all to pay,*
> > *It's Goodnight at the door.*

> *Goodnight and good dreams to you, —*
> > *Do you remember the picture-book thieves*
> *Who left two children sleeping in a wood the long night through,*
> > *And how the birds came down and covered them with leaves?*

> *So you and I should have slept, — but now,*
> > *Oh, what a lonely head!*
> *With just the shadow of a waving bough*
> > *In the moonlight over the bed.*

Hardy, it seemed, had copied out the poem, and Sidney, finding it among Hardy's things, had taken the time to post it to her. Charlotte, overcome with Hardy's compliment and Sidney's thoughtfulness, sat and wept.

When she recovered, she reread the poem as if a stranger had written it. It seemed curious to her now that in the second stanza the speaker would turn to the memory of a fairytale. Could she have been thinking of Henry and of Freda, lost for all those years as if sleeping in the wood? It didn't matter, did it, as long as Hardy liked the poem enough to copy it out in his own hand?

The pot of tea sat untouched, and the afternoon light of winter had waned. Charlotte agreed with the poem's sentiment, whatever she had imagined when she wrote it. One paid for her joy as well as for her sin, and at the end of one's life as at the end of a day, one rested alone in a solitary cot with only the scrape of a tree bough on the windowpane or a note from beyond such as Hardy's for occasional company.

CHAPTER 63

In the beginning of January, as her one New Year resolution, Charlotte drafted her will. She had little of any monetary value to leave, but what she did have she left for the care of Freda. Picking through the leavings in the studio made her gloomy, and she didn't want anyone else to have to do so. The sparse furnishings — Charlotte's wardrobe and vanity, the small dining table and three chairs, along with the silver and china, and Anne's canvases and painting supplies — could be salvaged or sold at auction for what little money they might bring.

She would like Kate, for whom it would matter, to have a piece of china she so admired. As for Anne's gold watch — Anne's most precious keepsake and now Charlotte's — Elsie, Edith, or Katherine Righton might like to have it. But Charlotte couldn't decide who might like it best, so she left that one burden to them and prayed they might forgive her. For now, Charlotte wore Anne's watch on her left wrist, but only when she was in the studio, lest she lose it.

In her haunting of the streets, Charlotte wore her mourning clothes — a black skirt and jacket over an (unfortunately) dingy, once-white shirtwaist, and a cameo broach at her throat, the one piece of jewelry she thought to adorn herself with. Of course, her boots, though needing new heels, carried her over the pavements. But she no longer bothered to brush or polish them, leaving them to look as worn and tired as her shirtwaist. Anne's clothes Charlotte kept in the wardrobe, and when she dressed after washing up in the small basin with water got from the ground floor's tap, she would touch a sleeve of Anne's favorite lavender dress and smile to herself.

The monotony of her days was a comfort. She might clean the studio desultorily, steering around the canvas-draped artifacts, a dust rag in hand, then sweep the floors of the dirt brought in on the soles of her shoes. She would wash the dust rag in the basin and hang it to dry. After Hardy's death, Charlotte expected to see little of Sidney, knowing how busy he was as literary executor of Hardy's estate. She knew, too, that Alida had her hands full with moving The Poetry Bookshop from Devonshire to Great Russell Street and how little help Harold could give her, despite his best intentions. So though she continued her correspondence with friends, she didn't expect to see anyone.

She hung a cardboard sign on the studio door that read, "In Mourning," and expected the other leaseholders of Hogarth Studios to respect her wishes, which they did, nodding as they passed on the stair but saying nothing. In this way, Charlotte saw no one she knew except a pale reflection of herself — dim and yellowish gray — in the mirror of the wardrobe. She thought she might live out her life in this manner, fading away like the scent of roses in the summer dusk. She continued her wakeful nights in her cot, listening for Anne's breathing and feeling as though she herself were floating disembodied on air.

She had all but forgotten her mother's brother, Edward Herne Kendall, until she received a letter in the post from his solicitor, James & James (like a solicitor's name out of Dickens, thought Charlotte). The letter said that Charlotte, now her uncle was deceased, was the lone beneficiary of her grandmother Kendall's trust. The figure was more than 8,000 pounds.

Charlotte, because it was a mild February day, sat on her favorite bench in the Gordon Square garden and read the letter a second time. Other Londoners, tempted by the fair weather, walked the paths in an unusually leisurely fashion given the calendar's date. She watched as an elderly man shook his cane at a squirrel who attempted to cross his path. The curmudgeon reminded her of Hardy, the only person who, when he was on this side of silence, could have appreciated the great irony of Charlotte's life at age fifty-eight, a well-to-do spinster, who had no one to share it with and for whom the money would have made all the difference years ago. She looked toward the Gordon Street house, where she, Anne, and Ma had lived below stairs, destitute, only ten years before.

The elderly man had made a turn around the garden and again passed Charlotte, this time muttering and poking his cane at the new leaves of grass. Charlotte laughed, and the man scowled at her and continued his mutterings, apparently full of contempt for the world. Charlotte laughed again, and she continued laughing, throwing her head back and guffawing at another of life's great jokes, until she scared a gaggle of pigeons, who flew up and away into the blue skies of London.

CHAPTER 64

Spring was so like autumn, Charlotte thought. This morning she saw a red tulip emerging from the decaying leaves of last year. She had been standing at a crosswalk looking down before stepping off the curb. The bulb grew in the boulevard, just as if it had fallen from a magician's shirt sleeve. A motorcar sounded its horn, and Charlotte looked up to see its driver, an old woman in a fur piece, motion to Charlotte to get out of her way.

Charlotte couldn't wait to tell Anne. But, of course, she could never tell Anne anything ever again. When Charlotte arrived at Hogarth Studios, the blue entry door glistening from the recent rains, a chill ran through her. She shook off her umbrella in the entry and took herself up the stairs, leaning on the banister as she went. Anne should be waiting, the kettle on. They could share their days over cups of steaming black tea and milk, and then Charlotte's head would clear. Before opening the studio's door, "In Mourning" swam before her eyes. She grabbed onto the doorknob to steady herself.

Now she lay in her cot, wondering where Anne could be. A band played beneath the window. Mr. Boynton's tuba carried the melody. How could they read their sheet music, wondered Charlotte, when there wasn't a moon? She drifted in and out of a fevered sleep. Days seemed to come and go, but the nights lasted an eternity. The sky was a blue door, and it was locked. There was someone knocking on the door, but each time she answered, no one was there except an angry magpie, who Charlotte knew was really Wek. She tried to come up for air, but Anne pushed her down and down. The Thames didn't have a bottom. She let go and sank, but where was Anne? Charlotte looked up from the bottom of the ocean and saw her at the top of a plane tree miles and miles above. Charlotte climbed the tree, but her hair, loosed from its chignon, got caught in the roots, and she knew she must drown.

Charlotte woke as though breaking the surface of water. She didn't gasp for air but listened instead to hear Anne breathing. A black curtain fell on the full moon and she finally slept.

"A spring chill. Nothing more," the doctor said.

"You're sure," Charlotte asked again.

"I'll have it analyzed," the doctor said, "to be on the safe side." He kindly laid his hand on her shoulder. "You mustn't worry."

She felt reassured until she saw he had left the specimen jar next to the wash basin. It was all Charlotte could do not to run after him in her chemise and stocking feet, carrying the germs that had killed Anne.

Charlotte had noticed them as soon as she was well. Little black specks no bigger than the head of a pin. They lay on the windowsill, and if it hadn't been for a full moon, she might not have seen them as anything more than soot. They appeared later on the Holland cloths thrown over the unused furniture, then on the gray tablecloth, and finally, even on the soles of her boots.

In between her gathering of evidence, the days threw themselves into spring. But Charlotte, though she told herself she looked forward to the return of Anne's flowers, felt as if she were moving in slow motion or trying to run underwater. Her mind was the estuary on the Isle when it lay cloaked by a dense fog. London's pavements, once a great joy, were only so much gray matter, like the fog that confused her thoughts.

She knew the black specks were the germs that killed Anne when she no longer wanted to eat. She had taken a walk to Doughty Street and stood in front of the old terraced house looking up at the attic rooms. For years, remembering the enchanted world under the skylight and stars had comforted her. But that day, in the rain gutters running from the roof to the pavement, Charlotte saw sapling growth, seedlings trying to take root in the downspout. She wanted to make it back to Charlotte Street or at least to Russell Square, but she vomited onto the pavement. She examined the soles of her boots and found the telltale black marks, and she knew she had been infected.

"Soot," the doctor repeated. "Garden variety soot."

"The laboratory could be mistaken," Charlotte argued. She hadn't slept more than an hour the previous three nights.

"I'd like you to see a specialist," the doctor said. When he laid his hand on her shoulder as he had the last time and smiled down at her pityingly, Charlotte felt as though she were a child.

She sat on her least favorite bench in the Gordon Square garden. She knew she was wrong, even as a child. What she excitedly called an old blackbird because of its white belly, her cousins said was really just a magpie. "And you know what the magpie does?" her cousins asked. "It steals the chicks of other birds and eats them." Indignant, Charlotte cried, "No bird would do that. All birds are good." Her cousins snickered. "Just ask Aunt Fanny, she'll tell you."

Now Charlotte watched as a magpie strutted out in the new grass. It walked like a soldier, throwing its black legs out to chest-level while jutting its head forward. But instead of an epaulet on its shoulder, it wore a white spot on its black wing. The magpie ignored her, just as Aunt did when Charlotte crashed into the kitchen demanding Aunt tell her cousins that magpies didn't steal other birds' chicks. Aunt, busy preparing supper, shushed her and gently pushed her out of the way.

Charlotte went to bed without eating, telling Nurse Goodman she had a stomachache. "It's no good telling fibs," Nurse had said. Charlotte squirmed and fibbed again. "I'm not lying. I hurt here," and she placed her hand on her waist, when it was really her chest that hurt. Nurse put her hand on Charlotte's forehead. "Perhaps bed without supper will do you good," she said. That night Charlotte dreamt of magpies and fairies stealing children who had been caught out telling fibs. They came in the night and snatched the child from its bed and hid it in the woods under a cover of sodden leaves.

When Charlotte woke the next morning, she was only a little disappointed that her dream wasn't true. It wasn't until days later that Aunt Fanny told her magpies like shiny things, so unless a baby bird glowed, the magpie would pay it no mind. That's when Charlotte learned that adults fib, too. Though it was to spare her feelings, it was still a lie.

She could only trust the specialist wasn't lying when he said Charlotte was distressed from grief and worry, but hardly certifiable.

That he'd spoken the word *certifiable* so lightly suggested that he didn't know Charlotte's family history, or if he did, he was either being cavalier or callous. Charlotte wished Anne were there. They hadn't needed words to reassure each other of their mutual sanity. They only needed to look into each other's eyes as a constant and failsafe mirror of truth.

The doctor delivered his verdict of "survivor's guilt" and sentenced Charlotte to a short rest cure at a nursing home on Beaumont Street. "An opportunity," he said, "to escape the cares of the world for a while."

It was as if she'd fought in a holy war, and though a victor, she had fallen.

She stood in the studio and surveyed the flotsam and agreed that she couldn't live here in this half-life another night. She packed a small case with toiletries, a nightgown, and her cigar box of mementos. Before leaving, she opened the door of the wardrobe to look at herself in the mirror. Its silvering was worn nearly through, and Charlotte appeared as a ghostly figure veiled by a sepia fog, so that she seemed to shift in and out of focus. She shut the wardrobe's door, put out the light, and left the studio, her case and umbrella in hand.

CHAPTER 65

Her small room on Beaumont Street sat at the back of the nursing home, so that the view from her one window was of the brick and mortar wall of an office building beyond. But if Charlotte stood at the window, leaned forward and looked up, she could just see a sliver of blue sky.

The room's furnishings suited her. A single bed with blue and white ticking on its thin mattress. A nightstand. A miniature chest of drawers, and next to it, a rack on which to hang her coat and suit. She spent her days sitting in a rocking chair, in a corner facing the window, willing the brown fog surrounding her to lift.

When Sidney wrote suggesting one of his diversions, an outing to see Queen Mary's dollhouse and its tiny library, with nothing but the finest English literature in miniature, she begged off, claiming she had turned a corner and needed only a few days of rest to feel like herself. While she knew this wasn't true, she also knew that she couldn't face London and all those people who hadn't yet realized that nothing mattered (short of the kindness of friends) and that at bottom everything was meaningless. She vaguely believed, as a distant memory or a desperate hope, in the restorative powers of spring and wrote so to Kate, who Sidney said was feeling better.

Today Charlotte rocked in her chair and felt numb to the possibilities of spring that she had so long kept utter faith with: the sky, the trees, the birds, Anne's flowers, Easter Sunday. She imagined herself in this room as a doll placed there by a child, who, having grown bored, had closed the dollhouse on its hinge and wandered off, leaving Charlotte alone in this brown light.

She remembered the Queen Anne dollhouse Fred Mew had made for her and Anne. Its wraparound porch and gabled roof, fish-scale shingles and latticework trim. Its bay window on the ground floor and diamond-shape window on the first, and its paneled front door. Best of all was the turret, whose craft Charlotte couldn't appreciate at the time, though she and Anne had loved it.

Now Charlotte realized it must have taken Fred Mew many long hours to build it. Their father had given Charlotte and Anne four houses. Doughty and Gordon Street, the farmhouse on the Isle, and the Queen Anne dollhouse. Had she ever appreciated them as her father's sacrifice? Had she ever confessed how little she had given him in return? And she cried until the brown sepia of her small room on Beaumont Street was that of dawn breaking in through the solitary window.

CHAPTER 66

It wouldn't be long now, she knew. Saturday Market always had its end, as did the circus and gypsy camp. Soon it would be time to move on.

It was a relief to think she needn't live forever. The thought of eternity exhausted her, even as she sat motionless in her rocking chair imagining the roots she had put down through the years. She closed her eyes and smelled the spring soil and tunneled in her mind down the length of a plane tree's roots. It was comforting to know that a tree's roots were as tall as its trunk. Plane trees four stories high were buttressed by roots four stories below ground.

She hadn't gone far. She had been as fixed as a tree, grounded where it stood. True, she had vacationed in France and on the Isle. But she had never traveled like Maggie Browne must have traveled in her secret life as a gypsy. Perhaps if Henry had been well, she might have flown away with him in his aeroplane. But she didn't think of birds or the sky. She thought of lying underground, quiet, and at peace.

When Alida came to visit, she talked of the labor of moving The Bookshop and of Harold being out of sorts.

"You mustn't trouble yourself, Alida, about things you have no control over. They have a way of sorting themselves out in time," Charlotte reassured her.

Alida sat in the rocking chair, Charlotte on the bed. Alida alternately crumpled and smoothed the spring scarf she wore, evidently preoccupied. Charlotte saw Alida's eyes were red, more likely from crying than from spring allergies.

Alida looked up. "It's awful loving someone so much. Spending your life with him, but never really knowing him."

Charlotte nodded, understanding that Alida needed to be heard, not given advice.

"Harold's the only man I could ever love, yet ... I can never see why he torments himself so, often over nothing, or at least what seems like nothing to me. Life needn't be as complicated as he makes it."

Charlotte smiled gently at Alida. "No, of course not. But in his struggles, he has you. You've made all the difference to him." Charlotte thought of Anne and how little she had appreciated her. She was sure Harold, though he loved Alida, couldn't truly appreciate her through the fog of his despair.

Alida let out a deep breath. She smiled at Charlotte. "Leave it to me to marry someone as inscrutable as Harold."

"You wouldn't have it any other way."

"No, I really wouldn't," Alida paused, "although some days I wish that he might notice the rose before spotting the thorn."

Charlotte stood. "There's something I'd like you to have."

Alida wiped her eyes.

Charlotte went to her chest of drawers and took out the cigar box. She placed it on top of the chest and opened it. From the box, she took "Fin de Fête" in Hardy's cramped handwriting. She presented the poem to Alida, who sat forward in the rocking chair. "Because of you, I met Sidney, and because of Sidney, I met Mr. Hardy and Florence."

Alida took the poem, then looked up at Charlotte. "I couldn't."

"You can and you will," Charlotte insisted.

Alida studied the poem, and for an instant, Charlotte feared Alida would ask her to read it. Charlotte knew she couldn't without giving herself away.

"I will treasure it always," Alida said, folding and placing the poem in her beaded handbag. "Next time, you must come and see Ham Bone, my new Westie, and we'll walk him on Great Russell Street, where all the other dogs will envy his good breeding."

"Of course," said Charlotte, taking Alida's hand. Alida held Charlotte's hand in hers. "There's nothing you need, Charlotte?"

Charlotte shook her head. "Only that you look after yourself, dear Alida, and stay true."

When Alida had gone, Charlotte felt just like a cut flower placed in a vase without water. Her head drooped and her arms and legs felt limp. She lay down on the bed and sensed herself tunneling stories and stories underground. Meanwhile, her trunk and limbs stood exposed as they cut a stark tracery against a perpetually winter sky.

CHAPTER 67

The March day was freshened by the smell of loam and birdsong, but Charlotte, in what she had come to understand was her posthumous life, was ignorant of it within her fortified room facing the brick wall. She had counted the bricks many times over and contemplated the handiwork of the mason.

However, the mortar was weathered by the wet London climate, and the wall needed tuckpointing. In another life, Charlotte thought, she might have been a builder like her father. She might have made something substantial that would survive her, something more than what she once termed her "immortal jingles." That world had passed on, and the copies of her books were packed away somewhere in the ruins of the studio, a life that she knew she could never return to.

On what would have been Henry's sixty-third birthday, Charlotte ceremoniously took out her cigar box and studied its mementos like a priest might examine the fingerbones of a saint. There was the rabbit's foot from Uncle. And, of course, there was Anne's gold watch. She replaced the items gingerly in the box, before closing its lid on the past.

Two days later, after more sleepless nights, she donned her black trench coat, barely noticing how oversized it had become, put on her black felt hat, and hooked her umbrella over her arm. She thought she would go to the corner drugstore for cigarettes. Though she seldom smoked except as an occasional force of habit, she used the cigarettes as an excuse. She knew what she would do, as certainly as she knew that the bright spring day was no longer her world.

She might have turned back for lack of courage, but in the bustle of London's streets, all the passersby bent on making their way, she came upon the sign she had not dared pray for. It was a piece of string, no longer than the length of her arm, and it lay on the pavement, directly in her way, between the nursing home and the drugstore. She stooped to retrieve the string and then admired it dangling from her outstretched hand. She could only smile.

Home again, she placed the drugstore package on her nightstand. She stood the umbrella in a corner, took off her coat and hung it on the rack, then placed her hat on the chest of drawers. From her suit pocket, she took the string, folded it, and placed it in the cigar box, next to the white handkerchief that held the ashes of a rose petal. From the box, she took the strand of rosary beads given to her by her cousin.

Charlotte felt singed through by the bright light of the day. There had been no breeze on her walk, as if the month were holding its breath until its tumultuous end. She drew the curtain from the brick wall and sat on her bed. Unlacing and taking off each boot in turn, she remembered all of the houses she had lived in during her life, and how now, at the end, she would at last live out of doors, like the gypsies and the birds, flying over country lanes by day and roosting in trees by night.

It was time.

She took the bottle from its brown package and poured the disinfectant into her drinking glass on the nightstand. "Our Father," she began, fingering the rosary beads as she drank from the glass. "Forgive us our trespasses," she continued. She saw the fiery roses across the way and felt them burning through her in all their painful splendor. She beat her wings against the windowpane and was released from the attic rooms of a many-storied house to fly away home through blue skies.

THE END
OF
BLOOMSBURY'S LATE ROSE

AUTHOR'S NOTE

Charlotte was buried in the same grave as Anne in Fortune Green Cemetery (now Hampstead Cemetery), Hampstead, England. Their headstone reads: "To the beloved memory of Caroline Frances Anne Mew, who departed this life on June 18th 1927. 'Cast Down the Seed of Weeping and Attend.' Here also lies her sister Charlotte Mary Mew, who departed this life on March 24th 1928."

Freda died in 1958 at Whitecroft Hospital, where she spent her entire adult life.

The Mews' home on Gordon Street stood just half a block from the house on Gordon Square where the Bloomsbury Group first met in 1905. In 1920, Virginia Woolf wrote of Mew and her poetry: "I think her good and interesting and unlike anyone else," but the two didn't meet until 1926 when they both happened to be visiting Florence Hardy in the hospital. However, the two women were too shy to speak to each other.

With few exceptions, the events of *Bloomsbury's Late Rose* are closely based on those described in Penelope Fitzgerald's biography, *Charlotte Mew and her friends*. These events include her childhood in the Doughty Street nursery and summers on the Isle of Wight; Henry and Freda's institutionalization for insanity; Ma's invalidism; Anne's visual artistry and her lease at Hogarth Studios; Mew's participation in Sappho's salon; her crush on May Sinclair and Sinclair's rejection; the aegis of Harold and Alida Monro; her many friendships, including those with Sidney and Kate Cockerell; Thomas Hardy's admiration of Mew's poetry and their meeting at Max Gate; her burgeoning fame in the 1920's; her suicide at fifty-eight years old following Anne's death from cancer; and their pact as young adults to never marry. Even Wek, Ma's parrot, is rooted in fact. A key exception is Mr. Antony, Anne's love interest. Little is known about Anne's life, and there is no evidence that Anne fell in love with anyone. However, I believe that human nature and the circumstances of Anne's and Charlotte's lives make such a romance plausible, particularly as Charlotte herself fell in love, first with Ella D'Arcy, then with May Sinclair. In imagining Mr. Antony, I aimed for the essential truth of Anne's and Charlotte Mew's experience, not for an indisputable history of their lives.

In short, this novel is just that: a fictional story. Though Charlotte Mew did exist, her presence in this novel is imagined, as are the scenes that constitute the novel, and despite my debt to Fitzgerald's biography, any errors of record are mine. In addition to Fitzgerald's biography and the scholarship of Mary Davidow and Val Warner, I drew on Charlotte's correspondence in the Berg Collection of the New York Public Library. Letters from and to Mew helped me appreciate her wry voice and self-deprecating sense of humor. They also revealed her attitudes toward various people and life in general. Visiting Mew's homes and haunts in London, even where buildings no longer exist, was equally inspiring. These sites include her childhood home on Doughty Street (which still exists), her adult home on Gordon Street (which no longer exists), Gordon Square garden (where a placard pays tribute to the Bloomsbury Group, but not to Mew), the building on Charlotte Street that housed Hogarth Studios, and Charlotte and Anne's grave in Hampstead.

What most inspired *Bloomsbury's Late Rose*, however, was Charlotte Mew's poetry. My appreciation of her poems began when I was an M.A. student in search of a female poet for the subject of my critical thesis. Among many American and British poets' work, Mew's poems alone asked to be read, reread, and then read again. From that introduction to this day, I admire her poems' poignant yet unsentimental view of life and their preoccupation with the haunting aspects of romantic love. But I most admire her poems' language. The sounds and rhythms are both colloquial and musical; the long lines are as original as the line breaks and diction. My favorite poem, "The Trees are Down," embodies these distinct characteristics, and its matter-of-fact pathos is heartbreaking, particularly when readers know the subject stems from Mew's life. Though her poems continue to be anthologized, collected, and treated by literary scholars, I believe Mew's poetry remains underappreciated today. I hope this novel helps pay a much-deserved tribute to Mew, and that it leads readers to Mew's poems and fulfills Thomas Hardy's prophecy that Charlotte Mew's poems will be read when other poets' work is forgotten.

I would like to thank ...

First and foremost, my late father, George, and my mother, Ruth; my siblings, Jim, Pam, and John; their spouses, Linda, Darrell, and Kay; and my nephews, Zach and Luke. I would be lost without you.

Penelope Fitzgerald for her illuminating biography of Charlotte Mew's life and legacy. Without it, this novel wouldn't exist.

The staff at the Berg Collection of the New York Public Library for access to and assistance with Charlotte Mew's letters.

Northern State University and the South Dakota Arts Council for grants that helped me to complete the novel, and my friends and colleagues at Northern State University, especially Lysbeth Benkert and Elizabeth Haller.

Ruth Mueller, Patrick Whiteley, Carol Graf, and Susan Breen for reading early drafts of the novel and offering invaluable feedback that guided my revisions and inspired me to finish the novel.

Donna Levin for reading a late draft of the novel and providing keen editing advice.

Steven Drachman and Chickadee Prince Books for believing in the novel and publishing it.

The mentors who influenced my love of literature and my writing life: Jeanne Emmons, Adam Frisch, Phil Hey, John Taylor, Paul Witherington, Michael Keller, Emily Haddad, Susan Wolfe, and especially Lee Ann Roripaugh.

My "Saturday Sisters" and fellow writers, Linda French, Cheryl Hartman, and Georgia Totten, who kept me going through many difficult years.

The editors of *New Writing: The International Journal for the Practice and Theory of Creative Writing* for publishing the first chapter of the novel.

John Sibley Williams, my agent, for his belief and guidance.

And Patrick for his insight, support, and kindness.

Pen Pearson
January 2019

The Changeling

Toll no bell for me, dear Father, dear Mother,
        Waste no sighs;
There are my sisters, there is my little brother
  Who plays in the place called Paradise,
Your children all, your children for ever;
        But I, so wild,
Your disgrace, with the queer brown face, was never,
  Never, I know, but half your child!

In the garden at play, all day, last summer,
        Far and away I heard
The sweet 'tweet-tweet' of a strange new-comer,
  The dearest, clearest call of a bird.
It lived down there in the deep green hollow,
  My own old home, and the fairies say
The word of a bird is a thing to follow,
  So I was away a night and a day.

One evening, too, by the nursery fire,
  We snuggled close and sat round so still,
When suddenly as the wind blew higher,
  Something scratched on the window-sill.
A pinched brown face peered in — I shivered;
  No one listened or seemed to see;
The arms of it waved and the wings of it quivered,
  Whoo — I knew it had come for me;
  Some are as bad as bad can be!
All night long They danced in the rain,
  Round and round in a dripping chain,
Threw Their caps at the window-pane,
  Tried to make me scream and shout
And fling the bedclothes all about:
  I meant to stay in bed that night,
And if only you had left a light
  They would never have got me out.

Sometimes I wouldn't speak, you see,
　　Or answer when you spoke to me,
Because in the long, still dusks of Spring
You can hear the whole world whispering;
　　The shy green grasses making love,
　　The feathers grown on the dear, grey dove,
　　The tiny heart of the redstart beat,
　　The patter of the squirrel's feet,
The pebbles pushing in the silver streams,
The rushes talking in their dreams,
　　The swish-swish of the bat's black wings,
　　The wild-wood bluebell's sweet ting-tings,
　　　Humming and hammering at your ear,
　　　Everything there is to hear
In the heart of hidden things,
　　But not in the midst of the nursery riot,
　　That's why I wanted to be quiet,
　　　Couldn't do my sums, or sing,
　　　Or settle down to anything.
And when, for that, I was sent upstairs
　　I *did* kneel down and say my prayers;
But the King who sits on your high church steeple
　　Has nothing to do with us fairy people!

'Times I pleased you, dear Father, dear Mother,
　　Learned all my lessons and liked to play,
And dearly I loved the little pale brother
　　Whom some other bird must have called away.
Why did They bring me here to make me
　　Not quite bad and not quite good,
Why unless They're wicked, do They want, in spite, to take me
　　Back to Their wet, wild wood?
Now, every night I shall see the windows shining,
　　The gold lamp's glow, and the fire's red gleam,
While the best of us are twining twigs and the rest of us are whining
　　In the hollow by the stream.
Black and chill are Their nights on the wold;
　　And They live so long and They feel no pain:
I shall grow up, but never grow old,
　　I shall always, always be very cold,
　　　I shall never come back again!

Fame

Sometimes in the over-heated house, but not for long,
    Smirking and speaking rather loud,
    I see myself among the crowd,
Where no one fits the singer to his song,
Or sifts the unpainted from the painted faces
Of the people who are always on my stair;
They were not with me when I walked in heavenly places;
    But could I spare
In the blind Earth's great silences and spaces,
    The din, the scuffle, the long stare
    If I went back and it was not there?
Back to the old known things that are the new,
The folded glory of the gorse, the sweetbriar air,
To the larks that cannot praise us, knowing nothing of what we do,
    And the divine, wise trees that do not care.
Yet, to leave Fame, still with such eyes and that bright hair!
God! If I might! And before I go hence
    Take in her stead
    To our tossed bed
One little dream, no matter how small, how wild.
Just now, I think I found it in a field, under a fence —
A frail, dead, new-born lamb, ghostly and pitiful and white
    A blot upon the night,
    The moon's dropped child!

The Pedlar

Lend me, a little while, the key
    That locks your heavy heart, and I'll give you back —
Rarer than books and ribbons and beads bright to see,
    This little Key of Dreams out of my pack.

The road, the road, beyond men's bolted doors,
    There shall I walk and you go free of me,
For yours lies North across the moors,
    And mine lies South. To what seas?

How if we stopped and let our solemn selves go by,
    While my gay ghost caught and kissed yours, as ghosts don't do,
And by the wayside, this forgotten you and I
    Sat, and were twenty-two?

Give me the key that locks your tired eyes,
    And I will lend you this one from my pack,
Brighter than colored beads and painted books that make men wise:
    Take it. No, give it back!

Requiescat

Your birds that call from tree to tree
    Just overhead, and whirl and dart,
Your breeze fresh-blowing from the sea,
    And your sea singing on, Sweetheart.

Your salt scent on the thin sharp air
    Of this grey dawn's first drowsy hours,
While on the grass shines everywhere
    The yellow starlight of your flowers.

At the road's end your strip of blue
    Beyond that line of naked trees —
Strange that we should remember you
    As if you would remember these!

As if your spirit, swaying yet
    To the old passions, were not free
Of Spring's wild magic, and the fret
    Of the wilder wooing of the sea!

What threat of old imaginings,
    Half-haunted joy, enchanted pain,
Or dread of unfamiliar things
    Should ever trouble you again?

Yet you would wake and want, you said
    The little whirr of wings, the clear
Gay notes, the wind, the golden bed
    Of the daffodil: and they are here!

Just overhead, they whirl and dart
    Your birds that call from tree to tree,
Your sea is singing on — Sweetheart,
    Your breeze is flowing from the sea.

Beyond the line of naked trees
    At the road's end, your stretch of blue —
Strange if you should remember these
    As we, ah! God! remember you!

The Sunlit House

White through the gate it gleamed and slept
          In shuttered sunshine: the parched garden flowers
Their fallen petals from the beds unswept,
          Like children unloved and ill-kept
                    Dreamed through the hours.
Two blue hydrangeas by the blistered door, burned brown,
               Watched there and no one in the town
               Cared to go past it night or day,
               Though why this was they wouldn't say.
But, I the stranger, knew that I must stay,
               Pace up the weed-grown paths and down,
               Till one afternoon — there is just a doubt —
               But I fancy I heard a tiny shout —
               From an upper window a bird flew out —
                    And I went my way.

The Quiet House

When we were children Old Nurse used to say
  The house was like an auction or a fair
  Until the lot of us were safe in bed.
  It has been quiet as the country-side
  Since Ted and Janey and then Mother died
And Tom crossed Father and was sent away.
After the lawsuit he could not hold up his head,
  Poor Father, and he does not care
  For people here, or to go anywhere.

To get away to Aunt's for that week-end
  Was hard enough; (since then, a year ago,
  He scarcely lets me slip out of his sight —)
At first I did not like my cousin's friend,
  I did not think I should remember him:
  His voice has gone, his face is growing dim
And if I like him now I do not know.
  He frightened me before he smiled —
  He did not ask me if he might —
  He said that he would come one Sunday night,
  He spoke to me as if I were a child.

No year has been like this that has just gone by;
  It may be that what Father says is true,
If things are so it does not matter why;
  But everything has burned and not quite through.
  The colours of the world have turned
  To flame, the blue, the gold has burned
In what used to be such a leaden sky.
When you are burned quite through you die.

  Red is the strangest pain to bear;
In Spring the leaves on the budding trees;
In Summer the roses are worse than these,
  More terrible than they are sweet;
  A rose can stab you across the street
    Deeper than any knife:
  And the crimson haunts you everywhere —
Thin shafts of sunlight, like the ghosts of reddened swords have
struck our stair

As if, coming down, you had spilt your life.

I think that my soul is red
Like the soul of a word or a scarlet flower:
But when these are dead
They have had their hour.

I shall have had mine, too,
For from head to feet,
I am burned and stabbed half through,
And the pain is deadly sweet.

The things that kill us seem
Blind to the death they give:
It is only in our dream
The things that kill us live.

The room is shut where Mother died,
The other rooms are as they were,
The world goes on the same outside,
The sparrows fly across the Square,
The children play as we four did there,
The trees grow green and brown and bare,
The sun shines on the dead Church spire,
And nothing lives here but the fire,
While Father watches from his chair
Day follows day
The same, or now and then, a different grey,
Till, like his hair,
Which Mother said was wavy once and bright,
They will all turn white.

To-night I heard a bell again —
Outside it was the same mist of fine rain,
The lamps just lighted down the long, dim street,
No one for me —
I think it is myself I go there to meet:
I do not care; some day I *shall* not think; I shall not *be*!

Read more poems by Charlotte Mew on the publisher's website:
http://chickadeeprince.com/Charlotte_Mew

OTHER BOOKS YOU WILL ENJOY

In Love with Alice, by Alon Preiss
ISBN 978-0991327454

"[A] spellbinding love story ... And I'm a little bit in love with Alice myself."
— Clifford Garstang, author of *What the Zhang Boys Know* (Press 53)

"Graceful, passionate, and earthy ... at once dreamlike and prosaic, poetic and practical...." — Kristine Morris, *Foreword Reviews*

He Could Be Another Bill Gates, by Donna Levin
ISBN 978-0999756935

A romantic comedy set in 21st century San Francisco, where differences are celebrated and everyone fits in ...
    Except when they don't.

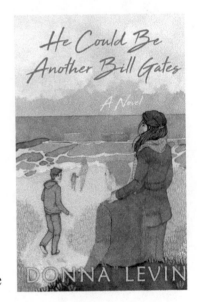

"Recommended for readers looking for a realistic story of contemporary experience, with a happy ending." — *Library Journal*

"[A] tender and realistic portrait of a nontraditional yet immediately recognizable family." — *Booklist*

"[A] complex and insightful rendering of contemporary love and family." — *Kirkus Reviews*

CPSIA information can be obtained
at www.ICGtesting.com
Printed in the USA
FSHW021255010520
69831FS